The Aviary

Emily Shore

THIS BOOK is a work of fiction. Names, characters, places and incidents are the product of the author's imagination or are used fictitiously. Any resemblance to actual persons, living or dead, business establishments, events or locales is entirely coincidental.

NO PART of this book may be reproduced, scanned, or distributed in any printed or electronic form without permission. Please do not participate in or encourage piracy of copyrighted materials in violation of the author's rights. Purchase only authorized editions.

THE AVIARY
Copyright ©2019 Emily Shore
All rights reserved.
Printed in the United States of America
First Edition: February 2019

WWW.CLEANTEENPUBLISHING.COM

SUMMARY: Serenity wakes to find she's be sold into The Aviary—an elite museum where girls are displayed as living art by day and cater to the lascivious whims of the highest bidder by night. In this elaborate and competitive world, girls go by names like Raven and Nightingale, and will stop at nothing to become top Bird. To escape would mean losing her parents, but to stay means losing herself.

ISBN: 978-1-63422-328-7 (paperback)
ISBN: 978-1-63422-329-4 (e-book)
Cover Design by: Marya Heidel
Typography by: Courtney Knight
Editing by: Cynthia Shepp

Young Adult Fiction / Dystopian
Young Adult Fiction /Social Themes / Sexual Abuse
Young Adult Fiction / Social Themes / Self-Esteem & Self-Reliance
Young Adult Fiction / Fantasy / Dark Fantasy

Authors Note:

I SET OUT TO WRITE The Aviary with one question in mind—what would the world look like if prostitution were legalized? After eleven years of involvement and research and volunteering in the anti-trafficking movement, this book has undergone many revisions and much evolution. It is not my intention to glamorize the world of prostitution/sex-trafficking/sexual exploitation in any way. However, I did want this work to target teenagers and to reach them on their level. While much of my book offers realistic glimpses into some of the deep complexities of the sex industry including dissociation, abuses, background of the victims and more, it is fair to offer a disclaimer:

The role of Luc as a trafficker is not a full portrayal. Traffickers do hire handsome recruiters. One could argue he takes on this recruiter role as well. But while Luc practices psychological manipulation and certain tactics of pimps/traffickers, he does not practice the physical and sexual abuse which saturates the sex industry. This is particularly important to note. While Serenity does undergo an identity struggle as well as issues with Stockholm Syndrome, this work is not meant to show how a good female protagonist can reform the bad boy as the false narrative of *Pretty Woman* exhibits.

What is also important to note is that Serenity's story is not normal trafficking. Trafficking does not normally equal forced abduction. That is extremely rare. Trafficking involves many methods, but the most common is trust and/or a romantic relationship—one reminiscent of a father figure—between trafficker and victim. The breakdown to that place of trust does not take long, which is what I attempt to portray with Serenity through her internal landscape.

I hope this series will offer some insight into this world, its complexities, and the state of its victims…not to discourage but to empower those who can to make a difference to prevent the sex industry from claiming one more innocent man, woman, or child.

For every book sold, a personal donation will return to Women At Risk, International, an organization working in fifty-three countries in awareness, prevention, rescue, restoration, and healing. To learn more about them, please visit www.warinternational.org and subscribe to their founder's newsletter.

For Terri,

Who invited me to the Women At Risk, International seminar that changed my life.

*You may choose to look the other way
But you can never say again that you did
not know.*

~William Wilberforce

One
SereNity

I shouldn't have left the hotel room.

"Gentlemen, we have a special treat for you today. Feast your eyes on this pure-blooded beauty!"

I feel colder than some featherless bird in the middle of winter, even after the spotlight scoops me into its glow. As soon as they unveil my cage, I hear murmured ripples of appreciation from the crowd. Though my display is segregated from the main district areas, I can still make out the other girls in their pittances of lingerie behind their own windows. Some kneel prostrate—younger ones, mostly—while others tap on the windows like a never-ending SOS, luring the attention of clients.

Every Glass District is different. This one is just fancier than most with its cobbled pathways, gothic fourteenth-century architecture, and expensive restaurants. However they dress it up, to me, every district is just a yawning cavern ready to swallow its patrons whole. The districts wear lust on their sleeves. Roll those sleeves up, and one will only discover bruises and brands on silken skin and needle marks confessing the arts of submission and coping.

Moving skyways crisscross above my head where more digital advertisements beckon tourists to view the district from the second level. Suspended just above my display are a series of viewing boxes where some of the skyways convene. Wealthier clientele—those interested in more than just one night, those with a more driven purpose—rent these. Some scout for theaters, others for

The Aviary

private clubs or brothels, and some for museums like the infamous Temple. I shudder to consider that notion.

Prospective clients already fill the viewing boxes.

Despite how much I want to, I don't shrink into myself when the auctioneer presents me. A few hours ago, I had ankle-skimming skirts and sleeves loose as rivers to my name. Now, there's nothing but panties and a lace camisole white as my own sunlight-starved skin. Ribbons drip from the camisole's hem onto my taut stomach, while the neckline overemphasizes my already-generous cleavage.

My hands yearn to cover my breasts, but I press them to both sides of the glass instead, lending my best icy stare to the encroaching crowd of men, both young and old. I'm grateful for the gated barrier between us.

"This little beauty was discovered in an old hotel in the center of the city."

Doesn't he mean *stolen*? After all, I was minding my own business, just enjoying a midnight swim. Who cared if the pool closed at ten? I still took precautions; I'd used the staff stairway instead of the elevator, then scanned the lobby and nearby halls to make sure there were no smugglers before sneaking into the pool. In hindsight, I should've waited for Sky, especially since he's looked out for me since the day I was born. Now, I'll never erase the feeling of their hands coming down on me even while I was still in the water. It was only happenstance they saw me in the dim lighting of the swimming area. I recognized them by their clothing, their Glass District insignias, but I still put up a good fight, thrashing water all over the place until they drowned my nose in chloroform.

"One must wonder if she was born right on the terrace of the lofts and raised in that very hotel."

It wasn't one hotel. It was...several. A lake house manor for a time, too.

"On the screen to your right, you'll find our medical tests have confirmed her virginity."

I want to punch my hand right through the glass. Glass chunks in my skin would be worth the pleasure of grabbing the auctioneer by his meaty throat.

"Watch out, gents! This hotel ghost may just be rabid," warns the auctioneer, motioning to my sudden crouch. I can see my green eyes reflected on one of the many viewing screens bearing my image. Not emerald in any way. They are far icier. Like Sky once said—the color of fresh mint held in frost.

She doesn't look like me. My reflection on the screen, a petite marionette with her birch-white skin, fairy blonde curls now shimmering in the sunlight, and burlesque body. She's always worn billowy skirts to soften her curves—curves Sky has always called downright deadly. Never so bare in public. Not since the first day of her existence.

My chest starts heaving for air, my breath steaming up the glass walls, which the crowd loves. It proves I am warm. But that is wrong; I'm not warm. And I'm nothing like the other girls here— the Breakables—a term coined by the first Glass District owner because of how many girls would break down over time. Cracked as easily as glass. I'm not glass. I am ice and wrath and electricity. Lightning. And I strike.

A few men step back in surprise when I spring forward, clawing my hands against the glass. Some walk away because I'm not their submissive cup of tea. Curious ones linger, though judging by their working-class or tourist clothes, I can tell they won't bid today. They might try taking pictures, but security prevents them, a reminder that Glass Districts have their own rules.

"Shall we start the bidding at one hundred thousand dollars?" the auctioneer commences. Auctioneers must be versatile and quick to deal with not only the crowd bids on the ground level, but also the electronic ones. This stubby, potbellied man doesn't seem like he can keep up.

Checking the holographic screen before him, the auctioneer raises his bushy brows. "Well! This is surprising. A first in our state, if not region. Thanks to a special patron, the leading bid is fifty million dollars. Would anyone like to counterbid? Going once? Going twice? Sold!"

He takes a gander at the screen below him and nods, and I wonder if he's receiving a message from the victor. If the final bid is meant to usurp all others, only a wealthier and connected client could have made it.

Fifty million dollars!

The Aviary

I might have been flattered…if the whole business wasn't disgusting.

Scanning the viewing boxes, I notice one man stand and tug at the ends of his smart suit jacket, which he wears with trim white pants and a loose scarf draped around his neck. From here, I can't make out his expression, but his controlled posture hints that he handles responsibility well. I will know soon enough.

While the auctioneer paces along the stage, preparing for the next auction, security arrives to remove me from the box.

They still haven't smartened up yet.

One opens the cage on the side. Ducking under his arms, I slide beneath him and around to the stage front where the auctioneer stands, his back facing me. Oh, it's far too tempting. In any case, it's not like I'm going to get far with the District meatheads behind me. Might as well have some fun.

I bring one leg up and kick hard, landing a flawless bull's-eye into the auctioneer's pudgy ass. Like uncooked bread dough, I imagine it will cave in, but I don't expect to see him topple over the stage. He lands belly down on the ground with a pained *oomph*. Bonus.

Well worth the security man jamming a sedative patch onto my arm.

Caught off guard by the tranquilizer, I stumble to my side, my arms feeling heavy, but I smile at my good fortune when I see it—a large fist-sized rock. Before the guards can lift me, I snatch up the rock and smash it as hard as I can at the glass, gratified when it shivers and breaks.

Murky fog invades my mind, and I gaze up at one of the skyways where my illustrious victor has paused to study my performance. Yes, God help him. I wonder what fate awaits me. Is he some high-ranking politician who wants me for a bride to share his bed? A museum director? An international graphicker with a famed studio?

Black cotton balls float into my head, collecting together, snuffing out consciousness and memory, and leaving me with one last recollection…

If he's from the Temple, then not even God can help him because I will die before I end up like my mother.

Two
The ImmorTal TreaTment

Despite my skin screaming from the needles boring into my arms, my paralyzed body leaves me no chance to fight. Instead, I crawl through webs of mental fluff and open my eyes to a disinfectant Wonderland.

I'm aware of several things at once.

Voices.

"She's coming to."

They sound suppressed. Like they're speaking through cotton candy.

"Not for long."

I teeter on the edge of the rabbit hole. Realizing I'm naked, all I can do is observe while nurses in starched outfits hover over me.

Another needle gives birth to a tear that tumbles down my cheek as the Temple skyscraper flickers in and out of my mind like a candle flame. Then, the machine beneath me hums and the laser lights above me begin to move. With purpose, they flow across my entire body, their warmth rippling across my skin like golden waves.

It's then I understand. This is part of the Immortal Treatment. How much have they done to me already? No doubt, they've detoxified my body and smoothed all its lines, as well as promoted collagen growth. A glance at my curls shows what they've done. Hair implants in my scalp to give it an even lighter hue. Almost white. Any blonde traces are now faint, bowing to a silvery frost. And it will never change.

The Aviary

So much like my body.

The Immortal implant is more of a program. I don't remember what the formal term is called. The trending one is the Immortal treatment. However the technology works—DNA sequencing, gene editing, nanobots—all I know is that it's age-reversing, or in my case...age-*freezing*. A chip injected under my skin. It is meant for one purpose: to keep me young forever. From now on, there will be no wrinkles. I will never lose my hair. I will never gain weight because fat will instantly dissolve. Have they strengthened my bones yet? If so, I'll really be opposite of the Breakables. I've heard some recipients can remain at their fixed ages for decades. At least one perk is that I'll never get sick.

I wonder how long I've been here. If I was kept in a perpetuated sleep stasis, what I think are hours could be days.

My mother won't abandon me. Not after everything she and my father went through to get us out of the Temple. They'll search for me.

Sky will figure it out. He may need some time, but he won't abandon me either. I don't care if he's spent the past three years pulling away from me. I don't care if he's not my blood...if he's *Family* blood. Whatever organized crime syndicate he belonged to in the past doesn't matter anymore. He's part of *our* family. It's always been him and me.

Fuzziness overwhelms me again. Sinking, I become a shipwreck in depth and darkness.

Three
TattOo

I'M LYING IN A HOSPITAL bed clothed in a white gown so light it feels like ocean foam. I struggle to resurface from whatever they've pumped into me. My body feels more sluggish than a drowned dumpling.

"How are you feeling?" inquires a person to my right. A younger voice. I recognize him as the man who bought me. Though his velvet voice doesn't tempt me, the midwinter blue steel in his deeply hooded eyes does. They demand my attention. Where I'm headed suddenly hits me. This might be my only chance. I won't let anyone put me behind glass again. I won't let any man have me.

So, I don't think. I just fly. Swiping the pitcher of water next to my bed, I chuck the contents in his face. Then, I leap out of the bed with my bare feet skimming the cold floor and swing toward the door. Before I can even touch the doorknob, his hand snaps around my wrist.

"You are nothing if not impulsive." Annoyed, he frowns and forces me back onto the bed, but one corner of his mouth lifts into a smirk as if he's secretly amused.

After his hands depart from my arms, the strings on the back of the hospital gown come undone, and one sleeve slips below my shoulder. Out of the corner of my eye, I notice the edge of a silver mark. I blink a couple of times before scrambling for the pitcher on the floor. The man huffs, but moves aside so I may grab it. Using it as a mirror, I thumb the image on the back of my shoulder, tracing the feather shape of the silver tattoo. It's like a noose tightening around my neck. Museum candidates are always tattooed.

He's already branded me.

A signature tattoo like this records my location, heart rate, blood pressure, and God knows what else! Maybe it's where they injected the Immortal implant.

My stomach churns. Bile splatters the butterflies in my stomach on its race out of my system.

On cue, the young man grabs a bucket and holds it underneath my chin just as I retch.

"At least it smells better than you," I snort.

When I hear him chuckle, all I want to do is dump the contents over his head. Show him who he's messing with.

Guess the joke's on me. It took him less than a second to thwart my attempt and knock the bucket to the ground, splattering me with some of its contents in the process. This man is not to be messed with either. Suddenly, I grab at whatever sheets I can, putting as much distance between us as possible. Pleased with his success, he relaxes back onto his chair, crossing one ankle over his knee and folding his hands in his lap.

Squeezing my eyes shut, I seethe. Amused, the man smiles. Definitely younger. I'd wager mid-twenties, but I can't determine. His brow bones are strong. All he does is exercise the thinnest effort and those sultry eyes narrow, betraying the gaze of one who wields control and influence. "Are you ready to listen?" Between his authoritative voice and youth, I assume he's with a Family branch. Only Family blood gives men his age higher status and position.

I stare down at the sheets, silent.

"Good. As you may have noticed, I'm well trained for situations like this." That's when he raises his hands. They are sheathed in black gloves.

My suspicions are confirmed. A Family director.

But which Family? Many branches run the country, but the most powerful one, The Syndicate, controls the Temple.

"The Guild," he says, answering my unspoken question.

Relief fills me.

"Where in the world have you been hiding, little girl? You look like you've been untouched by reality."

I shift my head in his direction. Glower as best I can. "You don't look much different."

He stretches his arm toward me. I have barely enough time to flinch before I realize he isn't trying to touch me. Rather, he unbuttons the cuff of his left sleeve, rolling it up so I can see the dozens of needle marks feasting on the skin. "Your condition is not so unfortunate. I have taken an oath that no needle shall ever pierce my flesh again. And I prohibit their usage in my museum. I felt the burden of narcotics, and the price is too high. Non-impacting hallucinogens such as Bliss, but not narcotics." He buttons his cuff again, asking in a casual manner, "Do you know who I am?"

I spit another bit or two onto my sleeve and refuse to answer, wincing a little from the stench, but he isn't so willing to let the topic slide. "You must have some idea, of course."

Holding my breath, I study him. I could very well choke on his beauty. Few have ever earned the right to compete with Sky, who is his own breed of handsome—earthy and rugged with enough muscles to be a demigod byproduct of Zeus. Sky has deep-set, dark amber eyes, not to mention hair that falls in abundant waves. In contrast, the man in front of me has a noble forehead and wears a crown of dark, swept-back hair. His eyes are scathing, along with the permanent curve of his thin but attractive mouth.

He only used one hand to stop my little escape attempt, so I know he's strong, probably strong enough to take Sky down if he ever attempts to rescue me.

Tired of waiting for me to respond, he sighs. "I am Luc Aldaine. Your new director."

So, the museum operator himself bought me and will escort me to his museum instead of a recruiter. Since he's the one who put up the bid of fifty million, it makes sense, but this is still unheard of. Most directors delegate auctions to recruiters. From what I know, directors don't usually take this much of a personal interest in the subjects of their exhibits.

I glance back at the feather brand. Is he already imagining feathers threaded together like a chorus along my body? Which museum does the Guild control? All I've ever concerned myself with is the Syndicate and its Temple empire.

I need to know where I'm going. "Which one?"

The Aviary

"The Aviary."

Birds. I will become a bird. His next words don't give me much opportunity to ponder.

"Your virginity alone would qualify you for Temple standing. That and your beauty, not to mention your spirit, would carry you to the Penthouse, but I have plans for you that will achieve what I have always desired—the Temple's envy. What is your name?"

The Glass District auctioneer asked my name, too, but I refused to give it. This time, I give the director my alias.

"Alice Trinity." The lie is instinctive. One thing Sky taught me well: never use my real name, but always keep it close. Alice Trinity. Serenity Lace.

"Alice Trinity," Luc reflects, wavering like he's uncertain whether he believes me. "I think I'll call you Trinity."

"Call me whatever you want. You'll give me another name soon enough."

Luc's laugh sprinkles the air. "Yes, indeed I will. Good to know you are so open to the idea."

I grimace. "Who says I'm open?"

"Yes, you've shown how open you are. Rest assured, I look forward to loosening that vise of yours."

"Don't hold your breath."

"Tell me, have you ever entered a museum before?"

I shake my head. Cringe when Luc approaches me. In the wake of my prior retching, he is far too welcoming, too inviting. I try to remember the other lessons Sky taught me. *Be numb. Don't show your emotions. Give him nothing he can use against you.* But unlike me, Sky could go outside our hotel rooms to understand the world around us. I never could. Too dangerous for a girl like me—too dangerous for most girls. Sky and my father are the only men I've ever known until now. Luc takes a match to the fuel of my curiosity.

He taps something on the flat screen behind him. "I have significant plans in store for you, Trinity. You've no need for concern. I will give you the utmost protection and respect." He rises from his chair, scoots it back to the wall. "But those terms are conditional to your behavior. Undoubtedly, you've heard of other directors who create addictions for their girls or beat them into submission. I prefer *other* methods. And you are a sculpture I will enjoy reshaping. Please keep that in mind the next time you consider flying off the handle."

He shouldn't waste his breath. He's no different from any other man who has controlled this industry of fear and abuse. No better than the politicians who opened the first district more than a century ago. This man who bought me for fifty million dollars isn't going to make an exception for me.

"There is a shower in the corner of the room." He motions to his left before picking up his suit jacket, which is draped over the chair. "And a dress for you to wear in the closet. Later tonight, I will personally transfer you to the Aviary, and you will begin."

"Begin what?" I spit out the words as he departs.

Turning back, he smiles. "Your new life."

As soon as he's gone, I jump out of the bed, careless of the undone strings of my gown, of how only air frames the backside of my body. For once, it feels nice—no long layers of fabric smothering my skin. Whether it was modesty, my father's glare, or Sky's muscles that kept recruiters, hotel employees and guests, or any other random men who crossed our path at bay, I'll never know. Maybe it was a combination of all three. But as I approach the window and gaze at the great city around me, I wonder if Sky has any idea where I am. Is he down there, several stories below, searching for me in the Glass Districts even now?

Views like this are familiar to me. I have spent many months staring out hotel windows. Except this one is far greater. I know exactly what city I'm in because I can see the Temple in the distance. It soars far above the gridwork of other skyscrapers. From here, I can make out humongous feeds of sexualized women and girls playing on the Temple's digitally enhanced windows. Temple ads. Other skyscrapers do the same thing for their businesses, along with the billboards sprinkled throughout the city. While the Temple is the super tower at the top of the food chain, the smaller towers are like fungi, parasitic growths, and the midsized skyscrapers are bottom feeders desperate to compete with the Temple city. None can. Not only is the Temple the most powerful and profitable corporation in the nation, it also houses the Centre. People travel from all over the world to use this medical monument,

The Aviary

which offers everything: organ sales, research and development, surgical procedures, and the largest breeding line in the country. Rich couples who want designer babies. Rich directors who want the same for museums. Not to mention supplementing the low birth rate.

In the distance is one of the Glass Districts on the edge of the city, strategically positioned before the bridges and checkpoints. Girls who escape the city without the right connections or the right money are plucked and dumped right into the nearest district. Runaways are the most common. My parents' precaution of keeping me in a hotel beyond the bridges didn't help much. Of course, if I hadn't snuck out of the hotel room to go swimming…

I should have waited for Sky. I went at midnight. After pool hours. Tricked the card sensor just like I'd watched him do in the past. I should have always assumed smugglers were everywhere, even in outlying hotels. They prey on spring breakers and bachelorette parties. Sometimes, they bring recruiters. Other times, they just don't bother. The lucky girls have rich parents who will pay a ransom, but close-knit families are sparse today. Real families have disintegrated—single parents, foster homes, and orphanages are more common. Families are now defined as any one of corrupt branches in the country that run everything from government to media to Glass Districts to museums. Our family might as well be a relic, whatever photographs we have worthy of an anthropological gallery.

Desperate to figure out what day it is, I turn on the holographic projection on the wall, cringing at the ancient technology, and find a news channel. Wall screens are old but cheap. Volumetric laser projection is the latest cutting-edge tech. Ironic. Technology was supposed to usher in a new world and make things better. Instead, it reduced the workforce and women took the worst beating. Without connections, few women have jobs outside the sex industry. I wouldn't doubt it was the intention of men all along…

Heart sinking, I realize I've been gone for seven days total. Two in the Glass District. Five here.

A reporter is responding to the chaos behind him. "For viewers just tuning in, as you can see in the background, security is carting away the lone activist and restoring order to the Glass District. After a three-day assault of carefully executed vandalism, the perpetrator will be brought to justice."

Justice. Bah. I press mute when I see black-gloved figures advancing toward the man. Activists were more common during the early days of legalization. No longer. Time bred conformity, then normality, and now any opposition is silenced because the Families won't have their commodities cheapened in any way. The money trail always leads back to the Families, where blood ties are thick and mandatory. They filled their pockets to the brim with lobbyists in the early days, marketing legalization to media moguls, who promoted it to Hollywood elite. Of course, more Family members run congress—all corrupt politicians serving their own corporate ends. Few laws are ever passed, fewer regulations imposed.

Sensing a slight ache on my shoulder, I needle my thumb into my silver tattoo and wince because it still hurts. I hurry to the shower, turn it until the heat blasts, snatch up the sponge, and scrub my shoulder. And I don't stop scrubbing. On the shower floor now, I bask in the water. More pours down the front of the hospital gown, rinsing any leftover bile from my skin, but the tattoo won't disappear. My hands tremble from the effort. I've scrubbed until my skin is raw, red, and chafed, but the silver feather proves to be a worthy adversary. Like a cackling ghost, it taunts me, and I finally slump down, cold and wet as a fish out of water.

Dropping the sponge, I smack the tiles over and over. Can't stop flopping around, can't stop fighting. Curling up with the shower streaming over me, I scratch at the tattoo with my thumbnail, wondering if I'm destined to follow in my mother's footsteps.

No, I won't become like the Unicorn.

I remember the photograph I'd unearthed, and though its image rises to the surface, cleaving to my mouth like chalk rubbed there, I try to spit it from my mind. Those eyes glittering lust don't belong to my mother. No, her eyes are purer now, thanks to my father and his gentle fingers that picked out the glitter fleck by fleck. But she didn't come away without scars.

My anger fuels the lightning inside me, keeps any scars from the Glass District at bay. But I feel a twinge of resentment that I must wrap up with guilt. Resentment my mother has left me unprepared for any scars, but guilt at knowing she never had any choice. Because we are the hunted ones. To this day, I know how overpowering my mother's love is; she's done everything she can to protect me.

I know I'm strong enough to escape sooner than she did. I won't spend years in any museum. And I'd tear the Temple down glass window by glass window before becoming part of the place that gave my mother nightmares.

Sky says I should've grown out of it by now, but I still curl up by their door every time to hear my father soothe her while she sobs. They never talk about the Temple. I do. I tell Sky all about my nightmares because it helps, because once I speak them, they become words and float away like chaff in wind. My mother isn't like me. She carries horrors on her skin, in her head, but no longer in her heart. My father stacked his love there until there was no room left for anything else. His patience is the thread wrapped around our family. A true family. If my mother is the broken survivor, he is the natural counselor, Sky's the protector, and I'm—the bat out of hell.

Four
The Avlary

"I CALL THEM MY BIRDS."

ON THE WAY OVER IN his self-driving-limousine, which is Family-branded so they have immunity, Luc gave me a digital tour of his Aviary, but seeing the building from the vehicles one-way windows was completely different than up close. Against the darkness, it was like a diamond sitting in a bed of ash. Grand spotlights and high-tech holographic images of birds light the entrance.

Now, it just looks like a giant glass dollhouse. From the observation deck within the domed ceiling of the Aviary where I stand with Luc, I stare down at the men flooding the lobby as they stray to girl-encrusted exhibits. If they pay more, they will advance to the second level. The ones with deep pockets continue to the third where the highest-ranking girls are.

It shouldn't impress me, but it does.

Luc motions to one of the screens stationed on the balcony's railing, gesturing for me to expand it. Voxel images like I've seen in some hotels. Better than holograms, these are interactive lasers manipulating particles in the air to create images. Volumetric technology.

Light as a cobweb, Luc's hand strays to my back as I lean over and magnify the sight, focusing on one exhibit. Two men stand in front of it watching, gesturing to the glass. Then, I see her. Frozen in place with her face, throat, and chest shimmering blue from an injected bioluminescent, her naked hips a fruitful purple, and a skirt fabricated of peacock feathers that flows behind her like a train. Even her hair is nothing but a straight waterfall of blue tresses that shine like dragon scales. Not a chemical dye, but hair implants like mine.

I step back from the laser lens, feeling a strange sensation in the pit of my stomach. Like all the butterflies that used to dance there are dying, wings fanning in and out, slow enough for heartbeats to pass through.

"Would you like to see one up close?" Luc offers as his hand strays to my bare arm, giving me another fleeting glimpse of the feather's edge. Thanks to the thin-strapped white dress I wear, the tattoo is prominent. My skin has already healed from my shower episode. I should count it a blessing. Breakables don't get this kind of treatment. Nor do they get smart fabric that regulates body temperature. These smart dresses are standard issue here. Not that I need one with my Immortal implant, which does the same.

As we walk deeper into the Aviary, the tattoo seems more like tree roots tunneling into my veins.

No matter how much I convince myself I'm not my mother, that I have more fight in me, every time I catch a glimpse of the tattoo out of the corner of my eye, it blows me a kiss, reminding me of its power. For now, I must hold onto my disgust. Remind myself of the girls in Glass District cages, and my mother's photograph. I cling to that image.

I follow Luc to an elevator, considering pressing the alarm button. He notices my gaze, but I lunge just quickly enough. His hand comes down on my wrist at the same time, flinging me back hard against the metal rail, but not before I jam the button.

Alarms blare, and the elevator stops.

Unperturbed by my action, Luc calmly presses the button again, silencing the alarm and rolling up his sleeve to reveal a digital tattoo of an owl. As soon as he presses the eyes, a screen appears, hovering above his skin. Skin interfaces are the latest in technology. Only recently legalized and expensive enough that only elites can afford it. Maybe he's canceling security.

After shutting down the interface, Luc adjusts his tie, surveys me, and then steps toward me, boxing me in before I can move. "Allow me to help you keep something in perspective, Trinity…

My security here is state of the art. The windows are constructed of unbreakable glass. A laser fence surrounds the property. I have dozens of security members on staff who are not the routine bodyguards you will find in the Glass District. I have exercised a good amount of patience with you thus far. You owe me some appreciation."

"Appreciation?" I try not to bend beneath his eyes. "You think you can just buy me off the street, turn me into your little sparrow? You're nothing but a flesh peddler!"

Luc cups my chin; his hand is an iron snare. "I find myself amused by your ferocity. But my patience is finite. And you do not wish to see me angry. Try to keep that in mind."

The thought of unbreakable glass causes me a moment of pause. But lightning can still burn anything with just one strike. "Do. Your. Worst." I spit in his face.

Not even cringing, Luc wipes his cheek before raising his finger in warning. "Please do not ask me to prove myself. I will if I must."

As the elevator ascends to the third floor, Luc takes pride in telling me more about the Aviary. "There's another museum on the other side of the country where they showcase flower displays; it's called the Garden. But mine is one of the oldest museums in the country. The Temple continues to grow, and they are our main competition, but I've revolutionized the Aviary and achieved the success only past directors could have imagined."

The elevator doors open, distracting us momentarily. Luc guides me down an empty hallway on our right to a separate wing for exhibits, and I know they must be quite expensive.

Luc can't possibly read my mind, but he always seems to voice some word, some idea related to what I *am* thinking. "Our wealthier patrons usually arrive after the normal rabble has left. They prefer their anonymity. Once they've viewed each exhibit and rated it, they place their opening bids for additional services." Disgust works its way upward from my stomach, twisting my intestines into knots. Every magazine, advertisement, even the virtual tour Luc gave me—they are all manipulative airbrushing. They try to paint roses over my eyes, luring me, enticing me.

I follow Luc around a corner into a room with all white walls, which won't divert any attention from the main theme: the glass exhibit. I feel my disgust, almost tasting salt and iron. Unlike my mother, who was born in the Temple with that glass film over her eyes—and so many other girls who have no choice—I refuse to accept this new home.

"The exhibits change weekly," Luc explains, joining his hands behind his back. "We have over a hundred Birds here. Unlike most museum directors, I take a special interest in each and every one. It's why I've achieved such success. First and foremost, I am their Owl because I am the ruler of the night. You will call me Owl or Director Aldaine. Did you know that owls were once believed to be keepers of spirits passing from death to another plane?"

Sky would come up with a good quip for that one. I try not to worry about him. He's the plotter and thinker. I'm the feeler. There is no doubt in my heart that I will see him again. Right now, Sky and my parents must be using all their resources to search for me. My parents are wealthy, and I wouldn't be surprised if they could buy me back. For now, I just need to wait, learn, and fight against the rose glass.

I half-expect to see laser peacocks strutting around as the lobby displayed a series of flying volumetric birds in the virtual tour. But it's evident by the white atmosphere that Peacock herself must demand all the attention.

When I see Peacock up close, my mouth turns dry. Like someone's ripped feathers right from a bird's breast and crammed them inside my mouth, forcing me to swallow them. I gaze at her teal hair, ripe and verdant along her shoulders in decadent waves. The curled ends are the color of plum juice, and her bare chest glows a salacious blue. All the butterflies in my stomach seize and die. Nothing left but crumpled wings, bits of antennae, and broken thoraxes. Then, her eyes move.

I nearly leap back, but Luc's hands frame both my arms, and he murmurs in my ear, "Careful. Peacocks are quite introverted and *highly* aggressive. Even so, her ratings are very high. Come with me. I will introduce you to some of my other Birds."

My old world is beginning to fade. I'm drinking in this new one where feather-clad girls are trapped. Frozen in the glass birdcages society calls exhibits. How long before I must perform the same sickening acts?

Overwhelmed, I follow Luc to another elevator, where he pushes a button marked *N*. There is no alarm button in this one.

"We're entering the Nest Wing. This is where my Birds live in their off hours—where they eat, drink, and play."

When we enter the Nest Wing, I see nothing but glass. Glass domed ceilings trickle starlight and moonbeams onto the heads of the girls like feathers dripping from the sky. One-way glass walls where glass sculpture gardens reflect off dancing water from glass fountains. Digital screens project a kaleidoscope of bird-themed art everywhere. In the lobby, it was exhibits of the past—a tribute to the Aviary's history. Even the walkways are made of glass with birds flying wherever my feet step as well as fused into the railings. I wonder if any of the glass is breakable. If I could shatter something, I could cut him, twist that bewitching smile off his face.

Inside the lobby of the Nest Wing are more girls than I've ever seen in my life. The ones who flit past me all pause to stare. For a moment, I forget about Luc. One girl has a tiny diamond bird embedded into her retina. They aren't Birds. None of them. They are more like dolls. Cracked dolls who dress in doll clothes, prancing about in one giant dollhouse they dare to call a museum. How many of these girls have disappeared into their Bird selves? The stitches holding my emotions together begin to rip.

"I run one of the top three museums in the Union."

"Let me guess—you're the third."

"I may be second to the Garden and third to the Temple, but I'm getting close thanks to my winged ones. Hello, Flamingo." He smiles at a wisp of a girl with white skin, flesh-pink hair, and eyes the color of freshly gutted salmon. She arches her neck, waves back, and flounces away.

I've seen other girls from my hotel windows and ones on television, but never so many at one time. Each one bears a tattoo just like mine on their shoulder blade, but mine is the only silver one. I have no basis, no sense of how to so much as speak one word to them. I can almost feel their eyes sinking past my pores, becoming teeth that gnaw on my bones. Did my mother ever have trouble with girls in the Temple, where competition is even fiercer? I wonder how she protected herself when she is so slight like me.

The Aviary

She must have some fight in her somewhere. Otherwise, she never would've escaped.

What unhinges me most is how Luc knows them. Every. Single. One.

"How's my little Mockingbird?"

A girl, smaller than me with rosy round cheeks and pearly gray hair, flitters up to him with her hands coyly strung behind her back. Her gray dress makes her seem smaller than she is, younger even, especially with her slender frame. Squeezing his arm, she pushes her plump lips into a pout. "You haven't come to see me in days, you naughty Owl."

He leans down to peck her on the cheek. "I've been a little preoccupied."

She peers over his shoulder at me. "New flesh?"

Stepping aside, Luc asks, "What do you think?"

Her eyes are pilgrims journeying down my body, across my hair, my arms, my hands, against my stomach and legs. "Where in the world did you find *her*?"

"She's a wild Bird. But don't worry. I'll tame her yet."

In response, I flip my bird, but all Luc does is smile with that same beckoning expression.

"You tame them all, Owl." Mockingbird's attention focuses on my face. She hasn't yet let go of his arm. "Look at all that white hair. Is it natural?"

"Ask her."

I narrow my eyes. "Most of it."

"Immortal Treatment." Mockingbird clucks her tongue. "So jealous."

She turns her attention back to Luc. "Egret?"

Luc just returns her question with a beguiling tilt of his lips.

"You don't mean…" Mockingbird flicks her eyes to me again before her widening gaze bounces back to Luc. "Does Nightingale know?"

Leaning over, he says in a singsong murmur, "Hush, little Bird, don't say a word."

"Aww, Owl…" She pouts. "You should know never to tell a secret to the Mockingbird."

"You're my hatchling." His smile is all sweet and syrup when he asks, "Just for a little while?"

"Anything for you, Owl."

Once he kisses her cheek, Mockingbird scampers away, but not before sidling up next to me and whispering, "I'd kill for that rack!" I fight the urge to glance down at the plunging neckline of my white dress.

Luc guides me through the wing toward the staircase.

"Feeling well, Gull?" he asks a girl whose skin is so white it looks like froth. Her eyes remind me of dead flesh and her hair frosted bubbles. Her fingers hold a cookie. From her hollow eyes to the way her back relaxes so far into the glass wall behind her, one would suspect narcotics, but Luc specified that he forbids them. Maybe one of those *safe* hallucinogens. Like Bliss.

"Nice to see you again, Hummingbird," he says to a girl who flutters about the lobby. Her hair is like spiced oranges, eyes like ripened cherries.

Some girls unnerve me more than others.

His Aviary with its sculpted-bird chandeliers unnerves me, too. It doesn't take long for me to notice a few empty exhibits sprinkled about here and there. I wonder why they are here in this wing reserved for the living quarters.

Luc touches my elbow, leading me toward the grand staircase in the center of the wing. Like everything else, the steps are glass, vast enough for dozens of people to stand on each side. Blown glass fused together with feather designs makes up the intricate banisters. When I step onto the staircase, it moves, giving the impression of flight. Halfway up, it splits into narrower ones on each side, one to the left and the other to the right. It ascends the two of us to the right one; Luc explains the other leads to more dormitories. The moving pathway stops, and I realize it's because of Luc. Midway up, he pauses to study the tattoo on my shoulder before fingering it in approval. I wish I could grow a beak right then and there. Peck his hand until it bleeds.

Before we reach the second level, I glance back to eye the lobby and the empty glass exhibits.

Luc beams, taking my observance for interest. "Those are for my Birds. Sometimes they need to use them during their off hours."

I can't fathom why they'd want to spend time in a glass cage.

"I am also an artist."

"How innovative."

Luc smiles. "Innovation is a necessity and a privilege here. All my Birds have a part to play. Just as you will."

"Which part? You haven't given me any clue as to what stupid Bird you'll turn me into."

"I will make that revelation in time."

"Ooh, a puzzle, then. The anticipation is killing me."

He laughs.

I hate Luc's laughter because it's the sort I could see myself wanting to wrap up in.

He's piqued my curiosity. From all the ads I've seen, I know there's no end to a man's fantasy. No matter how ordered, how pristine, the thought of posing scantily clad in one of those glass cages nauseates me.

"This is an ideal situation for you," Luc says. "Far preferable to the Glass Districts. You could have become a Breakable." He refers to the stereotypical term for Glass District girls. I've often used the word, but after learning more about this place, I wonder if there's more to district girls. Breakables...no one cares if they're broken or if someone else did the breaking. Older generations still call them hookers.

"As I've mentioned," Luc continues, "I prohibit all narcotics here. Though they are free, decriminalized, and available for all outside these walls, I order monthly blood tests. Any Bird with narcotics in her blood is suspended without wages."

I snort at the comment. "As if they get to spend anything since you probably take eighty percent of their pay."

Luc pauses, posture tightening. "As well I should. The funding it requires to run a museum such as the Aviary is astronomical. And since I provide them with anything they may need from food to clothing to caretakers to the latest fashion technology to protection, I assure you their wages are more than generous. But no drugs on my property whatsoever," he redirects the subject. "Not even at a client's request."

I don't comment, considering I've never had any experience with narcotics. Sky tried Bliss only once. A ground-breaking hallucinogen that produces all the effects of street-drugs but with no long-lasting negative impact. Then, he flushed the rest down the toilet after he woke up to discover I'd managed to get a tutu around his waist and paint little hearts all over his face.

"The second level of the Aviary houses bedchambers for each one of my Birds. Your room will overlook the grandest part of the sculpture garden, which covers twelve acres."

"Lucky me." I don't reveal how much I love flowers or how much I enjoy walking. Any time we stayed at one of my parents' seaside villas or country manors, I always spent as much time as I could outdoors.

"You will not be permitted outside the Aviary walls…for now" Luc crushes my hopes, but I consider the last part of the statement. "But you will have access to the adjoining aviary. I house some of the world's most exotic collection of birds. Many enjoy interacting, particularly if you bring bird food." He leans over, humming in my ear.

"An aviary within the Aviary. How fortuitous." I try not to show how the prospect of visiting a true bird sanctuary is thrilling.

"I have a chamber on the same level. My room is located directly across from yours, since I have a personal interest in preserving your future here." He pauses to survey me once when we reach the apex of the staircase.

"I'm sure you do."

He ignores me. "The staff here attends to all my Birds' needs. Sheets will be changed daily, food prepared fresh. You will join us for breakfast and dinner. Lunch is served in your room, and the rest of the day is yours to fill."

"Will I ever get my old clothes back?" I ask.

He shakes his head. "From now on, your clothes will be provided. Each Bird is defined by her color. Some alternate color is permitted for exhibits, but not during free hours. You will wear nothing other than white."

I rack my brain, searching for images of white birds. Pelican? Snowy Egret? Ibis? Goose—no, not a goose. Dove, perhaps? Dove seems like a safe assumption.

He touches a screen to our left, and a frosted glass door opens.

It's more than just a bedchamber. More like a penthouse suite. Like the hotel rooms Sky and I grew up in, it has its own bathroom, bedroom, and attached sitting room as well as a kitchenette. But no refrigerator. Of course not. There is a digital screen on the kitchen wall with *Menu* glimmering in bold font with a 3D printer directly under it. Whenever we stayed at a hotel with one, I'd sneak off in the middle of the night and print cupcakes.

Upon entering, I notice one side of the room has a large circular window with an alcove hollowed into it. That ledge will be getting a good deal of company soon. Staring through windows and daydreaming about the world beyond them is a frequent hobby of mine.

The door clicks shut. I spin to see Luc standing behind me, hands lingering at his sides as he tries to determine my reaction to the room. He takes a step toward me, hand advancing to my shoulder. I know some directors mix business with pleasure—none as egregiously as Director Force—but based on the way the other Birds treated Luc, I don't think him the type.

But if he is… it will be over my fifty-million-dollar body.

I grab the hardest and heaviest thing I can find—which happens to be a metal trash can—and smash it against the floor-to-ceiling mirror right behind me. To my surprise, it shatters and I lunge. I'm seconds too late from getting my hands around one single shard of glass that would've served as a worthy weapon. Now, Luc's hands are around me, strong and purposeful, dragging my kicking body backward. He doesn't yell. There are no frustrated words or insults. Not so much as a groan.

I'm still flailing when he gets me into the bathroom, releases my wrists, and locks the door behind him. While I collect myself in the far corner, he paces back and forth with a fist trained at his side. His reaction is a shock. He *laughs*.

"One of your best attempts, I must confess. But, Trinity, I'm afraid I must show you that I am not your enemy."

I cringe when Luc grazes a finger across my cheek, capturing a tendril of my fairy hair and rubbing it between his fingers. "You think this place is a cage. But where you came from is the real cage. You don't understand this yet. Anyone can tell you have not been groomed for this world, unlike the vast majority of girls. In the Glass District, girls are beaten when they don't perform. Most are drugged into compliance. Surely you must recognize your good fortune here."

Jerking my face away, I hiss a threat, "Get your filthy hands off me, Luc!"

"Owl," he corrects, then takes my face in his hands and rubs his thumbs across my cheekbones. "You are so feral. We've never had such a wild one. It's why I chose you. I could see it in your eyes. I knew it was not a mistake. Confirmed when you had the gumption to thwart district security and attack the auctioneer."

"His ass looked better in the dirt."

Chuckling, Luc tucks a curl behind my ear. "I have no intention of breaking your spirit. It is what makes you great. But you must learn respect. It's required in a place like this."

I want to harm him. When I snap my teeth at one of the hands on my cheek, he's quicker and seizes my hair, thrusting my head back. "I'll harness that spirit of yours. Today, I'll let you taste your worst fears. A visit to the Isolation Room will be an appropriate lesson."

He circles my wrists with his hands again, but I don't stop fighting. I will never stop. My worst weakness is my own physical fragility—a far cry from my spirit. I curse how strong Luc is when he drags me through the exit door. I don't like the sound of this Isolation Room.

Luc has no problem controlling me the entire way down the long hall and to an elevator. Only one other person has ever handled me like this, but that was when we were little, and Luc is far different from Sky. The elevator propels us downward. My anxiety increases with each floor.

Luc reaches out to cup my chin. "Remember, I have other methods of restriction. But after your visit here, I hope they will not be necessary."

He loosens his grip on me at the same time the elevator doors open. After shoving me into a pitch-black room, he grins, slow and steady. "I will see you at dinner, Trinity." The doors begin to slide together. I leap for them, heart in my throat, but my hands only connect with cold metal.

There's an electric hum beneath my feet, and the darkness around me lights up with a freckling of stars. Then, as my eyes begin to adjust, I'm able to make out a row of glass cages filled with

The Aviary

half-naked girls. Men view them from a glass walkway.

All at once, I understand the beastly horror that awaits me here…

The Isolation Room is a virtual-reality fear enhancer.

Five
The Isolation Room

AN ENDLESS ROW OF GLASS cages displays dozens of girls before the crowd. Once, after I turned thirteen, my father brought me to a Glass District. But the Isolation Room is learning. Its artificial intelligence needles its way into my brain, so it can parade my fears into the open. Desperate, I begin to run, doing my best to prevent myself from thinking, from betraying anything else. But when I raise my head, it's too late. The glass cage boxes me in like the rest of the girls, a glittery Glass District prisoner wearing nothing but transparent lingerie made from plastic.

I close my eyes, willing the image away. When I open them again, it's worse.

A hall of mirrors in a nightclub.

The mirrors reflect nothing but the deadened eyes of many girls. Spectral pupils gaze back at me, naked necks arched, mouths ravaging necks, skin starved for touches that will never satisfy. I feel a hand on my shoulder. Jerking away, I stumble until the images around me change and I connect with a moving walkway. A spinning walkway.

A carousel.

The Isolation Room dances on the edges of my basest fear, seeming to understand how I see my mother's face in each girl who is anchored to a carousel pole. They mimic the horses men pay to ride. Music—intoxicating medleys from band organs—bombards my ears as the girls wince from the flicks of riding crops.

The Aviary

Frozen just like them, I'm lost in a whirlwind of skin painted like porcelain. Men clap their hands from the stands. Others toss clinking coins onto the carousel. A sick ode to showgirls in history. Mouths suck in aroused inhales. No girl can survive like this for long. Mom once told me most of them did drugs just so they could cope. The desperate ones used them to escape the only way they could—by overdosing.

Finally, total black.

I don't remember starting to cry, but I can feel the hot tears on my face. My heart thuds fast as fevered drumbeats. Relief engulfs me until I realize I've been fooled.

Lying on the floor, I raise my head to see a room I don't recognize. A window appears before me, and I realize I am in the tallest building, peering at the skyline. No other skyscraper dares soar higher than the Temple. I stare at my hands painted white with silver speckles. At my naked skin, my breasts bound by ropes. A diamond-encrusted bridle imprisons my face and neck. A horn planted in the center of my forehead. I am in the Penthouse. Delicate earthquakes erupt in my fingers, causing my hands to tremble as I struggle to my knees just as I hear footsteps behind me.

No, don't think. Wish it away. Will it away. He's not here. He can't hurt you.

But his hot breath already feasts on my neck as he leans in to murmur just one word…

"Unicorn."

Air escapes my lungs. In the same moment, light pierces the room, growing brighter and brighter as I try to stand, but my legs are too shaky. Like I'm standing on quicksand. One more moment passes before everything once again turns black.

Six
FaMilyBrAt

"Sky!" I come to, crying for my... I don't know what one would title him. Closer than a friend—even closer than a brother—he's always remained the one constant in my life. The one by my side when my parents would leave.

"Hush now. You're waking up just fine." It sounds like something my mother would say, but the voice is not hers.

The windfall of snowy strands sweeping the woman's neck is my first anchor to reality. There's a hint of creaminess to the strands, nothing silvery like mine.

"Who are you?" I ask. To me, her identity matters.

"I am a ghost of Birds past, and I am your mentor. My name is Dove."

"But you're..." My words hinge on the edge of insulting her.

Dove rolls her eyes, but she doesn't seem offended. "Shocking, isn't it? Time makes fools of us all. And the Immortal Treatment was not invented in my Bird era."

Sitting up, I feel silkworm sheets encasing me as I finally start to get my bearings. But my compass is busted, and I don't know how to get home to Sky. This isn't a nightmare. The sorrow inside my chest and the ache in my throat are all too real.

"Director Owl assigned me as your mentor, and I am happy to take on the task. Of course, if you want me to leave—"

She starts to stand, but I grab her hand. Having another feminine presence in my room comforts me, especially when she appears to be the same age as my mother. "No, please stay." She's not as gentle as my mother, but she's not as guarded, either. Dove acts like she has nothing to hide. No secrets to keep. After a deep breath, I ask her where she came from.

She helps me get settled. "Some of us are born in this Aviary. For us, it is our home. For others, it is more." Traces of memory seem to curl into her words.

She turns to me with pearl-drop eyes, pale as her hair but with a hint of silver I almost don't catch. "I would rather hear about you. We need to discuss your place here."

"There is no place here for me."

Dove stands up, then sweeps toward one of the windows. Her white dress falls in layered wisps, plumage-like, to the floor, sliced in thin cuts along the sides to display just a glimpse of skin. Her tone is gentle as she feebly tries to make me understand. "I know you see this place as a prison, but Owl is your protector, not your jailer. I don't know much about you yet, but judging from your hands and your body, you cannot begin to fathom what scars a place like this can leave on you."

Dove smooths her hair to the side, turning around so I can see the jagged black line dirtying the back of her neck. "I received this more than a decade ago from another working Bird. Ostrich's handiwork. She came at me with a knife." She releases her hair, but I notice a tattoo on the other side of her neck: a tiny white dove. "Before he was even a director, Owl found me and stitched me up himself. He saved my life. And now, Ostrich and I are both caretakers. Nightingale will be your lethal enemy here."

Crossing my arms, I look away, choosing to ignore the name. "It wouldn't have happened if you hadn't been here."

"Can you really be so naïve? If you'd stayed in the Glass District, your modesty, your dignity, your virtue would've been ripped from you just like that. A Breakable in no time flat. The Aviary is a dream by comparison."

"So, I should be thankful for the Isolation Room?"

"In order to survive this place, you cannot cling so closely to your old self."

"It's the only way I know how to survive."

Dove reaches out to touch my cheek, but I reject it. She sighs. "This is your reality now. For most of these girls, this place is the best life has to offer. Some have been groomed for this since birth."

As Luc said, I have no *grooming*.

I don't want a new life. I am Serenity. Not some Bird. Not a body to be used. My mother was born inside the Temple, and she lost herself in the Penthouse.

"You are so different from them," Dove remarks, angling her head in curiosity. "I was...like you. When Owl asked if I would become your mentor, I said yes because you remind me of how I was long ago. And my daughter..."

Her daughter.

"Was she born here?" I ask, but Dove doesn't explain.

Her confession surprises me. In these times, the birth rate is low thanks to all the narcotics and chemicals pumped into girls. More miscarriages and stillbirths occur than healthy births.

Since she doesn't answer, I pose another question. "How did you survive?"

"I wised up. I became careful, and I am quiet."

"I've never been very...quiet." Or careful, for that matter.

"Some girls depend on the guards. Some offer them favors in return for protection."

My stomach churns at the word *favors*, but I keep quiet as Dove continues, "It's not something I'd advise in your case. You will have high-ranking clientele, and certain restrictions will be required to set you apart."

I want to bite the pillow. Let the feathers clog up my mouth at the thought of a client.

"I cannot protect you in this place," Dove goes on. "And you will *need* protection."

"Why?"

"Because of what you will become. He wants to announce it himself," she says, answering the question steeping in my mind. "Owl will give you his protection until your first client. Until then, play your right cards when it comes to your competition. From the broken mirror, I can tell you don't scare easily, but is your body strong enough for this place?"

It's a fair question. My will certainly is.

Dove takes me by the hand, "Come now, I will prepare you for dinner. I want to be your friend if you'll let me. But if you refuse, other hands will prepare you until you are trained. If I had the chance, I would go back and listen to my mentor, but I didn't. That night is burned into my memory forever. Those hands…" Her slight shudder tells me that no matter how long ago it was, it's still fresh in her mind.

I want to tell her that I'm not afraid of the hands, but the truth is something she can read in my eyes, so I slip out of the bed and stand before her. Despite her speech, I will hold onto my own reality for now. I won't shed myself like a cicada. Won't become a ghost to whatever creation Luc deems for me. But I will also go to dinner of my own will. The Isolation Room has cooled the lightning just enough. Tonight, I will stand at Luc's side and let him name me however he wishes.

"Serenity." With my head raised high, I announce, "My name is Serenity."

Dove doesn't respond. She only nods like she understands what I'm doing when I give my true name to her before saying, "We don't have time to waste."

I allow her to lead me to the mirror, then strip out of my clothes just as she asks, but I must take my time—the first time I've undressed for anyone. She even gives me a white towel to tuck around myself, though it leaves much of my legs, arms, and upper chest bare. Meanwhile, she taps the mirror a few times until a digital screen appears, but this one is different. It flashes once. A body scanner. In less than a minute, my body is projected on the screen with my designated costume, makeup, and hair for the evening. There are multiple options, but Dove doesn't ask me if I want to select a different one. Not that I should care… Lips tightening, I square my shoulders. I do *not* care.

After seating me in front of the mirrors, Dove paints the skin of my arms in elaborate white feather designs. The paint has no incandescence or gloss, but when she's finished, she attaches pearls onto random spots on my arms and even my hands. I decide not to look in the mirror yet.

"We only do this for first introductions—and exhibits, of course."

"Why a human? Why not automatic? Like NAILS?" I refer to the abbreviation for the technological invention Neuro Applicator for Individual's Live Structure. A fancy long name for the upgraded 3D body-art printer. It began as a simple process for painting nails before it was expanded.

"Temple tech," Dove clarifies, moving to my neck. "We are equipped with the facial ones, but Owl prefers to maintain a supply of mentors who are practiced in this art to interact with the present Birds."

More grooming, I think snidely, *because getting used to people touching your body is a requirement.*

"My skill as a painter manifested at an early age." Dove continues, sliding the brush over my skin. "Everyone has a skill that can be used to satisfy the needs of our clients. My painter's hands impressed my clients, but I enjoy this more."

I wince, trying not to picture her client time, while Dove grows quiet in her work. Despite the paint she applies over my tattoo, the feather still glows through. Again, I feel the overwhelming urge to cup my hand over it, to scratch my nails across it, but the luminescent ink will never come off. The implant beneath it is wired into my nerves.

Next, Dove brings the dress I am to wear. White, of course. The corset and off-the-shoulder sleeves are made of cobwebby lace. Strung loosely together, it is held by delicate stitches. At my waist, hundreds of white feathers overlay each other into a great skirt that sweeps the floor.

When I face the three-way mirror, Dove stands behind me to admire her handiwork.

Tears fill my eyes. Undone by the gown, I raise a pearled hand to my face and to the skin that seems so alien revealed this way. It's not supposed to be this bare. "I've never felt so…"

"Exposed," Dove finishes. "I felt that way at first. But I learned to appreciate it. Beauty is nothing to be ashamed of."

"Even if it's exploited?"

She cups my shoulders. "Tonight, you are just a girl going to dinner. Put all other thoughts out of your mind. This is your beauty to hold and to own. If *you* feel beautiful, what else matters?"

I don't need all this to know I'm beautiful, but since the Immortal Treatment intensified my hair and softened my skin, these clothes make everything…astonishing. Sky's always reminded me how dangerous my beauty is in this world, but it's the first time I've seen that come to life. All at once, I feel powerful and vulnerable.

Peering at Dove in the mirror, I bite down on my lower lip. "I've tried to cover myself all my life…"

She places her hands on my arms. "If it helps, Serenity, consider all the other girls on the outside who would scavenge for just a few of these feathers." Images from the Glass District play in my mind, and I nod. Every memory of those shriveled girls with their mouths ever silent but eyes screaming like lost banshees warning of District deaths became pieces of the armor I've donned for years. Armor that has shrunk from wandering eyes, resisted any advance, restrained any unwanted touch, and refused even the thought of intimacy with a man.

Somehow, I must reinforce that armor. No chinks allowed.

I can't break away from the mirage inside the mirror. "I don't know who she is."

"It doesn't matter. It is the girl inside who matters. She knows who she wants to be. She can be the one from the past, from the future, or she can be both at the same time."

I don't ask Dove how I can be the last person. Dove still bears her Aviary name. She still uses her skills from her days of working with clients. Has she learned how to blend both lives together? Could she teach me what my mother never mastered? If I carry any of my mother inside me, will I become a ghost to some Bird?

Dove pins portions of my renegade hair to the back of my skull with pearls. Picking up a miniature set of white wings, she pins them onto the edge of my head so they accent my silvery, dripping curls until there is more Bird than girl.

"Who am I?" I ask once she finishes. "I have to know. Am I an egret? Or an albatross?" I close my eyes. Picture the great white flying bird I found in a book once.

That's when I realize Dove is gone. My breath battles through the labyrinth of my lungs; his fingers roll across my neck instead. He leans over so his mouth can frost across my curls. So his nose can inhale my scent.

Luc's hands depart from my neck, leaving in their wake a silver chain with a silver charm—a white bird, tiny diamond-encrusted eyes with a long, graceful neck. Curved.

I recognize the bird before the director speaks the words. But his whisper still chills the blood beneath my skin when he addresses me. "You are my Swan."

CONFLICT STIRS THE WATER INSIDE me when it comes to Luc. To say I am attracted to him would be a grievous understatement. Something about the way his fingers nibble the skin of my neck and how he speaks, not to mention the way he is dressed. A long-sleeved white shirt with a collar and simple white pants accentuate his becoming facial features all the more. I am drawn to the blue kingdom of his eyes, the dark underworld of his brows, and the ever-present upward curve of his mouth.

Sometimes, the body wants what the mind does not. Fortunately, my mind is stronger.

"You are devastating," he breathes.

He turns me toward him, touches once again the swan charm at the hollow of my throat, and draws my arm into his. Perhaps I can muster up every part of my strength and push him down the staircase, but between the threat of the Isolation Room and Luc's tantalizing demeanor, I err on the side of caution. Maybe this fascination stems from him playing the hero; maybe he's already brainwashing me. I wonder if Director Force ever tantalized my mother.

Luc leads me through the halls, then down the grand staircase to the ballroom dining hall where the rest of the Birds flutter in yet another massive glass cage. Hawks watch them from behind the great bird-shaped table—security guards, men wearing black eye masks to sequester their identity.

Tonight, I am on Luc's arm.

Some Birds watch me in obvious envy, and I finally understand what Dove was talking about. All eyes turn on me, murderous like battlefields waiting to taste blood when Luc seats me next to him, cups my bare shoulders, and proceeds with his announcement.

"We have a new addition to our Aviary today. After all these years, the Swan has come to us. I trust you will treat her with the same respect that you treat me."

Every eye is a crazed whirlwind while they murmur amongst

themselves.

I hear a few whispers rush through the crowd, the most prominent being...

What will Nightingale do?

Nightingale.

Dove warned me about this Bird. My most lethal enemy, she'd said. Can I really see a fellow girl as more of an enemy than Luc? He's the one who plucked me from the Glass District. He's the one who ordered the Immortal Treatment. He's the one who trapped me in this glass prison.

I remind myself of all these things, but every time I glance at Luc, he never fails to notice my gaze. His eyes always converge on mine at the exact same moment. Every time, he renders me paralyzed. His very eyes can leach the warmth from my blood. Fill my veins with frost.

I can barely focus on the meal when it arrives. Instead, I watch the Birds, their feet bare like mine, many with skin dyed in unusual colors to suit their titles. No skin dyes ever conceal their tattoos.

"Where is Nightingale?" Luc asks from my right side, his question directed to Ostrich, who stands with her back braced against the south wall. Or I assume it's Ostrich since she has the bird tattooed on her neck. Caretakers all seem to have birds tattooed on their necks. The rest of us have feather tattoos on our shoulders. Dove remains at the east wall behind me.

"Fashionably late," chirps a voice like champagne bubbles.

My skin shrivels. Everything about this girl is my opposite. She doesn't wear dress. Instead, her pale patina of skin is arrayed in black feathers as if they are sewn onto her. Two black birds cover her chest, wings drawn into their bodies and heads curling inward, beaks camouflaged inside the plumage of their breasts. At first, I think they're props, but when I see the telltale inhale and exhale—the movement and the flutter of feathers—I realize the birds are real. Either well trained on a whole different level, or very convincing synthetic ones. Nightingale's hair is black, shadowing her back with a vestige of mystery and magic. She seems foreign. Inhuman.

I don't dare lower my head. Not even when her black eyes imprint mine.

Luc takes her hand in his own, fingers rubbing knuckles,

mouth bare against the back of her palm. "Nightingale."

"I see someone has finally filled the last chair." Her words are pointed as she sits at the table.

"The Swan." Luc's quick smile accents the two words, but Nightingale is unimpressed.

"And tell me, *Swan*..." she sticks her fork into the suckling pork on her plate, "what is your gift?"

If she wants to play this game, I will rise to the occasion. "I'm a dragon in disguise." If this place is a matter of survival, I'm not afraid of showing my true colors. For me, my words are my weapons. My mouth will do what my body cannot.

Beyond the rim of his wineglass, Luc observes the conversation. Everyone waits for one of us to capitulate.

After putting down her fork, Nightingale picks up her wineglass, leans back in her seat, and eyes me from across the crimson liquid. "I suppose clients will find that most...*appealing*. A body of scales," she speculates.

"Not scales," Luc interrupts. "Fire."

The room is quiet. I am grateful for my captor in this moment, a feeling I'm not quite sure what to do with.

"Nightingale," Luc says, breaking the silence. "Will you indulge us in a song?"

Nightingale narrows her eyes at me before dabbing the corners of her mouth with her napkin and announcing, "I would be honored."

Why I assumed she was randomly named the Nightingale, I can't fathom. When she stands and opens her mouth, her voice is high as the ever-rising clouds, as mournful as a lost angel with a broken wing. One who wanders around the table, eyes occasionally pinning mine. If a vacuum sucked away every speck of her physical beauty, she would still remain exquisite because of her voice.

Everyone applauds when she finishes. Luc's eyes skim all along her body as she strays back to her seat. However, I recognize that he seems to regard her with the eyes of an artist admiring his work, not the hungering gaze he adopts when he looks at me. That notion fills me with wonder—not disgust—and I can't fathom why.

"I am eager to determine what your talent is," Nightingale says to me. Her voice is incomparable; I could never possess such beauty.

"I'm sure you are." I reach for my glass, idly inspect the contents.

Luc clears his throat. "Remember, my fledglings, you've had a fair respite this past week. But vacation time is over. As many of you know, this Saturday is the beginning of a busy month. Over the next few weekends, important clients will be visiting. Your performance will be judged at the end of every weekend. The grand opening of the Swan exhibit will commence soon. Some of you will undoubtedly attend as escorts; the rest may come of your own accord."

Nightingale merely raises her glass, taking a sip, her deep-set eyes like two black thorns ready to pierce anything and anyone. Not intimidated, I match her gaze while focusing on Luc's words.

"The arrival of the Swan has prompted me to bring in extra security." Luc inclines his head to the double-door entryway where a number of black-uniformed guards appear. All masked in the same black, except one whose eyes are hidden by red.

"As all of you know, my head of security met with an accident. Meet his replacement." Luc motions a hand to the red-masked man who approaches the head of the table.

This newcomer is tall. He's a couple of inches taller than Luc, putting him well over a foot above me. His arms are impressive with eddies of muscles there. Some girls murmur and giggle while ogling him.

"You will address him as Vulture. In addition to acting as my head of security, he will serve as Swan's personal guard." Protecting his investment, it appears.

Despite Vulture's mask, he could never hide his identity from me. Those warm, roan eyes are too familiar. Nutmeg locks pulled back into a familiar ponytail, his indelible muscles could never be unrecognizable. I am one side of a coin, and he is the other. If we were melted down, we would still be one. If one side is broken, so would be the other.

I must bite hard on my lip to keep my grin from spreading. So hard I draw blood.

Sky has arrived.

Seven
AttacKed

H*E'S HERE TO BRING ME* home. The thought nearly melts me like snow in a campfire. But even as I strip all the feathers from my skin after dinner, my certainty wavers. His eyes never once skimmed mine tonight.

Still, I will wait. For the moment, I will hope.

"Are you thinking about the Isolation Room?" Dove wonders as she holds up a light cotton nightgown.

Until now, I hadn't realized I've been frowning. I press my lips into a straight line, attempting to rearrange my face into neutrality before staring in the mirror. Dove wipes the Swan away, scoops out the pins one by one, and scrubs away the paint until I am Serenity again. After, she helps me into the nightgown.

"How many times were you sent?" I want to know.

"Plenty." Dove buttons up my collar and the edges of my long-sleeves. "The Isolation Room gets to know you better over time."

One thing I do understand—I never want to return. I can't handle another visit to the Penthouse. All my life, I've avoided any press releases or articles about Director Force because I never want to know what he looks like. Thanks to the Isolation Room, I've felt his whip. I'll be damned if it ever shows me his face. If that means cooperating on the surface, then I will accept that. But I still have to get to Sky, get him alone somehow.

Dove turns down the sheets, but I'm not ready to sink into them yet. Instead, I drag a brush through my hair, turning my curls into frizzy waves. "Luc says my display will be finished tomorrow, whatever that means."

Dove clasps her hands in front of herself. "It will be better if you address him as Owl or director," she advises with a sigh. "And just like every girl gets a glass cage in the District, all the girls here get a display. Owl designs each one himself; it's the stage he sets for each Bird's exhibit."

"Like a set for a TV show," I say, and Dove nods. I tug on a tendril of hair, coil it around a finger, anxious. "I've heard of temporary…paralysis?"

Dove sighs. "It is a museum, Swan. The girls here are art. That is why the displays are called exhibits."

Whether I'm conflicted about Luc, I will rip out his beating heart before he can inject anything inside of me to freeze my limbs. Hopefully, Sky will get me out of here before I have to find out.

"Owl has searched many long years for his Swan. Even before he was director," Dove says, looking me in the eye. "Innocence is rare in this world. I never imagined he would find it until now." She gathers my hair in her hands, then lets it fall again. "You may be naïve, but you are fierce all the same. You'll need that ferocity." Nodding, I consider Nightingale, the blood and poison in her eyes.

Tonight is not a night for sleeping.

Once Dove is gone, I turn on the interface that controls the room and discover voxel-screens will play on the windows as well as the walls. However, the settings are not manual, and all the projected images are Birds past and present. Hundreds of different exhibits flash before my eyes. The only other available images are swans. Awe overcomes me as a swan flutters right above my head. I reach up, my hand interacting with the cooled laser image, which looks so real. The swan is motion sensitive and responds to my touch, bowing her head, beak curving toward my lips to impart a kiss.

Turning the displays off, I try the ambience instead and groan, ready to rip my hair from my scalp. Nothing but bird calls and twitters. Instead, I stray toward the fish tank in the other room. The opposite of birds. The water reminds me of the fountains that grace the courtyards of the hotels Sky and I grew up in. I spread my hand against the glass, where a fish kisses one of my fingers before promptly darting away.

A moment later, I feel other fingers winnowing through my hair. I don't turn around. I know who they belong to. He leans closer, breathing in my strands. "Your performance tonight was exemplary."

I place my other hand against the glass, arch my spine so my stomach flattens against it and away from him. Still, his hand eddies along the back of my neck, and he twines his fingers around the necklace he gave me.

There is only a handheld mirror sitting on an end table nearby. If I could reach it, smash it, I could… but that would only land me back in the Isolation Room.

Breathe. Control yourself.

I watch the fish, gypsies trapped in a crystal ball. No choice but to swim in endless, fathomless circles because they can't understand the world beyond the glass. Like my mother before she met my father.

The Aviary director strays to my side. "The Swan embodies what every museum has sought for so many years. Ever since the days of innocence were lost."

He scoots closer, preparing to cup my shoulders, but I scramble away from him. "And what good is innocence in a place like this?" *Where men devour it in one night?* I almost say.

Luc leans against the fish tank, crosses his arms. "After you've spent some time here, I believe you will think better of me."

I pause before answering, which is not in my nature. "I highly doubt that."

Luc does not respond, only picks up the tray from the table. It holds a glass of some algae-green substance. "It's a sleeping supplement," he says. "I give one to all my Birds at bedtime."

Tentative, I accept the glass, sniff its contents, and take one sip. It tastes like chalk. For one moment, I consider dumping it on his head, but I remember the Isolation Room and think better of it. Then, I realize there could be anything in the concoction I've just sipped—perhaps a paralyzing agent, all the better to make me into a statue, inanimate as some doll. I let the glass drop to the tiled floor, pleased by the way it shatters and admiring the dark green puddle I've just created.

Luc shakes his head, but smiles. "I'll let that one go." He

places an order for maid service. Guilt rises when I consider the poor sap who must clean up my mess. Only to realize the room is equipped with electronic claws that charge from a nearby wall and take care of the glass and puddle.

The fish are lucky; their forgetful lives are a blessing compared to mine.

I walk away from Luc and approach the bedroom, knowing he will follow. After stepping down from the solid floor of the adjacent sitting room, the luxurious rug in the bedroom cushions my feet. I brush my fingers across the length of white sheets, of pillows filled with feathers.

"I want you to know I will never paralyze you." Every word of Luc's is like a vessel of oxygen breathing life back into me. "Why would I? When you are so much more *real* like this? Can you not understand how long I've searched for someone like you?"

"So, you'd never let me go?" I challenge. "Not even for a beautiful price? I've heard about the Centre searching for girls like me, for breeding."

Luc's eyebrows furrow, expression like a cannon igniting. "You are too young." He uses a flimsy excuse. My mother was younger than me when she gave birth.

I back against the bed frame, lean my head against the white wood. "What does the Swan mean to you personally? Why have you searched for years?"

Luc's hollow gaze signals I will receive no answers tonight. "Get some sleep. Your display will be ready tomorrow. I'm eager to see how you take to it."

When he turns his back, I yearn to throw something. Or scream. But I restrain myself. "You don't even know me—and you never will."

He turns. "Oh, but I will learn."

I shake my head. "You have no right."

"Perhaps we could begin with something simple—your real name."

I want to say my name. I want the confirmation I am nobody's Swan. Even if I give this to Luc, it's my power, accepting my own beauty.

"Serenity."

In a voice that skims the breath of a whisper, he repeats my name like a chant. Then, he grins. "Ironic."

I try not to force a smile. "You have no idea."

"Goodnight, Swan." Reinforcement. He won't use my real name, but he still holds it.

When he leaves, he doesn't lock the door. Is that a token of trust? I realize Vulture must be right outside my door, guarding me, and the thought kindles a fire inside my chest.

I straighten, the urge to speak with him too strong to ignore.

Outside, the hall is empty. I flick my head back and forth. Where is he? I wander down the corridor to the staircase. This place is a haunted mausoleum of glass and darkness, the stairs just as empty and voiceless as the halls. No security waiting in the main room underneath the domed glass ceiling. No staff disguised in the corners. Why hasn't Sky come?

Behind me, I feel sudden body warmth, but I don't even get the chance to turn my head.

Hands push hard against my body. I try to regain balance, but the glass staircase rises to meet me. At the last second, I grab onto a clump of dress, and the girl's body tumbles down with mine. I land sharply, painfully, and each new collision with the steps brings a fresh surge of pain. If my bones are moaning and my body is screaming as we roll together, at least the girl who pushed me is experiencing the same.

Pain poisons all other senses. Besides, it's too dark to see anything, but I hear her groan before she gets to her knees and hobbles away. She's taller than me. That's all I can make out, but that hardly narrows it down. Dove was right. I have more to fear from the other girls than Luc.

"*Don't move.*" I recognize the voice. I've heard it many times. Any time I tried to sneak out of the hotel, any time I bent the rules. He's angry with me. He has every right to be. It was stupid of me to leave the room. Should've waited for him—then and now.

My body pulses with pain, thrums with tenderness. "Sky!" I smile despite the pain. Tears threaten to choke my words.

"Shh!"

"Sky," I whisper. My body is on fire from the pain, but my heart burns hotter because that's what hope does. It lets people

The Aviary

stand again.

Pain explodes in my leg when I try to get to my feet. My vision blurs like I'm under water, and I tumble to the ground, memorizing his eyes through the red mask.

"You always find me."

My consciousness shatters, unleashing black fog that pulls at my eyes and snuffs out all light.

Eight
My Old Life

"Mmm. Breakables can't do this."

"What?" Sky remained in his pool chair, averting his eyes.

Sky stopped joining me years ago. He would only watch me swim from one of the pool chairs while I reveled. Like I did tonight. I braced my hands along the side of the pool, wondering if I'd ever get to swim with him again, wondering why he'd put so much distance between us these days.

"*This*." I motioned around the pool atmosphere. "They can't sneak into the hotel pool after hours, strip to their undergarments, and splash around. Girls in the Glass Districts can't swim in the moonlight or steal towels." Or even shiver without permission.

"Don't let your mother catch you saying that word."

"Breakables?"

"Yeah, you know how she feels about it."

"Everyone says it." It was all the latest rage back when the Red-Light District was renamed the Glass District. Now, it is common. My mother never bothered to explain why she hated it so much.

"You know what Kerrick will do if he sees you wearing that." Sky cocked his head back to his book while a ringlet of his hair, a lighter shade of his earthy umber eyes, tumbled onto his cheekbone.

I rolled my eyes because Sky was right—my dad would probably burst a blood vessel if he saw me. "Next best thing after skinny dipping. If we were back at our lake house—"

THE AVIARY

"This isn't the lake house. If he were here, he'd give you a lecture."

A lengthy one filled with a mass of colorful vocabulary that would probably just get stuck in the network of cottony fluff in my head. Unlike my mother, actions were more appropriate when it came to me. My mother needed my father's words. Sky provided action, which was why our dynamic worked so well.

I thought about the Breakables again, living their lives like ghosts in obedience and fear or blind belief.

It was probably better to let the conversation rest. After all, I could end up talking to him about girls in museums, and then there would *really* be some trouble. Museums are Sky's kryptonite. Maybe because they're a Family business. Maybe because just the mention of the word made him wonder if his Family owns one.

As I swam, I let the water disturb those thoughts until they dissolved like popped bubbles.

I would never become a ghost.

Devious, I smiled at Sky just before splashing him.

Rage contorting his face, Sky stood from his chair with the full height of his six-foot-five shadow towering over me. He shook out his shirt, glaring.

"Serenity." He took one look at me before grunting and turning around.

Sky might not be my real brother, but he is still my everything—always enough for me. We are paper flowers in the attic. No sunlight to help us grow; we've held on to each other for warmth, our lives tethered in nothing but each other.

With the Temple never giving up its search for my mother and me, discretion was paramount. My parents always brought us to hotels when it was busiest to avoid smugglers. For some reason, they'd never bothered to just leave Sky and me holed up in one of their isolated country cabins or seaside condos even though they were so paranoid about my safety. My father came from wealth and was well paid during his time working for the Temple, so I knew they had the money to buy a house, rather than just rent one from time to time. If my mother wanted to hide from the Temple director so much, then why did she and my father always return to the Five Boroughs?

I sank into the pool, rejoicing in the sensation of my curls floating behind me in the water. With the moonlight bathing me, I imagined I was some sort of mermaid, but it had to be a dark mermaid, the kind with silver hair journeying to her hips and white skin befitting her dark inhabitance that swam in deep water far away from the sun. The kind who could drag men down to the depths with her.

"Shouldn't Mom and Dad be back by now?" I asked.

Sky grunted, and the muscles in his neck tensed as he responded, "Typical." Familiar body language he only used when he talked about my parents.

"Where do you think we'll go tomorrow?" I wondered just as Sky braced on the armrest of the lounge chair, flexing the muscles that could make a gladiator weep. The moonlight sewed its rays into his golden skin, the polar opposite of me.

Sky didn't answer. It was getting annoying.

We returned to the hotel room. Along the way, I received numerous stares, some curious but others hungry. But Sky kept a firm, almost possessive hand on my back during the entire trek. When he inserted his card key, I could already hear the sobs from inside. My mother sat on the couch, face tucked into her hands with my father just next to her, cupping her shoulder, body leaning into hers as he murmured into her ear. It wasn't abnormal to see my mother crying. What was abnormal were the bruises flowering on her arms. Sky shut the door behind us even as I rushed into the sitting room.

"Mom!" I cried, making my way toward her with the towel still tucked around my frame.

My father retrieved a throw blanket from the couch, then wrapped it around her to conceal the bruises. He also scraped away a piece of neuro-latex still sticking to her skin. They changed their features when they went outside on one of their missions, ones I was forbidden to know about. My mother had taken some skills from the Temple with her. Skin masks of all kinds was one of them. It could alter her features within moments.

"Serenity," my father said, taking my arm. "It's nothing to be concerned about. Your mother just needs a moment of space." She always needed space. Always kept a blanket over her past to muffle its secrets.

"What happened?" I asked her, sinking onto the couch. "Where did you go? Who did this to you?"

This wasn't the first time she'd appeared with bruises after one of their excursions. It hadn't happened in months, but we were in the Rome of our country, so to speak, and men were far more aggressive, confident, and demanding here. And my mother was still young and beautiful.

My father interjected again. "Serenity, go take your shower. Your mother will be available after that. And we will also discuss your midnight swim."

I heaved a sigh but didn't waste any time. The sooner I showered and dressed, the sooner I could talk to my mother. Sky's and my room were connected by an adjoining door while Mom and Dad shared the master bedroom on the opposite side of the main room. While I showered, I wove through the different options of what could've happened.

All throughout the years, I'd never asked many questions. Homeschooling, moving from place to place, sneaking out to swim, and spending time with Sky kept me preoccupied from wondering too much about where my parents went during the night and why they returned during the wee hours of the morning. Every now and then, Sky would leave the hotel for a couple of hours, but he'd always return and tell me everything about where he went.

The knock at the adjoining door prompted me to dress quickly, tease my fingers through my hair, and collect myself before permitting Sky to enter. In his open palm was a small glass snow globe.

"For your collection." He winked.

I snatched the item, fingering it for a moment before shaking it again and again.

"Hey," Sky protested while leaning against the door. "What'd that poor thing ever do to you?"

I liked these old-school ones, too. Not the digital ones that had animated snow flurries, negating the need to shake. Shaking was the fun part.

My smile crooked when I said, "Thank you, Sky." I paused to study the miniature city in my hand before kissing his cheek. He knew I enjoyed bringing a piece of each city with me wherever we traveled. Home wasn't one place. Home was chunks of skyscrapers, hotels, lake houses, seaside villas, and mountain cabins. These were enough for me. I may be wild, but I'm not dumb. I know what happens to girls on the outside. I know what happened to my mother.

Sky relayed the message. "Your mother's ready for you."

That was an understatement. She was never ready for me.

"Are you going to go work out?" I asked, knowing Sky always used the hotel weight rooms every night and morning. Another thing I never complained about since he was so hell-bent about it—part of his protector frame of mind. My father also trained him from time to time; the Temple had higher standards for its security than the Secret Service. Temple guards were practically ninjas.

He shook his head. "Later. I'd like to finish my book first. Be on the couch." He squeezed my arm once, leaving a pinch of warmth there before I approached my parents' bedroom. Guess Sky and I had something in common: he liked old-school books.

Inside, the curtains were drawn and lights turned off. Ironically, my mother feels most comfortable in darkness. Part of me imagines Force kept the lights on when he came for her at night. Maybe the darkness is her shield.

"Serenity," she mumbled, gesturing to a place on the bed next to her.

I concentrated on the object in her hands, which was a small chest. More of a jewelry box—one my father had given her years ago so she could store the items she'd escaped with when she'd fled the Temple. Forbidden to me. Her thumbs rubbed the wooden lid, but she made no motion to open it.

As I sank onto the bed next to her, she placed the box back on her nightstand. Her nightgown strap slid down her shoulder, betraying the edges of her scars. Each one was like a silver thread. When I was a child, I'd stepped in on her showering by accident and saw them all. A patchwork pattern of old lacerations and gashes healed into threadlike scars on her back. That was the first day I understood what a monster Force was, what he'd done to my mother. From that day on, I didn't ask her any more questions even though my hands ached to open her chest.

"Where were you?" I hoped it was a safe enough question.

My mother isn't a good liar. Still, some of her words bore a chime of truth, so I sighed and listened. "Your father and I met with some activists. But some Family discovered us. We got out, but others weren't so…lucky." Her last word is clouded in shame. I couldn't ever bear the weight of regret like she does. Instead, I plunge headfirst and fight my way out, regrets left far behind me. They're too slow to catch up anyway.

"Mom, why don't you tell me the truth? I'm sixteen now. I can handle whatever you need to tell me."

My mother shook her head. "Your strength is different from mine. You wear yours so proudly. You don't keep one bit of it tucked inside you. But I have to. My secrets are the only thing, the only way I can…cope. I wasn't allowed to have any secrets back at the…" She wasn't strong enough to say the word.

The Temple was still a ghost taunting her, drifting in and out of her memories. But I couldn't push her no matter how much I wanted to. Secrets were my mother's only bit of power. I couldn't take them away from her. She had to give them at the right time.

"Daddy." I peered at my father when he entered the room, a relaxed smile on his face. He cupped my shoulder once and nodded, signaling it was his turn.

My father and I didn't have many words for each other. He was a master at reading expressions and body language, part of his expertise when he worked in the Temple. He always seemed to register what was in my head. Unlike Sky, my father didn't have a temper.

Just before I turned to leave, he called my name and motioned to his cheek. I let out an airy giggle caught halfway between a sigh and a chuckle before rising to kiss his cheek. Before closing the door, I paused to watch my father gather my mother into the bed, draw her against his chest, and hold her in the fetal position while she whimpered into her pillow. He would make everything better. The best thing he ever did for my mother was stay with her. Stuck with her even in the dark days of the Temple until she realized he wasn't going to leave. The second-best thing he ever did was love her.

I closed the door, noticing Sky out of the corner of my eye. He sat on the couch reading the same book he was earlier.

At first, I said nothing and perused the magazine tablet on the side table by the couch, huffing every so often. Most were filled with interviews of Temple girls. Many I recognized from film trailers because they were often loaned to Hollywood.

"I don't know why you read that stuff. It just puts you in a foul mood."

I chucked the tablet at his head even though he was right. Pity that Sky's reflexes were too keen. He caught the tablet, then swept to the last page I had marked earlier just before narrowing his brows to look at me. "Like you need a magazine to determine your attractiveness. You don't even need me to remind you of that."

Or any other man from hotel guests to staff to passersby, who stopped in their tracks to ogle, drool, leer, flirt, and check me out in all other forms. I wasn't sure why I was always singled out when my mother was with me. She's every bit as beautiful as I am, if not more.

"It doesn't matter. I wasn't even reading it. I don't care."

"Yes, you do," he states.

I balled my hands into fists, leaped over the side of the couch, and crouched. "No, I don't! You know I'm going to my grave a virgin."

Sky eyed me from the opposite cushion. "Still holding to your mantra? Your *armor*? What if you change your mind?"

"Not. Going. To. Happen."

"What if someone changes it for you?"

"*You*. Won't. Let. That. Happen." I pointed out the obvious, relaxing a little.

"Meaning I'm your indentured-servant bodyguard for life."

I feigned a yawn. "You say servant. I say slave. Tomato, tomahtoe."

"Guess I can live with that." He shrugged, turning a page. "I've been under your power since you were an infant anyway."

"Never forget it," I warned with a smug smile before turning and flopping back so my head hit his leg, curls spread like dozens of spiraled halos.

Sky stared at me. "I'm serious." He rubbed his thumb against my cheek as if wiping at a smudge, expression softening, eyes deepening.

I didn't like his change in attitude. "Cut that out. Why don't we play a game?" I leapt off the couch, then targeted the playing cards on the kitchen table. Sky sighed behind me.

"Whatever you want, Serenity."

Just as I grabbed the cards, I turned back to him, my curiosity adopting his seriousness from a moment ago. "Sky, what if you're not there? Someday?" I wondered.

Sky turned then, eyes brutal and tense. He stood from the couch to approach me, leaned forward until our foreheads almost touched, eyes darting back and forth between my own to say, "I'll search for you. And I won't stop until I find you."

Nine
RecoVerY

UPON WAKING IN THE MORNING in the Aviary, my fingers meet with soft flesh.

"Dove…" She sits on the edge of my bed, holding my hand.

"I…what happened?" Sky. Sky happened.

What I wouldn't give for him to hold me right now. I almost forget he stopped holding me months ago. No hugs. No light pecks on the cheek. I can't so much as nudge or poke him without him wincing like my fingers are lightning rods. At least he kept his promise.

He found me.

"You've slept most of the day in recovery." Dove motions her head to the windows where the sun is stretched to its full height. "Owl has checked on you multiple times."

"Recovery?"

Seeming annoyed, Dove sighs. "He does not warn girls idly. He can't be there to protect you all the time. He told you to stay in your room. After Vulture found you, Owl had you transferred to the medical wing."

When I take inventory of my body, I discover all traces of pain are gone.

Dove must see the confusion on my face. "Your skin has been pigmented, and the bruises and lacerations are healing at an accelerated rate due to the Immortal Treatment." She glances away from me, the shadow of apprehension in her eyes. "The only reason you don't feel them is due to the remedies in your system."

The Aviary

Remedies? I peel away the narrow wad of cotton concealing the needle prick. "Pain medication," I say. That explains the numbness.

"An organic compound that will help block your brain's pain receptors. Luc insisted on non-synthetic compounds in your case."

While I'm mulling this over, Dove suddenly snaps, "You were foolish to leave your room. Did you really think you could escape? And what do you think would've happened once you were outside? You would've been taken to the Glass District in no time."

I don't tell her it wasn't my intention to escape. Don't breathe a word about searching for Sky.

I ponder how much has changed. My life was simple before this. I wished I'd appreciated my time behind hotel glass more. Better than Aviary glass any day of the week. No competition but my pillow fights with Sky. No emotional manipulation. No mind games. No sense of threat.

I discovered last night that the other Birds are just as dangerous as any man, even if I still don't know who my assailant is.

"Do you know who attacked me?" I ask, thinking there must be security cameras.

Dove shakes her head. "That is not my business. From what I've heard, the darkness would have impeded that. Someone must have known how to turn off the light sensors."

My cage used to be the hotels where I grew up. There, I knew what to do and how to act. Now, I would choose to spend an eternity inside those walls, just being Serenity instead of a caged bird. At least in the hotel, I always had one constant. Sky.

Who will I become here? Girls have adopted their feathers, seemingly as easy as zipping up a jacket. But I wear my lightning on my sleeve, and I always will.

After Dove departs, I thumb my silver tattoo. Like flames and frost, it taunts my skin. Somehow, I must keep the Aviary from conquering me.

Falling back against the bed pillow, I hear something crunch. Without hesitating, I reach beneath the pillowcase and withdraw a crumpled piece of paper. I recognize Sky's familiar chicken scratch:

Don't ever do that again, Serenity. Let me come to you. Be patient.

An hour later, Dove helps me dress. Thanks to my treatment, I'm healing well and can walk. By now, the numbness has subsided, and I feel the burden of the bruises with each movement. Sluggish, I put on the white dress Dove has laid out for me. It is more casual than the formal dinner ensemble from last night. Even so, there are still feathers stitched into random places on the material, which is light and decorated in lacy patches at the bottom. Anyone can see the skin of my knees where the hem stops.

I don't tell Dove how free my legs feel—no longer slaves to weighty pants or long skirts. When I sit in front of the mirror, she creates a certain magic in my hair, weaving the strands into a twisting sort of braid that cascades down my lower back. The braid is lovely and loose. Dove leaves the recalcitrant tendrils, oblivious of any order, to their own bidding. It's no surprise she interlaces white feathers into the braid.

"Some specialized pieces were custom designed for you." Dove motions to the assembly of Swan jewelry. A couple of wrist and arm cuffs, rings, earrings…I finger the arm cuff, the delicate swan wings, and the diamond-encrusted eye. Another gift from Luc. Pursuing my misguided desire, I slip it onto my forearm, flinching in surprise when it latches onto my skin, molding to my arm's curve. As soon as it's in place, the swan wings begin to flutter in slow, even movements while the diamond eye shimmers.

I sigh.

It's just a cuff. A very high-tech, impressive, expensive cuff.

"Did you always know how to do all this?" I ask, distracting my thoughts.

"To a degree. But when Birds are no longer fit for museum service, we are trained in the art of beautifying those who are. It just so happens I have a skill that coincides with it." Dove motions to the bottles of white paint on the counter near me.

For a moment, I think about refusing, but I remember this is something that holds meaning to her. These designs belong to Dove. She'd said she'd come close to becoming the Swan herself; I wonder if painting me causes her pain.

I don't ask to look at myself when she's through. I don't want to see. Don't want to remember the photograph of my mother as the Unicorn; I'm afraid of how similar my reflection might be. Instead, I curl up on the window ledge and stare outside at the garden.

"Owl will be here soon," she says while corking the paint bottles. "Your display is finished, but from what I've heard, he has something different in mind today."

I want her to define *different*, but Dove exits in short order. Bracing my knees to my chest, I lean forward against the windowpane.

"Would you like to see the gardens?" Luc utters from behind me.

"I'm looking at them now," I say, not bothering to take my eyes off the magnificent landscape. I hadn't heard him come in, but I'd seen his wavering reflection in the glass.

"Up close, Swan."

I say nothing, refusing to answer to Swan. Unfortunately, he's holding the cards and he knows it because I hear his footsteps getting softer as he walks away. More than anything, even more than I want to stubbornly cling to my pride, I want to get outside these glass walls.

"You said I was restricted to the Aviary," I point out, finally moving to look at him. He turns to me slowly, triumph in the creases around his smile. "And what about my *display*? Aren't you going to show me to my cage?" Like drawing an arrow back from a bow, I stretch the sarcasm in my voice.

"There is time."

Almost against my will, I study him. He wears another white shirt, one without a collar this time, and silver wings are embroidered into the fabric. Wings that flutter whenever the light hits them.

"I've arranged a suitable punishment for your behavior last night. Remaining in your room at night is one requirement I refuse to bend."

"Punishment?" I incline my head to him as my heartbeat quickens, thinking about the Isolation Room.

"You could have been taken… or killed." Luc's voice cracks. Worry lines crease his brow, but almost before they fully form, his face is stern again. Back to being nothing but the museum director once more.

"We'll discuss it later tonight. But for now, I am offering you a chance to see the property outside these walls."

I sit up a little taller. "You're taking me somewhere?"

"My museum is one of the few that houses a number of gardens. Most prefer to use their funding for oyster houses or chocolate shops since such aphrodisiacs provide more return on investment. But those are prominent in the town nearby, and the gardens are for my own personal enjoyment. Not many girls here are interested in flowering artwork. Perhaps you are like them?" He voices it as a question, but I can tell he is goading me. The flicker in his eyes makes it evident he's aware how badly I want to go.

When I do stand, I wince. Luc's face tightens as if he feels my pain, too. It's unsettling, how much attention he pays.

"Your dose has worn off." He scowls at my obvious discomfort. "I told Dove—"

"It wasn't her fault. I'm healing. That's what's important. I don't need anything for the bruises. I don't want anything else inside me."

I can't tell whether his smile is one of approval or if it's sardonic.

"No, I don't suppose you do."

WHEN WE REACH THE MAIN wing, I can see a few girls huddled inside the makeshift exhibits. My instinct is to herd myself closer to Luc, but I know hiding my gaze will only convince them of my vulnerability. I can't tell whether they are practicing or coping. Some of their movements beyond the glass seem forced, like they're trying too hard to be natural.

Luc guides me to a hallway with a moving walkway, which opens into one of the main exhibit areas. I tense until I realize this is just preparation time; there are no visitors yet.

In one exhibit, an iron park bench sits in the middle of a cobblestone road. Neutral colors paint the girl's skin, and she wears a transparent shift that clings to her subtle curves. Subtle if only because of how tiny she is. Smaller than me and thinner, with spindles for legs and arms. She is young, with childlike features, but I can see the hawk in her eyes.

"Did you know pigeons are among the strongest fliers?" Luc remarks.

There is a plaque of information about the bird next to the exhibit. Anything about the girl herself is limited to her ranking, which is nowhere close to others. I imagine she must be new. Nothing else. As a piece of artwork, she becomes an object, part of the décor. Girls lose themselves.

The moving walkway ends just past another display—the Blackbird exhibit. She's in the top five.

I pause.

Luc watches as I smooth a hand along the digital plaque. I read about the Bird before studying her. Her skin is black. For once, I recognize it as her own skin rather than paint. It is beautiful—the only visible paint on her skin is where yellow circles have been drawn around her eyes to evoke the pattern of the bird. All around her, flowers rise in exotic fiery reds, oranges, yellows, pinks, and purples. She stands with hands wrapped around their stems, neck arched to the side as if she's smelling them. Her only covering is the bit of black feathers strung across her breasts and bikini line.

"Perhaps I can introduce you to Blackbird sometime." Luc places a hand on the small of my back, sending a warm tingle up and down my spine. He leads me toward the door at the end of the walkway. "Interesting you seemed to connect with her exhibit. You're complete opposites. She has a tough exterior, but she doesn't make trouble. And I've never had a complaint about her services."

Each exhibit is so unique, complex, and eye catching. I can imagine why this is one of the most popular museums in the country. The last one I see is Flamingo's. Her hair is snow white, but her naked skin is dyed bright pink and stuck with pink plumage along her bikini areas. She stands on one leg in the middle of a shallow pool of water surrounded by tropical trees. I wonder how many requests she receives.

I wonder how many requests *I* will receive. My stomach

clenches at the thought and my shoulders roll forward, caving my prominent chest inward.

Luc pauses before the door, rolls up his sleeve, and summons the technology humming beneath his skin. After a moment, the door responds.

"Is the entire Aviary in there?" I ask, glancing back at the door as it closes behind us.

Luc beams. "Yes. I am connected to every part of this Aviary."

After he's escorted me out of the museum, I realize how vast the facilities are. The city is quite some distance past the winding drive. From this vantage point, I can see the skyscrapers in the distance. A few other buildings pepper the area, and my guess is they include some restaurants or shops strategically placed near the museum to attract clientele. If I squint, I can make out the Temple miles beyond the city. It's still the tallest structure in the nation. A silver needle from this distance.

At the bottom of the drive is an enormous iron gate, and trees line either side of it. It's a prominent selling feature—the Aviary is an oasis of secrecy and wonder. No one can see anything beyond those trees and the lasered border fence, and no one could ever sneak in. Or out.

I wonder, not for the first time since dinner last night, how Sky managed to secure his position here.

Diverting my thoughts, Luc leads me from the courtyard to the first garden pathway, which creeps toward a white bridge. The structure arches over a pond with a trickling fountain. Only when we near it do I realize that what I first believed to be white marble is actually a mosaic of flowers. Some centrifugal force must hold them together, but all I can see are the pale blooms fused together, coating the bridge.

Luc pauses, turning back to extend a hand to me with those sultry shadows bathing the skin above his eyes.

More out of curiosity than anything, I follow him, but refuse the hand he offers.

Wind robs some petals from the branches above, distracting me from Luc's closeness and his hand once again on the small of my back. A few land on my shoulders, but I don't brush them away. On the far side of the pond, a translucent waterfall weeps

THE AVIARY

over jagged boulders. Luc leads me across a stone pathway in the shallow water that passes in front of the waterfall. Moss garnishes the stones where I stand. Mist sprays the ends of my dress. I reach out a hand toward the waterfall, longing to touch the steadfast stream.

I can't stop beaming even though I try. It's obvious Luc can tell how much I love this place.

This time, Luc doesn't offer; he just takes my hand when the stones come to a gap between the water and solid ground. I'm not remiss in noticing how his other one idles on my waist.

"What do you think?" Luc asks. "Could any girl compare to the natural beauties here?"

I answer his question with one of my own. "Could girls compare to birds?"

Luc draws his hand from my back. "Have you seen any birds in real life?"

"Only from a distance. Some of the courtyards had peacocks, pheasants. I've seen pigeons in a park. And up close, seagulls..." I reminisce about a few years ago when Sky and I were staying at an oceanside villa, and the seagull that had perched on my windowsill. A smile tugs my lips. "It kept pecking at the windowpane."

"That reminds me of you." He raises my hand to his mouth. "Always pecking at the glass. Never quiet."

He rubs his lips across the back of my knuckles, and I try to ignore how my skin prickles there. Instead, I look around for something else to focus on. The property of the Aviary is extensive. This garden alone is acres long. Part of it feels like a flowery prison, but better than a glass one. And no natural bird art here.

Rich and fertile, the trees ripen all around me, broken only by clusters of vibrant wildflowers. At my request, Luc permits me to pick one, so long as it's white. He explains the Birds are territorial about their colors. If I so much as pluck a pink flower to tuck in my hair, Flamingo will have every right to take offense. Color is only allowed in exhibits for background and makeup. Sometimes paint.

Luc is relentless. He seeks my hand again and again until I give up, allowing my fingers to tangle with his. From the fading sunlight to the early spring breeze, there is too much to enjoy without concerning myself with Luc's proximity. Despite knowing it's another subtle tactic, I don't care too much. He can hold my hand all he wants. Soon, I won't ever see him again.

The gardens and trees clear to a wooden cottage built atop the lake water in traditional Japanese fashion. Handcrafted wooden lanterns float around the house while willows protect the surrounding pathways. Millions of tiny pebbles decorate the foundation, flanking slabs of black stone for us to walk on. The front overlooks the lake, but toward its right side is a floor like marble where the glow from candlelit lanterns shimmers and frolics in random patterns. Two panels on this side slide apart to reveal the interior.

Luc steps onto the floor. "This is a solace house. I come here for retreat and meditation. You are the first I've brought here."

I flex my fingers at my side. "How many others have you whispered that lie to?"

At first, I think he might be upset, but Luc only chuckles. "It also happens to be a bathhouse."

Almost wincing, I withdraw my hand from his and form both into fists. I quickly manage to change the subject. "Some would disagree with you."

Luc tilts his head to the side. "Disagree about what?"

"Some say peacocks are the most beautiful bird."

Luc sniggers a little at my argumentative comment, then glides a hand along one seamless wooden panel. "Yes, indeed… beauty is in the eye of the beholder."

He closes the distance between us, his hands smoothing the skin of my arms, brows screwing down to command my attention. "One thing that is irreplaceable is innocence, Swan. I don't know how you came to be, but innocence is most valuable—so please believe me when I tell you I will preserve yours at all costs." His eyes are a tornado of shadows. Intimidating, bordering on menacing.

I open my mouth, ready to tell him I am not so innocent. My body, perhaps, but my heart and my mind are far from pure. But Sky interrupts us, and I lose my moment.

"Pardon me, Director Owl. There's been an incident that requires your immediate attention."

THE AVIARY

Luc's eyes are on me, hands still braced around my arms when he asks, "What sort of incident?"

"One of the girls has collapsed. She's in a coma."

Ten
BlacKbiRd

"Escort the Swan back to her room," Luc orders. "Take the garden tunnel through the aviary, please. Not the lobby." Another moment later and he's gone.

I reach for Sky, but my hopes sink when he turns his back on me. Until he whispers, "Wait, Serenity. Cameras." His eyes dart back and forth.

I want to shake him silly, but I restrain myself, following him past the bathhouse and into the aviary. Here, the twittering ambience doesn't annoy me as I take in the kaleidoscope of dozens of birds fluttering around the exotic trees, hopping from branch to branch, and others soaring above the trees just under the domed glass ceiling shedding sunlight everywhere. A colorful parrot flits down to a nearby branch and cocks his head at me as if curious, maybe wondering if I've brought bird food. More than anything, I want to stretch out my hand and see if he'll roost there, but it's not the time.

Sky still says nothing, leading me deeper into the aviary. The sound of rushing water grows until I see the tunnel ahead with the manmade waterfall in front of it. Inside is a viewing fence so I can watch the falls gush over rocks into a steady stream where a few birds sip and wet their wings. As soon as we enter the tunnel, Sky's hand catches my arm. He pulls me closer to the edge of the fence, then presses me against the rock wall just near the baying water. The rocks conceal us, the falls drowning out any noise we make; I understand this is one of the rare places with no cameras.

THE AVIARY

As soon as he signals that we are clear, I throw my arms around his neck and he winces. Though tempted to call him out on the hurtful action, I just pause, wondering what it is about me now that seems to bother him. I drive the thoughts back, tackling the more important matter.

"Sky," I say after I finish hugging him. "You've got to get me out of here. What happened? What are you doing here...like this?"

"You need to stay." It's the last thing I expect to come out of his mouth. "*We* need to stay."

I shake my head. "Do you know what he's planning? What I'll be used for here?"

"I can take you out of here. But if I do, we'll be on the run. Hunted."

"We've been hiding all our lives; it's nothing new."

"They have your DNA now. They know your face. If we leave now, we won't make it."

"Where are Mom and Dad?" I can hear the urgency and emotion in my own voice. None of this is what I'd hoped.

The shake of Sky's head and the deep mahogany in his pinched eyes inject panic straight into my spine. "Gone. They never came back to the hotel."

Fear shoots into me. "Why aren't you out there looking for them?"

"I *am*. And the best place for that is right here." He circles the air with his finger.

I don't understand. "Why here?"

"It's not safe for us to talk much longer. Listen, I'll be watching out for you. But whatever you do, don't pull another stunt like you did last night. I just barely got there in time. If you do it again..." He drops his eyes. "Just don't, okay? You'll get us both into trouble."

"What are you talking about?"

I take a step toward him, only to slip on the path, stones slick from the spray of the falls. Reaching out, I grab Sky around the waist to stabilize myself. He rights me, but thrusts away at the contact, arching his back and wincing.

Foreboding roils in my gut. "You need to tell me what the hell is going on," I seethe.

Reluctantly, Sky turns and lifts his shirt so I can see the bruises soiling his hard abs and the lash marks covering his back. Deep cuts of dried blood are like an intricate latticework there. These are Sky's brand, like my tattoo. Except he didn't do anything wrong.

My heartbeat skitters out of control, and angry tears fill my eyes.

Sky drops his shirt, not meeting my gaze. "I'm your guard. If anything happens to you, I'm held responsible."

At my involuntary gasp, he looks up. Noticing my expression, Sky taps my cheek. "Serenity, I'm all right." He straightens, rolling his eyes. "Takes more than a little beating to rile me up."

I wonder what would. Sky's always kept his temper in check.

"Look, I can handle myself," he goes on. "But try to placate him until I can figure out a few more things. Just…try to play the part of the docile Swan, okay?"

I can see a hint of a smile on his face while he considers whether I could actually accomplish docility. Ironically, swans are the furthest thing from docile. Their temperaments are quite aggressive.

"We couldn't go on the run with you in this condition, anyway. You need to keep healing. In the meantime, here—" Sky thrusts something hard and rectangular into my hands. "Hide this. Whatever you do, don't let anyone see it. It should give you some clarity."

I finger the small book with the leather-bound cover, recognizing it as my mother's journal. "How did you get this?"

"The truth is complicated. It's going to be hard for you to swallow, but it'll give you some answers. Read the pages I marked first. They'll explain everything."

When I open to the first page, something drops out. I catch it in my fingers, recognizing it instantly. It's my mother's photograph. The Unicorn.

"I remember this."

"What?"

"Remember that time I snuck into Mom and Dad's bedroom and tried to break into Mom's chest?"

"I also recall catching you."

I huff, conjuring up the images of Sky hauling me over his shoulder and planting me back in my bedroom, ordering me to stay right where I was.

"What did you say when I tried to follow you back in? That I had all the impulse control of—"

"A mad baboon," Sky finishes with a grin. "Not much has changed there."

Studying the photograph, I ponder that day. "This was all I saw at the time."

I want to reel at the thought of what could happen until Sky is ready to get us out of here. "What do I do now? Tell me what to do."

He smooths aside my hair. His eyes seem wild and desperate, as though he wishes he could keep me from all that I'll have to face in the days or maybe weeks to come. He glances around to make sure we're still alone. "There's a chocolate house in town. It's called Lust and Cocoa. Sometimes, they give passes for good behavior."

We both know it's a stretch.

"Wait!" I grab his arm before he can move. "How are you here? How did you get this job?"

Sky crooks one side of his mouth. "Do you think there's another man alive who could prove how much he wants to protect you?" There is something else lingering behind that statement. He pauses and winks. "Muscles didn't hurt either." Sky leans forward, reaching to tuck a stray curl behind my ear. Then, he murmurs low, "You're not who you think you are. Read the journal."

More than ever, I want to open my mother's journal and learn the truth behind his words. She's always kept me closer than a pearl in an oyster shell, but her secrets have always kept me at arm's length.

Until now.

Sky's words about the chocolate house haunt me. I don't know how I'll manage to get a town visit, considering my behavior so far must cause Luc a fair amount of distrust. I wonder if there is more than one chocolate house in the city, but it's doubtful. Through the years, chocolate houses have taken a back door to opiate ones. With the legalization of narcotics and stimulants, opiate houses thrive. For most, getting high is more common than satisfying a sweet tooth.

When I enter the Aviary with Sky following close behind, the other Birds show me their disgust. Noses raise high in the air, brows knot, and eyes narrow as I walk into the main lobby where Dove greets me. My attention isn't on her but on the Blackbird exhibit I'd passed only a short time ago, now empty. I was so caught up with Sky and the diary, I'd forgotten all about the Bird in a coma. Girl in a coma.

Upon seeing my muddled expression, Dove explains, "Blackbird collapsed, and has succumbed to a coma. She's in the infirmary."

"Where is the infirmary?" I try to ignore the threatening way some of the other girls pause nearby to watch me.

"In a separate sector attached by a glass tunnel."

"Will you please take me there?" I request politely.

Dove hesitates, regarding me curiously. "We should be getting you ready for the unveiling of your display. Director Owl has specific instructions—"

"Screw the display!" I exclaim, aggravated. "Take me there."

Dove's cheeks flush like cherries bursting inside her skin. "Why? I've warned you about the other Birds here, and so has Director—"

"I don't know," I answer truthfully. "I just feel..." I can't tell Dove what I myself don't understand. I just know that I need to see Blackbird right now as everything else in my life unravels.

"The infirmary is open to visitors at this time of day. But I will inform the Owl of your insolence."

Guess he'll have to tack it on to my punishment later.

Part of me believes I should avoid all the other Birds here, but another emotion, one always so powerful inside me, beckons—curiosity.

The infirmary is connected to the main wing by a glass tunnel, just as Dove has said. Adjacent to the second and third floors are more wings with rooms upon rooms. Before we can see Blackbird, we both must wear a digital shield patch that will encase our skin and prevent any bacteria from leaving our bodies during our visit.

As soon as I enter, I see her.

The Aviary

Blackbird—black skin, tiny black braids raining down to her breast—lies on a sterile white bed, her hands tranquil at her sides. Around her eyes, the yellow paint is gone, scrubbed clean, and I notice the basin of tinted water sitting near the bed. Luc rises from the chair where he regards Blackbird from a safe distance. Traces of yellow smear his hands.

Luc doesn't acknowledge us until Dove announces our presence, "She insisted on coming here."

His face bears a mere feather of surprise when he turns to me. He indicates a hand to the chair next to him. "Please, Swan, sit." After I've accepted the chair, he informs Dove, "You may go now."

She retreats immediately.

He also dismisses Sky.

I am too close to him. That much I know by the way his leg glides against mine when I sit down. If the hairs on my skin stood up, I wouldn't blame them; everything about Luc magnetizes me. Choosing a safer route, I inch my chair closer to the bedside where Blackbird sleeps. Underneath the sheets, she's dressed in a black shift that can't veil the beauty of her skin. I don't tell Luc why I feel connected to her because I don't understand it myself. For some reason, the way she looked in her exhibit—she reflected outside what I'm feeling inside. Like she has lightning, too.

So far, Luc says nothing. I stretch my hand forward to her ebony one gracing the sheets, then close it around her palm. Hers feel softer than mine but colder. Maybe due to the skin shield.

"I must say..." Luc says, "...your fondness for her fascinates me. After all, you haven't even spoken to her. And you've seen her only once."

"It doesn't matter."

"I still plan on unveiling your exhibit tonight," he informs me. "You should prepare yourself."

In a voice no lighter than a wisp, I say, "I think that's Dove's job." I twist my fingers lightly across the fragile skin of Blackbird's, hurriedly speaking before Luc can say anything. "What happened to her?"

"All the tests are negative. She just collapsed inside her exhibit." Baffled, he pushes a hand through his hair, lips parting from this puzzle.

"Is she taking anything?" I ask.

He sighs. "Blackbird is different. She doesn't buy narcotics from the street vendors or shops when she's on town visits. Some Birds will use on town visits, the types that leave the blood before testing. But not Blackbird. She enjoys Bliss every now and then, but mostly she indulges in the oyster shops in the city. There is no reason for her coma."

Luc moves forward to touch my braid. I freeze, numbed by the winter blue of his eyes. He tries to soften any loose, willful strands that have escaped, but they refuse to be tamed.

"City visits must be earned," Luc explains while lighting his hand on the swan charm. "I have every confidence you will be allowed to go soon enough. Trust me..." He inches the loose clasp to the back of my neck where it belongs, finishing with, "No one desires it more than me. And your punishment later, for last night's disobedience, will be no pleasure for me, either. Come, I will escort you to your room. You may return to check on Blackbird later."

Eleven
TheSwAnExhIbit

Before Dove arrives to transform me, I have just enough time alone with my mother's journal to leaf through it. I huddle behind layers of clothes in a corner of the closet so I can travel across some of the pages, eager and demanding answers. Instead of turning to the passages Sky marked for me, I start at the beginning. It seems disrespectful to read the middle pages first. I smile, reflecting on my mother's beautiful handwriting.

> I played my part well. I never want my daughter to find out how well I played it. She knows only what I give her. She hears the stories, the fantasies that always end with my escape, but she only sees the surface story of what gives me nightmares every night. She doesn't know the things I've done...or the things that were done to me or how I convinced myself to love them.
>
> She's such a sensitive thing, journal. How could I ever tell her about how he chained me to a post, directed the artist to paint my naked skin white as porcelain and paste real gems onto my body just so he could rip them off later? I became his Unicorn on the sick carousel that is his Penthouse.
>
> How could I ever tell her that my lips twitched into a smile when he brushed the riding crop against the back of my neck or when he braced his whip if I didn't perform to his satisfaction? How could I tell her that I shook my mane for him whenever he desired? How I slipped far into the back of my mind, letting the Unicorn take over because she wanted the flick of his whip and the touch of his chest against her back when he took her from behind? How the Unicorn loved Director Force...

My smile fades, sickness roiling in my gut. We were never allowed to say his name. My mother just called him the Vampire. I never knew what he did to her. Only that he bled her dry and my father brought her back to life.

I hope no one will ever bleed me dry.

Dove's voice, muffled from behind the door, interrupts my thoughts. "Swan? Are you in there?" She knocks a little, and I bury my mother's journal behind a bunch of stockings in one of the closet cabinets before opening the door.

After a medic confirms my bone has healed and they give me a required anesthetic, Dove transforms me into the Swan once again.

Tonight, my gown is slit all the way up one side to my lower thigh while the other side cascades to the floor in spectral beds of white fabric, swathed in hundreds of crystals equipped with glowing optics. Dove patterns those same crystals into a circlet for my hair. No simple task when my ghostly tresses adorn my face in chaotic, fluffed curls. From the white cliff of my breasts on down, the dress is nothing but swan feathers stitched together into an elongated, magnificent corset. Chiffon swathes make up the strap on my left shoulder, connecting in the back far down to my lower spine to deliver a teasing peek of skin there. Even the gloves are lace and swan feathers, though smaller than the ones coating my body.

Once my costume is complete, Dove paints elaborate curving designs along the panes above and around my eyes. At the end of it all, she stains my lips white and places me before the mirror.

I feel like I could fly away.

I feel like the Swan.

For the first time, the glass walls around seem more like a cocoon than a cage. I'm ready for my metamorphosis.

For the first time, I see the girl I've always wished to be—the girl I am on the inside—reflected in the mirror. Hauntingly beautiful, she is a goddess of starlight, trailing silver and secrets in her wake.

I feel mysterious and powerful. But the source of my power perplexes me. Nothing inside me could ever appreciate this place or what Luc has done to me. Could it?

The Aviary

Dove inhales sharply and steps back, admiring her work. "I was wrong. You didn't just walk in off the pages of a fantasy book. There is no better explanation than magic for your existence. You are some siren, and you don't even need a song to lure men to their deaths. You could tempt an angel to sin."

I stare at my reflection. "I've never looked like this before," I say, stunned but grateful.

"Your beauty doesn't come from some paint and chiffon, girl. It comes from within *you*. Make it your own. Remember, this is your body. Only you can make the choice when to reveal yourself to the world."

Dove departs, and I rush toward the closet, desperate to scoop up a piece of my old life.

"Please, Mom, give me something," I beg. I turn to a random entry, hoping for anything that will keep me grounded.

> I miss those days when she was young. When Kerrick would hoist her over his shoulder and dump her back into the water again and again. Every single time, she would ask for more. Our daughter, the daredevil, our little water baby. Nothing could keep her from the water—the ocean, lakes, pools. Not even when Kerrick did his best to put some fear in her by letting her sink for a few seconds in the deep end when she was only two years old. She came up laughing.

A silly memory is *not* what I need.

I scramble for another entry, but the knock on the closet door prevents me. He doesn't wait before opening it, but I manage to toss the journal in a dark corner just before he enters.

"It's almost time," Luc announces.

Without asking me why I'm in here, he draws me out of the closet, observing my trembling hands. Then, he positions me before the mirror once again.

I can't bring myself to look.

"The moon herself would quake in the silver shadow of your beauty." He fingers the swan chain at my neck.

I try to still my chest while he warms the naked skin of my back with his palm. Again, I feel the temptation to embrace his touch. Everything from our garden visit together, to watching him with Blackbird, and now the way his fingers linger on the space just above my cleavage where the charm rests…

But then, I remember.

I remember the slices and bruises on Sky's skin.

The punishment Luc promised to inflict on me later tonight.

That I'm just an investment to him, that he bought and paid for me.

I remember my armor.

Instantly, I step away from him, mentally spitting out any sense of appreciation for him. I will never be his Swan.

I am Serenity, and that's all I will ever be. Except my mother's words in the journal haunt me. Is my blood my own? Or does too much of hers run inside me? What if the Swan is really there, lurking inside me like the Unicorn was inside my mother?

"Come with me." Luc's fingers touch my wrist. I shirk from his grasp, from the cold sting it gives me. He tries again. This time, I yield.

Instead of leading me to the main lobby where all the other exhibits branch out, Luc guides me to the door at the end of the hall, which opens at his command. It's so difficult to walk in this dress. My left leg is completely free from the thigh-high slit, but I keep trying to coax the other—unsuccessfully, as it's trapped in fabric—to my left side.

After a few more moments of watching me struggle, Luc finally pauses. "Take it like this." Snatching up a bundle of fabric, he lifts it to expose my right foot. "Leave the left. You don't need to hide it."

I'm still self-conscious about my leg, but I concentrate on the crumpled fabric in my hand. Part of me wants to rip it, tear it, delay this exhibit somehow. But I want to trust Sky, remembering his words about the chocolate shop in town, secure in the knowledge he will find a way to help me once I earn a city visit.

Bottling up my resentment, I play my part. So much of me wants to fight this, but if I do, Sky will reap the punishment.

Luc leads me to an entirely different wing where a winding glass staircase descending to a lower level greets us. I accept his hand, my other hovering above the railing as we traverse the steps. Upon my descent, the dress forms a V at my lower thighs, the long train on the right side flowing behind me. I am careful not to get it caught inside the gaps.

The staircase seems to descend for ages.

At its end is a door painted with the insignia of a swan.

When we get to it, Luc stops and turns to me.

"I have waited for this night for many years." He steps toward me, leans closer and breathes in my scent. I tremble, knowing what's about to happen. His hands cup my shoulders. "Shhh..." He curls a few fingers under my chin, raises my trembling jaw. "They will worship at your feet."

I can't stop shaking. He kisses each one of my eyelids. Whispers, "My Swan."

Then, he opens the door.

Inside, there's a steel swing suspended by cables. It's surrounded by black walls so close I can touch each with my arms. This is the gateway. Here, he directs me to sit, to keep my hands braced around the cables. To hold tight.

"Be still. Be brave." And he closes the door.

Hysteria attacks me.

I don't have a moment to breathe. Above me, a series of pulleys crank the swing, and I ascend. After a few feet, I'm lifted above the room to see walls of water behind glass on each side of me. Pulleys continue to lift me until I'm well above the water, and once I'm through the gap, I hear a mechanism thundering as the floor descends back into place, shifting the waters below me. Deep enough to form a manmade lake.

The pulleys raise me until I'm level with trees. A rush of wind stirs my hair, but when I look around, seeing nothing but glass walls on each side, I know it's artificial. Still, the glass domed ceiling above my head allows for stars, stars that are shimmery teardrops reflecting the water's surface. I see myself there, too.

So, this is my exhibit. From hotel pools to the manor lake Sky and I swam in when we were young, water is my glory. How could Luc know that?

I glance to the shore of the lake not far from my swing. Behind glass windows, scores of people dressed in fine clothes watch me. Curious Birds, men, some women. All their heads crane up to see me. In their hands, each person carries a candle—something I assume was Luc's idea to benefit the effect.

This is my grand opening.

I swallow back the panic threatening to cleave me in two. *Be still. Be brave.* I have to make this good. If I don't perform well, will he sell me off to the next highest bidder? Worse, if they love me, will I become the Swan the way my mother became the Unicorn? It scares me to think how easy it might be.

I search for Sky, but can't find him because there are too many faces.

Instead, I remember the time we snuck out of the lake house after midnight. Sky walked two miles with me through the woods to the old Sycamore tree swing.

I embrace the same feeling of childlike glee I had then.

And I pump my legs to swing.

Even from this height, I can hear the pleasured voices of the men. I must force the retch down when I consider how many will imagine me in their escorts' places.

My dress becomes the tail of an enormous cloud swinging behind me, long enough for its edges to skim the water. I should be cold until I realize the wind easing around me is strangely warm. But this is still one gigantic display case just like all the others. I don't know why I expected anything but an illusion. Luc would never allow my exhibit to be outside.

The sound of snapping alerts me. Somewhere, far above me, something is happening to the cable. The people, not thirty feet from me, must see what is happening because alarm strikes their faces.

After another crack, the swing dips, the last cable breaking. The swing drops, and my body sails through the air.

Twelve
GiFtoftheSwAn

URNS OUT THAT SILLY MEMORY is exactly what I need. Chilly water engulfs me. White sheaths of fabric pirouette around my vision. I am grateful the water is so deep. So grateful because I don't want to surface. From somewhere above me, I can hear shouts of mayhem. But down here, it's peaceful, quiet. Calm. Down here, it's another world beneath the Aviary. A magical one. So, I hold my breath just like I've always done growing up.

I swim deeper.

The dress threatens to drag me back, to return me to the air, but I deny it. I rip off the gloves, then swim more. All at once, the optic crystals come to life so they wreathe my body in a soft glow. Underwater, I can see both my legs, white shimmery stalks. My hair is like glorious silver serpents coiling and twisting around me.

My lungs start to ache. But not burn. Not yet. I skim my arms through the water until my hands connect with a thick pane of glass. No. I pound one fist against it. Heat siphons the air inside my lungs. I fan one hand along the glass. As I do, I make out bodies behind it. Dozens upon dozens of men and their Bird escorts stand there, watching me swim.

I choke on the liquid slipping into my mouth, close my eyes, and fit my feet together, pushing the water down with my hands in an attempt to rise to the surface, lungs constricting with the need for oxygen. As I near the surface, an arm reaches down into the lake. Since my lungs feel like a thousand pillows are smothering me, I accept the hand waiting for me. So pale and nowhere near Sky's brawn, Luc's generous muscles are still enough to yank me out of the water and into the boat beside him.

"You were glorious." After he situates me, he stands, perfectly balanced in the shifty boat, and stretches out his arms. Loudly, he declares for all to hear, "Ladies and gentlemen, I present the Swan!"

The air explodes into a thunder of endless claps and cheers. Once I have stolen a few more breaths, I look behind me and see the monstrous voxel-image lighting up the starry night background of the exhibit. There is a projection of my performance from the swing—my swan dive—and of me swimming beneath the surface.

It was all staged: the cable snapping, the swing giving way, my plummet into the depths of the water. And they are still watching me.

Amidst the applause, Luc lowers a hand to my chin and tilts it up to his face. "You don't need to stand. Simply raise your neck to look to them. They adore you."

Slow and stunned, I twist to see the hundreds of people gathered to watch my exhibit. All I do is stare, wide-eyed and terrified. Another sensation crawls inside my skin, multiplying like a bacterium. Adoration. It takes all my willpower not to tip the boat and drag Luc down to the depths with me. I want him to feel the whirl of emotion I am right now.

As they applaud, I find myself reacting to it. I'm supposed to revel in this, but I can't latch onto anything but revulsion. Instead, my lightning hinges on this moment, fuses with the cheers of the crowd. I hate him even more for this. More than anything, I hate myself for loving this sick and twisted performance.

I CONTINUE TO SHIVER LONG after Dove undresses me, removing the Swan from my skin and clothing me in a white nightgown. She orders dinner, which appears through the little door in the kitchen, delivered via hover-drone. Just after, Luc appraises me once before checking something on his arm interface.

I am only faintly aware when his words squeeze their way into my fogged mind. "Your blood pressure is a little elevated, but you will recover well."

The Aviary

The nightgown is soft and light, but I shiver because my long hair is damp and cold. Slowly, my itchy fingers regain their warmth. And I try. I try so hard to raise my fist to Luc's jaw, to strike him.

"Now, Swan." He catches my feral attempt to harm him. His hand is warm compared to the ice that is the rest of him. "You need to save your strength." When he rubs his thumb against my lower lip, I try to bite it. He taps my nose in response, then wags his finger in front of my eyes. "Follow me."

Fully ready to accept my punishment, I think about the marks on Sky's back and my stomach rolls. I want to share the burden, the pain, with Sky. If he was punished, I should be punished, too. This will make us stronger, unite us.

After taking an elevator to a separate wing and down a back corridor, Luc inserts an electronic card key into the slot and opens the door in front of us. Inside, the room is dark. Luc closes the door behind him, snuffing out any hallway glow.

"What is this place?" I ask, stiffening at the sudden darkness.

I hear the sound of one click. Light pours forth—not into this room, but the one right below me, which I can see through the glass floor.

Once I see what's taking place in the room below, I quickly look away. But it's too late to undo the images; they will be forever stamped into my memory.

Another click, and I hear them. Moans rack the room, a low growl here and there, winded breath, shuddering gasps, a whimper, yells building momentum, an occasional scream. The whole floor is glass, and through it, I can see the private client rooms. Hot breaths from their mouths steam up the glass under my feet.

I back up against the wall as far as I can, but I can't escape the glass. Even with my eyes squeezed shut, I can't escape the noise.

Above the sound streaming in through the room's speakers, Luc approaches. "I come here to monitor the appointments if I suspect any wrongdoing on the part of a client or one of my Birds."

I lunge for him. "You sick, demented—"

Luc seizes me by the arms, pulling me close, pressing the full weight of his chest against mine. "Consider this a gift. Tonight, you will remain here as a witness to what I've been keeping you from. Perhaps when this is over, you'll understand how lucky you are that I have not yet allowed you to take clients of your own."

No, because he's waiting to sell me to the wealthiest bidder.

"All night?" I whisper, trying to block out the awful sounds.

For a moment, Luc hesitates, and I feel hope he might change his mind. But then his face hardens. "All night. I will come for you in the morning."

"Please don't do this, Luc." It's the first time I beg him. The first time I pinch my eyes together, summoning tears. It's the first time I find myself clinging to him like a blood-starved leech.

His eyes seem to swim for a moment, but then he turns away, clearing his throat. "I've told you before, Swan, Luc is too personal," he says, his voice catching. Finally, he moves to face me again. "You must learn to call me Owl or Director Aldaine. I've invested a great deal in you. You must learn control, governance. My intention is not to break you, only to help you to understand that certain actions bear consequences."

I sob just a little, hearing a long, languid moan below me. "Please! I'd rather take a beating than this."

A muscle jerks in his cheek. He seems furious at the notion.

Suddenly, he levels with me, bends with brows low, his words solidifying like ice. "Out of the question."

He doesn't tell me goodnight when he leaves, locking the door behind him.

Overwhelmed by all the near-deafening sounds around me, I scramble to the switches on the wall, but they don't turn off. My eyes survey the room. No table, no chairs, no objects. All bare of anything but the glass and the bodies beneath it, bodies that will twist and bend and moan and scream all night long. Even if I *could* fall asleep, I know the sounds will haunt my nightmares. I will never forgive him for this.

The only things that bring me comfort or distraction are my memories—one in particular.

"It's not your fault," Dad had told me after he and Mom convinced me that I wasn't hemorrhaging—that I didn't need any sort of stitches.

"You're growing into a beautiful girl, and we love that," he'd said. "But you have to be careful. You have to watch how you dress and what you watch."

For years, I remember feeling angry. Angry because girls were raped every day, and it didn't matter what they wore. Ridiculous because I didn't want to dress like museum girls even if it seemed… fun. I was more comfortable in loose clothing. No, I was angry because Sky could leave the hotel rooms without permission or anyone watching him.

"Sky must watch where his eyes wander and how he treats women," Dad had argued. "It will be different because he is different."

I started wearing longer skirts after that day. Peasant blouses to hide my breasts, but it didn't help much. Eyes still devoured me wherever we traveled, which showed me how little my wardrobe mattered to them. The fact I had an extra X chromosome was enough.

Sky stopped watching television because everything showed skin and parts now. He started reading more.

When I hear another moan, I crumple into a ball, covering my ears with my hands. Still, I hear the heavy breaths that crawl from the speakers and squeeze their way past my fingers. Instead, I try to imagine my mother's voice above the speakers. Remember how she picked up the frame with the butterfly trapped behind the glass. I caught it in a bottle when I was nine, but it died. Since I wasn't willing to part with it, Dad decided to pin it in a glass frame for me.

I hear my mother's voice.

"So many girls are like this butterfly. They feel dead inside, but they look beautiful on the outside. Some are trained to smile. To look pretty from birth. Others are forced or manipulated to look that way. The last thing we want is for you to be stuck like this. The last thing I want is for my own daughter to feel trapped, to be trapped like I was in the Temple."

A scream startles me. Ear-splitting from the speaker volume. I peek through the threadbare gap in my fingers at the source. All I see is the girl's face. Neck arched back, mouth beaming as her head rocks back and forth, but her eyes are just vacant. Emptier than a winter bird's nest.

I cover my eyes again.

Dad once worked at a graphicker studio. He explained how they took photos of girls to put in their digital galleries. Every time they did, she was no longer free. He said the electronic frames of screens flashing pictures still haunted him even after he found my mother. Because those girls were still stuck there in that gallery behind their screens.

"You can never lose the memories," my mother had told me in a soft voice.

"It was like having a monster inside me, Serenity," Dad finished. "Once it got its claws in me, I wasn't satisfied. Just had to feed it more and more. Your mother was my saving grace. But I never want you to become some monster's fantasy."

All these girls are fantasies. They're not just exchanging skin. They're exchanging blood and flesh and bits and pieces of their souls. Feeding the monster of desire over and over again even though he'll always starve.

I spend the night sobbing, my gut wrenching, trying new ways to twist my body away from the sounds and movements of the client rooms below.

I don't open my eyes again for the entire night.

Thirteen
The ToUr

"As promised, Luc comes for me in the morning. It feels like days since last I saw him. Even though the client rooms are empty now, the sounds from last night still swarm inside my ears, like dying bees stinging me again and again. I hadn't looked once after I saw the girl's face.

Sleep deprivation, combined with the whirl of noises confusing my senses, forces me to yield when Luc unfurls me from the fetal position, then hoists me upward. When he realizes I'm dead on my feet, he picks me up and carries me. In his arms, I feel my armor weakening.

I don't hold on to him. Instead, I curl back into myself. I press my face into his chest because the sound of his heartbeat helps to quell the awful sounds in my memory.

"Mmm…" I murmur when he shifts to open the elevator.

He tilts his head against mine to whisper, "Shh… you'll rest today. You can join me at dinner." Luc is a mess of conflict because while his body language has softened like the ice there has thawed, his mouth is twisted into a grimace.

I don't struggle when Luc gingerly places me inside my bed, then covers me with blankets. Sleep comes quickly, but at some point, I must've thrown the covers off because I wake up later feeling cold, but free all the same.

I fear for my daughter every day. She can't have a normal life thanks to him. And I worry if the Temple were to ever discover her, that she would become like me. She has too much of me—and too much of her father—in her. I see his ferocity in her eyes, in the way she moves and the way she talks. But I see my longing in her, too. I fear she will want it like me.

I close the journal. Her words befuddle me because my father's never been fierce. Just the opposite. Even more controlled than Sky. Even after my mother escaped with my father, she didn't come out whole. Over the years, I know she's tried her hardest to shed her Penthouse skin and forget the Unicorn, but much of it is still stitched into her. Only my father can kiss the seams, help her forget their pain.

It's almost time for dinner, and I see Luc enter the room out of the corner of my eye. I don't look at him. Instead, I focus on the fish in the tank.

"You enjoy the water," he says.

Each fish flits like moving stained glass. "How perceptive of you," I snap, wishing I could pour my poisonous words down his throat. But I also remember his touch, more gentle than fawn fur when he'd carried me to bed, when he leaned his head against mine, when he'd whispered a goodnight against my lips.

With a smile, Luc folds his hands behind his back. "I had my suspicions, but your rather intoxicating swan dive last night confirmed it."

"It wasn't fair, the way you threw me in that exhibit with no warning about what would happen."

"It wasn't supposed to be fair." He draws my hand away from the tank, cradles it in his before raising it to his face so his lips can rub against the back of my palm. "It was supposed to be effective. Just like your punishment."

I don't want think about that. "Was my exhibit well received?"

His smile spreads into a grin. "You soared where others merely flapped."

Something twists in the pit of my stomach, two different emotions vying for dominance. One feels like I'm treading water with a boulder attached to my neck while the other has me straightening into the prim pose of pride, which is the inner voice of the Swan tempting me.

I remind myself that to avoid farther punishments—for me

The Aviary

and for Sky—it's safer to play along. Stop fighting. Just endure.

I TAKE MY PLACE AT Luc's side at the dining table. All the Birds compliment me on my illustrious debut the previous night—all except Nightingale, of course, who continues to regard me with crow-like eyes. Halfway through dinner, I realize I'm picking at the food; I have no appetite. I'm also not used to eating with so many people.

Just then, a fork, quicker than a bird pecking at seed, nabs one of my sand-dollar-sized crab cakes. Brow raised, I turn to my left. Where the chair was empty the other day, there is now a girl—a child. Her curls remind me of my own as they wildly ravish her body to her hips, but they are copper, like coins gilded in the sunlight. A fresh-yet-snarky smile illuminates her face when she stuffs the cake—whole—into her mouth before sticking a crumb-covered tongue out at me.

"That would be Finch," Luc says, motioning with a sweeping finger to the girl. "She's a hatchling. A trainee. Finch," he scolds, wagging a finger with a teasing smile on his face, "Remember your manners at the table, dear. You should know it's not very polite to stick out your tongue or steal food from others."

Enchanted, I scoot my plate toward the girl in offering. "Here." I've never seen a child up close, but I love her nose—small and white with a splatter of freckles like a cinnamon-glazed macadamia nut. She's skinny, more skeleton than flesh. Greedily, she jabs her fork into my offering, then swallows it in clumps.

During all my years, I've never gone hungry. My parents have seen to that. If for some reason we missed a meal, Sky always figured out something. I wonder where this girl came from.

As if reading my thoughts, Luc leans over and murmurs in my ear, "A recent acquisition. A carnival owner tried to outbid me at the Glass Districts for her."

I try not to cringe at the statement. With the birth rate plummeting lower and lower, children are a prize indeed, especially young girls. They are a commodity for anyone.

I take a drink of water to keep my voice from cracking before asking, "How old is she?"

"I'm seven and a half!" the girl surprises me by exclaiming loudly.

Luc wipes his mouth with a napkin, eyes on the child. "Inside voice, Finch."

"Will...will she...?" When I can't finish my sentence, many of the other girls regard me with curiosity, others with disbelief.

Luc's hand quivers, and I almost wonder if he will strike me. Before he can answer, Nightingale does. "If you knew anything about this place, you'd never ask that. Exhibits are only constructed for Birds who are sixteen or older, *Swan*." Her eyes are two sharp beaks jabbing into mine.

Many museums break the rules. Just like clubs have done for decades.

What will happen to Finch during the eight-and-a-half years she has left? More grooming, I'd suspect.

Mockingbird, who is seated opposite me, rises to my defense. "Give her a break, Gale. Anyone can see that Swan is as fresh as they come. She doesn't know any better."

Turning to Luc, she plumps up her lips like I saw her do the first day. "Owl, I know it's customary for you to lead the tours, but can I give her one? Pleeeeeeease?" She expertly bats her eyelashes—a feat I've never managed to master.

Luc hesitates, but Mockingbird continues. "I could show her the way of things around here, introduce her to some of the others."

At the last suggestion, all the girls crane their heads toward Luc in anticipation. I can't help but wonder if Mockingbird is eager to know more about me... or if she wishes me harm.

Luc dabs at his mouth once again, finally replying while lifting his water glass. "Yes, I'll give my permission—"

Delighted, Mockingbird squeals, and the other girls chime in, thereby exhibiting her popularity and influence.

Luc raises a finger while spreading his dangerous brows lower in warning. Everyone quiets. "I give my permission, but Vulture shall escort you. And of course, you must ask Swan herself if she wishes to accompany you."

Mockingbird turns toward me, cupping her hands together beneath her chin in a begging fashion. In her simplistic gray dress with capped short sleeves, she would look vulnerable if not for her chipper blue eyes and round, rosy cheeks.

If I say no, I can imagine my popularity will severely decrease.

As I survey Mockingbird again, I discover I don't want to say no. Especially if it means Sky will be close. So, I purse my lips together and nod.

Numerous girls express their glee, including Mockingbird; she claps her hands together like the quick beat of tiny wings. Nightingale takes a sip of her water, then puckers her lips to eye her reflection in the glass.

Finch dips her tiny hand into mine, smiles in gratification, and points to her plate. It is wiped clean.

AFTER DINNER, AN EAGER MOCKINGBIRD flutters out of the dining room with her hand anchored around mine.

"Let's go explore," she singsongs.

In no time, I've already lost track of where we are in this gigantic place. Our first stop is the library where, I learn, there are more than just physical books. Here, books will fly into your hands at the mention of their title, pages digitally enhanced to display the scenes inside. Sky follows in our wake as Mockingbird shows me the attached VirtuRoom. The virtual environment is fairly popular with the other girls, especially since they can tap into their FaceSpaces, check out the latest feeds, Temple and Hollywood gossip, and show off their last exhibit photos. Any other pictures are banned for museum girls. We are commodities first and foremost.

The girl with the pink hair—Flamingo—enhances her holographic FaceSpace screen before sending a message to someone. She has multiple other correspondences, some she speaks to.

"Prospective clients," Mockingbird explains, gesturing to Flamingo. "Many Birds have to work during their free time to attract more clients. Still gotta fill our quotas if we want to keep living here. This place doesn't come cheap. And none of us want to end up in the District."

Swallowing back the urge to vomit, I hurry to follow Mockingbird out of the library. She doesn't spend much time there.

None of the girls do. Books aren't popular, not even the flying, animated ones, as they are rather antiquated, but apparently, Luc is an amateur historian.

His mystery grows and grows.

We have to step onto one of the many moving glass walkways in order to reach our next stop. Mockingbird informs me that the kitchens alone take up one whole wing of the house as we travel what feels like an obscene amount of time on the contraption.

"Owl employs several full-time chefs and servers to cook for us," Mockingbird says as we step into the food prep area. "He's also got growers for the gardens and fields. A lot of our vegetables and fruits are grown on Aviary property. We're lucky. Most museums do this synthetic 3D-printed tasteless crap that have a ton of supplements and vitamins. But Luc likes to keep things organic and healthy, says fresh is better for us. And also something about helping the economy by employing more people."

"Do you ever go into the city?" I ask as she closes one of the swinging doors after she finishes showing me around, leading me back down the moving walkway.

Behind me, Sky is alert, attentive. He must be listening to everything we say, gaining as much information as he can.

"All the time, with a security guard," Mockingbird says. "Why? Need me to get something for you? Some Bliss maybe? Oh, never mind, you can only have those on town visits." And I haven't earned mine yet.

"I don't take Bliss or narcotics." I change the subject. "Are you happy here?"

Mockingbird flashes a quick grin, twists her lean body around, and presses her back against the walkway railing. "Sure. They got lassos here."

She didn't really answer my question. Denial, maybe?

I'd heard of lassos. Lasers that could target temporary contact lenses and project films or any imagery onto them. Sky and I have never had anything quite that high-tech.

"Sprite-light shows are pretty fun, too. The theater is next to the library," she says.

"You mean voxel-shows?" I ask, wondering why she hadn't shown me the room when we were over by it.

The Aviary

Mockingbird cackles. "Hardly anyone calls them voxels anymore except for media outlets. It's all sprite lights now. Some people still call them volus. Only old farts call them voxels or volumetric stuff."

I was never allowed a FaceSpace account. "I guess most of my terms are more formal."

Mockingbird shrugs. "I sort of hatched here. It's my home."

"What do you mean by hatched?"

"Owl found me when I was a baby. He was only ten at the time, but anyone could see he was born to take over this place. Not like that evil brother of his, or his sisters."

"Wow," I say. "You sure do know a lot about Luc. And what do you mean—found you?"

"Owl?" She seems confused by my using his first name. "Pretty much everything about him. I grew up here."

Mockingbird speaks so fast it's hard to keep up with her, and though she is shorter, she moves with such a flighty alacrity I must lengthen my stride to keep up with her.

"My mom, whoever she was, left me on the doorstep here, which is where Owl discovered me. I don't remember anything about her. Probably messed up or something, but obviously, I turned out fine." Twirling around, she stretches out her arms. I grin. "You turned out even better," she says. "What's your mom like?"

My words catch in my throat. I hadn't expected questions about my parents. Not that I would dare to mimic the timeless tale of my mother's escape from the Temple. And stories of my past are precious to me. Instead, I'll spin something on the spot like my mother's done in the past with all her fairy tales.

Fortunately, Mockingbird waves a hand and bites her lip, embarrassed. "Sorry, probably shouldn't have asked. I talk a lot. If you get tired of it, you can just ignore me."

I shrug my shoulders. "Sometimes, I talk too much, too."

Mockingbird's lips curve up into a beam before she faces forward, hand trained on the banister as she leads me to the second floor. "Trust me, I'm an expert in talking. You don't do enough of it."

"Luc will probably tell you differently."

Mockingbird pauses to look back at me. "Is that so? Hmm… I'll have to ask Owl sometime."

"My mother's special," I finally say to Mockingbird, who stops at the top of the stairs to listen as I continue, "You know how some mothers will buy pancakes and others will make them?"

Mockingbird raises one eyebrow. "Sort of. One of the cooks here is like a mother to me, and she makes me pancakes from time to time."

I reminisce on the special times of my childhood. "Well, my mother wouldn't just make pancakes. She'd make chocolate-chip pancakes, then she'd make sculptures out of them every time. Whenever she's home, I beg her to make them for me."

"Whenever she is home?" Mockingbird blinks. "Is she some graphicker star or something?"

Out of the corner of my eye, I notice Sky stiffen, and I take it as a signal not to say too much. "Whenever they come home from a trip. They travel a lot. And my dad always brings home pictures, dozens of pictures from wherever they travel."

Mockingbird starts walking again. "Where's home for you, Swan?"

Right behind me, I want to say, glancing at Sky. "Nowhere, really." It's close to the truth. Raised in hotels, on the road all the time, Sky and I became each other's homes.

"Oh, how was the Immortal Treatment?" she asks, flitting to the next subject. "Only the higher Birds get it. I'd kill for that! If your skin darkens a little too much in the sun, *bam*! Your implant lightens your pigmentation. Genius!" Mockingbird gushes. "I have to go to the restoration room once a year to help regenerate my skin. It's painful as hell. Nothing like the implants."

"Mockingbird!" The girl with orange hair I'd observed the first day bounces toward us. I remember her—Hummingbird.

Behind me, Sky takes a step forward out of caution, no doubt because the newcomer's fingers are clenched, but she loosens them a little to reveal a pixie stick.

"Easy there, sexy," she teases Sky. "It's just some Bliss. Maybe you should have some, might relax you a little." Hummingbird trills flirty fingers up his chest. I want to break them knuckle by knuckle. "Okay, well, maybe another Bird will catch your eye

The Aviary

sometime."

Even though my first instinct is to wince at the thought, I catch the hint of a smile toying with Sky's mouth. Still, he doesn't look at Hummingbird any differently than he has any other woman or girl for as long as I've known him. It's one thing I've always loved about Sky. Even when we've passed animated ads or he's come across a magazine cover or article for museums or Glass Districts or carousels all featuring risqué girls, he doesn't stare, ogle, or so much as part his lips. No, he pauses, gazing at a fixed point, just like he is with Hummingbird and Mockingbird now. It's the first time I finally understand what his sight is rooted on—their eyes.

My heart ignites both in anger and confusion because Sky's eyes spend far more time avoiding me. A few years ago, without warning, our old dynamic evaporated like a bubble popping on the surface of a lake. When he stopped wanting to spend time with me, stopped showing affection toward me in any way, I was devastated. I used to know every thought in his head, but I suddenly had no idea what he was thinking. Maybe I should embark on those marked pages of the diary. Maybe they explain why he's still going out of his way to avoid so much as looking at me, much less touching me. When he does eye me, that subtle upturn of his mouth hints at something else. I know we're not blood brother and sister, but I tell myself I've deciphered his body language wrong.

"I doubt it." Mockingbird crosses her arms. "He hasn't looked at any of us since he got here—except for Swan. You're lucky. No one wants to mess with him. Not with those muscles or that death glare." She leans toward me to whisper in my ear, and I'm mad as a wildflower in a storm that they keep talking about him that way. For some reason, I feel more possessive than ever when it comes to Sky.

"Want a hit, Mock?" Hummingbird holds up the pixie stick.

"I'm good," Mockingbird says. "You'll get punished if Owl catches you with that thing in the Aviary."

Hummingbird rolls her eyes before sucking on the stick. "Owl this, Owl that. Everyone knows you'd un-fan that little tail of yours for him if he asked you."

I glare at Hummingbird, curling my fingers tightly into one

another. After all, my good behavior doesn't have to extend beyond Luc. I come to Mockingbird's defense; she's been nothing but welcoming to me. "How about I un-fan my fist in your pretty little teeth?" I ask.

Mockingbird seems stunned by my display, but after the encounter above the client rooms, I need this. Last night shrunk me, crumpled me like a wet piece of paper. I need to dry out.

"Someone's touchy about her museum director," Hummingbird singsongs.

She shrieks when I grab a clump of her hair and jam her face-first against the wall. Out of the corner of my eye, I notice the proud glint in Sky's eye and both corners of his mouth curling.

"Ack! Let me go, you crazy chick," Hummingbird protests, struggling hands clawing at mine.

I lick the back of her neck to well and truly show her what crazy looks like. I'm disappointed she doesn't taste as orangey as her hair. Outraged, she squeaks, sounding like a hungry baby bird.

"Oh, trust me," Mockingbird defends. "She's definitely not a chick."

"No…" I hum in Hummingbird's ear, drawing it out. She shivers, trying to twist away. "I'm much younger."

"*Mock!*" she screams.

"Don't look at me." Shrugging, Mockingbird casually leans back, seeming to enjoy the display. "You're the one who decided to get your cloaca in a twist."

"Better than keeping yours open all the time," Hummingbird accuses. I nip her earlobe, reveling in her flinch and the sound of her squeals. Laughing, I give her a little push to release her. She whirls toward us, wiping the back of her neck and warily watching me as she exclaims, "Fine, whatever. I'm going!" She backs away a few feet, arms practically flapping as she hurries off in the other direction.

Mockingbird rolls her eyes, tossing her hair back. "Fledglings. That's what we call girls like her. Transfers from other museums. So puffed up. Think they're so smart, but I've been in this business all my life. Thanks, by the way. That was awesome."

Just as we round another corner, I bump into Finch. Nothing about the child is shy when she grabs me by the arms, yanks me down to her level, and licks the side of my neck before scampering away with a wave. I chuckle a little at the little mimic of a girl. She doesn't speak much, but her actions could stock a library.

I grin as I walk with Mockingbird again. "When did you start training?"

"I learned a lot of things when I was younger. It's easier to train girls when they're little. I'm a higher level here because I can do a lot of things. I have a lot of talents: dancing, singing, playing music...can't say swimming's among them, though. That was pretty impressive, what you did last night. Where did you learn to swim like that? Your eyes were open underwater and everything!"

We've arrived at a dormitory hallway. Girls' faces appear in the upper glass circles of the doors every now and then, curious to catch glimpses of us.

"My mother was born with water in her veins. And my father's part fish. I visited his parents once. Scaly folk, they are."

Mockingbird erupts into giggles. "You're funny. I wasn't expecting that. Anyone could see you were a hellion from the first day, but funny, too? You're the whole package, aren't you? No wonder so many girls hate you so much."

"And you?"

Mockingbird grins, fluttering a hand. "Oh, I'm like the mascot. People like me way too much. Clients *and* girls. Middle status is good for that. I don't get anywhere near Nightingale or Peacock's territory."

Pausing, she inspects her clear nails before tapping them in a sequence that turns them to an ash gray and then closer to a metallic pewter gray with an imprint of a tiny bird—a mockingbird, of course. From what I've seen, Mockingbird enjoys changing her makeup and nails every day but keeps her gray dresses simple.

"It's funny. I wouldn't have expected you to be able to pull off that wildcat move you just did. Sure, you got the ice eyes, but you're so tiny...except for your rack, of course. That's why it's probably going to be trickier for you."

"Because of my rack?" I raise an eyebrow.

Mockingbird giggles. "No, I mean girls here will underestimate you. You'll have to be on guard all the time. I might be able to spread the word for you though, tell everyone what you did to

Hummingbird."

I remember Luc's words to Mockingbird the first day. *Hush little bird, don't say a word.* She seems to be the Aviary mouthpiece.

I pinch my lips together and nod, accepting the offer. "One thing people should never do is underestimate me."

"In the meantime, watch out for Nightingale, Blackbird—if she wakes up—Peacock, and Raven. You don't want those girls as enemies."

I make a mental note of the Birds, but I hardly feel threatened. After all, what's in a name? Like the Swan… "People don't want me as an enemy, either."

AFTER MOCKINGBIRD DEPARTS, I DECIDE to return to the infirmary for what's left of the evening. Once there, I recognize Peacock. At my entrance, she rises from her seat, spanning a height far surpassing mine. Without a doubt, she is one of the tallest girls in the Aviary, though not as tall as Sky, who keeps his shoulders braced as she approaches me.

"Just what do you think *you're* doing here?" Her sultry green and blue irises glower as she tries to pen me in.

"Don't do that," I warn.

She crooks her mouth into a sardonic smile. "Let me tell you something about peacocks, darling. We don't mix well with other birds." A gold peacock winds around the outer curve of her ear, but its eyes must be mood-changing stones since they turn crimson from anger. Suddenly, the peacock tail of dozens of tiny gemstones fans out in a half-moon just as Peacock pinches the left side of my thigh. Hard.

Her assault triggers something in Sky. I recognize it before he even moves. His lips thin just like that day when a hotel employee made a move on me last year. Just one moment is all it takes for him to lash out, grabbing hold of her arms and pinning them behind her back. I rejoice in the sound of her squeal as he yanks her away from me, dipping his head low to hiss at her.

"No one touches Swan."

Not to be left out of the fun, I advance toward her. "Doesn't the name pea*cock* refer to male birds? Aren't females called pea-

hens?"

I pause just so I can see her lips pinch as thin as a crescent moon. "Owl will hear about this!" She struggles against Sky before he releases her.

Fury poisons her features. She raises one finger in warning before spinning on her bare heel to depart without another word. I wonder for the first time if she is the one who attacked me the other night. I wouldn't put it past her.

I shoot Sky a grateful smile. "You seem to make enemies with ease," he says, nostrils flaring just a little.

I widen my eyes, feigning innocence.

He draws a circle around the room in a casual fashion. "No listening devices here. Everything else is monitored: vitals, heartbeat, blood pressure. He takes extra care with his Birds."

Relieved, I slump into the chair near Blackbird's bedside. "So I've noticed."

"You should be more careful with the other girls here."

Taking stock of his frustrated mouth, I roll my eyes. "You're telling me to be careful? Really?"

Sky flares again, but settles a moment later. "Just try. I might not be here next time."

Just in case we have any other visitors, he positions himself against the back wall. I turn to Blackbird. In this room, she looks peaceful. When I take her hand, I feel warmth heating my skin, something I did not expect.

"I want things to be the way they were," I tell Sky, softening my gaze.

"I don't."

I trickle my fingers across Blackbird's knuckles, trying to ignore the wounds his words cause. "I'll never get used to this place."

"Your little Swan swim last night could have fooled me," Sky scoffs, defiant arms crossed over his chest

"I was just playing my role, like you told me to," I protest.

"Your acting skills are extraordinary then. Seemed to me like you were trying to impress him."

I retort, "Do you have any idea what he did to me after?"

Sky tenses, and I do my best to explain. I don't tell him about how Luc picked me up and carried me back to my bedroom, or how his heartbeat subdued me. Nor do I tell him how Luc's possessive yet tender arms managed to enslave me and melt my armor while he held me. Maybe that's why Luc terrifies me so much; he doesn't need to use his fists to pacify me.

After I've told him everything, Sky doesn't move, but he continues to wear his muscles tight, body tense. I recognize he's using more effort than normal to control himself. I'm almost surprised he hasn't marched right up to Luc and body-slammed him. "Did you close your eyes?"

I nod. "But I heard everything, all night. Please, Sky…tell me you have a plan."

Sky's gaze settles on me, steady. "I can tell you more if you can get to the chocolate shop."

Just then, he stiffens, his eyes hardening back into Vulture's. I focus on the door. Luc enters, striding toward me with his hands folded behind his back. I don't let go of Blackbird's hand. It's the only thing keeping me anchored.

"I saw Peacock on the way in. You made quite an impression." He flicks his attention to Sky. "I appreciate your dedication to Swan, but I care about *all* my Birds. Keep that in mind, Vulture, and tread carefully."

Sky nods in acceptance, retreating from the room. I imagine he'll be right outside the door, in guard mode.

Squeezing Blackbird's hand a little, I ask, "Have you figured out yet what happened to her?"

After settling in a chair at the foot of the bed, Luc leans back and surveys me. "Did you enjoy your time with Mockingbird?"

"Yes, she was very helpful," I say without looking at him.

"At times, Mockingbird talks too much."

"I like her." I spit out the words. "She's different."

"Well, she has lived here quite a long time."

"She said you found her when you were ten," I reflect on Mockingbird's story. "And now she's…how old?"

His voice betrays his amusement. "If you want to know how old I am, Swan, all you need to do is ask."

I turn to scrutinize his blue eyes, too stubborn to ask. Damn him.

"I'm twenty-five."

Nine years older than me.

He must know what I'm pondering because he directs the same question on me. "I'd wager you're sixteen, but only because of your youthful spirit and stature."

"I'm short. You don't need to sugarcoat it."

"I never sugarcoat anything." Wicked grin. "And you're not short. You're petite."

He waits.

I decide to give him a little help. "I'll be seventeen in the winter."

Clearly unconcerned by the gap in our age, Luc folds his hands behind his head and comments, "I still find your visitations with Blackbird fascinating. I am uncertain as to your motivation."

"You don't need to know my motivation."

Luc hushes for a few minutes, but I ignore him, giving all my attention to Blackbird. I can feel his eyes, but whether he stares at me or her is unknown. Coasting my fingers from her hands to her wrists, I glance at the inky feather tattoo on her shoulder, the polar opposite of mine.

And then, Luc starts to sing. A lullaby of his own.

Here is my ditty to bring you to trance.
Here is my tune to force you to dance.
Here is my lullaby so lovely and deep.
Here is my song to sing you to sleep.

Suddenly, Blackbird squeezes my hand...hard. The movement does not escape Luc's notice because the air around my body thins to make room for him when he hurries over.

He pauses to address me, hovering over my shoulder. "Whatever you are doing, don't stop."

My fingers create webs of circles along Blackbird's skin. I trail them along the side of her arm, and Luc repeats his lullaby. This time, her eyes crease, wrinkling the eyelids. Once again, her hand squeezes mine.

Luc is so close behind my chair I can feel his body warmth. Holding my breath, I touch her shoulder. Roused from whatever land is inside her head, Blackbird slowly opens her eyes and turns them on me, despite Luc hovering just above my head.

Blackbird cranes her neck. Her eyes sharpen against my hand, which still cups her shoulder. Under her gaze, I quickly remove it, feeling uncomfortable, but she shakes her head and murmurs, "You're the one I felt?"

Luc moves to my side. I lick my lips, glancing at his rather surprised face for a moment before nodding.

Her eyes don't stray from mine. "I remember you. You stopped to look at my exhibit. What happened? Why am I… Owl?"

Finally. I breathe a sigh and lean back in the chair, glad she's moved on to speaking to Luc now.

"You will be fine now," Luc assures her, voice brightening. "I will explain more later."

"I think…I'm hungry," she informs him, sounding a little confused.

Luc smiles and tilts his head just a little, speaking into some sort of device inside his ear. "A dozen oysters on a half shell to Blackbird's infirmary room immediately. And strawberries and cream."

Her smile reminds me of the edges of a fan spreading out to reveal alabaster paper beyond. She licks her dry, slightly chapped lips and whispers, "My favorite."

The next thing Luc does is call for a doctor to double-check Blackbird's condition. I linger nearby as he advises more rest and sets up another round of fluids. The doctor also attaches a device across her neck, shoulders, and arms. It looks like plastic to me, but he explains it's a new technology equipped with stimulation sensors that help the body recover its muscle memory quicker. Though oysters are not recommended, Luc proceeds to ignore that part.

After the doctor leaves, Luc starts to question her, "Blackbird, do you remember anything before your coma?"

She shakes her head. "No. Just being in my exhibit and then… waking up just now."

"Yes, you collapsed in your exhibit. Do you recall encountering anyone beforehand?"

"Just my artisans. I didn't speak to anyone else." Blackbird's words become more assured.

The Aviary

"Thank you, Blackbird." He glances at me for a second. "I have some business to attend to."

"Luc…" I try to object, a little unhinged at the thought of being alone with her, but he interrupts by cupping my cheek. That touch sends chilled tendrils needling into my skin, but somehow, I still flush.

"Owl," he corrects me. "You have earned your first town visit. Vulture will accompany you whenever you choose." He raises a finger in warning. "But only one place. And you will use a skin shield."

I understand what it means. No one can touch me. An electronic field around my body.

Before he leaves, Luc adds, fingering a curl of my hair, "When you decide where you wish to go, alert Vulture, and I will arrange for the place to be private. Free of any other customers."

I think my very blood vessels will burst, crack from how they've frozen. As soon as he exits, the room begins to warm, but I don't stop feeling cold. He's left his ice inside me.

Fourteen
AnsWers

"I can't believe you called him Luc." Blackbird points a finger at me, much more alert now. "We all knew you were special the first day you arrived." She stretches out her arms. Flexes her hands. Winces. She must be sore. "I tried to ignore it. Not like it'll affect me that much, anyway. Was I out for the grand opening of your exhibit?"

I nod.

"Figures."

She dumps a good portion of the blankets off her body. Beneath the white fabric, she wears a black hospital dress that pools past her thighs. She draws her knees toward her chest. I avert my eyes from her lower half as she situates herself, attempting to regain the use of her stagnant limbs.

"Why did you wake up?" I wonder, thinking back to a few minutes ago. "Was it Luc's song?"

Blackbird shakes her head. "No. It was more the feeling. I've never really been touched like that before." She gestures to my hand.

I shrug. "It wasn't anything special. Just...normal."

She winks, trying to tease, I think, but it falls flat. "I haven't had normal touching in a long time." She stretches her arms again, changing the subject. Her face is drawn, tired, but she's restless "How was it? The exhibit?"

"Luc was happy," I say.

"Good. You've ruffled their feathers, you know? The high-

The Aviary

er-up Birds."

A waiter enters with a rolling cart containing the ordered meal. He removes the bulbous silver cap and prepares to serve her, but Blackbird snatches the plate from the cart—an action I know wouldn't be possible without the sensory attachments she wears. She immediately cradles one of the oyster shells in her hand. Seeing that his presence is unneeded, the waiter leaves the bowl of strawberries and cream on the table at her bedside.

I observe her as she dips the shell toward her lips, tilts her head back, and slips the sleek and slimy oyster into her mouth. She doesn't chew.

"Aren't *you* a high Bird?" I ask.

Blackbird grins, holding up three fingers. "Third. Peacock's second. Nightingale's first."

"Peacock hates me."

"Good," Blackbird mutters while grabbing another shell. "If she were here, she'd gag. She hates seafood." Slipping another oyster into her mouth, she swallows effortlessly. "You're good for them. They haven't had any real competition in a long time. And they've let it go to their heads."

"You're not friends with Peacock?"

Blackbird shakes her head, reaching for the third oyster. "She's a show-off. Fortunately, her taste in clients and mine are completely different."

"What do you mean 'taste in clients?'"

Blackbird pauses, quirking a brow. "He didn't tell you?" She rolls her eyes, smiles a little. "Should have known. Owl's really sweet, you know." I bristle, but manage to listen as she continues.

"We get to choose our clients, Swan. Most of us get at least a dozen claims a day. Higher Birds can get up to thirty, but they don't make us fill that quota. That's the way it's done in the Glass Districts—quantity over quality. Museums are…different. They charge a flat rate at the door, and the prices go up with each level. I'm a High Bird, so I cost more." She winks. "Has Owl told you how many claims you've had yet?"

"No."

Gratified by her dish, Blackbird sighs, licking her plump, dark lips. "He's probably drawing it out. Ugh…" She yawns, her energy seeming to have run down. "I'd give anything for an energy patch right now. They're my favorite."

I nod, thinking of the patches Sky and my father used from time to time for training. Similar to an adrenaline shot, but lasts for at least twenty-four hours.

"So, you like it here?"

Blackbird reaches for a strawberry embellished with puffs of cream. "What kind of question is that? I mean, have you tried the *food*?"

"But…what about the rest?"

At first, Blackbird sucks on the strawberry, pondering my question. Popping it from her mouth, she finally remarks, "Sure, the job isn't glorious, but the clients aren't bad. They bring in a lot of extra money. Right now, I just send it to my mother. She lives in the town nearby. Besides, feed me and I'm happy. And I'm always hungry."

"But you're so—"

"Skinny, I know. Good genetics from my father's side."

"Your father?"

Blackbird shrugs as she sucks the juice from her fingers. "I guess it's an antiquated term. I'd say he doesn't deserve the title, but most men don't stick around these days. Just the way of things."

Cupping my hands together in my lap, I think of my father. He stuck around. He stuck with us through everything.

Before I use my town pass, I take a few minutes to read more of my mother's journal. Thanks to my conversation with Blackbird, thoughts of my father keep nagging at me. I think it's time I sifted through the pages Sky marked even if his foreboding words still hover in my mind.

And then, I see the first passage.

It crumbles my entire world.

Doctor Moby told me to push. It was the most important thing I had to do just then, if I wanted to escape. I remember how much I wanted Kerrick to be there. As far as I am concerned, Kerrick is Serenity's real father. Not Director Force.

THE AVIARY

I swallow back the lump polluting my throat, struggling to breathe. Her words answer every question I've wondered about for a long time. How I take after my mother but have never found an iota of Kerrick in me—physically *or* emotionally. Both my parents are calm wind and deep water. Sky is earth and thunder. And I am pure lightning—just fire and electricity.

How long has Sky known? For so many years, I've taunted him, calling him a Family brat. The name couldn't be more hypocritical. We are both Family brats. One more thing we can share.

No wonder my mother hid me all those years. Director Force would be searching for his child.

The words on the page stick like burrs in my mind, poking at the false security that has protected me all these years.

I continue reading.

The first birth was quiet.

The first?

I heave just a little, more frustrated than ever when my mother doesn't provide immediate relief.

Serenity came out mewing louder than a cat in labor, expressing distaste for this fractured world when she was perfectly happy an hour ago in the warm cocoon of my womb. Even as Moby wiped her off, she refused to stop screaming. Moby gave me a few minutes to feed, double checking that Kerrick was in his proper place. As soon as I started having contractions, Kerrick severed the call lines to the Penthouse and left to pick up the limousine. The Family Syndicate was on location that day. It meant I didn't have much time before Director Force showed up to inspect his baby.

I stared down at the child suckling at my breast. Severing us would be more impossible than a flag remaining still during a windstorm. Invisible roots crawled from every inch of her—mighty as thoughts—and wove straight into my heart, fusing with the strings there, doubling love and life and soul in the span of a single moment. When I looked at my child, there was no Temple, no skyscraper walls imprisoning me, no memory of Director Force's stink hovering over me there were just these unbelievable, unshakable olive branches of peace growing around me. Perfect Serenity.

I'd been unaware I was rocking myself until the action causes the tear on my cheek to tumble onto the page below.

A balm of forgiveness drives out the burrs in my mind. My mother always told me Kerrick was my father, and it makes sense why she said that. Even if he isn't biologically, he is still my dad. He's always been there behind the scenes, supporting us. Loving us. He loves my mother the most—I can see his devotion every time he looks at her—and that's always meant more to me than anything.

Moby gave me everything I needed. Medical scrubs and a nurse's mask for a disguise, along with a medical bag to conceal the baby. As soon as we said goodbye, I knew I would never stop missing the doctor who helped us. But I could almost taste freedom.

I knew Force would hunt us. He would comb whole countries for me and my child. But the thought of freedom from his ravenous mouth and his vengeful whip kept me moving forward. As did the thought of waking up to Kerrick.

I used Kerrick's security chip to get me to the freight elevators. When the doors opened onto floor one instead of the ground level, I panicked—until I saw him.

I turn the page, and a little note falls out of the book, but I crumple it up so I can focus on the next words.

A little boy with almost golden eyes, too wide for his small face beneath those cropped tufts of tawny hair. I asked him what his name was. Skylar, he told me.

When I slam the book shut, the pricking burrs return, competing with watery soft forgiveness. My attention turns to the note I crumpled, and I smooth it out to read Sky's familiar scrawl.

You deserve the truth about your past. Sorry it's late.

I shove the note into a nearby pocket before gripping clumps of my hair, yanking them so hard my scalp moans just a little. My hands quake. My fingers tremble, itching to reach out and break something, to throw something and watch it smash into a thousand pieces. To cause destruction.

Now, I know where my lightning comes from. Where I get my violent outbursts, my quick temper.

I am my father's daughter.

Though Dove says my decision to use my town pass right away is ill advised, I ignore the warning. I have to speak with Sky in private. He must have more answers about Force and my parents.

Luc bids me a fond farewell, entrusting me to Vulture's company. I try to ignore the feelings I conjure when I picture Luc's eyes, which haunt me even from the security transport car—his unyielding arms around my body, luring me in.

It doesn't take long to reach the downtown district of the city. Closer to the Temple City, the gigantic tower looks more like a blade's edge compared to the long needle from the Aviary. I know we're somewhere over the bridges, but I suppose I never paid attention to the Aviary's location when I caught the occasional advertisements or digital brochures.

As soon as I step outside, I catch salty whiffs of air curling into my nostrils. I imagine the only reason I can't smell the ocean on Aviary property is because of all the fresh oxygen pumped through its walls. I pause to look around me, one hand on the transport door even as Sky patiently waits for me. Just before I get out, I hear the telltale hum and feel the vibration of the skin shield. If I flutter my hand, I can see the shield flash and shiver when a wave vibrates like a rippling soundwave. It's an odd feeling, but necessary. Even with the private entrance and the chocolate house closed to the public.

The area echoes of the Aviary—from the glass retail businesses, luxury hotels all boasting glass architecture to the stained-glass decorations hanging in the windows, evoking bird patterns. Bird-patterned fashion haunts every fashion house and clothing outlet, no doubt exorbitantly priced due to their proximity to the Aviary. I press my lips into a thin line when I notice an employee erecting a mannequin dressed in a white ensemble that is reminiscent of a swan. Digital ads reveal swan jewelry, perfume, shoes, makeup, and more. Glad to know I'm having such an effect.

Before entering Lust and Cocoa, I notice black leather-gloved figures standing sentry across the street. The gloves are a distinguishing feature of Family security known as the Black Hand; this entire area, if not county, is Family-controlled. Guild-controlled. When I'd first seen his gloves, I'd assumed Luc was one of them—until he revealed himself as museum director. I wonder how high up in the food chain he is. No telling, considering the Families have their fingers in all sorts of revenue—nightclubs, shopping outlets, restaurants, and more. Family elders thrive as corporate moguls, surveying the world from their bulletproof skyscraper glass or luxury hotels. Borders here have far more security checks than cities without museums.

No wonder Sky can't get me out. The Guild is everywhere.

A few people pause to eye me, but Sky quickly dodges in front of me when they try to take pictures. Whether it's because they recognize me or just think I'm some sort of Family celebrity, I can't tell, but it's probably best to move on.

Lust and Cocoa is an older building. Vintage, unlike so many of the others, it isn't built of glass, but brick, though stained-glass pictures decorate windows. Inside, the sweet aroma overwhelms me.

I can understand why Sky enjoys this place. If it were inside a hotel, we'd sneak out together early in the morning to sample its wares and keep the secret from my parents like mischievous children. Immediately upon us walking in, he lets his guard down, relaxed like normal.

It's lunchtime. As Luc ordered, it's empty, and we have one hour to speak.

On display behind a wall of glass, the gold vat of churning chocolate causes my mouth to water. My eyes devour rich brownies decorated in dark frosting and assorted truffles. A woman behind the counter greets us. She wears a brown uniform with black hair tied back into a tight, thick bun, and her gold-tinted skin is set off by her lips, blushing red cherries.

Sky smiles as he approaches the counter. "Theodora." He nods to the woman. "Two Chanticos, please. We'll be at table sixteen. The Aviary tab."

She trains her gaze on me. "Are you certain you don't want

THE AVIARY

anything else?" She gestures to the menu screens above our heads. A moment later, they flash to featured delicacies that equal the price of a hover car. My jaw drops when I eye the items—from strawberries dipped in edible gold to cupcakes filled with champagne jelly and topped with exotic vanilla caviar to creations decorated in crystal and stained glass.

I glance at Sky, puzzled for a moment, before Theodora adds, "You may choose anything." From the way she says the words, it's almost as though she'd be insulted if I didn't.

"Those." I point without delay to the chilled chocolate shells housing an array of thick, dark chocolate ganache. Dusted with edible gold flakes. Not as expensive as others, but I'll be sure to include a worthy tip on the Aviary tab.

Table sixteen is actually a booth in the far corner of the cafe near the entrance to the kitchen. Before we sit down, I start to put my fragile arms around Sky. Even with my shoes on, my head can only find its way to his chest.

"Sky, if we don't leave soon, I'm going to be trapped in that birdhouse forever."

"Serenity." Sky doesn't touch me, just urges me into the booth. "Sit down and try the Chantico."

I remember the skin shield. The wearer can touch others, but not the other way around. No wonder he can't hug me back. The shield will shock him.

When we slide into the booth, I loosen my hair from its bun. I let the curls fall down my back, purposely using them to conceal the tattoo on my shoulder.

"How close are we to the Temple?"

Sky keeps his hands to himself, more conscientious of the shield. "Couple of hours' distance. You know you're on the island, right? The well-established. Not the urban sprawl. You're smack dab in the middle of billionaire alley. Congratulations."

"It doesn't seem too busy."

"It's still spring, but we're right around the corner from summer. And let's just say this island is the queen of summer. It's a playground for trust-fund kids and celebrities."

"But we're near the sea," I point out, surveying him.

"No escape there." He shakes his head, understanding my

meaning. "Guild Family controls this entire region, including any charter, private yachts, fishing, or tourist boats. They even have their own coast guard, believe it or not."

My hopes sink a little.

"Wish we were near the marina. They have a great cottage café where they keep the live lobsters in an antique bathtub by the front door."

I make a face, and Sky chuckles, knowing full well my distaste for seafood.

"Remember the time you stepped on a sea urchin?" I remind him of our seaside retreat when I was ten, remembering it was the first time I ever saw Sky so angry. Or cuss so much.

"Yes, and I also remember how you swam out too far, and the current carted you farther out to sea."

"But you dragged me back to shore."

"Under protest." He rolls his eyes. "Too fearless for your own good."

Our ability to find humor even now reassures me of our familiarity with one another. And how an apology is due before we get down to business.

"I'm sorry. I should've waited for you. You were gone all day, and I just...wanted to swim."

"I was delayed. My fault." He shouldn't blame himself like that.

"I did everything you showed me. Snuck out at night, took the stairs. I figured we were far enough away from the city, but there were smugglers."

"Probably a scout. Doesn't take more than a phone call to tell his contacts about a score. Too big a score for them to turn down." He observes me, eyes blinking down for one moment before settling on my face again. I know I'll remember that momentary glance.

"Thanks for the journal, by the way," I seethe. "And for lying to me all these years. Where are *my* parents?"

Sighing, he clenches his fingers into a fist on the table. "I might have a lead, but I can't be certain."

Theodora arrives with our order. Thick, decadent, creamy, and exploding in sweet richness, the drinking chocolate warms the passage of my throat and heats my insides to a delirious deliciousness. When I set it down, I immediately notice the object sitting on the table.

"An apology token." Sky motions to the snow globe housing the familiar network of glass buildings.

At first, I just study it, unsure whether I want to pick it up and shake it like I've always done with every other globe Sky has brought me.

His words seem to lead where my thoughts stray. "The Aviary's no different. It's part of you now. Just like every other place. You'll be taking it with you."

I don't want to believe that, but I pick up the snow globe and tip it over once, watch dozens of mini birds start to swirl before I start to shake. And shake.

"Careful. Don't want to kill the poor thing."

I meet his eyes in a deadpan as if to suggest 'what if I do?'

"It's just a snow globe," Sky reminds me.

Sighing, I set down the bird globe and fix my gaze on him. "Start talking."

"I believe the Guild branch has taken Kerrick and Serafina into custody."

Sky inches his hand forward to take a piece of my chocolate shell, but I slap his hand away and nearly shout, "You're not finished talking!" I cup my hands around the ganache, threatening him with my eyes. "Start explaining or I'll stab your eyeballs with this fork." I brandish the utensil. "How did this happen? They keep a low profile. They use disguises."

"As far as I know, it happened in the Glass District. Same one you ended up in. I don't know all the details, but they lost a bid on a girl there. Sounds like your mother made quite the scene."

"But she never does that." Unless it's in private.

"Can't begin to say. All I know is the Guild leader was on scene, and I guess he didn't believe they were just some ordinary sterile couple looking for a child to adopt. That was their cover. Anyway, by now, their DNA has been flagged in the system."

"Why do they want my parents?"

"I'm getting to that." Then he confirms what Luc once told me. "The Guild runs the Aviary. Second to the Syndicate that controls the Temple."

"But isn't the Aviary number three?" I interrupt, a little confused.

"Profit, yes. Power, no. The Garden brings in more revenue thanks to its location and its size, but the Garden is independently owned, inherited. No Family affiliation, but the only reason they're in business is because Force lets them. Anyway, the Guild and the Syndicate have always had a power struggle, and they could be using your parents as leverage."

"After all these years, Force still wants my mom, doesn't he?"

"Yes, but it's more complicated than that." Sky's eyes focus on me. "I need you to understand and trust everything I'm going to tell you. Because if you don't, we're all going to be in a world of trouble."

Fifteen
The GuiLd

"Your parents work for the Sanctuary."

"Come again?" I plant my hands on the table. "You always, *always* told me it was an urban legend!"

"I lied. Your parents didn't want to get you caught up in their world. They were afraid you'd insist on getting involved."

I want to be angry, but I know they were probably right about that. Thumbing the rim of my Chantico glass, I ask, "Are all the stories true?" When I was little, I concocted idealistic images of a paradise with a great castle where girls were treated like princesses and rode unicorns all day.

Sky sniggers. "Not the unicorn ones. But girls can live in freedom and peace away from museums and Glass Districts, and that's the important thing. They run off strict secrecy."

I nod. If the Sanctuary's secret network is ever exposed, the Families would bring down their hammer. Any number of branches would unite to destroy the Sanctuary and reclaim the treasure hoard of lost girls inside.

Sky leans back in the booth. "Your parents have spent years building connections to rescue girls from every diseased place in this twisted world. If they fall into Temple hands, the things they know about the Sanctuary could unravel it."

"If they work for the Sanctuary, why haven't they just kept me there? Both of us?"

He interrupts me, "I've asked myself the same question. My guess is they didn't want to take any chances. They just wanted you nearby."

"My mother wrote something about 'the first.' Was I a twin?"

Sighing, he kneads his eyes. "Yes. Firstborn wasn't breathing when she came out. All I know. Stillborns are common. Your mother has never talked about it. She's had enough demons in her life. Figured it was better not to ask."

I can't argue with him. And it's better to touch on our common ground. "So, I guess you and I are both Family brats."

Sky shrugs. "Bummer, huh?" He brandishes a smile, his eyes turn to liquid amber, and he adds, "Welcome to the club."

I recognize something else other than the humor there. Something that would explain his avoidance of physical contact over the past few years. At least I know we have a more important goal in mind: my parents.

"I don't understand. What does the Guild leader want with my parents?"

"It's a power play against the Temple. According to my sources, once you became Aviary property, they had your DNA on file. The system flags DNA if it matches another's in the system, so the Guild knows who you are. Who your parents are."

I shudder, imagining what the Guild might do with the knowledge they effectively own their fiercest competitor's daughter.

"I'm guessing the Guild leader is probably setting the stage for bargaining. He knows he's found a diamond in the rough in you, but I don't think he anticipated your exhibit to excel as much as it already has."

"Does Force know who I am yet?"

Sky shakes his head. "No. He's heard of the Swan, but hasn't discovered your true identity. The Guild leader wants to keep it that way until you get more popular. Show how valuable you are to Force when the time comes."

"What the hell am I supposed to do with all this?"

"Don't curse. Your mom wouldn't like it," he scolds. "Look, I don't like this any more than you do. It's going to take time for me to go through Aviary records. The more I do it, the greater the risk of getting caught. It's going to require more time inside the Aviary. And I'm…" He rubs the back of his neck and finishes, "I'm going to need you to play along. Maybe even convince Luc that you're letting him in. That you trust him."

"No! No! Uh-uh—no way." I shake my head violently. "Do you even know what you're asking me to do?"

Sky softens his eyes, angling his head, and I grimace. I can tell it hurts him more than he'll say to have to ask this of me. "Don't give me those puppy-dog eyes," I plead.

"If you keep getting as popular as I think you will, it'll buy me the time I need. The Swan is the perfect bait to draw the Guild out and recoup your parents."

Paint me into a corner, why don't you? "I'm not good at behaving. You *know* that."

"All I'm asking is that you do your best." He can't meet my eyes any longer. As he says his next words, his expression is one of pure revulsion. "The closer Luc believes he is to you, the better our chances he'll trust you enough to take you into his confidence. Maybe he'll even tell you something about your parents that will help us find them."

We sit in silence for a moment. Finally, he looks me in the eye.

"Ser, you can't imagine how critical Kerrick and Serafina are to our cause."

"*Our* cause?" I question, cocking an eyebrow. "You're not telling me something. How involved are you?"

Sky's voice deepens, a tone that registers he means business. "*Very* involved."

SKY RETURNS ME TO THE Aviary shortly after our talk. I need time to consider his words and what to do about them. As soon as I can, I slip inside the walk-in closet with its ocean of white clothes and settle down in the corner to read my mother's journal again.

Back then, he was just Force. He never let me use his first name. Now, I call him the Vampire. At night, I was his Unicorn. By day, I was Serafina. We were trained from childhood to never let those worlds touch. Serafina and Unicorn could never meet. But somewhere along the line, Unicorn took over, and Serafina became a ghost. I tell this story to my daughter because she's a child. It must always feel like a story to her. A fairy tale with a happy ending. I can't let her see the horrors I face every day.

It seems ironic, considering my mother was never particularly good at hiding things. Of course, it was easier when I was a little girl, but as I've grown older, I've picked up on more things. I remember my mother's beautiful face, a dim echo of my own—her silver hair is straighter, shorter, and embraces her cheekbones rather than smacks at them like my voracious curls. Melancholia etched in her gray eyes, with their fog of secrets. She doesn't have the same fierceness as I do, but every once in a while, I catch warships passing through her irises. Like she's still fighting some unknown demon. Now, I know it was for the Sanctuary.

Unicorn loved the chaos: the tangle of white dresses, silver horns, and gold bridles they used to decorate her. The way her skin smelled like blood and cologne in the morning. She even loved how his whip left marks on her skin.

But one day, everything changed.

It wasn't a crash. The Knight had to chip away at the Unicorn little by little. She bucked and kicked, but she finally stood still long enough for him to unlock the door in her mind. And that was when I broke the Unicorn, tamed her, and she became the ghost. The Knight and I eloped in secret, and we dreamed of escaping, but the Vampire came every night. I tried to imitate Unicorn, but my tears flowed like a river. And the Vampire seemed to love it even more.

Then, I felt life move inside of me. I knew the Vampire wouldn't bite me until after my baby was born. He never discovered the truth about us because we were very patient, and we waited for the exact right moment.

I know the rest of the story. How my parents had to keep moving from place to place, running from the Syndicate Family who hunted them. How many lost girls had they rescued along the way? No wonder we were constantly moving; it would have been an asset to their work with the Sanctuary. What will happen to all those lost girls if the Sanctuary comes crashing down?

I think of the Breakables and my first visit to the Glass District.

After my mother's explanation with the butterfly in the frame, my father thought it would be good to take me there so I could see firsthand. Some had nothing but flimsy limbs with loose skin.

Others snapped their hips back and forth, summoning eyes with come hither fingers. Other faces oozed jealousy from my father's protective stance next to me.

When we came home, I didn't want to hear about the Glass District or Breakables ever again. Instead, I clung onto my parents and their escape from the Temple. Every time they returned from one of their trips, I begged my mother to tell me the story over and over again. Sky never wanted to hear it because he knew things I didn't, things my mother didn't want to share. All these years, I've made excuses for him, said it was just a byproduct of his genetics, some of his Family blood trickling into his aloof body language and harsh words.

For so long, I've just heard the pretty story about my mother's past.

Now, it's time to read between the lines.

AFTER HIDING MY MOTHER'S JOURNAL again, I retreat to the fish tank, wishing I could become like those fish—with their forgetful minds and ever-moving mouths. Instead, I am a fish out of water, flopping around, struggling to breathe in this birdcage air.

If Sky is right about Luc's intentions not to sell me to a client, I know I can keep this up. In fact, I am in danger of keeping it up all too well. But if he isn't planning on selling me, what are his intentions?

"It was how I knew," the voice behind me murmurs. I flinch, but don't turn. By now, I've accustomed myself to the fact he can enter a room without making his presence known. "You never concealed your attraction to water." He sidles his body to the other side of the tank to better observe me.

"You suspected. You didn't *know*," I try to correct Luc, but his next words shred mine.

"I never assume, Swan. Gamble, yes, but never assume."

To play this charade Sky wants, I will need to plunge deeper into the Aviary director's world. Luc needs real pieces to believe my charade. Buy Sky time or...could I win Luc's trust enough that he would give me answers?

Swallowing back the knot of disgust in my throat from answering to Swan, I confess, "I learned to swim early. I grew up having access to water—mostly pools, but sometimes lakes. Once even the ocean."

Weaving the edge of my finger into a circle, I watch a wayside fish twinkle about from the motion before flitting behind some faux coral. Luc focuses on my every move, and I find I enjoy this new power. No matter how much I tell myself this is for Sky, my desire to share this with Luc surprises me.

"When I was eight, I went skinny dipping in the waves at night. I saw a shark under the waves. They feed in shallow water, but I was so thrilled to swim in the ocean for the first time I didn't care. I laughed. I actually *laughed* in the face of a shark. All these bubbles floated around my face. I was so sure it was going to attack, but it didn't. It's almost like it sensed I wasn't a threat. Like it knew…"

"…how pure your heart is," Luc finishes for me, but I keep my eyes on the fish. "Do you enjoy the ocean?"

I like swimming in lakes better, but I nod anyway.

"Perhaps I will take you to the old lighthouse situated on the outskirts of the island. Or our state park dunes trail. I'm certain you'd find scaling the dune mountains challenging but worthwhile. I look forward to seeing you in the water again. You are never more my Swan than when you are underwater."

"I will be Swan again tonight…but I still don't see the point."

"What do you mean?" My hand becomes a slave to his, my fingers pressed against the cages of his lips when he kisses them.

I remember his heartbeat, the warmth of his chest, the surety in his arms. At the same time, nothing makes sense with him. Everything becomes warped like a carousel twirling me around and around. That is how Luc makes me feel. Dizzy with no sense of grounding, capable of shedding my old skin and becoming whoever he wants me to be.

Finally, I raise my head, eyes on his, to tell him, "I don't think anyone could desire me as much as you already do."

ALMOST MIDNIGHT. MY PRESENTATION IS even grander. Dove decorates my skin with individual feathers all knit together to form

The Aviary

a dress while she paints the rest of me in a milky white cream. In the center of each feather is an optic opal so when the exhibit spotlights bathe me, I will shine like sun on snow. She's collected all my curls into a magnificent knot, one that will unravel in the water. To top it off, she gives me wings. They are heavier than I expected, and they curve around my small body. Once more, I begin to shake, doing my best to calm the tremors inside my hands.

"Please don't make me dive," I plead with Luc as he leads me to my exhibit.

He pauses before the door to observe me, suspicion rousing his features. I explain as best I can. "I don't like falling."

"Try to think of it this way—the fall is only for a moment." I realize that Luc, for the most part, has always been honest with me. "I wish there was more time so I could tell you—"

"Tell me what?"

He opens the door, motions to the swing. "Be brave, Swan." His hands alight on mine as I ease my body onto the contraption.

Clutching the rope, I try to hold fast to the frost of Luc's skin. I whisper motivating words to myself. "Just…wait for the water."

I never do.

His next words take me by surprise. "After the exhibit, don't close your eyes."

Before I can determine what he means, the pulleys start to propel the swing upward. Luc releases my hand.

More people this time.

Breathe.

The swing reaches its destination. Silence reigns. Everyone waits, holding their breath for me. I remember Sky's words from earlier—*Do your best.* Once I earn Luc's trust and gain popularity, it'll allow Sky more opportunities to find my parents. And then, I can go home and forget I was ever here. *Do your best.*

Instead of pumping my legs, I rise, maintain a firm grip on the ropes, and come to a standing position atop the wooden slab under my feet. Tonight, I will fly for them.

No one seems to be able to rip their eyes from me. If I close my eyes now, I will become a child again. Free and unbridled on the hotel playgrounds of my girlhood, swinging beneath the protection of night. With Sky beside me.

Sky...I inhale.

And I dive.

My wings catch a rush of wind just before the lake folds me into a watery trance. Just as Dove predicted, my hair unravels as soon as my body punctures the surface. The white jewels from my hair spiral away as I dive deeper, deeper. Behind me, the wings are my only hindrance. They seek the surface, trying to best me, their burden becoming too great. Like a savage, I tear them from my back, bit by bit until feathers whiten the water around me. Liberated, I continue my plunge through the depths.

I revel in the spell of the water. How it lulls my body and strangles all other sounds. When I pause to see the glass, I notice the drunken gazes of those beyond it for the first time. I can't hear them talking, but if I close my eyes just once, everything will disappear. But I don't. Down here, I am weightless and light.

Staring at my audience, I set one hand to the glass and fan it against the pane. I observe the spectators' hands copy my action. Thrilled by the attention, I place my other hand on the glass, watch them mimic me again as they yearn to touch.

What made my mother Director Force's favorite? She is a dancer. For years, she only danced for him...reared and bucked and kicked in elegant pirouettes. Her performance must have been stunning.

I am becoming just like her.

All my air is spent, so I leave them, close my eyes for the first time, and shimmy through the water to the surface. Luc waits for me as I gasp my first inhale of air. More exhausted and out of breath than before, I let him do most of the work of pulling me into the canoe. This time, he has a blanket for me.

For one moment, he cups my cheek and smiles. "Wondrous, Swan," he whispers above the applause. "I need you to be brave now. This is just the beginning."

Dove prepares me again in the customary simple dresses all the girls wear. She leaves my hair wet and dripping down my back because she says there is no time.

"What's happening?" I want to know.

The Aviary

Her hands work fast, faster than I've ever seen them work before. She wrings out my hair as best she can, braids a few strands together. "They only come three times a year unless it's a special occasion. *You* are that special occasion."

I try to stop Dove's hand. "Who?"

"Swan..." I spin around to see Luc waiting at the doorway. He peers at Dove. "Is she ready?"

Dove drops her hands to her sides. "I guess she will have to be."

Luc extends a hand. "Come with me. They're waiting for you."

Something in the way his brows plunge lower, forcing his eyes to don their hoods, something in the way his hand dominates mine...I ask no questions.

All the Birds of the Aviary stand in specified hierarchy along the staircase. Luc places me at the top. Right next to him.

The audience is gone. In the lobby are dozens of men dressed in black. Security. The symbol of a hand is embroidered into the right side of every uniform sleeve. They form a line on each side of the staircase while four figures issue through the center in detailed succession.

The first is an older man. He is handsome in a way, rugged, with scrubby chestnut whiskers shadowing his strong jawline. Behind him is a much younger man, only a few years older than me, whose muscles can rival even Sky's. His broad shoulders and muscle cording every trace of skin make him a beast of a man; his hands are so big, one could wrap around my head and crush it like an acorn. Behind him walk two girls, similar in age to me. They are identical. Both are horrifyingly beautiful, dressed in scarlet dresses that hug their lithe bodies. Silver hair braided like crowns frame their porcelain skin.

Suddenly, I understand. This is the Guild hierarchy.

The older man, the patriarch, reaches the top of the staircase and approaches Luc. Right away, I notice his eyes. I try not to let my astonishment show. Though everything else lacks resemblance, Luc's eyes are identical to this man's.

The Aviary director bows his head to the older man, and the Guild patriarch cups Luc's right shoulder and smiles.

"You have done well, my son."

Sixteen
GrapHickers

"Tonight's performance was spectacular," the Guild patriarch commends Luc in a deep but serene voice, something else Luc has inherited. "You've secured the envy of the Temple with this latest acquisition. I'm proud."

For once, Luc is silent. He nods, bowing his head once more.

The patriarch—Luc's father—turns to look at me. Where I feel like a child beneath Luc's scrutiny, this man turns me to an infant. When he takes a few tendrils of my drenched hair, I hold my breath like I'm underwater again.

He smiles at me. "She is quite a find," he tells Luc. "You will preserve her until the grand event?"

"Just as you've stipulated, Father."

Grand event?

Luc's father keeps his eyes on me, fingers pausing at my waist before straying to the feather tattoo. Everything about me freezes when he brushes the mark. He renders my whole body to ice. "Enchanting, child. I hope you appreciate how valuable you are. In fact, no museum in this entire region has held an international auction in the past fifty years."

At the word "auction," I lash out. Feel my lightning split the ice on my skin from his father. Luc gets his arms around me, but not before my nails sink into the Guild leader's arm.

Shocked murmurs ripple through the Birds, and the twin girls gaze back and forth from each other to my spectacle. The brawny man steps forward.

THE AVIARY

I buck against Luc, but he manages to derail me, forcing my knees to the staircase floor. He tethers my arms behind me, compressing the pressure point on my neck to keep me still. "*Swan.*" Luc's voice hardens like iron before he addresses the Guild leader. "I apologize, Father. It won't happen again."

The Guild leader eyes his arm once before shrugging it off. "No need, son. This one will become a thing of legend for the Aviary. Perhaps we will immortalize her with a diamond statue." When he brushes his fingers across my cheek, I throw my damp curls to one side and struggle against Luc's firm grip. "With word of our auction spreading fast, I'll be providing you with heightened security beginning next week."

He turns his body away from me toward the younger man, for which I am thankful, but Luc does not release his grip.

"Larke." Luc's father addresses the brawny man. "You and your men will remain here for now and learn under your brother's tutelage. Perhaps he will finally break through that thick skull of yours."

Larke's mouth compresses into a narrow line. Bowing to his father's authority, he steps down in submission.

Once again, the Guild patriarch turns to face me. Placing two fingers under my chin, he peers into my eyes. Did Luc learn that from him?

"I look forward to your next exhibit, my dear girl."

Finally, they depart.

Luc releases me to bid his Family farewell, but the sudden sound of a delicate shriek diverts me.

At the bottom of the staircase, I see a giant hand locked around Finch's neck. Her legs kick vainly in midair.

"She should learn her place." Luc's brother snarls, putting her down and pointing to a scratch on his cheek that is just beginning to drip blood.

"Finch is a hatchling," Luc says, clearly angered by his brother's behavior. "I bought her from a Glass Auction. The Glass Districts lack the sophistication of museums; she is still learning."

Only I know the truth: Finch has been mimicking me since that first dinner, when she stole food off my dinner plate. These past few days, she's practiced swimming through air while shadowing my every move. I did this.

"She's old enough to know better," Larke counters. He draws Finch's face closer to his.

Luc's father steps forward, observing Finch. I bite down on my lip. "Lash her once," he says. "And she shall know her place from now on."

When Luc's father speaks, everyone obeys.

Larke prepares to do the deed, awaiting Luc's consent.

Luc hesitates, but I know he will save face. His nod confirms it. Luc stands in front of her, then raises a single finger. "Finch, step forward."

Squeamish yet brave, the girl does as she's told, but I know better. I recognize throes of panic in her eyes. It reminds me of my own when I woke in the Glass District, when I entered the Aviary, when I had my first exhibit.

It feels like a swan is ramming my stomach, pecking at the lining as it begs me to do something. There is no way I can reach her in time to stop them. Only one thing will deter them. Only one thing will bring everything crashing down.

Before Larke can lash Finch, I do what is by far the most foolish thing I've done since coming here. I throw my body down the glass staircase, reliving the familiar pain I encountered that first night I snuck out of my room when some nameless, faceless Bird pushed me. But even if the pain is familiar, it's not as sharp or intense because it's mine, my choice, and it brings the response I desire.

Luc rushes worriedly to my crumpled body at the base of the stairs. Finch scurries away, and I watch through dazed eyes as some of the other Birds hide her behind their elaborate dresses.

I smile as Luc calls for a medic. I've succeeded.

The pain only lasts an instant longer, before I pass into unconsciousness.

"I KNOW WHY YOU DID it," Luc growls when I stir.

The infirmary reminds me of the hospital with its white sheets, sterile white walls, and white medical gown.

One touch from Luc's hand crumbles my resolve. "Do *not*

THE AVIARY

move," he orders, and I steady my head against the pillow. "You have more bruises than skin, but the implant is healing them."

As if knowing I'd want to ensure he's done nothing else, Luc raises a mirror to my face. Save for the violet shadows under my eyes and some other random fading ones, it looks untouched by injury.

"Do you have any idea what you did to me?" There is a sense of urgency in his voice. When I look at him, I see for the first time that his eyes look haggard, burdened by invisible weights. "I was afraid you were in a coma."

My voice is cracked and dry when I ask, "Finch?"

"Swan." He's so calm. Even when he smashes the mirror against one of the walls, causing me to flinch. He drags his hands through his hair before turning back toward me. "How can I make you understand they are none of your concern? You are singular. You are not like them. They will never accept you! You are my Swan!"

"Blackbird—" I try to argue, but Luc cuts me off.

"Where do you think she is now? One of your darker hours, and do you think she is here trying to visit you as you did her? No, she is attending to a client. Inside this Aviary, you have one advocate. You have *me*. Never forget that." He turns, shifting his gaze to the glass shards. Then he starts to chuckle. "You must be a negative influence. Look at what I just did."

"You should try it more often," I say. "It looks better that way. Reminds me what the Aviary really is. Broken."

Luc doesn't react the way I think he will. "I have to agree with you. You are the only unbroken Bird I have ever found."

Shifting in the bed, I raise my head a little. "I'm still trying to figure you out, Luc. Whether you're broken or whole."

"Owl. And trust me, I'm just as broken as the rest of them." He leans forward. "But when I'm with you, I'm whole again."

LUC STAYS BY MY SIDE most of the day, but leaves me alone at night to ponder his many facets.

The Aviary director: the master to whom all must bow.

The Owl: protector over the Birds.

The son of the Guild: a threatening Black Hand.

And finally, Luc: whose steadfast hands lull me and create masterpiece exhibits where I come alive.

Maybe one of his other roles can still benefit me. Like the Guild leader's son. With his father's approval resting on him, Luc must know about my parents, must know where they are and about their connection to me. Maybe all it would take is one request. If I ask him for a favor, he might not be able to resist me.

I lose my chance when *they* come. Footprints as quiet as shadows tiptoe into the room, and a small bottle is thrust against my nose. I try to rise to defend myself. Even when the chemicals whip my consciousness, taming it to submission, the last one who invades my mind is Sky.

My body feels like one giant eggshell just waiting for some uncaring boot to crack it. Whatever Luc gave me to abate the pain is gone.

"The agents will be here this morning. Pictures must be done now if we want to market her!"

"I know, Anders," returns the voice like shaved gravestones. "We'll take them now, edit later."

"While she's sleeping?"

"Oh, she's not sleeping." The smile is apparent in his voice. "Are you, your Swanness? I've done this enough times; I can tell when they're awake or asleep."

I am awake enough to register how my bare legs are curled into the fetal position, and when I stir, whatever holds me shakes. Beneath my body, I feel several soft and light things, but when my hands move, the objects flutter. Feathers. Hundreds of feathers, and below the spread of feathers, I feel a cold and metallic surface. Opening my eyes, I realize I'm blinded by a scrap of black fabric. I jerk it away.

"Careful," the first voice warns. "She may bite. Or peck."

At first, I'm confused. Whatever they put me in is far too small for me to stand up. I can only crawl to my knees, but that's far too much effort, especially with the giant white wings attached to my back, so I manage to sit. Gold lacquered bars block my body from the men in front of me. When I look up to see the bars shaped into a dome above my head, I recognize it. I'm inside the mouth of a birdcage.

Pressing my cheek against one cold bar, I struggle to gain control of my breath. Wilder than a trapped lioness, I target the two men.

One of them raises an object to my face that flashes. The first one grins approval. "Perfect."

Undoubtedly graphickers.

Ignoring the pain throbbing under my skin, I grip two bars and begin to shake the cage, which dangles from a chain fixed to the ceiling. All that produces is more flashes, more photography. Ancient compared to holography. He must be new at this career. Or retro is back in style.

"Don't shake too much, Swan girl," the first graphicker warns me. "Wouldn't want to shake those feathers right off now, would we?"

The second one eyes me with a hungry expression. "I wouldn't mind, your Swanness."

I've only focused on my surroundings, my disgust for the graphickers, and the pain under my skin. Now, I look down at the mere strips of lace harboring my lower regions and the feathers pasted across my breasts. Other than that, I'm naked.

I cross my arms over my chest, curling my legs closer to the rest of my body. Anger pecks the tears from my eyes, and all the emotions from the past few days cause them to flow freely.

"Now, now, don't spoil that pretty face, Swan. The Temple will take good care of you. We had just enough time to disable the alarm system, kill the guard outside your door, and smuggle you out."

No! Which guard? I start to panic.

"Been canvassing that place for weeks. So lucky you dropped in when you did. Far bigger prize than the other Bird we were going to steal. Graphicking is much more lucrative than smuggling, but I haven't lost my smuggler's touch, have I?"

I don't give them the benefit of speech. They can capture my body, incarcerate my form behind the glowing screens, but they can't cage my heart—can't tell me not to cry. What I wouldn't give to return to the Aviary. Luc and Sky are both right. Outside, the world is a cage. Worse than anything I'd ever experienced in the Aviary. Luc would never do this.

"Swan."

I peer up just enough so I can see the head graphicker close to the cage now, staring at me. His smile is sinuous and sultry as he lifts the digital printed photograph to the cage.

"Hush now," he whispers to the tears in my eyes. "Do you understand why we need to do this?" He traces a finger across the outline of my body on glossy paper. When I don't respond, he barks an order to the other man, "Open the cage."

"Come on! You know how long it took me to set that up?"

"Open it," the lead graphicker dictates again, taking one step forward. The other man flinches just a little before producing the keys.

Even after the door is opened, I make no move. I shrink away when the lead graphicker extends a hand to me. Right now, the cage is my only barrier from them, and I plant one hand on each gold-lacquered bar, closing my fist around it in an iron-tight grip. My new position prompts more photos.

The lead graphicker approaches me, and I arch my back farther against the cage just as he tosses a collection of photos inside. Each one is mine. Each one imprisons me.

"It is not about desire," he continues. "Desire will never be satisfied. It's about control. Right now, I control everything about your body. But trust me, you're not powerless." He motions to the photograph again. "We can do whatever we want to your body, but it's because of you that *I* will fail to control my addiction. I'll surrender whole-heartedly. I become a slave and you the master. And I will keep coming back for more and more."

"You're wrong."

The invading voice is savage yet melodic, brutal yet angelic. Sweet as a nightmare's lullaby. "*I* hold your fate."

In Luc's hand is a dark barreled object of shiny, silver metal. A gun.

"Release the girl." He calls me a girl. Not his Bird, not his Swan. Girl.

The head graphicker steps forward. Withdraws a gun from his jacket. He targets Luc. "The Temple owns her now, bird man."

The Aviary

"No one owns her, porn pusher. You have one. Last. Chance."

The graphicker raises his gun, and I realize it's smaller than Luc's. "Get out of my studio!"

"So be it."

The cannonades inside Luc's eyes thunder with the force of a thousand curses. He speaks three words to me. "Close your eyes."

I do what he says.

I hear the ricochet of bullets followed by a sickening crackle. Two frantic, panic-induced screams. Then…nothing but the stench of blood and burning flesh.

The next thing I hear is Luc's voice once again commanding, "Do not open your eyes."

One able hand encompasses my waist and the other roots itself just under my legs so he can hold me. His arms feel just as I remember them. Like he's holding something light and precious, as though fearful I will float away to where he can't find me. Except, I could never float away. In this moment, I feel him bending back my wings, taming me just as he predicted he would.

As he carries me out, I smell smoke in the air. I've heard of weapons the Families use. Certain, specialized guns that can shoot bullets that will explode after burrowing in flesh, or ones that will split apart and poison victims with a black, venomous liquid, making a slow and brutal example. I know I should keep my head tucked into the asylum of Luc's shoulder, but this is my chance to learn what I can about Luc. Not the Guild progeny. Not the Aviary director. Not even the Owl. Luc.

As soon as I open my eyes, Luc catches me and hisses, "Serenity!" He's used my real name, evoking how enraged he is.

The charred bodies reek of cinders. Hot oil oozes out of every orifice. Lethal, precise bullet holes are embedded in their heads.

Once I tear my gaze away and into the eyes of my rescuer, all I can do is whisper, "Who are you?"

Seventeen
BIRdsFalLing

*N*IGHT AGAIN.

After he returned me to my Aviary room, Luc left for the rest of the day. Whether he did that on purpose so I could process his actions in the studio or he did it out of shame, I couldn't tell.

Dove helped to scrub the graphicker feathers clean off my body before letting me rest, which was simple with Sky standing outside my bedroom door now. There was a shift change. Otherwise, the graphickers never should've managed to take me without Sky's notice. As it is, Luc has heightened security due to my abduction. Upgraded the Aviary's system.

After sleeping through most of the day, I linger in the heat of a bath, drawing the warmth from the water into my bruised body. Thanks to another dosage of pain reliever, I feel much better. Even if pride touts I should feel the bruises I've received for Finch, I'm far too tired to care. Besides, Luc would never have it.

"How did he find me?" I ask Dove, who sits behind me on the tiles. Her fingers fish through my hair, deciphering the tangles.

"Most girls are equipped with tracking devices, but your implant is linked to his personal interface. Owl always finds his Birds. I simply cannot brush your hair like this. You must come out."

Surrendering, I nod. There is more water than bubbles now anyway.

"I'll fetch your robe."

After securing me in the cotton folds, Dove motions to the

bed so she can comb my strands. "You gave us quite a scare."

"Does everyone know?"

"Owl told me but no others. Some secrets must be kept for the house to function."

"I understand." Images from the studio scratch the surface of my memory; the echoes of their scars will forever linger.

Luc is always in control. The puppeteer in everything. And now…I owe him. The first day I arrived, the thought would've sickened me. Now, it's like he's managed to noose one wedge of my heart. It's as though I've given part of my lightning to him. What he will do with the electric currents, I cannot begin to imagine.

"Dove."

It's the first time I don't flinch. Instead, I turn to find Luc, hand extended so he may take the comb from her. Tonight, he is dressed all in white.

I remain where I am while Dove exits my room, and Luc holds the ends of my hair and begins to comb them.

"Are you afraid of me?" he asks. I can hear anguish in his voice.

I curve my neck ever so slightly, but I can't see his eyes. "No," I say, hoping he can hear the resolve.

"I told you to keep your eyes closed."

"I'm not very obedient."

He continues brushing and remarks, "Yes, I am keenly aware of that."

"Are you going to punish me?"

He pauses. "No." I breathe a sigh of relief. "I believe the studio was punishment enough. Do you understand now how the Aviary is a safe haven?"

Too conflicted by Dove's voice competing with my parents', I don't say anything.

Luc plays with a few strands of my hair, coils them around his fingers. "They were correct on one level," he says, referring to the graphickers. "We all seek pleasure, but rarely does that pleasure ever fully satisfy. Even what I do for my Birds…there is *some* satisfaction, but only on the surface." He pauses. "This is the first time in my life that I've found someone who satisfies my heart."

I stare down at my hands. To prevent them from trembling,

I squeeze the ends of my fingers. His words cause me to consider my own heart. How my will has tried to strengthen my armor, but I've underestimated that formidable foe in my chest. Still, I refuse to accept that the fickle organ will beat me. Reminding myself of my parents helps keep my feelings in check.

Luc's voice hums to a whisper before he pulls up a chair next to me, then places two fingers beneath my chin to turn my face to him. "Swan."

I don't shirk this time, but I do change the subject, "What you did in there…I knew I was more than just an investment to you."

He nods.

"But what you did to them…"

He pulls away, and I let go of my breath at the same time he utters, "You said you weren't afraid."

"I'm not."

He tilts his head to look at me. "Then, what?"

"Who were you before the Aviary? How did you even *do* that?" I refer to the graphickers.

He smirks. "Ahh…you're curious. Why should I share anything regarding my past when you refuse to oblige me? All I've seen of you is an obstinate girl who laughs at sharks underwater."

I know less about Luc's background than he does mine. But do I risk revealing more of myself? Do I risk letting him capture more of Serenity so he can twist her into the Swan he desires?

Every time I think of his arms around me, the prospect is less and less horrifying.

But can I trust him?

Luc closes the distance between us. His scent cradles the breath around my face. "You want to know who I am. I want to know who you are, and who you want to be. Perhaps we can compromise. We ask one question to each other every night. Nothing but the truth."

I think of Sky and his proposal. This could be the chance to get what Sky needs. Still, the risk of losing myself in this Aviary, of becoming like my mother, terrifies me. But if it means finding my parents…rescuing them…

I nod. "One question. But…" I raise a finger, brandishing

THE AVIARY

it like a conditional blade that impales him, "you must call me Serenity."

He frowns right before the corners of his mouth lift like the spreading of wings. "If you will call me Owl."

One word. "No."

He waits.

I shake my head, stare at him dead on, two birds of prey measuring each other, waiting for the other to blink. I'm almost dumbfounded when he relents, sighing.

"Very well, Serenity."

"Good. I'll ask first. Who were you before the Aviary?"

Luc doesn't hesitate. "I took an interest in the Aviary at a young age. My father came here often to recuperate from the drudgery of Family business, and I always joined him. I spent my youth wandering the glass hallways and sketching the girls in the exhibits, memorizing their shapes...their curves...their anatomy." Luc studies my reaction, but all I return is a blank stare.

"My father did not originally train me for a career as its director. First, I was a smuggler. Then I was a transporter, then recruiter. I excelled in weaponry and marksmanship. With those unique skills, my father found the best use for me as a contract killer." He pauses again, but I still don't react because for the first time, I understand the reason his skin seems to breathe frost into mine. I may not accept it yet, but I understand.

"Between assignments, I always returned to the Aviary. On one such assignment, I didn't follow the rule of never leaving a witness behind. All I could see when I pointed that barrel in her face was her potential. Her dark hair, creamy skin...it would've been such a waste. So, I brought her to the Aviary.

"At first, my father was displeased. Until he saw her exhibit and heard her sing."

I knot my hands together. "Nightingale?"

Luc nods. "She excelled. Counted my sparing her life as a mercy and dedicated herself to the Aviary. Her exhibit helped the Aviary to join the ranks of the elite museums in this country. Shortly after we made headlines, my father placed me in charge for a trial period. I used my artistic ability, appointed artisans like Dove to carry out my visions, and the Aviary soared all the more.

So, after the trial period ended, my father officially designated me Aviary director. I've carried the title for three years."

Luc is generous. He could've given me a one-sentence answer, but he didn't. Part of me is worried because what if he asks me the same question? By now, I'm fairly certain Luc can tell whether I'm lying, but do I dare risk telling him anything about my parents, why we've always moved, my mother's escape from the Temple?

"And now for my question." Luc folds his palms together, fingertips forming a steeple. After a few moments of silence, he speaks. "What do you want most, out of anything in the world?"

His question catches me off guard, but I'm too relieved to even think about filtering my words. "I want my family back, and I want to live where no one else can find us."

"Where no one else can find you? Are you running from something?"

I grab one of the pillows on the bed, place it in my lap, and crook one side of my mouth into a playful smile. "That's another question."

"Point well made. But would you at least elaborate? It seems only fair, in exchange for what I gave you." He opens one of his hands, inviting me, pleading with me. "Please, describe this place you dream about."

Luc coaxes me like a firefly landing on the edge of a petal, willing the night flower to open. "There are no mirrors. It doesn't matter what I look like there because everyone already thinks I'm beautiful—no matter what time of day it is or what I'm wearing. It's surrounded by water. I can't step outside my door without seeing and smelling water. I'm barefoot there, too, but instead of cold glass floors, I just feel damp mud between my toes." When I close my eyes, I'm almost able to feel the soil squishing. I imagine Sky there next to me, rooting out a stubborn weed from the ground. "We live off the land, just the way it should be. And we swim in the water during every sunset until we can't stop shivering. But there are warm hands to tuck me in every night."

"Do you know of such a place?"

I glance down to see Luc's fingers touching the pillow on my lap. His eyes linger on mine, waiting for my response, but I shake my head. "I don't even know if it exists."

The Aviary

"If you ever find it, I will come with you."

As soon as I lift my head, he is there to meet me. His attractive, unwavering mouth dives beyond the edges of mine. I find myself welcoming his lips, but his hands, a frantic grappling on my arms, are too much.

Arching back, I force his mouth against my chin and to my neck. I shiver when his lips connect with the skin there. Mustering up the breath to exhale, I close my eyes, retreat into the sheets. Luc mimics my movement but only halfway.

Stretching out his hand, he rubs a thumb across my lower lip, smiling. "I want you to sleep knowing I've kissed you. Goodnight, Serenity."

He turns off the lights and leaves the room, and I am suddenly aware of the sensation deep inside, past the core of my stomach, the one that drives the goose bumps to the surface of my skin and causes my teeth to chatter. Desire.

The Swan inside me fans itself in the wake of my first kiss. Her wings flutter as fast as a hummingbird's. I struggle to maintain my reality, bucking against the craving, trying to deny what I feel because it's the first hint of surrender. Stupid, fickle, formidable foe.

Luc is the first man to ever needle his way into my heart. But as I surrender to sleep, I can't help but wonder if he will rip me open and spill all my secrets while I'm still trying to learn his. I feel both longing and horror at the notion, and I don't know what to do with either.

Due to my impromptu capture, additional security is expedited. Luc becomes preoccupied with tutoring his brother and the new men. Knowing his background, it makes the most sense that he trains the new security.

For the next few weeks or so, every security member undergoes strict background checks and extra training, which means I don't see much of Sky. Or Luc. True to his word, he keeps his promise of one question per night.

Though neither of us offers up a long story like the first time, we take slow samples of each other's lives night by night. At first, he tried to gorge himself on details about my life before the Aviary. He pushed too hard, too fast, but he's learning to nibble now. Without naming names, I manage to relate to him memories from my past, days spent in hotel rooms, nights swimming in pools, skinny dipping in lakes outside country houses.

During the day, Mockingbird becomes my confidante. It's rare to find us apart, and we take our lunch hours together. Mockingbird's appetite is as hearty as mine, but she enjoys everything. Since she doesn't have a food printer in her room, she helps herself to mine whenever she's here.

As Mockingbird prints a soufflé, she tells me about the eerie screams of a girl from down the hall.

"Her name is Gull," Mockingbird explains. "She has pretty bad nightmares and sleepwalks every now and then. She's a lower Bird. Most of the time, one of the guards just escorts her back to her room, but she still stirs up things."

"Does anyone know why she has the nightmares?" I ask.

Mockingbird shakes her head, bringing the soufflé over to the table.

Other than Gull, I've lost track of all the Bird girls in the Aviary. At one point, I catch a glimpse of Stork, the official breeder for the museum. Since she's spent much of her time in the infirmary or transferred to the Centre, no one sees her that much. Too often, her babies don't live past infancy, or they are stillborn thanks to her time in the chemical-laden Glass Districts.

None of the other girls here are even fertile. Unfortunately, it's quite common nowadays.

"Can I have that?" Finch startles me with her question, motioning to the half of soufflé Mockingbird placed on a plate in front of me.

Ever since my stair-plunging action, I've had a Finch-sized shadow trailing me wherever I go. Though Mockingbird gets annoyed with the child's interruptions during our lunchtime, it's hard to dislike Finch.

"Go ahead," I say, feeling a hummingbird-wing-like flutter in my heart.

"Want to see a magic trick?" When Finch nods, Mockingbird leans down and waves her hand back and forth until a coin materializes in her fingers. "Take this to the amusement room. It's a digital one. Will give you unlimited access. My treat."

Finch kisses Mockingbird's cheek, squeezes me tight, and then scampers away with the soufflé.

During open hours, I'm restricted to my wing, the kitchens, the amusement rooms, and the aviary, of course. I can't enter any Exhibit rooms, which means I can't visit Blackbird, who keeps busy between her exhibit and clients. After my second showing, Luc took great pains to ensure I wasn't for public viewing. If it weren't for Mockingbird, I'd have little interaction with anyone— other than Luc and Sky, of course.

Mockingbird waves a hand after Finch. "She's cute, but it's hard to talk about certain things around her."

I wonder what sort of things she refers to.

She doesn't get the chance to answer right away since Dove opens the door to the main room holding an armful of fresh white dresses. Though she is one of the top artisans here and sees to other girls, I personally requested that she be the only staff member allowed in my room other than Sky, who's technically security. It's my way of keeping Dove close. Her familiarity is always welcome from her no-nonsense attitude with a motherly twinge behind it to her artist's tender fingers. She pauses upon seeing Mockingbird and me together, nods once to the other Bird, and then strides forward again.

"I brought you some fresh uniforms," she says, addressing me as she approaches the bedroom to our right.

"Thank you, Dove."

Mockingbird surprises me when she voices her question well within earshot of Dove. "You've been pretty docile over this past month. No outbursts or anything. Has anything happened to you lately?"

I taper my brows. "Like what?"

"Like…?" She opens a hand in indication.

"No!" I shriek in refusal. When Dove comes out from the bedroom again, I soften my voice. "No, nothing like that. It's just…"

"You trust him now, don't you? Don't feel bad about it. Owl is easy to trust that way."

"Mockingbird is right," Dove interjects while approaching our table. She sets a hand on the other girl's shoulder across from me.

"But I told you that the first day, didn't I?"

I nod in surrender, noticing how Dove's hand lingers longer than I thought it would.

"Mockingbird, are you happy here?" I ask once Dove has exited the room.

She nods. "It's my home. And he's good to me."

It's the second time she doesn't really answer the question. It confirms my suspicion that denial is her coping mechanism... along with all the other distractions here.

"What do you mean?"

"He takes care of me. I like that Owl doesn't fraternize with his Birds."

Obviously, he made an exception in my case.

"Has he ever punished you?"

She shakes her head. "No, I'm his little Mockingbird. Why would he? He's had to punish Peacock a few times for aggressive behavior. Blackbird's got one or two on her record. Not Nightingale. Not me. Why? What did he do to you?"

I bite my lower lip before explaining about the client rooms.

"That was a punishment?" Mockingbird asks. "I mean, sure, you lose a little sleep, but—"

"What's it like?" It's the first time I've asked such a question. It's the first time I've ever been curious enough. Luc hasn't kissed me since that first night, and I haven't breathed one word of it to Sky, but I find myself waiting, catch myself staring at Luc's mouth every now and then.

Mockingbird tilts her head, raising one brow. "Mmm," she grunts. "You have your good ones, your bad ones, your regulars, and your not-so-regulars. There are panic buttons on the sides of the beds in case any of the clients get too…excited."

I don't want to think of how often the panic buttons are pushed…or not pushed when they should be. "How many regulars?"

"Not as many as the not-so-regulars. But the regulars pay well, especially for all-nighters, but those happen in the intimate rooms, which are *way* bigger than the normal client rooms. Men don't tend to stick around much, though. This is their world. I'm super sore by morning. Bliss takes the edge off whenever I get a town visit. It is what it is."

"What if it could be something more?" What would Mockingbird do if she could leave this place? Live somewhere safe? My parents certainly found another way. I consider my daydream. A fool's daydream, really. *One Luc could never fit into,* I try to tell myself.

"Sometimes, I just wait for us to implode, you know?" Mockingbird pauses, gesturing an explosion with her hands so I can almost envision smoke riding off her finger. She turns back to me. "There are no limits in this world now. We've come so far. So, what else is left? What comes next?"

"I don't know."

Truth: I don't want to find out.

Before Mockingbird can say anything else, an announcement issues from the Aviary speaker: *All girls not entertaining clients must immediately return to their rooms. The museum is in quarantine until dinner.*

A steady staccato blare sounds next, and Mockingbird exclaims above it, "We've gotta go!"

I am close on her heels when she gets up, tugging on her dress. "What's going on?" I ask at the same time the lights start to dim and flash.

"The only time they call a quarantine is when something happens to one of the girls."

"Like what?" I say once we are inside the elevator.

"Another coma, maybe?" Mockingbird says solemnly. She opens the door to the hallway. "I don't know. I need to get back to my room. I'll see you at dinner."

Sky waits just outside, ready to guard the entrance for me, and I try to ask him what's going on. For the first time since our interlude at Lust and Cocoa, he speaks to me, and I have a feeling it's only because of the blaring alarm in the background.

Leaning over, he says in a voice just below the alarm, "Another coma." Not once does he reach for me though every cord in my body flexes to touch him, to feel his warm, familiar brand of comfort. "I need to speak with you. Get to the waterfall tonight without Luc. We need to talk."

Somehow, I have a feeling that will be much more difficult

due to the new quarantine, but I hope I can convince Luc, particularly since I've behaved myself lately.

I can't help but wonder at the urgency of Sky's message. Does he have news about my parents?

THAT NIGHT, I LET FINCH steal even more off my plate than she normally does. I'm so anxious about what Sky has to tell me, all I can do is pick at my dinner.

Luc doesn't notice because everyone is picking at their food tonight. Flamingo's chair is empty. I barely know her, but the absence of her pink rose hair and salmon flesh eyes looms large in the room. Other than Mockingbird, she's been the most neutral of the girls, the one everyone recognized as a part of this place with no threat. Like Blackbird once was, she is now lost somewhere between her mind and the infirmary, pink hair nestled on white pillows. Cotton candy on cream puff clouds.

Blackbird is the first to gash a hole in the melancholia of the evening. "Nightingale, perhaps you could indulge us with that song you told me about earlier? The one you wrote for Flamingo?"

Luc regards Nightingale. "You could certainly ease the others' discomfort, my dear."

Not one to disagree with Luc, Nightingale rises, her beauteous body lithe like a jungle cat. Her hair is shinier tonight. Like onyx. As she wanders around the table, her notes lilt around the heads of all the girls. To me, every movement is painstaking because I know she will end her serenade behind my chair.

Scarce and rare
Your unimaginable hair
Perched in pink to make us stare
Without a care
Your plumaged eyes bared
Of fleshy wings so fair
And arms that dared
Crane beyond the client lair
To birds ensnared
You gave us air

The Aviary

On the last stanza, my prediction comes true. Nightingale's voice bleeds to a somber high note just behind my neck.

I don't turn around to see, but I feel every sweet, snapping note probe into my skin. Other than Peacock's, mine is the only chair she doesn't touch. As if I don't warrant the right to hear the song because of how little I know Flamingo.

After the meal, I approach Blackbird to ask her a few questions, but it is she who takes the lead.

"Walk with me," she says, directing me to follow her. "I don't have long before my exhibit opens for the evening. My artists are waiting in my room."

"She's so spiteful," I say, glancing back at Nightingale. "Why did you ask her to sing?"

I follow Blackbird up the stairs to her room.

Her hand glides across the glass banister. "We might be competition, but I can still appreciate her talent. I know what death is like. I know it can tug at you. If Nightingale's song helps with that, why not? And we're called Birds, not girls," she reminds me. Because they all become what they need to be. "Nightingale is the favorite among the Birds. You might want to be careful with your questions."

"Why do you think I came to *you*?" Mockingbird might've twittered.

Blackbird smiles back at me and opens the door to her room, which is on my floor but at the opposite end of the hall. Just as she said, her artists are waiting.

"You can stay," Blackbird informs me. "I'm not shy. It's one reason I don't mind using the artists. Not that creepy body printer."

Even so, I turn around when they strip her of the simplistic black dress. Every so often, I glance back to see what they're doing, though I keep my eyes above her chest. At present, they are smearing her skin in gold glitter.

"Which girl, er...*Bird* is the most hated?" I ask.

"Other than you?" Blackbird chuckles when one of the artists return with black fishnet thigh-highs, which they roll over her legs. She muses for a moment before replying, "Probably Raven or Peacock. But trust me, you only have Peacock to worry about."

"Why?" I ask.

The artists retrieve a few strips of braided black ropes, then begin to loop it around Blackbird's chest and bikini area.

"You'll find out why eventually."

Taking clumps of the tiny braids in her hair, the artists begin to un-braid them one by one. Arching her neck back, she gives them access. She looks comfortable, relaxed, even though she wears nothing but the stockings and rope. With so little on, I know I could never be so at ease in the company of others.

Blackbird holds out a few braided strands, offering them to me. "You want to? Go ahead. I don't mind."

"Really?" Eagerly approaching her, I begin undoing the braids. Whether she's doing this because she thinks I woke her up from her coma or some other reason, I don't know. Maybe this is normal behavior for girls in the Aviary.

"Don't forget," Blackbird reminds one of the artisans, "my oysters better be on my kitchen table when I get back."

Her room is similar to mine, not quite as large. The only other difference is the lack of a fish tank. My hands are definitely not as skilled as the artisans, but I admit how much I enjoy the task. At the end of it, with all the braids undone, it becomes a black mass of crushed waves—a crimped eclipse on her back. Above her eyes, the same gold shimmer dusts her lids.

"How do I look?" she asks.

One of the artisans begins to speak, but Blackbird snaps, "I'm asking the Swan!" She turns to me with a smile.

"I love your hair," I comment—a poor attempt at neutrality.

Blackbird sniffs it from a mile away, and she orders the artisans to leave. "That doesn't answer my question. I want to know what *you* think."

I wince a little. "What do you want me to say?"

"This is what we are. You have to get that through your thick skull. I do it because I have to. No other reason." Blackbird plays with one of the strings of rope on her chest.

"I was taught that everyone makes their own decisions."

"Would you like to know what my mother's decision was? She's gorgeous. And she spent most of her life in the Glass Districts. She was born into them, drowning in debt since birth. But she never wanted that life for me, so she worked hard, taking more clients because she wanted to find a better place for me. And she did. This place. And I've never looked back. This is my choice. I live with it."

"I *didn't* have a choice," I snap, a storm budding inside my mouth.

"A lot of girls don't, especially pretty ones. But you have one now." She tugs at one of her thigh-highs. "There's nowhere you can go now without someone wanting you. You wouldn't last one day outside."

"Well, I know this much—I'll *never* let anyone turn me into some sort of doll." I want to take back the words as soon as I say them, but it's too late.

Her eyes swell, black irises like charging stallions. "Glad to know what you think of me. Now get—"

"Blackbird, I—"

"*Out!*"

LUC OFFERS TO JOIN ME in the aviary, but I tell him I want some time alone. He agrees, provided my personal security joins me, which is just fine. Luc is still in the process of determining the source of the comas, scouring video feeds, which keeps him distracted.

Sky and I go to the spot where he handed my mother's journal to me a month ago. The waterfall is the only break in security. This is where we taste a sample of freedom together. We can just be Sky and Ser. Not Vulture and Swan.

"Your last exhibit was impressive," Sky says first, though I can hear the disdain in his voice.

"It feels like so long ago," I say, reflecting on the month that has passed.

"He's an artist. Takes his time. Obsessive just like he is with everything else. And it gives his father more time to invite international clients to the auction." His words are soaked in loathing.

"This is your idea," I remind him. "You told me to play along, to be the Swan, and get close to him so we increase our chances of finding Mom and Dad. That's what I'm doing."

"Yeah, I've noticed."

Narrowing my brows, I straighten. "What's that supposed to mean?"

Sky ignores my question and changes the subject, bracing a hand against the rock wall. "Luc's father, er, Malcolm—he's been in contact with Director Force, especially after the Swan's performance the night he visited. He wants to capitalize on Force's interest in your next exhibit by driving Force's curiosity to the breaking point."

"Why is it so important for Force to want me?"

Sky's mouth creases tight, and his bulging muscles tighten before he packs one hand into a fist. "Leverage. The Guild wants power, position. If you become as big as I suspect, they'll use you and your parents and blackmail the Syndicate into getting what they want."

"So, I'm just a bargaining chip. Wonderful." I lean against the iron fence, across from Sky.

Defensive, Sky braces his hands against the rock wall behind him, nostrils flaring. "You think this is easy for me, Serenity? Watching them eat you up whenever your exhibit is open? Parading you around like some sick spectacle? Seeing the way *he* looks at you? Seeing the way you've begun looking at *him*?"

I lift a finger in warning. "I didn't ask for any of this, Skylar Lace. If I had my way, we'd have run by now."

"Could have fooled me."

My back digs into the iron behind me, the falls misting my bare shoulders as my blood reaches its boiling point. "Stop pretending this is my fault!"

"It *is* your fault!" Sky raises his voice, but keeps it below the sound of the waterfall. "You're just too damn...beautiful."

"How about we mangle it up then?" I reach for the knife at his belt, but Sky is always quicker than me, and his hand comes down on mine.

"It wouldn't even matter if you did. You know they can fix anything." He releases my hand, then turns around.

"That's not true." I soften my voice, and he twists his head back just enough to hear me. "They can't fix you and me."

His shoulders slump, but he says nothing.

"Why do you keep pulling away from me? You've been doing

it for years. The older we get, the farther I feel from you." Why doesn't he just admit it? Or is it something else than what I suspect?

"It's complicated."

"So, I'm just your pawn now. Is that it?"

Sky turns around and rolls his eyes, his eyes darkened to brown muslin. "You don't know what you're talking about, as usual. You're just overdramatizing."

"Least I haven't changed."

I'm about to walk away when Sky grabs me by the arm and pushes me back toward the rock wall in the shadows, despite my struggling protest. "I wasn't finished," he says.

"Spit it out, then!" I sigh, aggravated.

"Being Vulture isn't a role I play easily. All these *girls*—I'm not used to this."

That's what this is about? All the other girls? I squirm a little under his gaze. "Do you think I can really help you with any of this?"

"After their shifts, the other guards all check out different exhibits. Something looks off if you don't because we get discounted services." He searches my face. "I just—I'm not—"

I struggle now. "Sky, I've got my own problems to worry about."

"Yes," he seethes, digging his fingers into the hilt of his knife. "I've seen your biggest one."

"It's not like that. And even if it was, he's different than the others. He's not going to give me to some client."

Sky grimaces, fingers grating into the rock. "No, I imagine he's got his own plans for you."

Too uncomfortable, I divert the subject back to him. "So, have you? Taken advantage of your discount, I mean. Which Bird…you know…catches your attention?"

A lurking smile crooks Sky's features—that conspiratorial grin he always gets when he toys with me.

"Do whatever you want!" More exasperated than before, I push him and practically bark, "It's not like you need my permission. I don't care."

Sky lowers his head toward me, but it's still a good few inches above mine. "I care."

His eyes melt into liquid gold. It's the same face he uses when I'm in a foul mood, and he's trying to get me to laugh. The closer he gets, the more emotions stir within me. When I think about him with another Bird, my chest tightens and I can feel a flush invade my usual pallor.

I move my head to the side, away from his.

"Do you know anything about the comas?" I ask, choosing business, a subject that feels far safer than the last.

He shakes his head. "Still investigating. It's becoming easier—Luc gives me a higher clearance level every day. Especially after the graphickers. If I'd been on duty, it wouldn't have happened. And I fixed the system so no one will ever be able to hack in again." Sky has always been good with technology. He's dedicated many years to understanding its marvels. "What happened that night? You never told me, and I never wanted to bring it up."

Almost unsure whether I should say, I bite my lower lip. "Do you know anything about Luc's background? Who he was before the Aviary?"

Sky shakes his head, a dark shadow passing through his eyes at the mention of Luc's name. "He's a ghost in the records; I've always assumed it was that way for a reason. What do you know?"

"He killed the graphickers to get me out. He told me to close my eyes, but I opened them. I…saw." My stomach roils at the memory. "Luc told me he was a contract hit man before he became the Aviary director."

Sky tenses, anger brooding in his eyes. "And when were you going to tell me this?"

"I—"

He slaps the rocks just above my head. "I don't give a damn if he saved you that night! I don't give a damn how kind he's been to you. You need to trust *me* first. You can't hide something like that from me. Hell, I don't know what's going on with you anymore! He comes to your room almost every night. Stays for half an hour or so and then leaves."

Sighing, I relate our question-and-answer bargain and how I've learned more about him and the Guild Family.

He raises an eyebrow. "Not bad, actually. The Sanctuary should've recruited you a long time ago." Leaning forward again, he cups the side of my head. "I should get you back."

Uplifted by his compliment, I'm ready to return to the Aviary, enthusiastic at the thought of finding out more about Luc.

I realize I'll have to change once I return to my room. The back of my dress is too damp from the mist, and water droplets ornament my hair.

"There's just one more thing," Sky says. Before I can step out of the way, he thrusts my back against the damp stone wall. He encloses my cheek with one palm while he runs his other hand through my hair, holding the back of my head. Then, he presses his lips to mine, taking my mouth hostage.

My eyes open as far as they can go. My mind reels.

Unlike with Luc, I don't bend before Sky, because Sky is too strong, too fast, knows just how to keep me still.

He crushes his mouth and body to mine, tugs at my lower lip, tasting me fierce and strong.

For a minute, I just let him. I feel the warmth in my mouth, my throat, my chest. Nothing like Luc's ice. Sky crams his heat into me, fuels my body with it, and my lightning knows exactly how to handle him. It welcomes him.

And then, I taste him back.

Like thunder, he rocks me, fueling my lightning, supporting me. His earthy scent, like soil damp from leftover rain, consumes me. The links between us strengthen. Not just merely connected, now they shackle us together. In this kiss are all the unvoiced explanations for the distance he forced between us over the past few years: why he stopped swimming with me, why he looks burned every time I touch him. All these years, but he's never acted, not once. Until now. Sky's resolve, his willpower, grinds mine into dust. And his kiss suffocates even the memory of the one I shared with Luc.

Finally, he puts space between him and my breathless mouth. He grins, dipping his head to the side to say, "You're my biggest problem, Serenity."

Eighteen
SkY'sAdmiSsIon

Throughout my childhood, there were stretches of time when Mom, Dad, Sky, and I would live in the old mansion. Even with the old water pipes that sounded like a miniature dwarf army was trapped inside them, hacking away at their pickaxes, it was far preferable than the real world because Dad had just showed me the Glass District.

"Let's go swimming," I'd suggested to Sky shortly after my District visit.

"No."

"Why not?"

"I don't want to."

"Come on. It's getting dark soon. Perfect time to swim." I'd tried to persuade him and grabbed one of his pillows, chucking it at him.

I remember he grimaced. After straightening out the pillow, he placed it back on the bed. His words were just as rehearsed as his movements.

"I said no. I don't want to swim with you anymore, Serenity. Go by yourself."

"Fine! Be an ass if you want," I'd shouted. "I'll go by myself!"

I giggle just a little, remembering how I'd slammed the door too soon and caught my long curls in the wood. Sky's chortle behind the door had been muffled. He was grinning when I opened it to free my imprisoned hair. I slammed it even louder the second time.

The Aviary

But after I'd waded into the lake water and pumped my body under its surface, rising only when I'd run out of breath, I looked back toward the house, and there was Sky standing on the shore fully dressed, arms folded, gaze steadfast on me...

Now, he pulls away, leaving me dumbfounded and panting for him. Despite my silent protests, finger jerking back to the waterfall, trying to get him to come back, Sky is unbending.

I have no choice but to follow him back to the Aviary. He knows full well I can't ask him anything once we step away from the waterfall hiding spot. Knows he's ripped through the pixie gossamer webs of my mind. He's slipped right past my armor and slammed his way into my heart. More than Luc ever could.

Guilt is close at hand. How can I feel like this, think about these things, when my parents are still in prison?

I don't want to go back to the Aviary. I want to return to the old mansion overlooking the lake.

My heart is burning as I walk through the glass doors. Right now, I'm a beast ready to bite. A bird ready to peck at whoever is foolish enough to open her cage.

I follow Sky, too lost in my thoughts to notice the feather-clad girls until they're in front of me. First, I hear them. Her moan, his growl.

The man's hands creep around the familiar Bird's waist, primed below her hips, while her lily-petal fingers stroke his chest. His mouth forages hers, but her hands are greedy, nails ready to impale him.

Until our presence catches his attention, and his hesitation alerts hers.

Nightingale pauses from kissing Larke—her mouth all blotted and swollen from his, red as a bleeding Cardinal. Her eyes whirl a little before they target me.

Staying close to the glass wall at the end of the empty hallway near my secret entrance, I keep my eyes as vacant as that hallway, but Nightingale's are as deep and black as snow drowning in ink.

She raises a delicate finger in warning. "Breathe a word of this to your precious Owl, and I will slit..." She pantomimes a slicing motion across my neck with one pointed fingernail, and I raise my chin. "...your pretty white throat."

Larke towers behind Nightingale as she speaks, but where Luc can command with one downward knit of his brows, all Larke's power comes from his body, packed tight and corded with muscle like some war drum.

Nightingale shoves her hand against my throat, pushing deep into the hollow. Sky steps forward, but I halt him with one pointed look.

I'm ready to claw straight through her black dress and stain it with her blood. Ready to split her wings, shred those black feathers, and leave them to rot in a scarlet stain. Maybe Sky knows this. Maybe he knows Alice holds the sword today. And I'm ready to chop the Queen of Hearts' head clean off. He lets me take the battlefield.

"*Enough*, Nightingale!"

I recognize the voice behind me, twisting my head to find Blackbird standing there and Raven marching down the hall toward us. I hadn't expected others to join me on the field.

I've only seen Raven at the dinner table, but every time I see her, I can't help but feel intimidated. She isn't just intoxicating; she is arresting. Prestige defines her as she sweeps toward Nightingale. Her faultless, endless legs far surpass mine, as do her long, lithe torso, ample bust, and aquiline neck. Her height alone—at least a head taller than Nightingale and two heads taller than me—intimidates, though it's clear Blackbird is the mouthpiece. Raven's wild tiger eyes attack Nightingale, but she says nothing.

"Watch your back, Nightingale," warns Blackbird just as Raven's brutal eyes spear Nightingale, who releases my throat.

Nightingale is graceful, but Raven is a vicious breed of beauty. No delicacy in her features. Thanks to her hair strained so tight against her skull, her rage is even more defined. Her ponytail flicks back and forth when she hisses at Nightingale.

"Watch yourself," Nightingale seethes, but everyone knows the comment is directed at me.

Blackbird approaches me once Nightingale and Larke leave. "Thinks she owns this place," she says, practically spitting.

Sky lingers nearby, still intent on my reaction.

"Why did you—" I begin to ask Blackbird, but I should've known she would cut me off.

The Aviary

"Why would we what? Look out for each other?" Blackbird says. "Because that's what we do here."

"Even after I...?"

At first, Blackbird seems confused. Then, she waves me off. "Oh, that! I don't hold grudges for long. Ask Raven."

Raven merely nods.

"Besides." Blackbird crosses her arms over her chest. "You've done the same for us."

Confused, I glance at Raven, unsure of what it is I was supposed to have done for her. She grabs me by the wrist, nest-brown hand swallowing mine.

She announces, "Your bruises might be gone, but the memory's not."

Blackbird explains, "Finch is her sister. I told you, nothing to worry about from Raven."

That's when I realize Blackbird is still wearing her exhibit ropes. She must have just come from there.

"My exhibit is tomorrow," Raven announces. "I need sleep."

Blackbird nods. "And I'm late for my client."

I stop her for a moment, understanding the sacrifice she made on my behalf. "Thank you."

After Blackbird has gone, I'm about to open the door to my bedroom when I recognize the figure at the end of the hall disappearing around the corner to the staircase. I'd think nothing of it, but when the second figure dances around the same corner just after him, I grow suspicious.

"Where do you think you're going?" Sky blocks my way. "Go back to your room."

I don't try to explain; I simply duck around him.

Sky knows if he were to touch me at all, if he so much as reaches a hand to my arm, the Aviary will see. So, I'm free to follow the figures down the stairs, out of the Aviary, and back into the gardens. Thanks to my good behavior, I've been granted access to the grounds.

I keep my distance, ducking behind glass flower sculptures, and observe as Luc enters his personal shrine, his solace house: the wood house on top of the still lake. Sunset has deepened the sky to a fresco of gold and crimson tongues, and the floating lanterns surrounding the house cast a lustful glow.

Luc weaves around the side of the building where the bathhouse is. The second figure follows suit.

"Serenity," Sky whispers.

"Not now." I shake my head and press my lips tight, willing myself to watch because in my heart, I know what happens under the cover of night.

Steam froths into the air when Luc slides the two panels on the side of the small house apart, and he slowly removes his shirt. It's the first time I've ever seen a man's chest other than Sky's. Unlike Sky, Luc is not tan. And though he's not as muscle-bound as Sky, he's well defined, his back braided with sinew. He rolls his broad shoulders back and forth and stretches his neck to the right and then left before stepping inside and discarding his shirt on the floor. Then, his hands travel to his pants and he unbuttons the top button.

I turn away, focusing instead on the second figure, who appears just outside the room. Her sweet legs, blonde hair falling in bubbles of curls to her chest, and transparent gray shift leave little doubt as to why she's here.

Mockingbird. She tiptoes inside, just behind Luc.

When she removes her dress, I wince and turn away.

Under Sky's watchful gaze, I retreat to my room. By the way his eyes follow my every footstep, I know he wants to speak to me, but the Aviary is an unbearable labyrinth of barriers between us. It doesn't seem significant when I add one more by slamming the door in his face.

I don't want to be lost in my thoughts. More than anything, I want to curl up inside Sky's arms, but I don't feel as though I'd fit there the way I used to, despite feeling more drawn to him than ever. I don't know what to do with this new Sky.

Instead, I read from my mother's journal. In no particular order, I flip pages, reading from the back.

Sometimes, I worry about Skylar. He has the Family in him, too—almost as much as Serenity. He deals with his anger better than she does, and that's why he's good for her. She has a childlike fire. Sky's fire is earthy, grounded, able to damage but can also be put to good use. It's why they've always worked well together. Lately, I see him trying too hard. Their dynamic isn't easy for him anymore, and I think I know why. I should've been prepared for this. I should've known this life wouldn't be easy for them, bundled up together all the time. Serenity's such a child. Oblivious to what I see. Too caught up in her own imagination and curiosity.

I realize my anger was a cheap shot at Sky. He doesn't deserve it, not when he's spent years respecting my mother's wishes. Could she have believed that things would always stay the same? That Sky and I would grow up and nothing would change between us? All she did was build a dam. That kiss broke whatever was left. And now, Sky is inside my head, his thunder competing against Luc's ice.

Sensing another presence in my room, I flinch when I see the figure leaning against the wall with his massive arms crossed over his chest. He dips his head to observe me.

"How did you get in here?" I rise from the bed, but it's too late. Luc's brother takes me by the shoulders, forcing me into the closet where the netting of white dresses waits to swallow me whole.

"You are going to keep your flapdoodle trap shut." Larke presses his head to mine so I can feel his hot breath on my face. "We're going to take a nice, casual stroll to your exhibit." He trails a large finger down my throat. My breath escapes in wicked pants. I'm prepared to scream until his firm hand clamps over my mouth.

Larke's hand voyages down to my waist and lower still. Panting, I feel salt tears gushing from my eyes, but they don't stem my rage. It bubbles up into my mouth, and I bite his hand. It only startles him.

Larke wags a finger in front of my face, "Naughty birdie. You spied on me earlier. Too curious for your own good. So, you're going to swim for me, little Swan. Understand?"

He pins me against the back wall, then jerks the strap of my dress down my shoulder to press a thumb to my tattoo.

A snarl hacks through my anger and fear. "Understand this—I will sever your brain stem if I *ever* catch you touching Swan again. Blood or no blood."

Rejoicing over the voice, I look over Larke's shoulder to where Luc is brandishing a knife. Relieved by his presence.

"Release her," Luc orders.

Larke grumbles but does as he is told.

"Get out. I'll deal with you later," Luc says, dragging his brother out of the closet.

Tremors shudder through my body. An earthquake seizes my heart, ready to collapse my lungs, rupture my rib cage.

"Swan." Softening his voice, he slips the strap of my dress back up my shoulder.

"Don't touch me," I say, retreating into the clothes behind me. My nerves are still shot, and the touch of another man—even Luc—comes too soon for comfort. "I'm Serenity! Not your Swan."

Surprised by my behavior, Luc steps forward until Dove sashays past him. Her presence brings the end of the earthquake inside my body, so I don't crumple in on myself. But I still can't breathe and I leap into her arms, imagining fresh oxygen is right there.

I sob into her shoulder. Dove settles a hand against my hair and turns to Luc, saying, "Let me be alone with her now."

"Alert me if she needs a sedative."

"What she needs is space and a hot bath. Go."

Dove helps me to the bathroom, setting me down on the tiles while she fills the immense tub with steam and hot water. By now, my cries have weakened to a whimper or two, and the cold of the tiles are a stab of reality again. It seems ridiculous. So foolish to be this upset over one assault when thousands of girls are raped in the Glass Districts every minute.

Dove removes my white dress, and I sink into the water. It's surprising how much it abates all my nerves. Dove soothes my skin when she soaps my back and massages the skin there.

"Men like Larke are common, Swan. I have to admit I'm impressed by your defense. You drew blood with your bite. An exceptional attempt, but an attempt all the same. I hope you remember that Director Aldaine is here to protect you, to guard you."

"How many clients did you have?" I ask, diverting the subject from Luc.

She scrubs my hair. "None at first. I was put on trial with private exhibits for the eyes of the director at the time to see if I could be Swan worthy, but no one can *become* the Swan. One is *born* the

Swan." Dove tips my head forward so she can reach the ends of my hair. "All your life, she's been there just waiting for someone to unleash her. Someone like Director Aldaine," she finishes, and she drops all my wild silver curls back into the water.

"And how many others has he *unleashed*?"

Dove blinks. "Owl doesn't fraternize with the Birds here. He treats his Aviary with respect, as well as the Birds inside it."

I want to believe her, but I know what I saw.

Once the bath is finished, I venture into the cotton robe Dove provides. My blood has stopped boiling. It simmers now, settled enough for Luc to return.

With wary hands folded behind his back and eyes judging me, Luc approaches my bedside before asking, "May I sit down?"

"There." I point to the end of the bed, far from where I sit at the head.

If he's disappointed, he doesn't show it—*unlike Sky*, I can't help but think, who always expresses his frustration with me. "Swan, you must allow me to apologize for the breach in security. I had called a meeting for all my staff and security, and Larke exited early. I had my suspicions regarding his motives. If I had not come when I did, I can't imagine—"

"Nothing happened," I almost hiss. "Please don't make me relive what could have been."

"Very well."

I turn to look at the indigo brine inside his eyes. They remind me of the water in my exhibit. No choice but to let it devour me, but beneath the surface, deep in its watery arms—complete escape. Shards of him are in me now. Him and the Aviary. That's undeniable. Like Sky said before: even if I leave this place, I'll take the Aviary with me. It's part of me. I just have to hope I can get out before I become part of it.

"I thought we'd come farther than this silence between us." Luc waits for me to say something. Too patient. Though always rational and logical, Sky doesn't have much patience for my antics or silent treatment.

After a few minutes, my restraint crumbles. Under Luc's eyes, I'm pinned like a butterfly. So, I tell him the truth. "I followed you."

"When?"

"To the bathhouse."

"You weren't the only one." He doesn't bother denying it. "Mockingbird attaches herself to certain people. She has latched on to me—perhaps because I rescued her as a babe. But I have found many Birds, and I have rescued many. Mockingbird simply has a proud, if not deluded, sense of entitlement because she was the first."

He pauses, sighs, and drags a hand down his face. "When clinical inspections are performed, I monitor them. I inspect each Bird to ensure their weight, appearance, and aging falls into the correct parameters." He trails on, using his fancy language, but I know what he means. He checks them to make sure they still look beautiful enough. "Mockingbird's inspection time was due, but she chose an unprofessional environment to approach me," he explains.

"You are the only one who has saved me," he admits, moving closer. "But every time you look at me, I feel like some worm wriggling on a hook. At times, I even consider releasing you. But…" He slows, his chilled fingers curving over my cheeks like hoarfrost. "That would mean letting you go."

Our second kiss is different from the first.

His mouth is more like fog as it seeks mine, light, entering to taste my secrets. When I kiss him back, I don't give him all of myself. Instead, I taste him on the surface. I take in all his scent from the cologne that hints of fresh water and an early winter dawn. Not one trace of warmth to speak of—no heated spices, no woodiness, no hearty musk. Luc is all pressed linens and cotton tufts. He's like a snowdrift seeking somewhere to settle, and for the first time, I want him to settle here, with me. I wonder—

No, I remember Breakables. I remember my parents. I remember Sky.

He pulls back and pauses. "I will go to extreme lengths to protect you, Swan. Especially given what has recently transpired. I must tell you that Flamingo has passed away. She went quickly, peacefully, from her coma. I'm still rooting out the source."

I push myself against the bed frame, then draw my knees into my chest. I don't know what to say. His eyes have lost any trace of

THE AVIARY

intensity. In fact, they seem hollow.

"I'm...sorry, Luc."

He sighs as if annoyed by my continued refusal to call him "Owl," but he doesn't correct me this time. "Tomorrow is the day of physicals," he informs me. "I hold them each month for my Birds. It's important to my father that Guild-owned Birds are healthy, too."

"And do I still belong to the Guild? Or could the Temple take me from here at the auction?" I almost say, 'Take me from you.'

Luc peers at the sheets, then back to me. "Is that tonight's question?"

"No. That question doesn't have anything to do with you. I have a right to know what will become of me."

"You're right. And I don't wish to lie to you. The Temple has a chance in the upcoming auction, but I'm doing everything in my power to see that you stay here."

"So, an international client could...?" I wince at the same time a snarl erupts from Luc's throat. I still can't help but interrupt, "It's not up to you, though, is it? It's up to your father."

He doesn't bother to deny it, but he doesn't confirm it either. "The Temple has a better chance than any client. They are the ultimate museum, and we could never hope to surpass them. My father wants the best deal, of course. But deliberations could last weeks, perhaps months. A blood feud would not be in the interest of either Family. They will take their time to avoid it."

I don't speak, just trace the fringes of the cotton on my knees. "If you can't let me go now, how could you let me go to them?"

"Ahhh." I hear the knowing sigh in Luc's voice. "How far will I go to keep you? Is the life of one girl worth the sacrifice of all the others? What are my boundaries?"

I wring the sheets at my legs. "I have my own boundaries."

Luc feathers his fingers across the backs of my knuckles, saying gently, "Yes, I've watched your boundaries, and I've seen them fall twice now." I know he refers to the two kisses.

Even if my spirit hangs loose off my body, I've always worn my innocence like a glove. An armored glove. All my life, I've daydreamed of a world where women command respect from men. Where men don't take advantage of the war raging with hormones as our feelings betray us. Luc knows just how to loosen my glove. Like many men in his *profession*, he takes advantage, knows every way to manipulate. Is it just a trick of the mind when he leaves the choice in my hands? It's getting harder to hold on.

My body is betraying me, forming a gap between it and my willpower. The Aviary doesn't help. This place brings out the best and worst of me: the emotional extremes. My mother was Temple-born, so I can't fault her for how simple it was to become the Unicorn. But I should be better at keeping one foot on solid ground. I shouldn't fall for Luc's grooming methods.

"What else do you want to ask before I leave?" Luc offers, easing closer.

I don't hesitate. "Have you ever slept with a Bird?"

Luc isn't offended by my question, but he does hesitate before answering, eyes narrowing. "Yes. Before my time as director, I slept with a Bird. I was a repeat client between my assignments. And I used to interact on a more…personal level with my Birds. But not since you."

"Who was she?"

"Now, that is another question. Perhaps you should save it."

"Is she still here?"

"Swan." Luc pinches his brows together. "It's *my* turn," he reminds me. "Considering your question, I believe I'm entitled to a personal one. What do you believe about love and sex?"

I inhale and plant my hands on either side of me, grounding myself. "I've seen love in my parents' eyes. That's the kind of love I want for myself. Love has always been deep to them."

"And sex?"

"I can't imagine having one without the other. After all, no one can have sex without forming some sort of bond. It's more than just physical. It's chemical. Feelings, emotions…they get all twisted up together like ropes. Even if you never see that person again, you still carry their ghost everywhere."

"People must carry many ghosts with them."

I nod, pondering the Breakables in the Glass District. How they must carry the ghost of every man who has stepped beyond their windows. How those men carry each girl inside them—taking pieces of their hearts—whether they realize it or not.

The Aviary

I steel myself. "I've never wanted anyone under my skin. I don't want to be anyone's ghost. I never have."

Forget ghosts. I have demons to reckon with. Sky's worked hard to fight those demons with me over the years. If there is one man on earth worthy of breaking my promise, it would be Sky. And I can imagine he's the only man who'd make sure I broke it at the right time. He won't let me throw it all away on an emotional whim. Especially not when our family is in jeopardy. Neither of us will rest until we are all safe out of the clutches of the Aviary and Temple.

He shakes his head and leans toward me, forehead against mine. "No, Swan, you chase all ghosts away."

With Luc's mouth fast approaching, tempting more, I can't help but consider the questions constantly running through my mind.

Could I ask you about them right now?
Do you know where they are?
Would you tell me if you did know?

"Luc," I say, just before his lips brush mine. "I want another question. Please."

He straightens and relents. "I believe I owe you, for Larke earlier."

"What's the worst thing you've ever done?"

Sighing, he rubs a hand down his face. "Okay, I'll answer that. Provided you go first."

I rack my brain, sifting through options, finally settling on one. "Swimming in the hotel pool during daylight hours when I knew I shouldn't. I didn't know smugglers were there that day, but I knew better than to go alone."

"I would have enjoyed seeing you fight that day."

"Answer mine," I pressure him.

"My addiction," he says. "It was the worst thing I've ever done without question."

I can feel the surprise on my face, even as I try to hide it.

"You seem surprised."

"It's hard not to remember what you used to do for a living."

"True, my hands have blood on them. I have the blood of an entire Family branch on my name. It's true I've created orphans, too, but I've also rescued others in the process. Have you heard of the Axis?"

I remember the title from newspaper headlines, the pattern of bizarre deaths that emerged within one month. "That was you?"

He nods once. "They were Guild competition. They were constructing a museum that would feature children only. Plucking girls as young as four from orphanages and the occasional district. They were already gaining momentum by marketing them in graphicker studios. For my father, it was a shrewd business move to wipe them out. For me, it was personal."

"That's horrific," I whisper, placing one hand on his chest.

He covers it with his own. "I don't regret one life I've taken in my time. My greatest regret is relinquishing control of my own body to drugs. I've never let anything control me since those days. Until now." He kisses my hand. "Goodnight, Serenity. Vulture will be stationed just outside your bedroom door should you require anything. After what happened, I am taking precautions. Unless I am with you, he will not leave your side except for a few hours of rest while you are still sleeping." He departs without another word.

A few hours of rest doesn't seem like enough, but Sky is resilient. A part of me wonders if he's getting injected with enhancers. With all the medical advances in the last hundred years, the possibilities are endless. Museum guards operate on a training level more advanced than Olympic gold medalists.

"Ser," I hear after the lights turn off.

"Sky?" I bolt up in bed only to find his warm body standing just beside the bed. "What—"

"We don't have long," he says in the darkness, and I smell his warm breath that reminds me of roasted vegetable stew before he wraps one arm around my shoulder and urges me close to his chest just like he used to when we were younger. "I've bought us a little time. Don't ask."

The first thing I do is punch his chest. Feeble attempt, but he takes it all the same.

"I can't believe you would kiss me like that and then leave me with no opportunity to speak," I cry, feeling hot tears soaking into the fabric at his shoulder.

"I know."

"You're an ass."

"I know."

I poke his chest, pressuring him. "You're good at talking. So, talk."

"I fell in love with you, Ser. I didn't plan it. Tried to fight it, but the harder I fought, the worse it got. And when I saw you in your exhibit for the first time…Just torn. Came this close to throwing you over my back and marching out the front door. No one should see you like that, except for…" He doesn't finish, the implication lingering like dust bunnies in the air.

I grate my nails into his clothes. "You should've told me."

"I've kept a lot of secrets from you. But that was the biggest one."

Sky's heat coils around me, thawing Luc's winter chill. It's too much. After a minute or two with his arms around me, I change the subject. "Have you learned anything else about my parents?"

He nods, solemn. "Got my hands on a memo. The Guild has them in custody, in one of their prisons."

"What's Luc's father planning?"

"Don't know yet. DNA tests have been done, so he knows who they are. Probably plans to use them against Force in a Guild/Temple power play."

My heart sinks. "Is there any way to get them out?"

"The prison is very secure, but your exhibit is giving me the time I need to get more information."

"I can't stay in limbo like this!"

"Oh, Serenity." Sky's voice is an amused reprimand. "You're the key in all of this. You're the one everyone's watching. And the Guild wants to gauge how much you're worth."

I lower my head, biting down on my bottom lip because the pain helps keep back the tears. Sky scoots closer, reaching up to cup my head so he can lean it against his chest.

"Tell me more about the Sanctuary," I say.

He nods, running his fingers through my hair. "The Sanctuary's network is called the Task Force. They find girls everywhere from Glass Districts to graphicker studios to carnivals to museums, and they get them to safety. We smuggle the girls from safe house to safe house. The Sanctuary provided me with everything

I needed to get here, to the Aviary. You know I'd never give up on you. And that's not just because of how I feel."

He pauses before explaining, "Your parents always wanted to be sure you were safe. I wasn't part of the plan the day you were born, but Serafina kept me all these years because of you. I loved you since I first looked into your baby eyes. I know she doesn't love me the way she loves you. But that's never mattered. I care most about who I am in your eyes."

"Why did you hide how you felt for so long?" I thread my fingers into his.

I feel him shrug. "Was trying to do right by your mother. It wasn't easy, especially since it's always just us and all."

"That's why you stopped swimming with me. But you still watched over me."

"Over the last year, it was almost impossible. You're more and more beautiful with every passing day." Sky's hand on my neck makes me flinch. "Do you mind me watching you?"

Snapping, I shove him hard, but I barely make a dent. "That's not fair. I'm still trying to process everything."

"You know what's not fair? Your damned exhibit. Seeing the way their eyes rake all over you. Knowing their sick thoughts."

"And what are you thinking, Sky?" I counter, striking him harder than I know I should.

He groans. "Not gonna lie to you, Ser. I've had some thoughts, 'cause I'm just as much a sinner as any man, but your mother raised me to be a gentleman. Hope that counts for something. Unlike your precious Luc, who's turned you into his little puppet bird," he adds.

"I'm no one's puppet, Sky. If you say one more thing like that, I'll—"

"Serenity," Sky interjects, "I saw him kiss you. More than once. And I know what he asked you tonight about *sex*."

"I'm getting close to him for my parents. For you. I can't help what he asks me. You know I'm not a good liar. Try being the one performing, not watching."

"I wish it weren't this way. The way you are in that exhibit…I can't stand all those eyes on you. Trust me when I say, if I could, I'd stab each one and serve them to you on a giant platter." The sweet gesture makes me smile. That's just Sky and me on the same wavelength. "The last time, I was close to hauling you over my shoulder and pulling you out of there."

"He would've killed you."

"I'd put up a hell of a fight."

"Don't curse. You know Mom wouldn't like it," I reprimand him.

Sky grunts but sidles up next to me again, and we both shift so our heads lean against each other's even if my feet don't make it past his shins.

"Did it scare you, when you saw what Luc did to those graphickers?"

"No."

"Figures. Not much does."

"You scare me sometimes." I pause, wait to see his reaction, but Sky waits for me to explain. "Sometimes, I feel like I can trust him more than you."

"How can you feel that way?" Sky questions, surprise in his tone.

"You know me too well. You've been feeling this way for a long time. But I'm coming to grips with it all. It's overwhelming with him—and now with you, too. And that's not fair."

"I never said I would play fair."

Nineteen
BlaCkbird's BeaUty

THE NEXT MORNING, DOVE WAKES me up early when the sun is still low on the horizon. Well before breakfast.

"What is it?" I ask while she shakes the sheets loose from my body.

"Monthly physical." Dove draws my groggy form to a stand. "The girls are all tested and inspected. The Guild reads the reports, and yours will be included in your auction records."

It seems odd, given my recent Immortal Treatment and implant, but I don't complain. After showering, I wear a simple white dress with lace trim at my knees. To prevent my hair from soaking into the dress, Dove intricately braids my strands and twists them into a knot at the back of my head before ushering me to the main room where Luc waits for me with Sky bringing up our rear.

My physical must be the earliest since he isn't escorting any other Birds. Apparently, Luc wants mine done and out of the way. From what I can tell from his rigid spine and squared shoulders, he's not looking forward to this examination. Only when we reach the Inspection Room where Luc directs me to a medical bed do I understand why.

I recognize the Temple uniform of the older woman who meets Luc inside the observation room on my left. Luc closes the door, leaving Sky outside, which is even more unsettling. Next, I hear his voice waft through the Inspection Room speaker as he explains the woman is an inspector commissioned by the Temple, a concession made by his father.

The Aviary

"A fine specimen," the Temple inspector remarks. She is a tall, thin woman with narrow, black eyes, a sharp, crooked nose, and hair with ends so pointed they remind me of nettles. "Force would be most pleased by this one."

I swallow back bile.

The room is dark, but I see a glow and hear faint humming sounds. Spotlights bathe me before the room darkens. The humming sound increases as the hospital bed moves forward, and a machine scans my body. I am instructed to remain perfectly still, but midway through the inspection, my stomach starts to churn like a hooked worm. This has nothing to do with me—just my body's reaction to the machine's wavelengths. I hold my breath until the sensation passes. Once the machine shuts down, I look through the glass to where Luc and the inspector stand behind a projected screen. Their voices issue through a speaker, and she informs Luc of how pure I am. Maybe they don't know it's turned on.

"I'm aware of her purity and what my father deigns for her. I would prefer her here."

I clench my hands into fists at my sides as they discuss *my* future.

"Her repute is growing. Force is taking a keen interest."

"I know what repute she has gained." Luc keeps his voice firm, but no matter how faint, I can hear the undertones of rage lacing it like poison in wine. "I have seen to her repute."

"Nonetheless, her results from today, along with her blood samples, will be shared with Force."

It won't be long before he discovers I'm his lost little princess.

"The Guild will continue negotiations with the Temple. My father will see to it," Luc says pointedly.

"I'm certain. Your repute is well-established," she compliments him. "Your museum is the only one I've inspected where the girls are healthy and without much signs of abuse. Some, but nowhere near the Glass District."

"I monitor the client sessions on museum feed every night I can," Luc explains, which causes my stomach to churn. It means he won't allow clients to outright assault girls. Glass Districts don't have the same strict regulations. Museums do, but it's ridiculous to assume clients will play by the rules every time. The inspector just confirmed it for me.

"There is another matter I must discuss with you. One of your girls is pregnant."

I listen closer even when they speak in lower voices.

"I found her in the bathroom. She tried to excuse it as sickness, but I could see the lump on her stomach."

"Yes, I've been aware of Stork's pregnancy for a good deal of time. None of the other Birds are fertile."

"You understand the Centre allowed you to keep her here because each one of her labors results in a stillborn. Any conception is so rare, it warrants our immediate notice. But it is not Stork to whom I refer. You need to turn this one over to the Centre as quickly as possible. The Aviary is not equipped with a breeding wing."

I watch Luc as he steps forward, lowering his voice to a hum. "Which one of my Birds?"

Even as her mouth forms the word, it takes me a beat longer than Luc to react to the news.

"Blackbird."

For some time now, I've been sitting on the ledge of the window that overlooks the garden. All I've managed to do is smother the glass with my fingerprints. Blackbird will leave. For months, her body will become the Centre's test tube, succumbing to whatever tests, injections, inoculations, and studies they deem necessary.

And I'll stay here. Alone.

More fingerprints than glass now.

"She wants to see you."

I don't look up at Luc. And I say nothing. I don't know he's so close until he tugs the swan chain at my neck and juts my chin forward. He tilts my head from side to side, allowing his eyes to drift along the skin on my chest, arms, to my legs and bare feet. Checking me over.

"Your eyes are cold." Luc's fingers circle my wrist, but his eyes devour mine. "Has my Aviary so swiftly worn you down?"

More and more each day, Luc seems to comprehend how to

THE AVIARY

get under my skin. And I loathe him for it.

"Let her in," I sigh while forcing my back to him.

Luc gives us a moment alone.

For the first time, Blackbird wears a black dress that dangles to her ankles with long sleeves. They seem to strangle her arms. But her eyes are the same. Still ferociously black, they haven't lost their luster, though she seems to carry herself with more caution than normal. As if she feels her skin is glass and can crack at any moment, destroy the budding life inside. Just a faint bump.

She eases herself onto the window ledge opposite me, takes note of the fingerprints kissing the pane before arching her back against the wall.

"Don't look at me like that, Swan. You have no right."

"They'll take you from here now."

"This place is part life and part survival. You should know that by now. You can't keep pretending it's something it's not."

I gaze up at her in scorn and deny, "I'm not pretending."

"Then stop dreaming. Girls look out for each other here, but that's all. It's about assets and survival, nothing else."

"But—"

Blackbird interrupts me with a glare. "But nothing. I'm not going to be able to look out for you anymore. If you keep depending on Luc or Dove to do it, you're going to get in trouble."

"I'm already in trouble." I draw my knees up into my chest. "I'm the white rose when all the others are painted red."

"If you keep talking like that, you'll wind up like Cuckoo."

"Just like you'll end up like Stork," I quip.

Blackbird pauses, and I watch her mouth pinch. "I'm proud of what happened. After generations of inborn sterility and stillborn babies, I am one of the rare few who could make a difference."

"And what if every time it's just another dead—"

"At least I'll have tried!" Blackbird gets to her feet. "Whether I carry him for just another day, a week, or just the six months till my due date, I'll have done something not every girl out there can do."

My mouth stitches shut, and all the words in my throat become broken butterfly wings fluttering back to my stomach.

Sighing, Blackbird runs a hand through her thick hair. "I

didn't expect this. It's not like it's common with how many managers and directors force girls to stop their fertility." Blackbird fans out her fingers along her covered belly. "Guess they never thought the population would die out so quickly."

I nod. That and the drugs just made it worse. Babies who got through paid the price. With defects or inherited infertility. "Too many busted girls…" I speculate.

Blackbird flutters her fingers in little circles along her abdomen before continuing, "I'm not busted, Swan. My mama wasn't busted. She worked hard in the Glass District for years to get me here. And now, I have a way to help her. The Breeding Line pays more than the intimate services here. She'll come with me to the Centre. She'll get to be a grandmother."

"But all the stories about the Centre—"

Blackbird narrows her eyes at me. "I'll take the risk. My grandmother did."

"Your grandmother was in the Centre?"

She nods. "My mother found her, spoke with her before she died. Told me stories growing up because she wanted me to know where I came from. Gave me some roots. My grandmother had a *purpose*. Even though she had to give up her baby, she said it was like a dream come true. She said that giving birth was the most beautiful thing in the world."

It's the first time I hear Blackbird giggle. Her reaction to raw oysters can't compare to the sprinkle of laughter inundating her lips and soaking up the air. "I'm looking forward to feeling beautiful. For just once in my life."

Blackbird does nothing else except stand and walk away. Not like Mockingbird, who'd give me a parting kiss on the cheek or an embrace. No, this was just Blackbird telling her piece and nothing more.

My thoughts jump around like chopped-off snake heads that won't stop snapping. When she was in the Temple, my mother was a chemical girl with her fertility forced back. Was I just a baby who got through? Some sort of glass doll with inherited chemical shards?

Maybe I am broken. No better than a wind-up doll.

Even at dinnertime as I hear the other girls cheer when Luc

announces Blackbird's pregnancy, I can't rid myself of the selfish thoughts. Later, I'll make it more about Blackbird. I will tell her in my own way how I am glad for her. It will be enough. Congratulations will come later. Maybe I can visit her someday.

As usual, Finch sits right next to me. I hardly even notice her until I see that much of my plate is now empty. Even after the meal, the little girl shadows me as usual. I should be thankful I'm not alone, but I'm too numb.

It's evening, the busiest time of day for the Aviary. I'm glad I can't see the line of men waiting outside the museum. This weekend, my exhibit will open again, and Luc is determined to keep the surprises coming. Maybe next time I won't wear a dress, and I'll just be covered with white feathers or paint. "Look but don't touch" is the ultimate thrill of all for them. The chase. And I am part of it.

Too much too fast.

I am sinking, enjoying the moments of all eyes feasting on my skin like my body is a carousel they ride. I shouldn't feel excited for that. It should make me feel like a half-eaten apple core kicked into a gutter. The Aviary is sucking me in just like the Temple sucked my mother. Luc, the other girls, the Swan—they've all fused and imprinted themselves like a seal on my skin, worse than the feather tattoo. I've become part of the act.

My mother's words: the greatest act of all time.

You give your client what he wants, she's always said. *He never sees the tears behind the smile.*

Finch's constant proximity begins to feel cloying. There are only so many places to turn in a glass prison. And everywhere I go, there she is, underfoot.

With all those thoughts jangling like a thousand loose keys in my mind, on my way back to my room, I finally snap.

"Get away from me!" I shout at the little girl.

She stops, momentarily shocked, but still pursuing. "I want to see your room."

"Quit following me," I say, trying to shoo her away. "I just need some space! You're always around me!"

Her bottom lip trembles; I can see she's about to cry. I read the dreadful emotion on her face and reach out, but she flees.

"Finch, wait!"

I growl and face one of the glass walls, stare at my reflection, and scrape my nails across the glass, wishing I could scrape them across my flesh and seal scars into my cheeks.

Feeling a presence behind me, I sweep around to see Sky. I want more answers from him, but the heat from his eyes and his stiff body muzzles my words. He's disappointed in me.

I walk down the hallway to my room to find Blackbird waiting for me just outside my door. At first, she regards me with a measure of reproach. More than likely, Finch has told her what happened.

She molds her fingers together before saying, "I want to explain more to you."

At this point, I know I should welcome company and not reject it. So… "Come in." I open the door, allowing her to go in first.

My action seems to meet with her approval, and she takes her place again on the ledge just overlooking the garden. Sky follows us inside.

Blackbird notices my gaze on her stomach. "I'm just starting to show, Swan. You want to see?"

I'm not sure. I scrunch up my knees, flatten my back against the wall, and eye her. "Yes." She shows me her bump, just a plump little thing. I touch it and ask, "What does it feel like?"

"My stomach won't settle." She shrugs and indicates, "I throw up a lot. I guess some girls don't get the sickness, but it's like when you have those dreams where you're falling from something. Multiple times during the day, whenever I think about it, I get that feeling."

I press my cheek against my knees. "I know that feeling." I think of my exhibit and falling from the swing, but a cold rush of soothing water isn't what will await Blackbird. All that is left for her is gray pain followed by rosy warmth. Unless it doesn't live. I hope it will, for her sake. For the first time, I'm seeing her in a new light. It catches her skin, creating an ebony glow. Like she's some beautiful temple. Soul and skin and spirit. Not just because of her pregnancy. It goes beyond that.

"I bet the Aviary made enough off your exhibits alone to keep running another year," she says, crumpling my thoughts. "Bet you got a nice amount of claims stacking up for your auction, too. Has he told you anything else about your next exhibit?" she asks me.

I shake my head. "No. Just that it's this weekend."

Our conversation is interrupted by Luc's entrance. Even from all the way down the hallway by my bedroom door, I can read the consternation in his eyes.

"Blackbird, Raven is asking for you. Finch has fallen into a coma."

Twenty
LoStFeaThers

ALL THAT IS LEFT OF Finch are feathers. She doesn't look like Blackbird did when she was here. Finch is a child, her body too fragile. Too much energy spent growing, nothing left to fight this off. Will her hands ever steal my food again? Her body is tender as an eggshell, pale with her copper waves dulled to rust from lack of sprite and spirit. And my last memory of her involved my brilliant rush of anger. If Raven knows, she doesn't mention anything. With all of us in her infirmary room—me, Luc, Sky, Raven, and Blackbird—I feel stifled. Silence gnaws on the air. Dread laces through me.

"*Here is my ditty to bring you to trance. Here is my tune to force you to dance. Here is my lullaby so lovely and deep. Here is my song to sing you to sleep.*"

All of us seem to understand Luc's treasured lullaby will do nothing. Most of all Raven, who seems paralyzed in bed next to her little sister. After years of separation, they were reunited in this museum, and now the child is lost again. Wandering somewhere inside the carousels of her mind.

I feel as though I don't even deserve to breathe the same air as she does.

It's like I've broken something with what I've done to Finch. Inside me, something has cracked, and shards whirl around, cutting my insides. I'm fracturing, shivering.

I can't stand to stay in the room a second longer, but thankfully, Luc doesn't follow me out, only Sky. I venture outside the glass doors of the Aviary, but instead of taking the familiar path behind the waterfall, I continue across the bridge to where a glass door reads:

Glass Garden

I open the door, then step onto a glass walkway. On each side, there are sculptures of frosted glass birds, some in flight, some perched on branches with folded wings. They increase in number the farther I wander. Beside each sculpture is a plaque with a digital screen revealing the girl behind each bird. One still-shot of her exhibit. Then, the glass sculptures retreat in the wake of a circle of glass trees, budding with glass flowers. All white, like icing.

In the clearing is one final sculpture, and I am all too aware of Sky tracking my steps as I squeeze through the spaces between the trees to study it. I shouldn't be surprised that it's a swan or that it's the largest of the sculptures. Luc had put me on a pedestal before he even found me. No wonder the girls despise me so. If it weren't for Sky, I'd probably already be dead at the hands of Peacock, Nightingale, or any of the other dozens of Birds here. Mine is the only moving video.

A part of me recognizes that Luc has done his fair share of saving me, too. Without him, my virginity would've been sacrificed long ago.

Who knows what else Luc has planned for my exhibit?

Twenty-one
SwAnsaNdSkY

Tonight's costume certainly gives a proud Dove cause to preen.

At mid-thigh, the dress splits down the middle. Around my legs, the fabric is translucent white and mingles with my fair skin to my ankles. Dove paints elaborate patterns across my stomach, my throat, but laces tufts of white feathers across my breasts. She does nothing to my arms. Instead, thin swathes of fabric swing down from just below my shoulders and from under my elbows, creating a flowing illusion. Strings of feathers twist together into straps that weave all around my back to the last vertebra of my spine. More translucent fabric coats my hips along with a loop on each side, which puzzles me.

Last, she tackles my hair. Somehow, she tames the wild curls. To think this process used to takes hours, but with the automatic flattening laser, my hair is now longer than ever within minutes, surpassing well below my hips—until she coils it into a towering ponytail. I can see her objective; she's imitating the curved neck of the swan. Crystal dust decorates one side of my face. Each tiny crystallized mineral is high-tech, made to shine underneath the water to illuminate my skin.

Still, I seem more naked. I should prefer something demure that will cover all my white skin, but I'm embracing the cold. It's as though Luc is injecting his frost into me, transforming me into the latest glass sculpture.

I know without a doubt in this moment that I am becoming

part of the Aviary.

"What's next?" I ask Dove as I approach the wall mirror. I finger the expanse of my bare stomach, touch the feathers covering my breasts. "How much more clothing can he take away?" When she doesn't respond, I continue to speak.

"Will you simply paint my entire body in feathers next time?"

Every exhibit, I seem to lose more fabric and reveal more skin. I wish I could know what Sky thinks as he stands guard nearby, rooted in his usual place.

In the mirror behind me, Dove cups my shoulders and smiles. "I think you will enjoy yourself tonight."

I narrow my brows, questioning, "Why?"

Dove's smile deepens. "A premonition." She looks to the figure who enters the room just off to our left.

Luc dismisses both Dove and a hesitant Sky from the room before striding toward me. He reaches forward to adjust the swan charm on my throat. "Please believe me when I tell you how much I dislike sharing you this way. You should be my Swan and my Swan only." I guess he and Sky have that in common. But Sky wants Serenity. Luc wants the Swan.

"Then, why don't you cancel the exhibit?"

Luc regards me with an amused smile in the mirror. "You misunderstand me. I am not referring to your exhibit. More than anyone else, I appreciate your performance because I am the only one who recognizes who you are beneath the water."

Other than Sky, I think.

"They may treasure your physical image for a time, but I will treasure the soul behind your physical image for all time. But there is another matter I've wanted to discuss with you. Finch. I've read your despair."

I flutter my fingers across my arms, linger on the thin planes of fabric under my elbows. "How is Finch?" I ask.

"Much the same, unfortunately." Luc places his hands on the backs of mine. "Stop fiddling with your costume."

Throwing my arms to my sides, I glower.

"You are special to me, Swan. I care about you deeply."

"You don't know me," I say. "Not really. You can read every move I make, every expression—" *every yearning in my body*, I want to say, "—but you don't know the real girl. You don't know Serenity."

Luc takes my arm, twists me around to face him. "Tonight, then. After your exhibit closes, you will wear whatever you wish, and you will swim for no one's eyes but mine. And you may ask me whatever you want, whatever favor you wish, and I will grant it. Until then, it's time for your exhibit."

THIS TIME, THERE IS NO swing. In place of it is the trunk of a tree—its branches disappearing somewhere above my head where it meets the surface of the exhibit. Attached to the base of the tree is a pedestal for me to stand upon. Two black ropes with hooks on the end dangle above. Luc offers no instructions, merely attaches the hooks to the loop on each side of my hips.

"It will hold," he murmurs gently.

Hold for what?

Something in his behavior has changed. He's distracted, and I wonder if it has something to do with his revelation from a few minutes ago. I can't think about that now. I'll go crazy if I try. *Stay in the present.*

I open my mouth to ask a question, but Luc, who always predicts my thoughts, alerts me first. "You will know what to do when the time comes." He closes the door.

Once I reach the surface—still anchored on the pedestal fixed to the tree—the floor shifts down just like last time to make way for the lake water. When I feel a tug on the ropes, I realize they aren't just ropes, but cables.

Luc wants me to jump.

Needless to say, I understand why Dove told me I would enjoy tonight's performance. There—circling in the lake—is a ring of five swans, not sprite lights, but real and trained and waiting for me to dive directly into their center. Cables tug on me again, propelling my body up ever so slightly.

He's waiting for me. Everyone is.

I want to search for Sky's face, but I know he's lingering somewhere in the shadows, as usual.

I press my hands together, close my eyes, and leap from the

The Aviary

tree.

Sheer sheets of air almost knock the wind out of me before the water cradles my body. Except, I'm still attached to the cables, and this time, Luc has no intention of letting me dive deeper. The cables return me to the surface. I flip my long hair back so I can see, creating a magnificent arc of water droplets above my head as I do so. Disturbed by my dive or trained to fly, the five swans soar all around me as the ropes haul my body through the air. Instead of fighting the inertia tempting my stomach to lurch, I succumb to the motion. Exhaling, I feed Swan, who's taken up root inside me while the real swans follow me into the air. We are flying together.

The applause thunders louder than ever.

Ferried through the air, I wonder what they see. White enchantment or white fury? Water droplets topple off my body and dress, sailing through the air before rejoining the lake. Above me, the cables swing my body, stirring me into some sultry, flying dance. Slow enough I can respond without feeling too dizzy. Gusts of wind clap my face, and I pretend the wind is water. Pretend I'm still swimming, moving my arms and legs to respond. The result must work since the applause grows.

I wonder how far I can take this. Thinking, I slip into a crouch and flip forward. The action is so fast because all the motion propels me up again, and the force of the inertia somersaults my stomach, but my flip turns the applause into a roaring cacophony. Whistles and candles sway back and forth to the music echoing in the background.

After my flip, the cables dip my body until my feet kiss the surface of the water. Aware it's being controlled, I'm unsurprised when the cables dip me in the water to my knees only to lift me to the air again. Luc must be controlling them. And he wants more.

On the next dip, I tilt my head back and curve my spine so my hair rolls into the water. I point my toes and keeping my long, white legs raised high so my back coils into a flawless arc.

The ropes snap, and I capsize into the water, finally free to swim and to dive. When I approach the underwater viewing center and see a thousand different eyes, hypnotized by my form, I get a sense, just a stirring, of the power the one graphicker referred to.

I am the master. They are the slaves.

I become one glorious Swan fantasy.

As usual, Luc greets me with a blanket inside the canoe along with a proud smile strutting across his face. Just like the last two times, he addresses the crowd, which roars even louder this time.

Then, he lowers his mouth to my ear and whispers, "I look forward to seeing the real Serenity."

I ASK DOVE TO LEAVE so I can undress myself. Staring into the mirror, I try to figure this out. *Any favor*, he'd said. How could he promise that if he knows the connection to my parents?

I remove the dress starting with the strap, which twists around my back, peel back the feathers on my chest, the sheath on my stomach, and the fabric on my legs until I'm just skin and hair again. All Dove's work to straighten my hair is ruined, but her painted designs remain.

With one leg planted on the bathtub, I soak a rag in water and soap and begin to scrub, viciously scrub, until every trace of swan white escapes down the drain. Except for that damned feather. I reach for a towel, to smooth it around my body. Finally, I collapse regardless of how hunched over I am with my head on the tub faucet and my feet on the floor. Didn't quite make it all the way. Panting, I clutch the towel around my chest, its ends falling around my lower thighs. Spent and tired. The exhibit always leaves me so tired.

My eyes are closed, so I hear the water turn off before I open my eyes to see the hand coming off the faucet—too tan to be Luc's.

He sits on the edge of the tub, leaning over me, touching a space below my shoulder blade. "You missed a spot."

I don't flinch when Sky touches me. It doesn't feel wrong when he takes the rag from my hand, then starts to scrub away the stains on my back.

"What are you doing here? What about the cameras?" I don't shift my face from the faucet, just eye him as he tugs at the towel around my back, edges it lower so he can get at the rest of the paint.

"Footage is on a loop for now. And Luc's preoccupied for the moment. Monitoring client appointments. But I overheard him muttering to himself. Something about seeing the real Serenity. Something you want to share?"

"If I show him Serenity tonight, just be me for one night, then he won't only answer any question I want. He'll grant me any favor."

Sky's hand hardens on my skin. "You're playing with fire, Serenity. You've *never* played with fire well."

"Ow…" I wince when his fingers dig into my skin right near the tattoo. "I know what the boundaries are. What he expects."

Sky's hands practically growl on my back, fingers snarling into my spine. "You know what he expects, but you don't know what he *desires*."

My lips are cold against the faucet when I answer, "And what about *my* desires?"

Abruptly, Sky stands up and turns his back to me. "You're sick, Serenity. I didn't think you'd be so weak."

"Sky!" Raising my voice, I pivot my body at the same time, "Don't you dare walk away from me!"

He doesn't turn around, which just enrages me even more until I rake my nails into the back of his neck. This time, he doesn't throw me off, he twists me around so I'm in front of him and pins me against the wall.

Then he raises one big finger to my face. "I haven't worked this hard for you to throw it all away on a whim. Your parents are counting on you. You're not one of his Birds, so stop acting like one."

Through my tears, I muster a nod. This is Sky grounding me. This is real. With Luc, I never know what's real.

His hands hold my tiny, toweled waist high against the wall. He is so strong. Always has been. Sky—strong in body and will; Serenity—strong in spirit and life. That's what my mother always said.

He stares at me for a few seconds, eyes drifting down a little.

I narrow my brows, sharpen my eyes harder than a dragon scale. "What are you *doing*?" Sky would never take it too far. Would I?

With a frown, Sky shakes his head and sets my feet down

again, glances away. "Nothing."

I cinch the towel tighter around my frame, not to be undone by his questing eyes. "You're not the only one working. You have no idea what I've been going through."

"You *really* need to stop talking." He tugs me out of his way, then makes for the door. "I'm doing a damn good job right now. Don't tempt me."

"You know I hate it when you do that," I say as I follow him into the main room.

"Yeah, well, I hate it when you do a lot of things." He doesn't stop walking.

"Fine! Be a stubborn ass."

I wander to the closet and fish out one of the white dresses, slam the door, drop the towel, and don't come out until I'm clothed.

But he's there, sliding into the closet behind me once I've finished dressing. Confused, I watch as Sky closes the door, clenches his fist at his sides, and eyes me. "You can't imagine how terrified I am." At his words, my body feels more grounded than ever. I pacify myself to hear what Sky has to say.

"Every time your exhibit opens, every time he shows you off for the world to see, every time he feels like he's closer to you…" Sky's words trail off, his breath a warm echo, but his hand reaches up to cup my cheek. It's so big it swallows half my face.

"Sometimes, I think it'd be simpler to help my parents if—"

Sky's eyes turn lethal. "Don't you ever think that! You *never* have to give him anything. You have no idea how men are or what they think. You've never seen the way the world works or what men do as soon as they get what they want."

I shrug. "You said they'll never stop wanting more. Everyone always wants more."

"Exactly." Sky palms my shoulders. "They'll always search for something more, something better. He'll just move on from you once he gets what he wants."

"He isn't like that," I say, defending Luc. "He's better than those other men."

"No, he's not. He's just good at what he does. Don't buy into it."

"But..." My tongue tiptoes on the words, hesitating before speaking them. I know how it will sound, but it means something to me. With his recent offer, Luc has shown just how much I mean to him. "I'm his Swan."

The rush of heat from Sky almost sears my skin.

I pause in the full understanding of what I've just said. Sky's hands leap from my skin like he's a rod conducting electricity, and he turns away from me.

I spin around so I can see his eyes, but he won't look at me. When I try to reach for him, he shoves me away. He's always pushing me away, but something in this world will always bring him back to me. Just like the day Sky pulled me back to land after I swam out too far.

"Sky–"

He cuts me off while moving toward the door. "I only had a few minutes to loop the system. He'll be coming soon."

I follow him out of the closet and to the main door. "Sky, it shouldn't be this way between us. It's too much. I don't know what to do."

"Neither do I." And he closes the door behind him.

"Give me your hand," Luc requests when he enters my room and shuts the door behind himself.

As soon as I accept, Luc produces something from behind his back and places it in my hand. My fingers curl around its edges, studying its porcelain curves. "Why a mask?" I ask. "I thought you—"

"First, I want to show you something. I need your help tonight."

I hesitate even as my fingertips capsize into his palm. "Where are we going?"

Touching the small of my back, he whispers low, "Just follow me."

After he leads me out through a secret exit, I discover Luc has ordered a limousine transporter for us. We travel away from the glass walls of the Aviary on a remote track along the outer edge of the city. It's much more extensive than I originally believed. The museum itself rests on the city's eastern edge in an upscale neighborhood that's popular with tourists, near malls and business centers, and wealthier, private residences. Now, we are driving toward the western edge of the city, where skyscrapers pepper the night and a metrodome interrupts the darkness like a white fist raised to strike. We pass them all, progressing to the western edge. From the tinted windows of the car, I stare at the city lights glittering like armies of dragonflies battling with fireflies. Two lone spotlights compete for attention on the outskirts, and the vehicle finally stops in a reserved lot near the center of the spotlighted area.

"No one will see your face," Luc reassures me, motioning to the mask. "They will assume you are an anonymous escort."

I suck in a deep breath, remembering the last time I visited the Glass District.

Because Luc is a wealthier and more connected patron, he is free to use one of the private viewing centers constructed above the shops. Others have already taken their places in various ones nearby when Luc escorts me into the glass elevator that transports us to his reserved viewing center. Even so, Luc is recognized. Other patrons and even security guards bow their heads in respect. Luc's status is well-known. There are even a few reporters who request interviews with him, but he declines. It shouldn't surprise me that the director of one of the most popular museums in the country should have a certain amount of celebrity status.

The room is only a little bigger than the elevator itself, but there are two chairs as well as a viewing screen on each wall. Luc switches on the screens. Off to my right and left are lines of mostly male customers, some female—probably madams, looping around various blocks, waiting to use the Glass District. The demand for bodies is just as high as ever.

When I look down through the mask's eyeholes, I can see the heads of some of the customers through the glass of the viewing center. I wrinkle my nose at the thought of why they're here.

Luc catches my attention, then motions to the glass displays of the windowed shops before pointing to the screens above our heads. Screens are outdated, but the districts don't have the funds for volumetric tech like museums. After the first presentation of girls, which lasts about a minute, the lights dim for a few moments, but it doesn't take them long to flash on again. At their signal, a new wave of girls has appeared. Like an assembly line.

None of them should be here.

Most of the girls' expressions are familiar—imprinted on my mind from my first visit, years ago. Come-hither smiles with blank mask holes for eyes. Nothing much has changed, just the viewing center and the sophisticated screens. Many girls' costumes mimic the pattern of museums from flowers wrapped around their bodies, to wings embellishing their shoulders, to fruit garnishing their chests. Above the shops is one giant screen portraying a profile of each girl, flashing from one to the next and the next, repeating an endless cycle. On each side of our viewing center, screens beckon with those same profiles.

Luc doesn't let go of my hand, even when he clicks the button on his remote. "Screens like this have always existed. They exist in homes, on the streets, in businesses, anywhere one can be a consumer. Every Glass District is simply a more palpable experience for customers who want it firsthand."

"Why did you bring me here?" I ask. My mask trembles.

"I hope this visit will ease your sadness over Finch. The Swan must be prepared for her exhibit, and…I do not enjoy seeing this side of you. There are more girls here. And more who want them." Luc gestures to one of the centers on our right. "You see that man?"

From here, I can only make out his features by the glow of the screen. He is dressed more extravagantly than Luc—his clothes remind me of fish scales—and it leaves little doubt as to who he is.

"A carnival owner," I say with certainty.

"He enjoys bidding higher than me. He knows I have a weakness for hatchlings, and he goes out of his way to outbid me on them."

"*Why* did you bring me here?" Repeating my earlier question, I scan the screen briefly as a few girls' profiles flash before us.

"Because tonight, you will be his house of cards and the ace up my sleeve. You are going to choose first."

He places the remote in my hands before I can respond, and the understanding of what Luc is gifting me trills into my fingers while more faces travel past. Some do not reappear, which means they've been bought—whether it's for one night, one week, or permanently. I know final sales are rare unless it's a special auction, like mine.

My fingers tremble as my eyes wander across skin and cheeks and mouths, flowers and wings and fruit and feathers and petals. And they stop. On moss and leaves, on skin and hair white as snow.

I hold the button down on the remote, and Luc places his bid as soon as my eyes pause on the screen. I catch the dull bell ring—a signal he is outbid. He glances to his right, and so do I.

The carnival owner turns to Luc, raises a hand in mock gesture, and grins.

Luc bids higher.

In the same moment, I stand and sweep toward the window, knowing I've caught the carnival owner's attention. At first, he tries to multitask. But then, I remove my mask and wink at him. He won't be forcing Luc to bid higher.

The bell signals that Luc has won the final bid—at a much lower price than he anticipated.

"Well done," Luc says.

I lower myself back into the chair beside him.

"Though I would have preferred you'd kept the mask on." His narrowed eyes soften when the screen shows us the face of the girl I've selected. "My youngest hatchling was Mockingbird, of course. But this one is the youngest I will have invested in since. You must understand something, Swan." Luc reaches out to cup my chin beneath the weight of the mask. "I do my best to preserve the innocence of my Birds until they are older. I have a place set aside for the younger ones. A flight school, as it were. You will not be permitted to see her. When she comes of age, she will be brought to the Aviary." Obviously, Finch is an exception because of Raven.

I memorize the color of the girl's eyes before nodding. "What will you call her?"

Luc examines the screen and then scrutinizes me, judging my reaction. "Ironic that you chose her. To me, she is the Fawn Zebra Finch. I know my Birds—their genetics and mutations."

"You won't call her Finch." My voice hardens.

"Of course not. She will go by Fawn Finch."

My eyes tilt back to the screen, and I nod as I study the girl's eyes, the color of a fawn's back; the name will be worthy. I wish I could see this flight school he's referred to, but as we descend back to the ground level, the carnival owner approaches us to express his distaste for Luc's method.

"Well played, Director Aldaine," he croons as Luc places himself between my body and the man with the face of a weasel. A weasel wearing a joker suit, considering the rash color palette.

That's when I notice a crowd of people moving toward the Glass District opening. The signs in their hands leave little doubt as to who they are: activists. On the opposite side, closer to us, is another crowd, but they are paparazzi with holographic cams. Some of the paparazzi cry out "Director," wanting to take holograms with Luc.

"You've always had a wandering eye, Willis. Pity the stench of deep fried butter will always waft from your person."

Luc's audacity almost catches me off guard, but the revulsion he shows toward Willis practically hisses off his body.

I turn back to eye the hoard moving closer to the entrance. Security hasn't arrived yet. No wonder the crowd chose now. Since much of the bids have been placed, security will be escorting girls to their claimers. It's an opportune time for a protest strike.

I consider another fleeting thought: *It's an opportune time for something else.*

The carnival owner clears his throat, alerting me. His eyes roam across my form.

"I trust you still have all your lovely Birds' wings clipped. Except for this one, I see. Is this your latest acquisition I've heard so much about? Surely you didn't take the risk of bringing the Swan outside Aviary property, Aldaine! What a surprising treat." He cups his hands over a decorative cane, then leans on it to eye me.

"I have confidence in my ability to protect what is rightfully mine," Luc says lazily.

"Of course." Willis bows his head before staring once more at me. "Perhaps I will visit the Aviary during my stay here. After all, I wouldn't want to miss her next exhibit. Not after having finally seen her. Until then, she shall haunt my dreams."

Count on it, I want to say before glancing at the crowd out of the corner of my eye. They are only a couple dozen feet from me.

It's risky, but I consider how so many activists have Sanctuary connections. If I escaped, it would be simple to get in touch with Sky. We could get my parents without Aviary interference. Without me sinking deeper into Luc's world. There's no guarantee Luc will keep his word about his favor. No guarantee he'd be satisfied with my definition of the real Serenity. Skeptical thoughts swarm in my head, advising me to play it safe, but then Luc turns his head from me. It's a chance I can't refuse.

I break away from him, making a beeline for the crowd. A few seconds later, I think I hear him shout, but by now, the cries and chants from the hoard waving their signs overwhelm me. I crash right through their barricade, but they don't part. Almost as if they can't be bothered with me. Like they're drones following their mission with no regard to anything else. Bodies cram me in, stealing my air. Voices assault my ears until they throb. A hip almost crushes me, and I stumble from the action, terrified I'm going to be trampled as the activists continue to move forward. Somehow, I squeeze through a pair of legs, tearing my dress in the process and getting to my feet. This was a mistake. Never have I felt more panic. Never have I felt more surrounded. My mind reels. Right now, I'm on a manic ferris wheel that has broken off its hinges—spinning out of control.

One of the protestors curses at a Glass District window. Curses the girl inside. More shouts and jeers follow as more bodies hem me in. I don't understand. Another body slams into me, and brutal fingers come down on my mask, ripping it from my face and scratching my cheek at the same time. One man pitches me to the ground. Shouts 'Breakable whore' in my ear before marching onward with the oncoming crowd.

They're going to trample me!

I shouldn't have left Luc's side. Better to be a flightless Bird in the Aviary than to be meat fodder for these activists. None of them are with the Sanctuary because Sky would never throw his lot in with them.

Just as I try to get up, another leg thrusts me back to the ground. More curses, more shouts, more sign waving. I whimper when another shoe bears down, stomping on my back hard. How long does it take to get trampled to death? I realize I won't find out when a strong hand latches onto my waist, raising me from the dirt. I recognize his hold. His expression confounds me. Not one trace of anger is in his eyes. Instead, they are laced with creased concern. He exchanges no words with me, just starts to pull me along, and I comply, treating his hand like an anchor. As it is, I'm little more than seaweed clinging to his body as he hauls me out of the ocean of people and away from the Glass District. Back into the Family limo.

Now, he shows his anger. Brows deepening the shadows around his eyes, which become thin as wires. "I should have enforced the skin shield. What the hell were you thinking?" He raises his voice and tugs on my wrist because he hasn't released me yet.

Panting, I shake my head and slam my eyes shut, trying to expel the feeling of the bodies smothering me. "I don't know. I—" I swallow to regain control of my voice, then find myself throwing my head back with a frail laugh. What *was* I thinking? "Can't blame a girl for trying, right?"

"Wrong." Luc's voice is the hardened edge of a blade. "Those protestors care nothing for Breakables."

I got that message loud and clear. No, they were *blaming* the girls, targeting them as if it's their fault the world is the way it is. As if it's our fault.

"Rest assured, you will be punished," Luc hastens to add. "But I intend to keep my word first. One favor for the real Serenity."

I nod.

More than ever, I want to return to the Aviary.

"So, THIS IS YOU?" LUC asks with fingers titillating the back of my neck.

In my head are all the thoughts, memories, of what Sky said about Luc earlier. They chip away at my resolve, at my ability to complete this, but Sky must know if he's willing to go to whatever lengths to save me, that I am willing to go just as far for my own blood. At least, I think I am.

I want to believe in the man behind me, the man who slaughtered graphickers for me, and the man whose eyes overpower me like a fever, whose arms lull me like the quiet eye of a storm, promising protection with hands transforming me into his fantasy.

"No. I won't let you see the real me."

Luc's hand cups the back of my neck. "Why?"

"Because…" I sweep my hand to my shoulder. "It's without this."

Luc doesn't move. "Without this…" His hand lingers on one of the straps.

I don't look at him. "You promised any favor, right?"

"On the condition you swim for no one's eyes but mine."

"I can't give you that, Luc. I can't show you, but I'll tell you. There was one night at this lake house…I snuck out and went skinny dipping. Nothing around me but dark water and the reflection of the stars. I hate walls. Walls are cold and immovable, and I hate drapes and blinds that hide the moon. I love water, though, because it moves beneath me and all around me, but it follows me, too. It holds me close. Lets me use it however I want. If I dive deep enough, I can't hear anything. I forget about glass walls and graphickers and swan dives and girls in comas. I forget everything but the quiet."

"It's where you feel free."

I nod.

"Serenity." I inhale when he uses my real name. "I will keep my word of one favor. But will you grant me just one in return? Provided my eyes remain closed?"

I hold my breath when his fingers light on the strap of my dress, and he urges it down the curve of my shoulder. The mirror of my virtue cracks. A hairline fracture. He slides the strap farther down, fingers brushing the tattoo, but he keeps his word and doesn't open his eyes.

I listen as his breath increases when he does the same with my other strap, fingers slow dancing on my arm. They don't quite press, so they're not as cold as usual, more like cool mist. It's the first time I shiver without reservation. He pauses, kisses his feather tattoo, and inhales deeply as his hands teeter along the fabric of my waist before he urges it down. The dress plunges lower, fabric sliding across my breasts to free them.

What does this mean to him? All I want to do is become water. Slip right through the hands gliding across my skin and leaving goose flesh there. Instead, I find myself warping the hands. I change them and make them rougher, bigger, more calloused. Not as gentle as they discover my hips. Sky's hands. The only hands I can imagine touching me more. They are familiar. I know every curved and straight line, every common blister and callous, every scar, the shape and contour of his palm and fingers as well as I know my own. Luc's hands are alien. He's already wheedled his way into my mind. Will I let him get underneath my skin?

I'm still holding my breath, watching him. His eyes never open once as he coaxes the fabric down my hips, knuckles gliding across the skin there until the dress pools at my feet. He doesn't stray once. Would Sky?

Water laps at my toes, returning me to my senses. I bite my lower lip hard. This moment isn't about them. It's about earning a favor, one favor, which I will use to free my parents.

I think Luc's finished until his fingertips curl behind my neck, causing me to shiver again as he removes the swan charm.

Luc whispers, breath dragging along my neck. "Serenity."

How can his hands feel so cold but his breath so warm?

I dive into the lake. No doubt he can hear me splashing, but I don't stop to turn. I don't want to know if he's kept his word. Just so long as he keeps his word about the favor. Everything is clear now. Dark water nurses every inch of my naked skin. Down here, I can think. With no one watching me, no hands on glass waiting for me to move, I can just think.

I want my family back, but for that to happen, I'm in danger of accepting all of this.

I understand one thing—in return for their freedom, I would exchange mine. I would stay.

If Luc can free my parents, I will become his most glorious Swan. My breath escapes in a hundred bubbles, and I dive deeper until there is nothing but darkness. My lungs are just on the edge of burning. Despite the water, it's the first time my body feels like it's burning, and I know it's the lightning inside me—the knowledge of what I'm going to ask once I surface.

If escape is possible, I would be breaking my word. Part of me wonders what is worth more: my word or my dignity. What of Luc's word? He said that I am the only one to satisfy his heart, to make him whole. Everything he has done for me has set me apart to prove his words from rescuing me from the graphickers to Fawn Finch in the Glass District to offering me the singular Swan exhibit. The thought of entering the exhibit and seeing what Luc unveils again and again used to churn the bile in my stomach. Now, my inner Swan considers not only embracing her exhibit, but also accepting Luc. Would he buy me himself? He said he would treasure my soul. If I could choose to stay, better Luc's bed than in the hands of Director Force.

My body presses against the underwater viewing center where I can see one solitary figure standing with hands in his pockets. For some reason, I don't panic when I see him there with eyes wide open in surprise.

I wonder what he sees without the spotlights dazzling my skin.

A white shape blurred at the edges by darkness? An outline? Curves? More? Whatever the case, he knows I can see him. Because of what was said earlier, it seems almost inevitable. I never realized what my exhibits meant to Sky until now.

He used to be the only one who ever watched me. Now, everyone has studied my every curve.

Every swan dive must shred his heart—I know he can't bear to share me. Sky has spent his life protecting me, but he can't protect me from everything. And tonight, I've let Luc in. Guilt floods me as I realize I've shut Sky out at the same time, keeping him at a distance because he kept the truth from me. He doesn't deserve it. Not after all we've been through.

I'm losing him.

Nothing should stop me from fighting or running. The stain of a broken promise should be easier to live with than losing my virtue, than breaking my mantra.

Even as I lose more bubbles, and my lungs pray on their last knees for me to surface, I stay to watch Sky turn and walk away.

Luc greets me with closed eyes and a towel. For a moment, I stand there in front of him, staring at the way he spreads the towel, fingers hovering at the corners…waiting. I let him fold the towel around me, after which he finally opens his eyes. To see my face, pale in the darkness of the exhibit.

"You seem thinner," he observes and cups my cheek. "You seem weaker."

"Finch, Blackbird, the exhibit..." *Sky.*

"What is your favor?" Luc asks. "What do you want?"

"I know you'll never let me go, Luc. I won't insult you by asking for that. But I will ask that you let my parents go. Please."

Luc's fingers drift from my cheek. "Your parents?"

"You have to know, Luc. I'll be your Swan, but don't let my mother become Force's Unicorn again. Don't let the Temple take any of us, and I'll stay here. With you."

Luc's hand retreats, fingers rubbing his temple.

"You said anything," I remind him.

"Swan," he reverts, crawling back into his director shell. "You're asking me to go against my father." So, he is involved. He's known all this time who I am and who my parents are. "You ask me to betray my very *Family*." He emphasizes the last word, so I know it means more than just mere blood.

Lightning pulses through my pores. "You gave me your word!"

"You know how long I've waited for you. This could jeopardize everything I've worked for."

"If I mean as much to you as you've said, Luc, you'll do as I ask."

After another few moments of silence and just staring at me, studying my unwavering gaze, Luc touches my shoulder. "It's time for your punishment now. But if you wish to visit the town, I will arrange for a transport. You performed very well tonight."

"But—"

His mouth covers mine, causing ice to spread into my blood like venom, rooting me to the ground. Winded, I part my lips, but he doesn't deepen the kiss.

"I will see what I can do."

I bite down on my lower lip, then pose another question. "What about your father? What if my next exhibit...I mean...what's next? What could you possibly do to top what we did tonight?"

"Never doubt my creativity." Luc pulls away, grin stretching before escorting me out of the exhibit. "I am an artist. And a supreme one at that."

For my punishment, Luc escorts me to the Isolation Room again. At least it's not above the client rooms, so I don't struggle when he opens the door and urges me inside. Spent from the night, I sink to the cold floor and wait for the electronic sound of the virtual machine.

The Isolation Room dims, and I recognize the long windows on one side of me, betraying the Penthouse. The brush of the whip on my back is familiar. So is the glitter all over my skin and the bits of horse fur strung along the sides of my face. I feel the horn sealed in the center of my forehead, and I hear the whip as it's uncoiled. Closing my eyes, I wait for it to come down, the seconds in between more excruciating than the action, but it doesn't land. I open my eyes to see my costume replaced. No more fur. There are feathers. Feathers everywhere on and all around me. The hardwood floor beneath me has been replaced by a bed, a bed suffocated by millions of fluffs of feathers. Recognizing them as swan feathers, I stir from the pillow beneath me, disturbing them, finding nothing on my skin but a plunging corset knit of the same feathers.

Then, I hear the familiar voice beside me. "My Swan," he whispers in my ear before plucking one feather from the bottom of the corset.

More than anything, I want to fight, I want to run, but the Isolation Room strangles my ability and pins me to the bed just as Luc rips at another feather. Worse than the whip from my father, this is my deepest fear—my armor dissolving like warm snow.

One by one, Luc plucks the feathers, taking his time. Every one reminds me of pieces of my old life that he's chipped away at since I entered the Aviary. Unraveling me little by little, discovering parts of me I wasn't even aware of. Only one other man knows me to such a degree. Luc doesn't deserve to share that, does he?

Fewer feathers and more skin now. He places a hand on the smoothness of my stomach, smiles down at me as if reminding me of the night with the graphickers and the time in the Glass District when I chose Fawn Finch, when he rescued me from the crowd. His fingers brushing my skin echo the day he bought me. He takes another feather, blows on it, and it lands on my cheek. Rubbing it away with his thumb, he turns my face to his.

When he kisses me, it doesn't feel new. Like a replay of every other time he's kissed me, but his lips sink lower onto my bare neck, and I find myself arching in response even as his hand lowers to grip multiple feathers and tear them off. Just the barest string left covering me, clinging to a fragile thread. Luc fingers the leftover feathers in between my cleavage, toying with them, toying with me just as he always has.

I clench my eyes just as he prepares to tear the final line of feathers, but everything disintegrates into voxels when the Isolation Room lights flood me, the sound of electronics humming down. I'm still lying on my back in my dress, but I'm on the metallic floor when Luc enters. Without waiting for me to speak, he raises me up and beckons me outside the room. His expression is all tight creases and hard lines, features bordering on dangerous. Did he see everything? Was he insulted by my subconscious fear paraded before his eyes?

He says nothing while escorting me back to my bedroom. By the time we reach the door, I'm convinced his demeanor has nothing to do with the Isolation Room. Something much more serious has demanded his attention.

We reach the door to my bedroom where Luc isn't gentle about pushing me inside. "Stay in your room and don't come out," he commands.

"Luc," I try to stop him. "What's going on?"

He prepares to close the door. "I need you safe. I'll send for Vulture."

I try to imagine all sorts of scenarios, but without any clue as to what's going on, I come up empty. After I change into one of the white nightgowns, I curl up in bed, too exhausted for anything else.

Sky arrives a few minutes later. Based on the way he carries himself, I understand the security system is very much engaged. He doesn't even look at me, just stands in the corner, in the shadows of the room near the door.

I scan the layers of night to where he stands. "What's going on out there?"

"One of the Birds is missing."

"Who?"

Sky doesn't give a moment to pause. Would he have cushioned the blow if he wasn't Vulture? I can't stop treading on the name over and over and over and over again.

Blackbird.

I reach for the object under my pillow I'd smuggled from the closet and open the book, holding onto it like it is a life preserver. Moonlight spills through the window, helping me distinguish the words.

Girls went missing from the Temple all the time. We weren't supposed to get attached to each other, but holding onto each other was the only warmth we ever felt. Spending most of my time in the Penthouse made it more difficult. Every morning, I had to rest, heal, and prepare myself for the Vampire to come at night. Before the Penthouse, I had one friend. We called each other by our real names. We whispered them at night beside indestructible glass windows where we could see the sky, the one thing in our lives that wasn't polished or airbrushed.

I remember Violet. She knew I was moving up in the ranks of the Temple, while she was on her way down. Violet came closer than anyone I'd spoken to about the Penthouse. While all the other girls on our level slept, Violet and I crawled through the ceiling shafts, lit virtual candles since real were forbidden, and pretended what the world was like outside. She called me Sera. She never talked about what happened to her on the upper levels, and I didn't ask. Every girl knows the clients are richer there, more Family-oriented.

People rumored I would reach the Penthouse. Each level, I was tested. My seduction grades were increasing, and the studios became more advanced and glamorous with every level. My artwork was popular. The faces I saw the most were graphickers and artisans. Unlike me, Violet never spoke about her artwork, but every now and then, I'd find a dab of purple paint on her shoulder like a tattoo left behind. I wondered if they turned her into a flower.

I never found out.

After my studio the next day, they announced they were moving me up to the Penthouse. The infamous Force had asked for me. A trial. I was thrilled. I hurried to pack my things, to tell Violet the news, but her bunk was empty. One of the other girls said she was taken to the Centre. Now, my better sense tells me that Force discovered our connection and snapped our thread, the first stage of his control. My imagination still thinks she broke the glass and flew away.

Twenty-two
FlyAwAy

*I*N THE MORNING, S*KY* IS still standing in the corner of the room when Dove comes in. She looks haggard somehow, not pristine as she always is.

"They still haven't found her," I say, reading her face. "Do they know anything?"

Dove shakes her head. "Owl has ordered a lockdown."

It means I won't be going anywhere today. Is there any point in getting out of bed?

"Let me paint you," Dove says, her appeal like a ragged echo. She was Blackbird's caretaker before she was assigned to me.

Too numb for much of anything, I let her lead me to the chair in front of the mirror. After setting up the screen, Dove uncaps a few different bottles.

One tear paints her cheek. Despite her attempts at neutrality with the Birds here, it's obvious Dove favors those she paints. And she painted Blackbird before me. Her voice cracks, but nothing more than a whimper escapes as she decorates me, brush twirling against my skin. For once, I don't ask to see. This is her moment more than mine. I've known Blackbird a pittance of time compared to her. I don't have as much right to grieve.

Dove starts looking better when she weaves my hair into a steadfast mass of twists until the strands resemble interlocking vines.

She retrieves a backless dress for me, and I wander out from behind the screen a few moments later. If Sky is surprised by whatever she's painted on my back, he doesn't react.

Looking seems too invasive. Even if it is my own skin. So, I just ask her instead.

"What is it?" I motion to my back.

"A serpent. A viper striking," she says simply, before catching a tendril of my hair and tucking it behind my ear. "It's how my daughter perished."

"Oh, Dove..." I murmur.

"She brought so much life to this museum. It took long years, countless clients, but she was mine. She came from my body. But her body was too little when it bit her. It took her in a few seconds, just long enough for me to see her eyes go still, for the froth to fill her mouth." How could a poisonous snake get here from the outside? Was it on purpose? I don't ask her for details. Doing that would only bring her more pain.

Instead, I ask in a small voice, "Do I look like her?"

"Yes."

"That's why you wanted to paint me from the beginning."

"Yes."

"Thank you," I tell her as she recaps a few of the bottles on her workstation. I don't tell her how she reminds me of my mother, but without all the secrets. The words in my mother's diary are like Dove's paint on my skin, but Dove doesn't hide her past from me. She doesn't try to protect me. She just tries to nurture me while doing her best. There are no secrets between us.

"Dove," I say, "may I see Finch? I want to visit her."

"All girls are restricted to the main wings."

Sky clears his throat. "Director Owl informed me Finch's room will be open to visitors, but only one at a time and under security."

I meet his eyes, brown as two acorns. No sunlight to warm them to amber. He nods, giving me permission. Dove promises to stay in the bedroom and wait for me. I won't be gone long.

Only when I enter the outer hallway do I realize Dove's grieving gift has become a curse. A familiar figure walks past me, her gaze settling on my back, and I hear her seethe before she turns and advances toward me, ravishing and dark as a child's nightmare. I don't move, but she does.

The Aviary

Nightingale is stronger than me, her curves hard-worked muscle. Her eyes are like wrought iron when she grabs me by the arm, shoving me against the wall before smearing the paint on my back with her hand.

"Black is *my* color," she snarls before wiping her blackened thumb across my cheek.

Before Sky can step forward, I throw my body back so she stumbles off me. "Don't you dare touch me again, you glorified crow. I never asked to be the Swan."

Nightingale's ready for another assault, but a figure interrupts, flitting down the hallway toward us. "Leave her alone, Gale," Mockingbird says, defending me.

"You stay out of this," Nightingale warns with a jut of her finger. "Don't pretend you're here to help her. You're only helping yourself."

I don't understand what she means by that until Mockingbird says, "You've always been jealous that Dove never chose to paint you. That she chose to paint me and the Swan over you."

"Let's see if that remains true after I speak to Owl. Perhaps he will demote her." She backs away from me, lustrous dark hair flicking over her shoulder as she does so.

"And who do you think Luc will listen to more?" I call out, and Mockingbird grins next to me.

Nightingale turns on one heel. "Just because you call him by his real name doesn't mean he belongs to you. Remember, you're art just like the rest of us. You just happen to be the flavor of the week."

Mockingbird tries to stop me, but I'm quicker than a lightning flash. I round a corner and flee down another hallway, outside to the aviary and the tunnel behind the waterfall. Once there, I submerge my hand under the water and splash it against my back, trying in vain to rub away the black paint. It sluices into my dress instead, staining it a dark gray.

Suddenly, the black becomes a plague on my skin. I want to scurry out of the dress. Get every last bit of paint off.

My arms and legs are bare. Next, I rip my hair out of the vine-like braids and let the strands cover my face as I sink to the damp ground. Dirt smothers the backs of my legs and dress, and

I grind my fingers into it, feel the mud sinking beneath my nails. It reminds me of Sky's eyes in the Aviary. Too muddy, too dark. Like the mud, Sky is the only one who can get under my skin and manage to stay there.

My filthy hands rise to grip my forehead. The falls pant, spraying the right side of my body, mingling with the dirt until mud starts rolling down the sides of my arms and legs, splattering my dress in murky droplets. On my left side, his body sucks up the air and replaces it with his warmth just before he wraps an arm around my shoulder.

"Looks like this is our spot." Sky leans over and kisses the side of my head, coaxing heat into my skin. The fine mist covers his hair. I love it when his waves fall all around his shoulders, damp like that. "Handled yourself pretty well back there." Then, Sky's fingers pause from tracing my shoulder. "I want to be there for you, always, but I—"

"Shut up, of course you'll always be here." I lean back into him again, distrustful of any gap of air between us.

"What makes you so sure? I saw you with him last night."

"You're not as smart as you think you are." I shove him.

Sky straightens, raising himself, nostrils flaring. "Smart enough to see he's clipped your wings."

Balling my hands into fists, I confront him head-on, my voice raising an octave, "What would *you* know anyway? You spy on me whenever you can, but you don't bother sticking around to hear anything important."

"I couldn't stick around."

When he leans closer, eyes almost bruising mine, I can't help but pause, confused.

"Why?"

I have to hold back the smile wanting to lift the corners of my mouth when his hands cup the air on each side of my head, fingers curved like they want to squeeze me like a grape. Exasperated, he grunts and groans. Flares once more. One more second passes before Sky suddenly reaches down, grabs a heavy stone at the base of the rock wall, and launches it against the other side. It thunks loudly enough to drown out the noise of the falls for two seconds.

He slumps back down next to me.

"Feel better?" I ask, bending at the waist.

"No."

I nudge him a little. "Want to throw it again?"

"What I want is to find your parents—to get you out of this damn birdhouse."

"And then what?"

He angles his head up at me. "What do you mean?"

"What happens after? We just go back to the way we used to be?" My voice is dubious.

Sky doesn't answer, but that's when I notice the blood creeping into his cheeks.

"Are you blushing?" I lift my brows. "You are!"

Sky raises a finger in warning. "Don't. Listen—" He pauses and drags a hand through his hair, groaning a little. "You're sixteen."

"That's middle-aged for girls nowadays."

"Not to your parents. And not to me. In any case, it won't matter."

"Why?"

Sky flares again. "Damn it, Serenity! What do you take me for? After all these years—" Pausing, he raises his hand to explain. "I couldn't stay. Your exhibits are bad enough. I could see where everything was going. Couldn't watch you with him like that. Knew it'd be too hard for me to keep my eyes in check."

Sighing, I reassure him, "Nothing happened. He kept his eyes closed the whole time like I asked."

"Got to give him points for his control."

Silence.

I bite my lower lip as I work out what to say next, then settle on a question. "How long would you wait?"

"As long as you want."

I wait a few moments before meeting his eyes, "Thank you for telling me."

"Will it make a difference?"

"It makes a difference to me." I settle closer to him without telling him about my bargain with Luc.

He leans over. Without saying a word, he cups the side of my head and urges it to his shoulder. I breathe in the familiar scent of him, wondering if all of him smells like this. If all of him feels like this. If it's possible to be closer than we ever have been.

"It's us, Sky," I tell him. "It's always been us."

Once more, his mouth tangles with mine. Hungry as a winter sun, Sky demands everything from me. His hands crowd my waist before he tugs on my hips, pulling me closer until I'm under him and he brings his full force down on me. Nothing but gold chains between us. Unchanging. Melt the gold down, grind it into dust, but it always stays the same, value never deteriorating. Leaning over, Sky kisses the peak of my shoulder, lips warm on the tattoo's cold silver. I don't shiver once. I'm a vessel to his flames. Lightning in a bottle knitting around his fire.

"Serenity." Sky stares at me like I'm a stag he's hunting. "I've held back from telling you everything. But I need you to listen *here*." He thumbs the side of my forehead. "Not here." He touches my chest where my heart beats. "Do you understand?" I nod, but it's not enough for him. "Swear it to me."

"I swear."

Searching me, he studies my eyes before pursing his lips and nodding. He takes my hand in his. "I know where Blackbird is… because I'm the one who took her."

Sky rises to stand. He produces a piece of paper from his pocket, then hands it to me. "She left this for you."

I unfold the note, ravenous to read her words.

> We're going to the Sanctuary. I can't believe it! I've never known if it was a ghost story the Temple used to frighten children or if it was the Promised Land. I'm hoping for something in between. Kyle is getting us out. I won't apologize for leaving so soon or not saying goodbye. I hate goodbyes. It's better this way. You'll have to learn to look out for yourself. I can't watch your back anymore. I've got someone else to protect now.

I'm glad Blackbird doesn't know Sky's real name. That he's used Kyle just like I used Alice.

"That child belongs to her." Sky jerks a thumb to the note.

The Aviary

"Seems like she should get to keep it, don't you think?"

I go to Sky, sealing my lips against his. It catches him off guard, but his strong arms wind around me, pressing me close. It's a hungry, mournful embrace—as though we're making up for all the time we will soon no longer have. Maybe our time is running out.

If we can't escape, I'm going to have to find a way to separate sex and love—which means breaking my own promise. Like my mother, I'll play the part. I'm already sewing the Swan into myself. I'm becoming what he wants me to be because I can bear it.

My mother can't bear another whip's lash. Her old wounds cannot be reopened without causing irreparable damage.

For my parents, I will become wholly Swan.

Twenty-three
FiReandWaTer

Upon returning to my room—Sky trailing behind me all the way—I catch the smear of black under my arm, realizing there is still a speckle of paint from Dove's handiwork earlier.

I wander into the bathroom to wash it away, then stare at myself in the far mirror. I'm too focused on my skin and washing away the paint to remember Blackbird's words.

Too focused to see the mirror off to my left opening, caving in on itself, and delivering the three Birds who have come for me.

It happens so fast I don't even get to scream.

They swoop down on me, fingernails pecking at my skin. They stuff my mouth with a rag so I can't speak. They will need more than that. Three girls are no match for me. They seem to recognize it when, instead of spitting out the rag, I bite down on it farther and peer at their necks, recognizing them from their colors, from their shapes—Cardinal, Parrot, and Robin.

Their six hands drag me from the bathroom and through the mirror.

"Oh, you're doing it all wrong!"

I whip my head around to see a familiar face that belongs to an equally familiar voice, but at the same time, one of the girls sprays my face with something. When the misty particles hit my nose, the chemical commands my body to sag and to bow. My mind floats somewhere in between reality and passing out. Not lucid enough to tell where they're taking me but enough to hear

The Aviary

the recognizable voice say something else:

"If you want something done right..." she warbles.

My head bobbles back when the three girls pick me up, carry me past the mirror, and shut it behind them while the ringleader leads them away.

All I can see is her hair, but it's all I need. I would know those ends of exalted purple anywhere.

Peacock.

Down, down, down they take me. My head topples forward so I can see nothing but stone steps, and I wonder what part of the Aviary this is. And how long before my implant raises an alarm due to my blood pressure spiking or heart rate accelerating?

Their voices sound like chiming bells in my ears. Peacock's is a kettledrum. What has she given me?

When they drop me, the dizziness clears, and my brazen hands get ready. I grab for the first thing I can find—their ankles. I bite down on the skin there, grin when I hear their Bird cries. I feel my nails tearing holes in their dresses. Finally, they pin me down and tie my hands behind my back with leather cord.

"Where are your pretty Swan wings now?" Peacock leers at me, eyes thinned to pin-width. In one hand, she holds a torch. "Look at me when I'm talking to you!"

One of the girls behind me propels my head back with a thrust. When she does, I spit straight into Peacock's face.

She flicks the spit off with her finger, growls. "You're going to wish you hadn't done that. When this is over, you'll be licking my feet, Swan."

I take in my surroundings. I'm in a circular stone room filled with Birds, about ten in all. Pigeon, Bluebird, and even Gull—shivering alone in the corner of the room, her nightmares still seeming to haunt her.

All around me, the sweet, sickening smell of incense curls in the air. As though purposely arranged in a sacrificial circle are torches, lit by blazing fire.

Peacock jerks her head to the girls in the corner of the room. "Bring the oil!"

Two girls advance toward me, beaming and pompous. Both carry two large pitchers.

"Dump it on her!" orders Peacock.

The girls oblige without hesitation.

The oil temporarily blinds me, marinating my hair, covering my shoulders. The thick, lazy liquid meanders into even the most forbidden places of my skin, rolling down my breasts, my underwear, between my fingers.

Peacock orders Cardinal to tug my head back so she can shine the torchlight on my face.

"So tiny." Peacock blows on the fire so it crackles a spark near my face. "Like a little bunting. How can you be the Swan? You're just a tiny white bunting with big breasts."

Oil oozes down the sides of my face, and I spit some of it out and force a laugh, "Jealous, pea*hen*?"

Peacock glares at me before commanding the other girls. "Light the oil around the circle."

One of them, Parrot, hesitates. "Maybe we shouldn't. I mean, maybe she's had enough. If Owl catches you—"

Peacock marches right up to Parrot. Slaps her hard on the cheek. "Shut your trap and do as you're told! I'm a High Bird; I can arrange you to have nothing but old men as clients for the next month. Light. The. Oil."

Shrinking away, Parrot moves to pick up the torch. Feebly, she lowers it to the ground, dipping the torch to the oil.

All at once, the fire rears up, yielding to the oil. It becomes a flaming circle, camping me in, rising to the height of my ankles.

Peacock dumps a little more oil just beyond the edges of the first circle so the fire inches closer to me. "Why don't you dance for me, Swan? Shake those pretty little feathers."

I fold my arms across my chest and shake my oil-logged hair, causing sparks to fly when the drops hit the flames.

"Careful now." Peacock waggles a finger. "Wouldn't want to get those pretty tail feathers burned, now would we? Where's all your precious water now?"

"That's your mistake! I am *so* much more than water, Peacock. I am fire and ice, water and electricity."

"Then, go through it," she dares me.

I laugh. "I'm not afraid of you. But I'm not stupid either."

All the other girls in the room start to glance at each other, and Peacock seems to realize that she needs to save face, so she pours more oil on the fire.

The flames gnash their teeth at me, only inches away. I can feel their warmth. I imagine for a moment what I would look like when it's all over. Like a black star exploded and left white cinders in its wake.

"You're the first one who got a moving exhibit. So, move!" Peacock says. She upends the container of oil, but there are only a couple of drops left.

The fire spreads.

"If the fire doesn't take you, the comas will. Just like Flamingo. Just like Finch. You don't deserve to be here. He just scraped you off the street. But *I* was born here. Just like my mother before me."

Fire is a fitting death for me, I suppose. Impetuous, passionate, feral.

Before I can even make sense of it all, Nightingale storms into the room, carrying two buckets of something. She dumps them over the fire, white powder raining like ash. All that is left of Peacock's smoldering circle is smoke and exhaust.

For the first time, I see Peacock shrink before someone else. Nightingale is regal. Other girls scramble toward each other in the wake of her crusading eyes.

She takes Peacock's hair in her fists, forcing the other Bird to her knees. Tears form in Peacock's eyes, and she whimpers.

Nightingale narrows her eyes at Peacock. "And while you've been wasting everybody's time here, Finch was *dying* up there."

Every single girl in the room, including Peacock, flinches.

I bow my head, heartbroken.

Because all I can think about is the little girl rusted away. And the last callous words I spoke to her.

NIGHTINGALE TAKES ME BACK UP the stairs after the rest of the girls have fled. Like terrified chicks, they flittered away at the news of another dead Bird. No wonder Luc didn't come for me. With his first ever hatchling dead…maybe he even turned off his interface. And Sky wouldn't have known anything was amiss.

"I'm going to stay with you for now," Nightingale says as she closes the mirror behind us.

Every inch of me smells like oil. I skid across the floor to turn on the shower as soon as I can, allowing the water to pour over me, even with the dress still on.

"Why did you do it?" I ask Nightingale, who is still in the bathroom.

She pays no attention to me. Her eyes are on her own reflection in the mirror, on the black dress she wears like fleshy sinew on her illustrious curves.

"I remember my first hazing," she says. "Before you, I was the one who showed the most promise."

Not once does she turn to look at me. Not even when I peel off the dress, rinse myself, yank the shower handle to the off position, and grab a towel to wipe my body dry.

"People came from miles away just to hear me sing. My exhibit was nothing like yours. Other than you, no one has ever *become* part of her exhibit."

Her eyes finally stray to mine in the mirror as I comb through my curls.

"They locked me in the Music Room when Owl was gone. The Music Room is spectacular, especially for someone with a gift like mine. I could see symphonies on the walls, all these ribbons and lights playing again and again. They dance when one sings. Anyway, after they locked me in there, they turned the music to blaring. And then, they turned it up louder. And louder. And… how can a Nightingale sing if she can't *hear*?" Nightingale stands up straight, staring dead-eyed into her reflection. "Owl found me there. The next day, I had a brand-new set of eardrums. It was like he resurrected me."

Nightingale tips her head to me. "Peacock couldn't get inside your head. Is there anything you're afraid of, Serenity?"

I narrow my brows. "How do you know my name?"

"You don't always see me. But I'm there." Nightingale turns slowly, feet skimming across the floor, which is slippery from oil.

"*You're* the one who pushed me down the stairs that first night."

Nightingale doesn't deny it. "And you took me with you. Then, you pushed yourself off the same stairs when Finch was going to be whipped."

With hands clutched at the edges of my towel, I back up against the shower. "Is that why you—"

"Changed my mind? Yes. It took some time, but yes. I couldn't hate you anymore, even though I tried. How do you feel?"

"I'm baking," I sarcastically joke about Peacock's flames, and I flutter a hand in front of my face.

Suddenly, the two of us are laughing. Real laughter, seasoned with understanding.

"You weren't afraid of them for a second, were you? Or the fire?"

I shrug. "Don't tell anyone." I cup one of my hands by my mouth like I'm telling her a stolen secret. "But my body's made of more water than normal people. Fire just won't catch."

"My voice can't even compare to what you do in your exhibit, you know," she says.

Stunned, I am grateful for the hard-won compliment. "Your song. My water. What's the difference?"

"Mine can be destroyed." Nightingale faces me, dark eyes bearing down, slaughtering me. "Mine will fade. You may have to find your gift, but you never can and never will lose it."

"What's your name?"

Nightingale looks up, a hint of a smile peeking through, but it fades when she glances at the floor. "She doesn't exist anymore. Just a scared, weak girl growing up in an orphanage who took a job in the Glass District to get away from the constant abuse she was in." She shrugs and presses her hands together, squares her shoulders. "Turns out, it's just the same there. But at least I got paid for it. If I was going to get raped anyway, I might as well get some money out of it."

Paid rape, I reflect. I wonder how many similar stories are out there. Mine is rare. Most girls are not like me. They're not getting kidnapped and dumped into the Glass District. Like Luc said, I've never had the grooming. Most girls do. Girls who feel like they have no other choice. Homeless girls, runaways, girls living from house to house like dominoes slow-falling, girls born in the Glass District and owned before birth…

How many of those same girls ended up here?

Suddenly, there's a realization that I don't have one of those stories. And I'm overwhelmed by relief…and guilt.

Finch's body is laid in a glass casket for all of us to see. Tonight, everyone wears black except for Finch, who is clothed in a white shift. A bed of roses bears her casket, and a circle of white daisies crowns her head. In death, her curls seem to have regained their splendor, all spread around her petite body like a circus of copper-gilded lights.

This is all new to me since I wasn't at Flamingo's funeral.

Next to me, at the head of Finch's coffin, stands Luc. He doesn't know about the hazing, and Nightingale will keep my secret, take it to her grave of black-winged melodies.

Tonight, only one thing is a silver lining. After what Peacock said about Finch and how Nightingale confronted her got out, Peacock's popularity ebbed, rolled out with the tide.

Raven is the first to place her feather on top of the coffin. Each Bird will give their own feather, gifts provided to them by the Owl. Each one is silk, so it will last longer. In my hands, I carry the only white feather, and when my turn comes, I hesitate. After my last words to Finch, it seems pitiful, unworthy, to add my feeble feather to the tapestry of others.

Luc regards me with sinking brows. With my hand limp at my side, I drop the feather to the floor and say to Finch, "My feather doesn't deserve you. It never did."

Whispers crush the air until Luc silences them, then dismisses everyone but me in short order. The entire time the Birds flutter to the stairs to go back up to their rooms, my eyes don't once leave Luc's. I want to show him I'm ready for whatever words will follow.

The first thing he does is walk around the coffin. Then, he kneels and picks up my feather. He nestles it into the featherbed resting on top of the glass. Folding his hands behind his back, he turns to face me. "What happened to Finch is not your fault. She was poisoned," he says. "Her food was poisoned."

I trip over his words in my head. Where Luc's revelation was supposed to bring relief, it does the opposite because I remember something. Finch stole *my* food. I lean over the casket, gasping in a breath before crunching into a ball beneath it.

The Aviary

I cry into my arms until Luc raises me up.

"Swan—"

"Don't you get it?" I ask. "You painted a target on me, Luc. The other girls… That poison was meant for me. She ate *my* food at dinner that night."

"I know."

"You *know*?"

"I did not know about the poison until I tested all the food from that dinner. I know it was meant for you. But *you* are here."

That's when it dawns on me. I tear myself from his grip. "You're glad! You're glad she died instead of me!"

Luc doesn't let me escape. He pins my arms, backing me against a glass wall. "I'm glad you are still alive, not glad Finch is dead. There is a difference."

I won't look at him.

"I will tell you what you are. You are my Swan." His thumbs leave shivers on my cheeks. "You are unlike any other Bird. You have something inside you that is different. You will never lose it because it's lightning. Don't you see that you're the only one who can light the fire in my soul?"

Before Luc can close the tiny gap between us, I summon all my strength, shove him away, rush for the stairs, and climb them two at a time. At the top, I turn back to where Luc is standing, smiling at me, but not following. Because he knows I understand now. I understand how well he sees me.

All this time, Luc wasn't just peeking into the window of my soul; he's shattered the glass. In this short spell of time, he's come to recognize what has taken a lifetime for Sky. Which means he's invading my heart, pushing Sky out, and possessing me.

Back in my room, I take out my mother's journal. It's the only thing keeping me sane, grounded.

Serenity is like a hurricane in a bottle. I wish she could go to school. I wish she could play with other children. But she doesn't have the identification chip they insert in all infants at birth. No papers showing her existence. No certificate of birth. I can't take the risk of her DNA tracing back to Force. I must keep her hidden. But I wonder how long she can go on like this. And I wonder how long Sky will be strong enough to endure her. Could anyone else ever manage?

Twenty-four
GuLl

*W*HEN I CUT MYSELF OFF from the rest of the world, my room becomes my drug.

All night long, I remain wrapped in my sheets, curled up in the alcove, staring at the gardens. Not once do I leave the window ledge.

I finish reading my mother's journal, in hopes I will be able to piece her scattered thoughts into some sort of advice I can follow.

> That night, he used the riding crop, the whip, and the spurs. He stockpiled my bruises, opened my skin like it was a cache, spilling my blood. I remember I felt warm before my muscles stopped working and went limp.
>
> I came close to death. But when I awoke the next morning in a Centre bed, both death and life were closer than ever before. Because that was the first time I saw Kerrick.

From what I know of my "father," he found my mother one morning passed out after the Vampire sucked almost all her blood away. Before my father was a security guard, he was a nurse. He did more than just rescue her; he healed her.

My mother told pretty stories to protect me, but in the process, she failed to properly prepare me for anything in this life. And even though she spent her whole life trying to hide me from the world, and hide the world from me, she didn't protect me, from life *or* death.

The Aviary

After reading through the journal for hours, I stand up and make for the door. Sky doesn't try to stop me. He must know I need to escape. He follows me wordlessly, keeping guard, even if I can see his neck muscles flexing with the desire to simply pick me up one-handed and deposit me safely back in the room.

Instead, he gives me some space and lets me go to the Nest wing, where all is quiet because it's the wee hours of the morning. Except for Finch's coffin, which screams at me, accuses me. The poison was meant for me. No possible way for me to guess, considering the enemies I've made here.

They will take Finch's body away tomorrow. She will be burned so she can truly fly away, and her ash will become like magical gray ships sailing her to silver shores. Just like my mother, I use my own pretty stories to cope.

"I'm sorry, Finch," I whisper.

Then, I hear the cry. It transforms into a wail.

The Bird's cry echoes through the hallway of the Aviary somewhere near the staircase. If she reaches the stairs, will she fall? Those stairs have felt too many bodies tumble.

Her next wail crawls into my very heart. Makes a bed there.

That's when I glance up to see her, wandering the edges of the staircase, in her gray nightgown, nightmare-drenched cry, tears wetting her cheeks, eyes closed and blind to the stairs. Gull.

Swifter than swan's wings, I race toward her. I reach her just in time, catching her in my arms before she can fall. Though she's thinner than me, she takes me down, her body crumpling into mine as we stumble to the floor.

When Gull opens her eyes, there's more black and white than anything else. Pupils dilated so much, they accent the whites of her eyes, drowning out the gray of her irises. At first, she thrashes against me, but when she senses my arms around her, Gull shuts down. Her skin cracks, letting some of my care seep into her. Suddenly, she's grasping for me, arms around my neck, fingers kneading my dress, face pressing into my chest above my beating heart. Yielding, I coil my arms around her till I've practically swaddled her body. She curls into a terrified fetal position.

I smooth away her hair, permanently dyed gray for her exhibit. But I freeze when I find the bruises. When I tug the long sleeve of her dress down the curve of her shoulder only to discover more bruises riddled all across her forearm, I gnash my teeth. Seemingly ashamed of them, Gull pushes the fabric up farther and nestles closer into my chest.

"Gull." I wrap my arms around her once more, whispering in the still darkness, "You're going to come back to my room to sleep. All right?"

Her head flicks to mine, and she begs me in a whimpering voice, "Don't leave me."

"I won't leave you." Not after Finch. I can't deny how selfish this is. How Gull is the balm to my crater-sized Finch wound.

I can't carry her, but I don't have to. Just behind us, I hear footsteps and turn to see Sky jerking into action. He rushes toward us as I try to lift Gull, but she buckles again. Without a word, Sky hoists her into his capable arms. I bite down on my lower lip, admiring how safe his arms look as he carries her back to my bedroom. He's not possessive of her the way I imagine Luc would be, because to Sky, Gull is just a girl, a human being. Not a commodity.

Once we arrive, Sky lays her in my bed. I crawl in beside her, then pull the covers around us both and kiss her eyelids. Sky disappears outside the bedroom door to give us space.

Never have I shared a bed with anyone but Sky. Nightmares were frequent when I was little, and he'd let me snuggle with him in his bed. But that was many years ago. Now, I am the protector.

Trembling, timorous, scarred Gull. I think about how arrogant it is of Luc to think he knows everything, and can control everything, that happens in this place. Like so many girls in the Glass District, Gull is scarred from crude client hands, from their hungry fingers. Where is he now when she needs him? Probably meeting with the Guild, I imagine.

Sky creeps back into the room after a few minutes. Under his watchful gaze, I fall asleep. I dream of breaking the fingers of Gull's abuser, one by one, by one, by one.

SOMETIME DURING THE NIGHT, I feel Gull shift in bed, and I kiss her cheek. By now, she's calm, and she poses a question. "Will you sing me something?"

I shrug. "I'm not very good at singing. At all."

"I don't care. Sing me a lullaby."

"Trust me, you don't want to hear my voice. How about I tell you a story?"

I select a random fairy tale. One beginning with darkness and blood but ending with hope and chiming bells. As I tell it, I ponder this girl, tinier than me, with a broken soul so determined to get to its knees and keep on breathing, so determined to piece itself back together after it has been cracked one too many times. She is so much younger than I am, and so much older at the same time.

"Did they live happily ever after?" she asks when I finish the story.

I nod. "Yes, they did. They still are."

Gull turns on her side, curling her body toward me with her hand tucked under her chin. "I'll tell you a story, too, Swan. My mother was really pretty. Prettier than me—she told me that. She told me I'd never be good for anything other than the Glass Districts. She and my stepfather trained me from an early age. It was training, but my stepfather took a piece of me with him. And every time I go into a client room, they take pieces of me with them, too."

I wonder how much is left of Gull, after so many men have taken so many pieces. How small can a soul shrink and remain intact? Can it ever hope to grow back to the size it's supposed to be? Not here. Glass walls and soft feathers and hurtful hands are no fertile soil. Gull is more nightmare than dream.

She takes hold of my hand, then squeezes my fingers so tight they whiten. I try not to cry when I listen because I know she's dying to tell someone, *anyone*, who will listen.

She licks her dry lips, then shrugs. "Swan, will you fly away for me? Promise?"

I promise her all the while, knowing I've chosen to sacrifice myself for my parents. Because I'm stronger than my mother. Nothing will stop me from keeping her out of the Temple. The most I can hope for is to stay here in the Aviary. Forever.

I wake with the scent of Gull all around me. Like seawater brine. I almost expect to hear ocean waves if I press my ear to hers.

Late morning sunlight streams through the windows, warming the room, and I'm covered in sweat from the extra body heat. I twist my head around but see no one. Not Sky or Luc or Dove.

Something must have happened.

It's not too difficult to get out of bed without disturbing Gull. She's had so many sleepless nights, it's time for her to catch up. And there's something I need to do today, especially since Gull will have an exhibit later.

Without bothering to change from my white nightgown, translucent from all the sweat, I throw on a robe and hurry to Luc's room.

To my great surprise, it opens when I knock. Luc's hair reminds me of a dark teabag, all wrung and rotten and sticking to his face. So different from how it always is—swept back and soft as sighs. His eyes are burdened with grief.

When he closes the door and his fingers seek my cheeks, I don't flinch or pull away. He looks like he hasn't slept all night. My grief clings to his, as his forehead kneels against mine. I feel his lips with my own, his numb mouth bearing down on mine. He drags his mouth to my chin, lingering on my neck, hovering above the Swan charm at the base of my throat. Then, he places one hand against the door behind me, flattening it on the glass while dropping his head to the floor, eyes pinched shut, pained.

Drawing me into him, his one arm coils around my waist and urges me farther into the main room, a mirror copy of my own.

I don't ask yet what his trouble is, and he doesn't give me an answer until we reach the bedroom and I see her.

Raven's body rests in the center of his bed. Hands folded over her stomach. Hair spread around her like a dark raiment. Sick, artificial lights shroud her skin, turning her lips so blue it's like melancholy made its home there. No wonder he didn't respond to Gull or me last night.

"Raven." I touch a finger to her arm, struck by how cold it is. "How long has she been here, Luc?"

"I found her after you ran from me. It's the only reason I didn't follow."

"You've been with her since? All night and all morning?" I almost trip on the words, feeling his body suddenly warm against my back.

"And a meeting with my father to notify him of the situation. I love my Birds, Swan." He rubs his eyes. "And I am losing them. I've interrogated the staff. I've checked every inch of my property for security breaches. I've performed room searches. Though I have access to the security feeds, some have been tampered with. If an outsider was hurting anyone in this building, I'd have discovered it by now. It can only mean…"

"One of the Birds," I finish.

Cupping my shoulders, he shifts me around to look at him. "What will happen if I lose you?" His knuckles rub my arm, along the fabric of the thin robe.

"Oh, Luc." I have to raise myself high on my tiptoes so I can kiss his lips, just once, and then I plead, "It's time to let her go. She and her sister are finally together now. Let them both go. There are others here who need you."

He shields one side of his face with his hand. "You alone matter most to me."

I shake my head. "You are *not* allowed to do that. I won't let you!"

"In spite of our bargain?" Now, his brows knit low, creating shadows of doom above his eyes. "I know about your fall with Gull last night. But I also know what happened in the basement. When will you listen to me and forsake this fruitless quest for friendship? It doesn't exist in museums."

Luc tries to take my face in his hands. "You are my Swan now. You agreed to that the moment you asked your favor. They are fowl compared to you."

The lightning inside me practically singes my blood.

"Stop it! Stop talking about them like that! If you would stop pretending for once! Stop pretending they're wings and feathers and beaks, nothing but pecking, pecking, *pecking*! Damn you, Luc, they are *girls*! Girls with thoughts and dreams and desires and heartbeats!"

He steps toward me, but I jerk back and throw my hands in the air. "Maybe if you look at them once, if you take your eyes off me, you'll see *them*! You'll see that Mockingbird needs one ounce of your attention. You'll see that Peacock needs more time in her exhibit—not in the client rooms. And you'll see the bruises on Gull's body because that's what gives her nightmares every damn night!"

Luc doesn't need more, but I do. My lightning is ready to set a forest on fire. Every emotion that has been stirring in me since the moment I was stolen from the hotel—since I spent an entire day and night thinking I would spend the rest of my life as a Breakable in the Glass District; since Luc bought me for his Aviary and then bought and sold my heart so many times since then I've lost count—every emotion since then seems to hit me all at once. It feels like a fire ready to burst forth from the chest. It all comes out as fury.

Fury toward him but fury toward myself. For not seeing these girls as they truly are. Not dolls. Not broken. No, in many ways, they are more whole than I am. Stronger than me. Beautiful no matter what.

I launch a chair at Luc's wall mirror, pick up one of the fragments, and hold it against the soft flesh of my wrist. He steps toward me.

"If you care about me—*me*, not Swan—you should care about each one of them." I blackmail him with one prick, one drop of blood. "Swan might be a part of me, but I'll always be Serenity. And Serenity cares about each and every one of them, too."

Luc tries to advance, but I push the edge of the glass down farther, so he stops, eyes creasing. "Of course I want all my Birds safe. I care for their protection and well-being more than anything."

"You want to protect them; you want them safe. But you don't *care*," I accuse him. "Caring requires love, and love requires effort *and* emotion." If he really cared about them, if he had any honor, he'd let them go. Take them to the Sanctuary. Give up this…life. Give them better lives.

"I care for *you*." There is a rabid desperation about his voice.

I lick my lips. "Luc, just put us aside for one minute. *Please*. I'm just like them. Just a *girl*."

He hangs his head and sighs, bringing two desperate fingers to rub his eyes. "Not to me."

I drop the shard of glass.

The Aviary

I don't expect him to reach out, to grab me by the arm. Nor does he expect me to slip out of my robe and leave it—and my anger—behind with him while the rest of me runs back to Gull.

When I enter my bedroom, Gull is stirring.

"Time to wake up, sleepyhead." I nudge her.

She stretches her arms, rubs one of her eyes, and then seems to register everything that happened the night before. Then, to my surprise, Luc swings open the bedroom door.

Gull shrinks into my arms, her body crumpling in shame. I keep one hand tight around her, sheltering and safeguarding her. At first, Luc's eyes are dark like thunderheads, but when he stops and really looks at the gray-haired girl whimpering in my arms, his eyes swell—wider than I've ever seen them before.

He steps forward, approaches slower. "Gull." If anyone's voice can turn from ice to lace, it's Luc's. "Please don't be afraid of me. May I see?"

I push her just a little, and Luc takes the sleeve of her shoulder to pull aside the fabric. When he sees the bruises gaping back at him, he winces, flicks his eyes to me, and regards me with brows knit low.

I keep my head high, eyes stinging him.

He turns back to Gull. "Why didn't you come to me? Why didn't you use the panic button?"

Gull swallows. "He threatened me. And I didn't want to end up like Flamingo or Finch. People outside have heard the rumors, and he said the same would happen to me if I told."

"Listen to me." Luc eases a finger beneath her chin. "I will *not* lose another one of my Birds. Do you believe that? Do you trust me?"

Gull glances back at me, eyes gray like windswept water, and when she sees my convinced nod, she turns back to Luc and mimics the motion.

"Good." Luc takes her thin frame into his arms. "Come with me now. I will take care of this. I will take care of *you*."

I watch them walk away, believing him whole-heartedly. Until Gull is missing from her room that evening and I learn she's being prepared for her exhibit.

Twenty-five
RetriBution

ALL THE GIRLS IN THE Aviary are called to watch Gull's exhibit that night—an occurrence I've only ever been witness to once before, for my exhibit.

To protect the Swan's anonymity amongst the crowd, Dove gives me a white mask to wear that night. With no feathers, gems, or decorations, the mask won't draw attention while I remain on the second level where I can see everything from the holograph since only higher-ranking levels have sprite-light screens.

Gull is more magnificent in her meager body than ever before. A gray pigment paints her skin, a color that reminds me of rotten roses, dried and sapped just like she is.

Gull isn't supposed to be here. Not after what Luc saw. Why is she here with her hair gray as fog skirting the floor from the new extensions she wears? Artisans have stuck gull feathers in her hair. Netting is draped across her entire body as though she's a fish caught by sailors. Gray pearls decorate the rest of her skin—save the two gray oyster shells, no bigger than my fists, cupping her small breasts. With her arms positioned to reach for the glass, she looks like a siren rising from the ocean. Face haunted, heartbroken.

Gull receives more claims tonight than ever before.

Sickened by the rolling of the men's tongues along their lips as their eyes seek the flesh I cuddled alongside just hours earlier, I finally march down the stairs after most of the viewers have gone and confront Luc, who is addressing Gull's claimer. I don't rip off the mask. Instead, I let my eyes penetrate his with my disapproval.

The claimer briefly glances at me when I approach, but Luc dismisses him before I speak from behind the mask. "What the hell are you doing to her?" I hiss.

"My words won't be enough. I can only show you. After tonight, I hope you will trust me."

"There is only one person I will ever trust. And you can be sure that it's not you. After tonight, it will *never* be you."

I storm away, but Luc doesn't pursue me. His duty to his Aviary will always come first, but I can't stand by and watch. Instead, I return to my room to stare at the fish shimmying about their tank, wishing I could join their world for one moment. I've let my fickle heart conquer me again. I sucked down Luc's poison.

Hearing movement, I look behind me to see Dove picking up the mask I'd left in the entry hall. "The exhibit is over," she says. "An offer was accepted."

Indifferent, numb, I wander away from the tank and scoot onto the ledge. "I don't care."

"Yes, you do. I saw you leave the exhibit hall after you spoke to him. Sometimes," Dove says, sitting on the bench across from me, "Owl is a puzzlement."

"No, he's not." Shaking my head, I meet her gaze.

"You're curious about him, though, I can see it when you look at him. You have been from the moment you arrived. He confounds you, but he makes you feel whole at the same time."

"How do you know?"

"My gift is not only painting; it's also perception. Perhaps it will be a consolation to you if the Temple wins your auction. Then, you'll never see him again."

I can tell she's trying to sound casual, but I'm not buying it. Perplexed, I screw my brows together. "What do you know, Dove?"

"Director Aldaine met with his father in the wee hours of the morning. I don't know what they discussed, but I'm certain it had something to do with you."

Because she knows nothing about our bargain. At least Luc kept his word. I hope he was securing my parents' release at that meeting. No doubt convincing his father to keep the Swan here. With him. No auction will happen now.

I consider what my life would be like once I begin seeing clients. I'll have an Intimacy Room segregated from the routine client rooms. When I try to think of what it will feel like to share a bed for the first time, even with Luc, I cannot. Perhaps it's better to become a ghost, to fade into the background, to save my soul by sending it away.

"I guess I'll start seeing clients soon," I say.

"I'm certain they will preserve you as long as possible," Dove says. Her words are comforting. "They will show you to the world first." Luc will be the first client.

I want Sky to get me out. I want to break my word, my bargain with Luc. If we confirm my parents' release, maybe Sky could get me out before anything happens between Luc and me. If I can get outside these walls, Luc will become a memory. My word is not worth more than my dignity. We can all escape together, and things will be just like they were. Well…almost. I smile as I consider the prospect with Sky, but…give it some time.

"What if I don't go to the Temple? What if I stay here?"

Dove touches her fingertips to my curls. "It would please me. I have never painted on such a beautiful canvas before. I'm certain Owl hasn't either."

I nestle my chin onto my knees, tilt my head to the side.

The corners of Dove's lips curve into a smile. "I hadn't suspected it would happen so fast, but this place does break one down, doesn't it?" She pauses, but then muses, "You formed bonds here, attachments, assets just as I explained the first day. I thought it would be more difficult for you. I knew of Blackbird, but I wasn't aware of Gull until tonight. Everyone else respected your love for Finch. Who else? Certainly not Peacock. And I wouldn't suspect Nightingale. Mockingbird, perhaps?"

I shrug, thinking of the flighty girl who has shared my lunches, but who also twitters about the museum with no regard to anything beyond these walls; the one who knows all the secrets inside each glass hallway, but who chirps them just as effortlessly. She would've loved to unfurl herself for Luc that night she followed him.

"Mockingbird is just a twit, really. She just tries too hard to get attention." My stomach twists at the memory of seeing her with

Luc, removing her clothes for him.

She's attached herself to me, Luc had said.

"I see." Dove lifts an eyebrow, then folds her hands in front of her. "But there isn't anyone else you've grown attached to?"

Could she suspect Sky? I shake my head. "It doesn't matter. There's only one thing that matters now." My family's freedom.

Dove doesn't ask, nor do I offer.

I can only hope Sky will find a time to come to me alone again. No matter what, we will figure this out together. Like we always do.

"Serenity."

At first, I think it's Sky. It sounds like him. Insistent, urgent.

But as soon as his fingers stroke my cheek, I realize it's Luc. He rouses me from my sleep, his arm curling behind to lift me from the bed.

"You must come with me now." Luc coaxes me to my feet. "I will carry you if I have to."

"I'm tired," I pipe up before closing my eyes again. "I don't want to go anywhere with you."

"Then, I will have to carry you. There's something you must see."

"Another exhibit?"

"Something like that." Luc gathers me up into his arms.

I slump against his shoulder, lean my head into his neck to breathe his skin; it smells like winter—fresh and crisp. When I hear his pleased snigger, I stop. Instead, I focus on my surroundings, how he leads me down the staircase and onto the moving walkway, out of the Nest wing and to the second level of the Exhibit rooms.

I don't open my eyes until he announces in a soft voice, "We're here."

There, in the center of the hall, is Gull's exhibit.

But there is a man inside, and he is clearly trapped.

Luc eases me to the floor.

"Gull?" Luc calls.

Dressed in her simple gray shift with feet bare, Gull emerges from one of the dark corners of the room to stand beside me. She shivers, but I can't join her, can't touch her. Frozen between the world of standing and sitting, it's all I can do to stay on my knees because I know what's to come.

Luc stands before the display just like he stood before the graphickers that fateful night he turned them to bloodied pulp and sizzled flesh. Beside me, Gull is unaware of what's coming as Luc enters the exhibit room. No gun in his hand tonight. Through the exhibit speaker, we can hear every word Luc says from beyond the glass.

"Do you know why you're here?" he questions Gull's abuser.

"For my private exhibit room, just like you said. I won the claim, didn't I?"

"Yes, you did," Luc says. "And tonight, you win the honor of being part of the display. You will become part of an incredibly special showing tonight."

"Is that so?" The man stands against one glass wall, arms folded, apathy coloring his features.

"Yes." Luc closes the glass door behind him, unbuttons the cuffs of his sleeves, and rolls them up his forearms. "Tonight, you get the opportunity to try to hit someone who hits back."

And before the man can assume a defensive position, Luc swings his fist—a strong uppercut to the man's jaw, sprawling him on the glass floor. But Luc doesn't wait for the man to get up. Nothing about the Aviary director indicates he fights with anger. To him, this is business. Pure violence —a means to an end. Retribution. Just like his contract killing in the past. A way to maintain control in his Aviary.

Except I am here, too. This is also Luc's effort to satisfy *me*. To prove me wrong.

Seizing him by the hair, Luc crams the abuser's face into the glass wall. The glass doesn't crack, but the man's nose certainly does. Blood gushes from his nose while Luc beats at the rest of him over and over and over again. The man is beyond the point of screaming; he is simply crying now.

Luc glances at me once, and I can see the memory of my damning words flashing in his eyes. And then, Luc erupts. He slams his fist into the man's mouth—a few of his teeth eject. Luc lands another punch, and I hear a sickening crunch.

Mania wracks Luc's body now. Taking the man's arm in his powerful hands, he twists until it cracks and hangs loosely from its socket.

It is like some vicious, graceful dance I don't want to interrupt, but I know only I have the power to do it. And by now, Gull has crumpled with her fingers pressed to the glass, crying, sobbing.

"Luc!" I call, rising from my knees.

Gull watches the massacre inside her exhibit, watches as her abuser's blood swims in rivulets along the glass floor.

"*Luc!*" I pound on the glass.

Pausing, he drops the man's other arm. It takes him longer to face me. After he opens the exhibit door, Luc shoves the man to the floor. He pauses, eyes remaining on the man but fingers summoning the Aviary interface. Security guards appear seconds later and seize the man, dragging him beyond the doors of the main hall.

When Luc finally turns around to face Gull with blood-covered hands and swollen knuckles, it is she who runs while I remain.

"Go after her," Luc urges, with a motion of his head toward the staircase. "She'll need you. She doesn't understand."

"I wish you'd done it for her," I say, taking a step toward the stairs.

"It wasn't for either of you. It was for him. Maybe now you'll see I am willing to go to any lengths to protect them. You're right—caring for them requires love. Something I've neither felt nor made the choice to feel—not until now."

For a moment, I only stand there frozen, allowing his confession to sink in. Then, I march toward Luc, smothering the air between us.

I close my eyes, touch my palm to his, and savor in the smear of blood wetting my fingers. He grabs my other hand. Luc doesn't need an apology. For him, I can see that this is enough. His hands crowd my cheeks, fingers leaving blood smears on my neck, and when his mouth bears down on mine, I kiss him back for the first time. Not to win his trust, not holding anything back, but because I truly want to.

He tastes like dark water, feels like frosted glass, smells like salt and iron, and he plunges his ice deep into my heart while his hands reach up to capture the back of my head, pulling me closer.

Hearing those words, sensing his claim sealing itself around my heart, his hands possessing my body, I know for certain he's kept his word and convinced his father to keep me here. Luc will be my first.

After the kiss becomes overwhelming, he releases me to Gull.

I find her cowering by my door. Sky is watching her, but waiting for me as always. At the sight of the blood on my face and hair, he angles his head, worried. Once he realizes the blood is not mine, he seems to relax. Even as he resumes his vulture-like stance, confusion dots his eyes.

Opening the door, I lead Gull into the bedroom where Sky follows. I almost want Gull to leave so he and I can talk, but when I see the way she caves in on herself, the way she shivers, I take pity on the girl. First, I wipe my face and hair as best I can before lifting the sheets to snuggle beside her.

Pressing her hand to mine, she traces the tips of my fingers, which still have a few blood smears. She doesn't pause at the blood. Her fingers drift across it, pondering, like she's hoping her own fingers can taste it like mine.

"It didn't make a difference," she whispers in the still of the room.

I shake my head. "Not to you."

"For you, right? I was hoping it was for me. But when he came out, covered in blood, and only had eyes for you, I knew."

"That's why you ran away," I say, realizing. "Then why are you here, talking to me?"

Gull shrugs, nudging me with her elbow. "Your bed's warmer than mine."

Rolling my eyes, I chuckle a little. "That's actually impossible, considering it's a lot bigger. The more space there is, the less warm it is at night."

"Unless there's another body inside it. At least it doesn't smell like nightmares."

I straighten, listening in the dark. "And how do nightmares smell?"

"Like sweat. Dried sweat."

The Aviary

I shake my head. "No, I happen to be an expert at nightmares. Sweat is a good thing. That's the smell of your body fighting the nightmare. The real nightmare sounds and smells sweet like harps and honeysuckles. That's when you know the nightmare is about to begin. And all you can do is hope your body's strong enough to make your mind wake up."

"Mine doesn't do a very good job," Gull complains.

"Give it time. Your body doesn't do so well when it runs off so little sleep."

Gull groans. "And how can it sleep when it keeps having nightmares to worry about?"

"Mmm." Leaning my head against the bed frame, I reflect. "If we were in my kingdom, I'd give you my magical sleep potion. I made it myself out of rose water and stardust."

"And where is your kingdom?" Gull asks, playing along.

I think of my imaginary island, but Gull needs more than that tonight. She needs a bit of magic to hang onto. "Far across the sea, there's an island hidden by fog so thick no one can sail through it. And if the fog wasn't enough, high cliffs surround the entire island. There's only one magical door through the cliffs, and it can't be opened by anyone but the fairy godmother."

Darkness dims the room as the moon peeps from behind the clouds, shedding a glow into the bedroom. Gull mimics my movement of leaning back, and little by little, her legs unwind themselves from her chest, loosen until they relax. "How does she decide who can come in?"

"Anyone who wants to enter must perform an impossible service to prove themselves worthy. It can be anything from dredging up a cup of salt straight from the sea without a drop of water, or singing a beautiful song without even opening your mouth."

"Those are impossible. How can anyone get in?"

I cross my arms across my chest. "The only other people she lets in are those born with fairy blood. Like me," I tease.

"You're definitely not a Bird. That's for sure." Gull straightens, then touches my back. "If you're a fairy, where are your wings?"

"Oh, I don't bring them out too often." I wave a hand in the air. "It's such a chore."

"If you ever do grow wings, will you promise to fly me away

from here?"

Stopping, I stare down at Gull. All this time, I thought it was just pretend. In the beginning, it was. Pretend to behave. Pretend to be his Swan. Pretend to smile. Now, it's more. I've become part of this glass birdhouse. Even if I leave here, I'll take it with me. I'll carry the Aviary like a scar on my heart forever. I'll carry Luc like a brand.

Gull is too scarred. Too broken, like a chipped cup once silver-plated porcelain. What I must look like to her, with the dreams I wear on my skin like sparkles. Am I sure enough to close my hand around hers? Am I strong enough to chase her nightmares away?

I ease my arm around her waist, lean my head against hers, and whisper, "Yes, Gull. I'll fly you away from here."

IN THE MORNING, I DON'T wake to the smell of Gull. It's late, and as usual, Sky is no longer here. If he watches me all night, he gets a few hours of sleep before joining me after lunch.

Since discovering the poison, Luc prepares and brings me food himself. No more Birds at breakfast. Today is different. Today, he eats with me.

Ignoring the bird ambience and how sprite-light swans sweep the air above our heads, I slip a thin white robe over my nightgown and join him at the table, briefly glancing out the window. Tossing my hair, which is even wilder in the morning, especially with traces of bloodstains I missed, I notice how different Luc looks today. Nothing left of the man from the previous night, but there's still an air of satisfaction in his eyes. In the morning, they seem bluer. Robin's eggs basking in sunlight.

"Did you send her away?" I ask.

"Who?"

"Gull." I reach for one of the white biscuits, spreading strawberry preserves in its fluffy bosom.

Luc dips a spoon into a small bowl of grits and raises it to his mouth, pausing just to say, "Gull is enjoying a well-earned reprieve with a visit to town."

"Hmm..." I help myself to the chilled peach soup and ricotta-smothered eggs. "I'm surprised I don't remember her getting out of bed."

"No dreams last night?" Luc asks. I shake my head, and he nods in confirmation. "Then, you slept well. And I can see you are famished from it." He sips from a pewter coffee cup with an attachment, so it will refill itself.

I don't notice how quickly I've gobbled up the biscuit, but I reach for a cinnamon roll as big as a baby's head. Nibbling first on flakes of icing, I finish it under a minute and start on the peach soup.

"Are you going to eat that?" I motion to the last biscuit on the plate.

Laughing, Luc shakes his head and offers it to me. "Though she be but little, she is fierce."

"I always thought Shakespeare was a little convenient," I muse.

He folds his hands, quirking a brow appraisingly. "Explain."

"Take *Romeo and Juliet*—two children die because of love, and their families join together in peace." I lather strawberry preserves on the biscuit till it's more red than white. "As if that could make people change so easily."

"Can a heart change?"

I press my lips thin and tight. "Some, maybe. But in general, people don't change."

"And your basis for comparison?"

"Generations of this…" I motion a hand to the air, to the atmosphere of the Aviary. "They just get worse."

"I thought we were past all this."

I sample half the biscuit in one bite, speak through the pieces. "I'm not saying this place is the *worst*, Luc. I'm just saying *worse*."

"What do you believe is the worst? What is your deepest fear in this world?"

I suppose this is our question swap today.

You I almost say aloud, but I keep my thought to myself because Luc is a different sort of fear than the other. A unique fear altogether, not just because of what it means for me but because of what it means for Sky and me.

Staring at my plate, I speak a simple answer. "The Temple."

Luc shakes his head. "There's more to that answer." He opens his palm, gesturing to me. "What is underneath that fear?"

"Force." I speak his name like a dagger.

Luc nods. "Your father." Just after I narrow my brows, he explains, "The lost Temple daughter has always been an urban legend in the Families circuit. But those with closer connections to the Syndicate know its truth. Aviary DNA tests are logged into the national system, scanned for biological matches. But you aren't afraid of him. Your anger is too palpable."

"He's a monster."

"You know I would never let you fall into his hands. But I'm still detecting the fear in your eyes. Tell me," he urges me.

Sinking my face into my hands, I rub my eyes before succumbing. "Losing myself completely to the Swan."

"And why can't the two unite—you and the Swan?"

I close my eyes. "I don't think that's possible."

Luc stands up from the table. He circles my chair before he kneels down, cups my knee, and reaches up to touch my cheek. "If there is anyone in this world who can become one with both, it is you. What is your favorite Shakespeare?"

That is another question but a small one, so I respond, chin high. "Macbeth."

Luc smiles knowingly. "Look like the innocent flower…" he quotes, "…but be the serpent under it."

I lean forward. "Not bad, but I prefer 'Stars, hide your fires; Let not light see my black and deep desires.'"

Luc pats my knee. "I am fond of Hamlet. A rich, intelligent prince driven mad by a ghost."

I see the parallel, but I choose to expound, "No, not a ghost. But a demon. The demon of his guilt for a past death he could not control and the sin he could."

Luc bristles once, but then, his eyes soften, understanding. "I owe you an apology for the Isolation Room, and for your punishment above the client rooms. I'm sorry, Serenity."

For a minute, I am stunned into silence.

"It was the safest option you had at the time," I say finally. "I understand why you *thought* you had to do it." There is a distinction between "thought" and "had to do it".

"Yet, there is no safe option left for you now. You're not safe from anyone here. Not from my Birds or my Family or the Temple who wants to possess you. Nor are you safe from all the claimers at the auction."

His thumb rubs my cheek, but I pull away. "What are you talking about?" I demand. "What auction?"

Luc rises to confront me. "The claims for you are vast. They are numberless. Middle class, politicians, dignitaries, foreign diplomats, even royalty—no rank is untouched. The Temple has staked a claim on you. My father has spoken with Director Force. He's seen every one of your exhibits."

As soon as he speaks the name, I scramble out of my chair, and get my hands on it. But Luc forces it out of my hands, back to the glass floor. It scrapes and squeals like the shrill cry of a swallow. Both of us bend over it, heads almost brushing, eyes contesting with one another's, but his height and muscles overpower mine.

"You gave me your word!" I seethe, but he flings the chair away.

"None of it matters."

"It matters to me! What now?" I struggle against him. "Are you too gutless to so much as try?"

I try to escape, but Luc holds me fast. He pens me in with his arms around my waist. Sky would be smart. He would pin me to the floor, stop my whole body even if it meant pinning me under his. Luc has much to learn; my legs and my head are unencumbered.

I use them both, thrusting my head into his nose. He doubles over from the pain.

"I should've known everything was a lie," I say. "I should've known you'd break your word."

Why had I believed him? Because of my stupid heart. Fickle, formidable foe.

Luc wipes at the blood dribbling from his nose before he marches toward me. From his tapered brows to the slits of his eyes, he is a force to be reckoned with, and he's going to show me. Show me that once again, he's the master of this birdcage.

With him like this, I am weaponless.

When his mouth comes down on mine, Luc ignites the fuse inside me. He tempts my mouth to open but then pulls back to stare at me, leaving my stomach on a cliff's edge.

"Careful," he warns. "I've shown tremendous patience with you. I've earned the right to keep secrets from you, and any plans I choose. I earned that right the day I slaughtered for you. Your life is not your own. Only your heart and your soul belong to you. I can help myself to one but never the other."

Like a ravenous beak, my nails ransack the skin of Luc's cheek, down to his neck, savoring the blood there and the rewarding curse from his mouth. At the sight of my handiwork, I smile just before Luc palms his cheek and moves ever closer.

I crouch, waiting. "I can do this all day, Luc," I beckon in a sultry voice, smile curling my lips as I rock on the balls of my feet. "And you're wrong. You can't have one without the other."

I am more than my body. I am more than skin and nerves and hormones all strung together. I am heart and spirit, mind and soul, feelings and choices. I am not just a girl. I am a human being. And it is because of that that I am worth something.

For one moment, he pauses, stops to let his gaze travel across the bare parts of my skin. He shakes his head, wry grin lifting his lips. "Where did they make you?"

"Now, you're asking the right questions."

We're so preoccupied with one another that neither of us notices Dove stepping into the room with a fresh set of white dresses in her hands.

"Excuse me." She nods to him after stopping short when she sees us. "Am I'm interrupting something?"

"Take the dresses to her bedroom," Luc orders, and Dove obediently departs. He shakes his head at me. "What am I going to do about you?"

"No one knows what to do about me." Glaring, I drop my arms. "Not even you."

Even as I turn my back to him and retreat to join Dove, I know it's a lie. All a lie, because there is one person in the world who knows what to do with me.

Twenty-six
My FaTe

"WHAT ARE YOU DOING HERE?" Sky asks after trailing me to the waterfall, the liquid guardian that protects our voices.

Dusk has already purged daylight and sunset. It gnaws on my heart in the wake of my failure—the auction will go forward. Luc won't stop it. He won't go against his father, his Guild Family. Soon, I will be the property of the Temple, and my father will have won.

"I failed, Sky," I confess.

Sky was right all along. I can't blame Luc for everything. What he roused within me, what the Aviary itself promoted…I let it all unravel me. Somewhere along the line, pretending became real. Instead, I held onto the Swan's wings and let her carry me away.

Sky doesn't bother sitting down. "There are things I can't tell you yet, but we're almost there. I just need you to be patient a little longer."

"Almost where? We're not anywhere! My plan backfired. And I just keep getting myself in deeper and deeper."

Sky flexes his fingers and huffs. "So, he didn't keep his word?"

"He lied, just like you said he would. It was all just manipulation. But you have to get me out of here. I trust you to do that."

Sky grins wider than ever.

"I don't know how much longer I can stand this. I'm falling apart."

He shakes his head. "No, Serenity, you've impressed me. How

you talked back to Peacock, how you behaved at Finch's funeral, and the whole Gull thing..."

"Can you get her out, too? Like you did for Blackbird?"

"I don't know."

"Why?"

He crosses his arms over his chest and cocks his head to the side. "Too risky right now. 'Sides, I don't think she'd go. Some girls are too...*used* to the cage. More afraid of what's outside than inside."

I press my lips tighter than the skin of a berry, tears forming. "I hoped we could. Just. Try."

Forcing the tears back, I change the subject. "I'm surprised you didn't get in trouble for not protecting me enough during the Peacock incident. For leaving me alone."

"You and Nightingale both agreed not to tell anyone. So, how do you think Luc found out?"

So, it was Sky! Luc must've rewarded him for the knowledge.

"How did *you* know about it?"

Sky leans against the wall, dipping his hand into the falls, spraying my hair more. "I know everything. I know you inside and out. And I've always believed the inner you is more beautiful than anything outside."

If I try to answer, my voice will break. Sky is the only one to see the real Serenity. Whatever power I felt I had in the exhibits was all an illusion. They could never see the girl behind the Swan. All anyone could ever see was their own fantasy. A fantasy I chose to be.

When Sky presses a finger to his head, it's obvious he's getting a message from his security ear implant.

"Luc's father just arrived in the Aviary."

"What's he doing here?" I ask.

"Private meeting. Things may be *changing*. I need to take you back now. We'll have to finish this conversation later. Meet me at the lake after the Guild leader is gone."

SKY THINKS I'M ASLEEP IN my bedroom, but the secret passage behind my mirror provides me with a prime opportunity to sneak out of my room unnoticed as it connects to the room next to mine. So I can eavesdrop on Luc and his father's conversation. I have to know.

Despite the fact I haven't eaten since lunch, my appetite has thinned to nothing. So, I don't envy the meal served during their discussion.

"Very well, son," I hear Luc's father say, sipping his wine. He thumbs the rim of the glass. "She has resurrected the Aviary. It's true. We have earned the Temple's envy, but we do not wish to make them an enemy. I am more interested in them becoming an ally—an affiliate. With Force's support, we could do so much more."

"She's only been here a month, Father. Think of how much farther I could take her."

"To what end? Yes, I'm certain even a royal would pay a tremendous sum and probably offer prestigious aid, connections, or strategic secrets to bed her. But afterward, her worth will diminish. I'm more interested in the long haul. I have too much invested in this auction already. It will not only gain us international attention, it will also secure our partnership with the Temple. We'll even be able to fund our own breeding line."

His words are throwing stars, sinking deeper into my chest with their hopelessness.

"You'll invite the world to see her, then." Luc seems to consider the notion, his fingers clenched.

The Guild leader eases his back to the side of the chair. "The world will fall to its knees. Once she reaches the Temple, her future will be in Force's hands. Either way, I trust you will ensure her last exhibit is sensational. Force enjoys usurping lofty bidders." He retrieves a cigar from his pocket, then slices off the end.

Deep inside me, a thousand serpents squirm, restless and hungering, snapping their fangs. If he doesn't stop talking soon…

"What if your own son was a bidder?" Luc asks. "What then?"

The Guild leader cocks his head in Luc's direction. "Not to worry, son. I've already spoken to Force regarding a Penthouse visitation. You will bed your Swan first. Afterward, he will use her for his own designs."

"Designs?"

"Why, the Face of the Temple, son. Imagine, one of our Birds—the *Face* of the Temple. Our legend will only grow when the world learns the Aviary brought the lost Temple daughter to life."

My skin is alive with lightning and venom, my emotion raw as the first day I arrived here. No good will come of this, but I can't stop it. I don't waste one more moment. Instead, I lunge from the drapes, my action stunning both men and causing Luc to immediately rise.

When I reach for his father, Luc stops me before I can attack. I manage to get a hold of his glass, though, and each shard sing-songs to me when I break it.

Luc's hands secure my wrists, seizing me so he can prevent me from breaking anything more. Meanwhile, the Guild leader scrutinizes me with the cockeyed grin that twists his features. I want to grab a shard, tiptoe the jagged edges against his face before slicing that mouth open.

"I apologize, Father," Luc tells him as he drags me out of the dining room.

"Do what you must. Remember, the Face of the Temple." It's the last thing I hear him say.

Luc really drags me now because I kick at him, legs thrashing. He uses a shortcut that takes us into the main lobby, which is dark with nothing but empty glass displays.

"So help me, Swan…" Luc wrestles me around and shoves me onto the grand staircase, so I fall back on the glass. "You will stop this childishness *now*!"

I begin to laugh. I laugh so hard I bend over the staircase, hands fanned out to touch the cold glass. My hair doubles over my face. "Congratulations, Luc!" I applaud him. "Excellent performance. Bravo! You did it. You turned me into your Swan. And after the auction, your wish will come true. I'll become the Face of the Temple and the warmth in your bed. How does it taste, knowing you defeated me? Knowing you manipulated me?"

"You continue to misjudge me." Luc says.

"Oh, there's no misjudging." Indifferent, I sprawl my legs on the stairs and tilt my head. "Your spine isn't so mighty as you'd like to dupe yourself into believing. I was stupid to believe you'd keep your word. Stupid to believe you had any trace of love in your murderous heart."

At my words, Luc strains like knots are pulling his neck tighter and tighter as I continue to address him, arching my head back in mad laughter. "I doubt you even *mentioned* my parents to him."

Luc doesn't make one move toward me, but he speaks so low I have to lean in to hear him. "*I* saved you from the District. *I* slaughtered for you. *I* created you. And I've opened myself up to you time and time again. But you still do not give me the benefit of the doubt."

"You're a fool." Jumping to my feet, I march toward him so I can look him right in the eye. "No, not a fool. You're nothing but a *coward*. You think you can pick me up off some street, pay for me like I'm some damn trophy, then dress me up in your feathers and I'll just become what you want me to be? You're just like the rest of them."

"Stop it!" he yells. He lunges toward me but stops short.

Inches from his eyes, I laugh again. "You know what the worst of it is? How much I admired you for the graphickers, for your answers, for Gull's abuser, for the exhibits. Your hands are so full of life. The way they create beauty from what you imagine in your mind. And even how they've carried me." Luc's hands grip my face, but I continue. "It's amazing how I've loved turning into your Swan. How much I love the lie. It's just so *beautiful*."

Luc squats down in front of me, then whispers low in my ear. "Auction or no auction, no one will *ever* have you."

"No one but you," I correct him, because we both know it's true.

I imagine what it will be like with Luc for the first time. My mind erupts into millions of bubbles of thoughts and images. I want to pop them all, but I can't deny them now. They're unbreakable. All this time spent with him has just been a buildup to this moment of acknowledgement. With the Temple's involvement, escape seems less likely. I will belong to Luc. Like the swan statue in the garden, I will become an Aviary legend. Soon, we will become each other's ghosts, haunting our bloods for a lifetime.

Luc leaves. Which is a mistake, because I slip out to meet Sky by the lake on the grounds where he said he'd wait for me.

Sky must take me away from here. Even with Force coming, I

have to know if Sky can live up to his word.

Somehow, I know he's disabled the security system. Unconcerned, Sky stands beside the lake—just outside Luc's bathhouse retreat—shoes off, feet bare on the shore. His loose pants are rolled up to the knee, black fitted shirtsleeves nestling above his elbows.

"What are you doing here?" I ask.

"Heard everything. I know what you want, and we're almost there. But I think we should do one last thing before we leave."

One blank look is all I can give him before Sky seizes me by the shoulders and then by the waist, bringing me with him into the water. That is Sky. Simple, wordless, effective. Always knowing what to do.

Exhilarated by our action, the lake whirls, splashing above our heads until the water canvasses us. We sink lower. Sky dives with me, and we pull each other down, a watery wrestling match that takes us back to our childhood…yet everything is different now.

Once our feet squish against the muddy bottom, our bubbles drift upward together like a flock of skittering birds.

I hold them back, better at the practice than Sky. Insistent, Sky keeps his powerful hands on my arms, stationing me under with him, showing me that he can endure the world underwater. His fingers travel upward until they tug my neck forward so his mouth can cram down on mine, feeding me the last of the air from his lungs. Giving me every last scrap.

Under here, there are no lies and no secrets, no feathers and no flesh, no glass and mirrors. Just Serenity and Sky, silence and touch, lightning and thunder.

He raises my body to the surface first, so I can breathe air again. A moment later, we come up in the deep water of the lake where my legs wrap around his waist, my arms snake around his neck, and my fingers thread into his wet waves.

Pressing my forehead against his, I close my eyes, pant into his neck, and my heart blesses him over and over for this. Sky lets my body weigh him down as he uses all his muscles to tread in the deep water.

The Aviary

"You swam with me." I gasp the words just under his ear.

"I never stopped wanting to," he says.

How could I forget Sky and I are two sides of the same coin? That Sky would walk barefoot through hell for me?

"I'll get you out during the auction. It will be the perfect diversion. Until then, I need you to hang on. One more exhibit. Hold your breath if you have to. Oh…damn." My lips only stop tilting on the edge of his when he curses.

Fear possesses me when I open my eyes, but it's not Luc watching us. And then I register how much worse it could be.

It's Mockingbird.

Twenty-seven
PeaCock

BEFORE SHE HAS THE CHANCE to open the door to the Aviary, I grab Mockingbird by the arms and drag her into the sculpture garden, forcing her back against a glass bird. I'm soaked in water, my white dress completely see-through, but I don't bother to cover myself. What's the point, when she's already seen everything?

I can see that she's frightened of me. Good.

I narrow my eyes like I'm a raptor. "Mock, if you tweet one word about what you just saw—"

Mockingbird shakes her head once, eyes wide. "I wasn't going to tell him!"

I hesitate.

"Why would I? All the girls exploit the guards."

"Not me. You know that. And you know what Luc would do." He would kill Sky. "And I know you enjoy telling your little secrets. That's how you survive, Mockingbird. Secrets make you feel valuable." I shouldn't be so hard on her. Mockingbird isn't made of the same stuff as me. Nor does she have any sense of identity other than who she is here.

Mockingbird juts her chin forward, marking me with her eyes. "It wouldn't matter if I told him. It wouldn't change anything. Once I saw him with you, I knew it was over."

"You'll get another chance soon enough," I tell her. "One last exhibit, Mock. And then, it'll all be over."

Mockingbird shakes her head. "He'll do anything to keep you

here."

I trade one secret so she will keep mine. "He can't fight the Temple." *He won't fight the Temple.*

Her brows lift at the hint. "The Temple?"

I smile.

"What about him?" She points back to Sky, studies my eyes, and discerns something for herself. "You have a history."

"You might say that." History is far too weak a word to describe what Sky and I have.

"They'll do another medical test," Mockingbird warns me. "If you—"

"It's not like that," I assure her. It's a half-truth. But neither one of us would act on anything until my family is safe and a thousand miles from Force. Even then… "Trust me, I'm still pure."

"I'll keep your secret."

When I release her, Mockingbird hugs me, and I breathe her in, unable to find a scent. Like her skin and clothes are as neutral as the rest of her. "When you're in the Temple, you'll have to sleep with one eye open."

I shake my head. "*Both* eyes open."

I'll GET YOU OUT DURING *the auction.*

One more exhibit. Just a little longer. I trust Sky.

I take the private entrance to my room, where I peel off the wet, clingy dress, change into the customary white nightgown, and retreat into the bathroom. Sky is in his usual place in the main room.

As I begin to unstring the wet tresses of my hair from my cheeks, I hear a light tapping from the mirror. Behind the glass, someone is requesting an invitation, not demanding one. The mirror doesn't have any hidden grooves or knobs, so my restless hands must explore its edges, pressing down until they find the right application until the mirror submits, unfolding to reveal the girl on the other side.

"Nightingale."

In one of her hands is a candle, its glow a golden web of gossamer pricking the darkness.

"Swan," she whispers. "Please, will you come with me?"

Trust is not a luxury one can afford in this place, particularly with Nightingale. Reminding myself what she did to me on my first night, I hesitate.

"I need your help," she says. "You're her only hope—and mine. Bring muscles with you if you must."

Sky would come after me either way, so I wave him forward into the bathroom. He doesn't hesitate, which makes me suspicious, but there's no time for questions. We follow her into the darkness.

Sky doesn't close the mirror behind us, and Nightingale walks ahead to guide the way with her light. The darkness is a devouring wolf, but the dark has never frightened me. Lightning does well in darkness.

What my drugged and blind state before could not register last time I was here is now apparent. At the base of the path, the tunnel spreads into a corridor lined with shelves, all sealed by thin, metal bars. But it's the heads on those shelves, heads choked by plastic tarps, that cause me to cringe. Each one is exactly the same. They are all models, mannequins, molds, and casts from the eras before this one—the days of wax. Luc said this was one of the oldest museums in the country.

The next corridor is much the same. Except inside these, the wax figures live on behind iron bars, wigs on their heads, clothes on their frames, some of which are moth eaten, hole-ridden. This was once a wax museum, until a prominent Family member concocted the idea of live models. Down here, they are just eerie ghosts from a time past.

Rounding the corner, we enter the same circular room where Peacock and her ensemble brought me. Except now, it's she who lays in the center of the circle, hair half-veiling her face. Alone, Peacock doesn't move, nor does she look up to see who's entered the room. For a moment, I wonder if it's some sort of trick, but when I near the circle, I understand what prompted Nightingale to come to me.

Peacock looks like a busted marionette. One of her arms hangs limp at her side with her left leg much the same. Her breath comes in light, pained inhales. Judging by the bruises on her chest,

THE AVIARY

I can tell her ribs are cracked, if not fractured. I smooth away her hair to see one side of her face, blanketed in a cocoon of dried blood. Sky inspects her just after me.

I whip my head around to Nightingale. "Why didn't you go to Luc?"

"Because I know who did this, Serenity. And if they find out I spilled their secret…I can't afford that risk." Who could Nightingale possibly fear here?

"But I can."

"Of course you can." Something in the simplistic way she says it, in the way she folds her arms over her chest, makes me believe she knows something. "We all know you're the reason Blackbird went missing. I don't know how you did it."

"I didn't." I glance at Sky.

Nightingale addresses him, "Can you help her?"

"Only if you turn a blind eye." He tilts Peacock's chin to the side to scrutinize the wounds on the side of her face. "She's not going to last much longer."

"Can you do anything?"

"I can. It'll be risky."

"Do it, Sky," I say.

Peacock's too injured to pick up on my use of his real name, but Nightingale peers at me, head tilted. If she intends to say anything, she doesn't get the chance.

"You girls better get topside," Sky tells us. "They'll be checking the rooms soon."

"Why?" I ask as he gingerly lifts Peacock into his arms. She whimpers when he does so. It's the second time I've watched him carry a girl for my sake.

"New security precaution Luc just enacted."

Or his father, due to the upcoming auction. I can't help but wonder if they are mounting security, can Sky still get me out?

As Nightingale and I prepare to part ways, I ask her one last question. "Why, Nightingale? Peacock is second only to you. And I will be gone soon. Why would you want to help the only one who stands in your way?"

Nightingale twists her form toward me, smiling as Sky disappears down a conjoined hall with Peacock. "No one stands in my way. Except maybe you."

For now, I accept her vague answer.

I take the stairs two at a time. Once we reach my room, Nightingale leaves. She is too concerned about her reputation; everything is about the Aviary for her. I close the mirror, sink to the glass floor, and sigh, second-guessing my decision. Peacock could wreck everything. Place Sky and the Sanctuary in danger.

After everything that's happened to her, will Peacock want to leave? Or is her identity too wrapped up in this glass birdcage like so many others? And why did Nightingale want to help her? There are too many loose threads, and I can't even begin to string them together.

I should've known Luc would check on me. As usual, he finds me sitting at my alcove, staring at my reflection through the window. By this time, my hair is dry, giving no indication of mine and Sky's swim earlier. He doesn't mention a word about Peacock or why she's not in her room, even though he always checks on me last. Odd. Tomorrow, I will get answers from Sky.

Luc shifts into a sitting position with his back against the other wall of the alcove, opposite me. The confident, controlled expression he wore earlier is now gone; I can see worry lines creasing the spaces of his forehead between his brows. On his cheeks, the scraped flesh where I'd dragged my nails earlier cackles back at me, proud.

Luc sighs, places his arms across his raised knees, and flattens the tips of his fingertips against each other. "Swan, I cannot cage you here any longer."

I don't take my eyes off my nail marks on his face.

Luc nudges his head so I can only see one side—the clean side. "The Temple will shatter you."

I grin, playing along. "Or maybe I will shatter it."

"Only what you tell yourself to keep the fire going."

I hug myself tighter. "It's not fire. It's lightning."

"Yes, electrical sparks inside water and ice."

"Mmm," I murmur in admission.

"For the hundredth time, I want to know where they made you. You have more fight in your little finger than thousands of girls have in their entire bodies, heart and soul included. I have admired that spirit from the beginning."

"And now you'll get to admire it from Temple publicity photos...and in the Penthouse."

Luc doesn't refute my accusation. Instead, he talks to me about my last exhibit.

"Your exhibit will be your final act in my Aviary. The auction will commence as soon it is finished. It's a private auction; you won't be on display."

He is wrong. My final act will be leaving this Aviary. No matter what security measures are taken, Sky won't dare let me go to the Temple. Little by little, I'm regaining parts of my old self. My butterflies are rising from the ashes, attacking the Swan inside me until she becomes nothing more than a ghost. Just enough to get me through one final display.

"When is the exhibit?" I ask while knitting my fingers into one another.

Luc traces the tips of his fingers onto my arm, slides them down to cord into my hand. "After the weekend, when all the other exhibits are finished."

"So soon," I say, staring through the glass. The sooner, the better.

"My father believes it will draw the most committed buyers, root out those less than worthy."

I twist my hand out of his. "We both know it will be Director Force."

Luc's brows are like trenches, dangerous and brutish when he grimaces. "This is your form of torture, isn't it? You play it so easily, like you enjoy it."

"I feel very alive right now." I stare at my curled fingers and opt for a more physical suggestion, reaching up to trace one of my marks.

Luc only chuckles. "No, thank you. You always feel alive, and I'd rather we retire your child's play for another evening." Standing, he extends a hand to me.

I sigh, reaching up to take it, and allow him to escort me to bed.

Twenty-eight
Obsession

There aren't any chances for me to meet with Sky before our escape. Luc barricades himself in his room, only coming out to attend to any necessities, and I learn from Nightingale it's because he's designing a new wave of exhibits for the weekend.

"His genius knows no limits," Nightingale says. I've invited her to my room for dinner.

I wanted a change from Mockingbird; all she does is gossip about other girls and talk about her client rendezvous. Nightingale is subtler. With the exhibit a short time away, the last thing I want to do is hear about clients.

Nightingale ignores the sampling of sweets I've printed, preferring her soup, which I've always seen her eat, but I greedily wolf down a pastry chilled inside by cream. Since I'm leaving soon, I only need the supplemental food once a day.

"I guarantee you he has all the displays finished. He must be adding something to yours," Nightingale says after sampling her soup.

Unlike most of the girls in the Aviary, Nightingale never leaves her hair down. She always keeps it in a tight bun, low to the back of her neck.

"He must come out some time," I say, gazing out the window. I wonder if I will see Luc walking to his private retreat.

Nightingale shakes her head. After finishing her soup, she strides about the room, observing what she can, pausing near the fish tank. "He takes all his meals in his room when he's engrossed in a project. Thank you, by the way, for inviting me to dinner. More like dessert, for you."

I shrug. "I'm taking advantage. Besides, Luc stopped our community dinners."

"Yes," she agrees. "It's the calm before the auction."

"Why do you always eat soup?" She even orders chilled fruit soup for dessert.

"Soothes my vocal chords."

Simple explanation. My appetite goes through phases. Sometimes, this place thins me, its tight walls constricting my appetite. I've skipped meals, stomaching only the sweetest of flavors like pastries and chocolate.

I decide to ask Nightingale the same question as Mockingbird. "Are you happy here?"

Nightingale blinks once, eyes curving down as if tentative, debating on whether to tell me. Perhaps because I am an outsider compared to her. Whatever happens, I know she'll tell me the truth. Not like Mockingbird and her denial.

"It's the same, you know? It doesn't matter where we are: Glass District, graphicker studios, carousels, the Temple. Our bodies are still being used." She lifts her head, but examines her fingers. "Our mouths, necks, arms, breasts, bellies—legs pulled apart to expose our insides. Wealth doesn't discriminate just like poverty doesn't. We don't get rich, handsome princes in here. We still go for whoever has the biggest paycheck because in the end, we still owe Owl." They always will.

Swallowing, I summon up the nerve to ask one more question. "What do you do about it?"

Nightingale takes one glimpse at me before focusing out the window. "I sing." She gestures to her temple. "In here. I go to my music room and I sing." Nightingale's coping mechanism.

"It's obvious what yours is…" Nightingale smiles, pointing to my sweet tray.

Up until now, I hadn't realized it, but she's right. I barely eat any normal meals. Dinners and lunches go untouched, but sweets are my indulgence. My Bliss.

When I glance out the window again, I see him. And I leap

to my feet.

Just as I'd predicted, Luc's resolve has finally crumbled or withered enough for him to take a break. There he is, crossing the bridge and hurrying to his bathhouse. I head for the door.

"What are you doing?" Nightingale asks while I skirt across the hall.

I turn the knob. "It's my last exhibit. I have a right to see whatever he's planning."

"Wait and ask him, then," Nightingale advises.

"Why would I ever do things the simple way?"

Besides, Luc has kept his distance the past few days, fraying what little remains of whatever twisted relationship we have. He would never show me. This time, I won't be surprised by snapped ropes, an underwater viewing center, or invisible cables to make me fly with swans. Because I will know.

If Sky were on duty, he wouldn't allow this, but we're right in the middle of a shift change, and I seize the opportunity.

Once I reach Luc's door, I place my hand against the opaque glass, feel the hum of the screen next to it, waiting…hoping…will it work?

I hear a click, and the door nudges open. After everything, Luc is still so trusting. When I first arrived, he'd set it up this way so I could reach him whenever I needed. But the last time I was in this room, Luc's bed had cradled a dead Raven. Back then, the room appeared haggard. Now, not one stitch is out of place. Despite having taken his meals in here, the room only smells like fresh linen. Not one curtain is ruffled, the bed is made, there is no dust on the hardwood. But there is certainly chaos, albeit organized.

All over the room are sprite lights of me in the exhibit. Or rather…versions of me since they are sketches. I notice a digital wand sitting on the table next to his bed. The kind with a built-in laser with terabytes of storage.

In one sketch, I stand in the center of naked, spindly trees. What looks like dust and feathers fall from the ceiling. And me, in the very center. Two ropes hold my body. There is nothing on my skin but ropes of pearls, and swan wings on my back. I touch a wing and it flutters, the sprite light responding to my gesture.

The Aviary

I tap another sketch. This one is animated. There I am, walking along the surface of the lake—iced and white as angel arms—while thick, white furs keep me warm. Then, the furs are removed just as the ice cracks and pits me into the water.

I wade through each sprite light. Nightingale is right; his genius knows no bounds. If Luc wants, he can keep the flame of my exhibit burning long into the night. It's not just his gift, it's his obsession. His identity.

All the images choke me, overwhelm me; I'm locked in a screen.

No, I refuse to think of myself as a victim. I'm not a slave. Closing my eyes, I hold my breath. In my mind, these are real. Paper. I crouch—the fairy with claws ripping them into a million pieces and turning Luc's room into one giant hamster cage. I could make ink bleed, paper wet and soggy. Or I could set them on fire. But I can do nothing to these but twirl my fingers through the lasered sketches. I focus on my eyes, on my expression. He's captured it well. Too well.

Each and every one is like a star. Over the past few weeks, I haven't lost an iota of Serenity, but she's more now. Swan feathers have fused with the lightning. Indestructible, they don't singe. Unlike my mother, I haven't lost myself in the Aviary—I've found myself. Even when I crawl out of the tunnel, I will take Swan with me.

Over Luc's bed, footage plays over and over on the ceiling, like a lullaby with no sound. Transfixed, I sink onto the mattress and watch. All from my exhibits, my preparations, and even footage of me lingering in the glass sculptures...it's all there. Just as he'd promised, he was always watching me.

"I saw you come in."

I curse under my breath. Sky is far too quiet for one so tall. I hear him curse, too, but he does it more openly than me. He reaches up and taps a finger to a moving image of me, studying it before dropping his hand. "Looks like I underestimated him."

"I did, too, at first. I haven't for a while now."

"And when were you going to enlighten me?"

"I thought it was obvious."

Sky curses again. "Not to this degree. Damn, Ser, how could

I have known you would be *this* good?"

"What are you talking about? You *wanted* this to happen. You planned—"

Sky holds up a hand. "I didn't intend for it to go this far. He's in love with you! I've been making plans. Arranging things, hacking the system, plotting out escape routes, but if Aldaine is this obsessed—"

When we hear the low hum of the door responding to the hand behind it, Sky resumes his guard position as Luc enters the room.

No! What did Sky mean? Is he still getting me out? I can't ask.

Luc takes one look at me, bristles, and puckers his mouth before glancing at Sky.

"I was reporting to her room for duty when I saw her come in here," Sky says.

Luc narrows his brows, stalking in a direct line to me.

"You always welcomed me here from the first moment you let the screen read me," I remind him.

"Leave us," Luc says.

"No," I protest and try to walk past Luc, but he hems me in, using his eyes to imprison me.

Sky hesitates while Luc addresses me. "I saw you in the window, Serenity. You came here just after I left. Don't try to pretend with me. Is this what you wanted to see?" He raises his hands, motioning to my surroundings.

When I say nothing, he asks, "Are you satisfied?"

My eyes wander toward the images, and Luc seethes once more. "Answer me!"

Behind Luc, Sky has tensed, and I notice his hands curl into fists. I know what will follow if Luc threatens me, if he so much as touches me.

So, I keep my voice soft as down. "Which one will you choose?"

Luc relaxes his shoulders. "I've already chosen. I keep the final renditions safe elsewhere."

That is why his visit outside was so brief. He wasn't going to his retreat to rest. He went there to finalize.

"No, I will not show you." He demolishes any aspirations I

have to the contrary. "No one sees it other than me. And Dove will only know how to prepare you when I tell her just before the unveiling. It's the only way the performance can fulfill itself. Do you understand?"

I nod.

"Are you going to say anything else?"

I narrow my brows, suspicious. "What should I say?"

"Say you will play the part of the Swan. Is that all it is? Pretend?" Luc touches me, but his fingertips shy away, hover above my arm. "How can my Swan fly if she is so numb?"

My fingertips trace one sprite light like a carousel. "I never fly. I fall, I swim, and then I sink. And I'm *never* numb."

Twenty-nine
ThEFiNalExhiBit

I ENJOYED GETTING PAINTED. ONE OF my artisans was a plump older woman who'd birthed thirteen children for the Centre, the highest on record in the past fifty years. She made me feel comfortable. Her body had endured so much I didn't mind when she painted mine, nor when she pasted the white gemstones in swirling patterns on my breasts. Hilda wasn't even soft, and I liked that. Her fingers were able and focused on their work, her mind on the art and not on me. The lack of attention was apparent whenever she twisted me one way or sharpened her eyes against my thigh to determine the best angle for the paint or jewels.

I think of Dove, and the contrast. Even at her age, Dove is beautiful. Though slender and strong, her body probably never had luscious curves.

I realize this is the last time Dove will decorate me.

Save for Gull's return from her sabbatical, nothing else has happened. Everything happens tonight. After what I said the other night, Luc escorted me back to the bedroom before arranging a private meeting with Sky. I hope and pray Luc didn't beat him, punish him for my invasion.

Immediately after my final exhibit, the real auction will commence. All other claims before this night will be rejected in favor of the high bidders.

Force will be the highest.

I'm almost finished with my mother's journal. She is good.

The Aviary

No information about their secret Sanctuary activities, no names of girls they've helped; everything is about me, Sky, Kerrick, and her time in the Temple. Sometimes, the words are like miniature spears, but I know I have to read them regardless. If Force ever finds me, I need to prepare myself. If Sky doesn't succeed, I will enter the Temple by the end of the weekend.

If we don't get out, will I become the new Unicorn?

"How long do I have?" I ask.

"One hour until the exhibit opens. Bidders are already arriving. Some want to see the display in person. Others who have entered are content to watch a digital display. Owl is giving the present bidders a tour."

What? "Why didn't you tell me?"

Before Dove can loosen the straps on my white dress and take a paintbrush to my skin, I jerk my body up and scramble across the room with Sky shrinking the gap behind us even more than usual when I open the door to the hallway. I stop just before I reach the stairs, choosing to only peek my head around the corner. It doesn't take but a moment to spot him entering the Nest Wing with Luc. Of course he'd get a private tour. Private as can be with his level of security.

Nothing about my father exudes order. From the untucked collar of his black shirt, to the white scarf casually draped around his neck, to the dark hair he keeps pulled back in a top knot above his head. Even the way he walks is light and without care, like he's stepping on spun sugar. Force is a man who doesn't play by the rules. No, he doesn't even know what rules are, and I suspect that is why the Syndicate is as powerful as it is. The saying 'no honor among thieves' is an apt statement for my father, one he very well could've coined. No honor among thieves, rapists, abusers, or sadists.

From here, it's hard to determine how old he is. He must have at least ten, maybe fifteen years or more on my mother. Physically, I have so much of my mother in me, like her silvery hair and petite body with plump bust, but never her gray eyes. Do I move like him, too? Like I don't care if I'm wandering across a sea of eggshells without any consideration to how many I wreck?

Luc leads my father around a corner to a different hallway,

and I return to my room so Dove can prepare me.

NAKED, I LINGER BEFORE THE mirror, watching my caretaker's eyes, feeling the slightness of the brush like a kiss on my body. Unlike my mother, I am glad Dove pays attention to my curves, because she knows just how to accentuate them. And I know when she looks at my body, she thinks of her daughter. In her eyes, I will always be an infant.

Tonight, she paints my skin in elaborate designs that remind me of embroidered lacework. By dusting my skin in silvery shimmers, she turns my body into a star. While it dries, Dove sees to my hair, for the first time plumping every harum-scarum curl until they are maniacal water serpents rising around my head with their tails restless and wandering down my back.

In the mirror, I am face to face with the intoxicating image of a delicate, sterling siren.

Dove seems to read my thoughts. "You will not be small tonight."

Two seamstresses arrive with my ensemble for the evening, both of their hands bearing the skirt because it is longer than anything I've ever seen in my life. It must be over a hundred feet.

From where it will collect at my hips all the way to its generous hem, the skirt is a serenade of swan feathers. It isn't one I step into, but it splits apart to twist around my hips where they tie it. I try to step forward, but find it oppressive to move. Pondering the heaviness of the hundreds of feathers, I wonder how I'll manage a dive.

Finally, they add two enormous white wings, but at least these feel lighter than a cloud.

"You will know what to do when the time comes," Dove reassures me. "These feathers are...different. Now." She holds two small white wings but with broad feathers that overlap just at the bottom and curve up toward my neck, which she presses to my breasts. With a sticky substance, Dove adheres them to my skin there, flattening the feathers into place.

To complete the look, Dove corkscrews my hair to one side, fastening it with white pins. Loose enough so my hair will unravel

The Aviary

in the water. Her next step is pasting tiny pearls to random areas of my bare skin, my arms, my neck, my stomach, and even my legs because the skirt is slit up to my thighs. Those same pearls she strings around my neck, forming a broad choker. Her last act is the mask of white wings, which she settles on my forehead. The feathery ends fan into the air, gathering on the edges of the holes where my eyes blink.

Finished.

Dove excuses herself just a few minutes until my final exhibit. I walk around the screen. All the seamstresses are also gone, but I am not alone. Not when I open the door to the bedroom into the main room where *he* stands. He doesn't suck the air from the room even if his presence is a swinging ball to my chest. No, all he does is spark the lightning inside me.

Casual hands, one lifted, fingers tapping his chin more amused than a hawk cackling over its prey. He strides forward with that same air of delightful chaos. Like his entire body is one network of spider webs and he doesn't care whose wings get stuck there.

If Sky were here, I could imagine the muscles in his neck tightening, jaw hardening with the same resolve I feel. No doubt Luc ensured this would be a private moment. Father and daughter for the first time.

When his eyes frost across mine, close enough for me to discern their color, it's then I notice the resemblance. It's undeniable—the same wintergreen infused in mine. Only Force's seem more embellished, glittery even, like sugared mint leaves.

I have no armor. I do not guard myself. Instead, I descend into a crouch, almost ready to pounce, but my father's body is an eerie reflection of mine. He plays my game with the corners of his devilish mouth twisting upward. Delicious as the devil. And my mother is his angel. Except he's met his match in the bat who flew straight out of hell along with his Unicorn.

When I stiffen from my crouch, he relaxes and nods to me in approval at the gap in our game. "Director Aldaine tells me your name is Trinity."

I only have one expression for him, and fortunately, my disgust covers any sense of relief I feel at my father not knowing my real name.

"I must admit, it perplexes me. You don't look like a Trinity to me. And your mother..." He smiles at the word, and the possessive curve of his lips is the strike of the whip, every brutal flick of leather on her skin. "Well, let's just say Trinity doesn't seem fitting."

"Force seems fitting for you, but the other name we call you is even more fitting."

He folds his hands behind his back, tilting his head toward me. "And what name would that be, *daughter*?" He emphasizes the word, practically hurls it at me like it's a shard of glass he can cut me with.

I catch it instead when I retort, "Vampire."

"Hmm..." He muses on the name for a moment before drawing his icy green eyes back to mine, shadows curtaining them while a lock of dark hair descends on his brow. "Come to think of it, your mother's blood tasted sweeter than any other girls I've ever sampled."

I should've known my father would play this game. It's what he enjoys. And it's where I've come from. Even so, I step forward, advancing toward him, but all he does is shift his weight, leaning back on his heels with his arms held out, inviting me but with eyes no less entertained.

I'm this close to jabbing my fingers into his mouth, snaking my hand down his throat to grab his black heart and yank it out. I imagine his aortas would feel relieved. After all, it must be a tiring job pumping that level of evil all the time. For now, I settle on a demand laced with a threat.

"Get. Out. Of. My. Room."

I'm not surprised when he begins to circle me, fist raised to his chin as he surveys my final Swan ensemble. "Aldaine has a fine eye. I offered him a position in the Temple just today, but he turned it down. Such a pity. A man with his talent, his ability to highlight the natural beauty that is already there, like a jeweler polishing a diamond, is rare. A diamond the world is just waiting to see shine. And it will," he finishes in front of me, eyes settling on mine, drawing down since he's at least a head taller.

Deadpan. "I am *not* my mother."

He throws his head back. Laughs. I resist the urge to push on his chest as a child would. Then again, I am his child.

"Clearly, Trinity. Clearly. Oh, so transparently." He puts his hands together, laughing again. "All these years spent looking for you and your mother, never did I in a million years believe you'd surface like this. It wasn't what I planned."

"Sorry to disappoint you."

"No. Not a disappointment at all." He stretches a hand out to me, but I shrink away.

"Touch me, you lose a finger. Swans bite."

"No, not a disappointment," he repeats. "You are more than I ever could have hoped for. You see…" He leans forward and whispers in my ear, breath like smoke rings curling, "I have big plans in store for you."

So close I could just turn and bite his nose off. But Luc would never forgive me if I got blood on his last costume.

"You will never have me," I hiss low, matching my father's eyes.

"Oh, I already do."

Dove escorts me this time.

Luc will never escort me again.

Not even my father's visit unhinges me. I'm ready for my grand finale.

This time, there is no swing. There is a glass pedestal, and onto this, she directs me to stand. As soon as my hands settle on the glass, the pedestal moves. Up and up and up. Ironic, because all I feel is down and down and down.

I just want the dive. I want the water, want to rip all the feathers off. *Don't close your eyes,* I remind myself.

The surface of the lake is alive with the fluff of thousands of white feathers, restless for my Swan dive. The ends of the skirt trail in the water, feathers kissing feathers. Notes knit a melody into the exhibit, speakers manipulating the sound like the music is issuing from the depths before it stirs in the branches around me, culminating behind me. The song is Luc's, but this is no lullaby. This is a new one he has written for me. For the finale.

In the midst of the first sprinkle of notes, the glass dome of sky above me begins to shed. Snowflakes, hundreds of them, float through air, each one like a tuft of magic as they frolic on the branches of the trees, prance across my skin and in my hair, while the rest pirouette onto the feathers below me.

I hear Luc's words, but out of Nightingale's mouth.

White Swan,
Bliss in lightning skin.
White Swan,
Hide me in your pinions.
White Swan.
Wings flying passion and pure.
White Swan,
Sin and guilt fading forever.
White Swan,
White Swan…

The last words are a naked whisper, becoming an echo. An echo of our conversation. Behind the glass, people freeze, stunned hands bearing down on the glass wall. Some curl their fingers like they're hoping to catch some of the purity, some of this astonished innocence. Instead, I will give them my lightning, my sparks, and water.

When the pedestal begins to shrink, I curb my body, bring my arms together, and dive. Water slaps me, softened by the feather bed. My act disturbs them. I wreck the feathers all around me… and *on* me. Now, I understand what Dove meant when she told me I would know what to do, because the bindings on the skirt break. It falls apart, becoming nothing more than a white sinking ship. It leaves me with Dove's handiwork, her white lace painting, the undergarment of pearls she's fastened around my pelvis, the wings on my breasts, and the ones behind me, but they do not inhibit me. Feathers float in front of my body, some tripping over the wings on my breasts.

A free Swan.

And Serenity.

My lungs haven't even begun to sense the stirrings of fire, but my heart does.

This is the last thing I expected.

He swims to me, his legs bonded by white pants, chest pardoned of clothes. His arms yank the water back to bring his body

The Aviary

closer to mine. It's the body of a dancer, muscles braided so lithe and graceful into his calves, into his thighs and shoulders.

No one needs to tell me this is the first time Luc has ever joined an exhibit.

Like me, his skin is painted white, and when his bubbles twine with mine, we crash together, my Swan body vying with his into a serpentine water dance. Luc moors both his legs around one of mine, liberating the other to rebel in the water.

Together, we sink.

The edges of his feet flatten on my ankles, causing the full force of his body to plunge me lower as I arch my neck, resisting the way his chest towers over me. Regardless of the spectators, Luc's hands become the cage for my face before his head anchors against mine, mouth trampling mine, opening its boundaries to taste me and to share breath. Like he's giving me a precursor to what inevitably will be if I don't make it out.

When the water vanquishes the last of my bubbles humming around Luc's face, I close my eyes while my hands wrestle for the surface.

Too long under. A particle or two left of air.

Close to fainting, my head lolls back, hellfire seizing my mourning lungs as their watery funeral approaches.

But Luc's hands grab me around my waist, and he tugs us up through the water. Just before we surface, he takes the sides of my legs in his hands, then thrusts me fast and hard into the air.

I gasp, chest heaving from its salvation. Just to my left is the boat, but this time, it's *my* boat. Bow protected by a swan figurehead, wings girding the sides.

Luc climbs the ladder to the stern, then turns around to take me by the arms and bring me to him. I realize I can't hear anything. Standing there, with my body pressed against his—furnished only by drowned white wings, pearl undergarments, and paint—I know we have left the audience in a spellbound stupor.

Luc's fingers cradle the sides of my head, burrow them into my hair, and then he whispers two words to me, magnified to the audience by the exhibit speaker.

"My Swan."

I faint to the sound of applause.

Thirty
GuLL's CracKs

Tonight, Dove is not in my room to help me un-Swan myself.

I am alone.

Briefly, I wonder if that was Luc's doing, or if the Aviary is on lockdown for the auction. Whatever the case, Sky is in my room just like always.

Even behind bedroom doors, I feel the need to hide behind the dressing screen while I peel the wings from my chest, unloop the pearl underwear, and comb through my hair. I tug on the customary white dress.

Tonight, I feel too white. The paint seems heavier than ever before.

Even now, I can imagine the auction progressing. In light of the exhibit, of the palpable desire between Luc and me, I know there is no competition. How long will it take for Temple transporters to arrive? Will Director Force speak to me alone first? *When will Sky act?*

The waiting is the hardest.

And the silence.

I was never good at silence.

Sky doesn't flinch when I yank the bedroom door open. I rush for him, fingers straining against his arms. "Sky! *Please.*"

All it takes is one nod to shatter me, to pour an ocean of relief into my skin. "Yes, Serenity. It's time."

He leads me out the secret entrance at the back of the dor-

THE AVIARY

mitory building, the one reserved for security. As we slip into the night, I think of the Swan. How Luc has trapped my image forever here. For the rest of the world to see, images from my exhibit will become illusions on the entrance walls just like the first night I arrived here.

On our way out, I pass by the sculpture garden. I think of the glass Swan statue—it will become a relic of this place. A living piece of history.

"One last thing," I whisper before he motions to the self-driving Family limo on the back road past a security gate. How on earth did he manage that?

With Sky following me, I hurry into the glass sculpture gardens and find the Swan in the center where it always slumbers. I wonder when Luc built this, how many nights he must have stared up at it, wondering if his beloved Swan even existed.

I can never go back to who I was, but this is my first step forward. This is my last act. I will show him she didn't have ultimate power. Though she will haunt me the rest of my life, I won't let her take me down.

I'll take her down instead.

Bracing my hands against the two magnanimous, frosted white wings, I feel the cool embrace of the glass on my palms and push hard. Harder still, but it doesn't give way. Then, Sky's steady body heat warms my neck, just before his hands cover my own.

Together, we push. It starts to slip and loosen, but the pedestal it's sealed to topples with it. Just like I am sealed to Sky. If he breaks, so will I.

The Swan sails and cracks and shatters. Not into fragments but into chunks—glass wedges the size of Sky's hands. Winded, I step back to admire them, lean against his chest and sigh just as he takes my hand, fingers threading into mine. In this moment, I feel more powerful than I ever did in the exhibits. Leaving here, I will have conquered Force, Luc, the Aviary, the Swan, and anything else that would tear me from my family.

"Are we ready?" I tilt my head back to his.

"Yes."

"Sky..." I freeze. "Shh."

I suddenly break away from him. The shadowy figure glides

past the archway of the glass garden, almost seeming to float toward the garden of trees and flowers.

Glancing up at Sky, I whisper, "What is she doing here?"

Sky tugs on my arm for a moment, pulls me back. "Something's happening inside the Aviary." Pressing a finger to his ear, he listens. "Get into the car and stay there. I have to get into the system again or the gates won't open. Someone's overriding the system. They've opened all the doors. The girls are attacking each other."

"*What?*"

"I'll tell you later. Go!"

I have no intention of going to the limo. Not after I see Gull stagger across the bridge leading to the lake with her hands shaking and trembling. Her gray hair swims down her back and chest in elegant waves, and she wears nothing but the designated Aviary gray dress.

Gull only stops when she reaches the shore. Pressing myself against the side of a tree, I peer behind the bark, finally comprehending what she's doing. She is meeting someone. Dumbfounded curiosity hollows every other emotion.

I have to force myself not to cry out.

I recognize the man with the bruises—the broken nose and his one good eye and the broken arm in a sling. He hands something to Gull, after which she smiles and presses the small item to her nose. When she inhales sharply, I realize she's taken something—Bliss, probably.

When he touches her, the full force of my lightning strikes.

I can't take it.

I throw myself forward, running toward them while crying her name.

"Swan." Gull raises her head with a fading smile.

"Gull, why?" I lament. "You wanted me to fly you away. Why?"

Sky was right. He's always right.

"The Swan." The man's one whole eye feasts on me, and I take a step back.

"Our bargain," Gull reminds him.

"Yes." He brushes his hand across her neckline. "Even after what the director did, I knew you'd come running back to me. You always do. What about her?"

"Let her watch. She should watch."

"What did he give you?" I ask Gull in confusion. "What are you on?"

Gull breathes deep with eyes closed, whispering the word in an exhale. "*Memory*. The most expensive. It stimulates what I need to remember. Those nights with my stepfather and the carnival owner."

I face them both, but my eyes are aimed at Gull.

Her eyes are gray eggshells, cracked but searching for someone who can piece her together. "My stepfather tried to drown me. After my mother died, he came after me. Struck up a deal with the carnival owner. They took turns. They *shared* me." She pauses as she closes her eyes, once again breathing deeply like she's remembering.

"They gave me Bliss after the carnival shut down every night. And took me to the lake." She stares down at her own hands, fingers fanned out, studying the gaps of air between them.

"One night, he told me he couldn't look at me anymore, said I looked too much like her. So, he tried to drown me." Gull says it so simply. "But he didn't know I'd started wearing a knife. I didn't mean to kill him, but his hands were around my neck, and I couldn't breathe. Through the water, I couldn't see where I'd stabbed him. In the throat. And then, Jonas found me. He took me away. Brought me to the Aviary. I promised him he could visit me. Just as he promised not to tell. And he never has. And I never have…until now." Turning to him, she announces, "I'm ready."

Gull walks a few steps, until the lake tucks itself around her bare feet.

"Gull…what are you doing?" I ask her, petrified.

Jonas eyes her. "You've been a naughty bird. Are you ready for your punishment?"

"Yes." Gull wades in to her knees. "I'm ready. It's what I deserve."

Jonas follows her.

I slide down the meadow slope to the shore, but inertia propels me to my knees. No girl deserves this.

Jonas wraps two hands around Gull's neck, then he tips her

back until the ends of her hair touch the water.

With her expression tranquil as snow clouds eclipsing sunlight, Gull shuts her eyes beneath the waterline. Jonas plunges her lower, and the lake closes over her nose. Bubbles gush from it and then her mouth.

Gull puts me to shame. She remains there with the water lapping against the curves of her body, her dress floating up to the surface, for an enviably long time. Her hands don't struggle once.

Is this her dissociation? A punishment and a coping mechanism? Reliving the nightmare of her life. Just like Sky said—some Birds can't fly because they are too used to the cage.

"Please...stop," I whisper, pleading with the man, but he only grins.

I lunge for them at the last minute, but I'm too late.

The water around Gull turns blood red, and I see the blade jutting through the other side of Jonas' throat. From other hands.

I gasp when Jonas falls into the bloody water.

Gull starts to surface, but this time, *she's* too late.

The other Bird's claws are too strong. They dig into Gull's skull, pinning her beneath the watery cage.

I scramble to my feet, splashing water around my knees, but the lake becomes barred glass, indestructible, soldered shut over Gull forever. By the time I reach her, tugging her by the arms until I've dragged her body to the shore, her skin is paler than egg whites. Her eyes are hollow as the first nesting doll without her family. More water than Gull.

I hold the drowned Bird in my arms. Kiss the cold skin of her cheek.

"*Why?*" I scream at the other girl. Cursing at the darkness that hid her as she swam from the other side of the lake until it was too late.

She rises from the water with a triumphant grin, a beguiling string on her face.

"Because it's finally my turn," Mockingbird says.

Thirty-one
Mockingbird's GiFt

I CRADLE THE SIDES OF GULL's face and tilt my forehead against hers, crying.

"I gave her what she wanted." Mockingbird approaches, water cascading off her dress, dripping to the grass beside me. "She always wanted to know what it felt like to drown. She drowned every night in her dreams."

I squeeze Gull's hand, drizzle my fingers along her arm up to her shoulder, to her neck, and finally her face as Mockingbird continues.

"Water makes everything quiet. You should know that better than anyone. You're the Swan."

"So, what? Are you going to kill me now?" I eye the blade in her hand, the one weeping Jonas's blood.

Mockingbird glances at me, her hands coddling the knife hilt, and she crooks her neck to the side just like a Bird hatched here would. "What are you thinking? I can see you figuring it out."

Thoughts scurry like feathers upset by a gust of wind. "Blackbird…"

"She wasn't the first. But she was the first high Bird I tried to kill. She was supposed to die, but she must've thrown up the poison thanks to her morning sickness."

"Raven?"

"Raven was a little harder," Mockingbird says as she wanders in a circle around me. "She took too much Bliss every day. Made my poison lighter. It didn't take right away. You know what my gift is?" Mockingbird suddenly crouches before me, her eyes wide and hyperactive, animated as two thieves with their hands smothered in gold.

She giggles, flicking her hands up, fluttering her fingers, all except two—which still house the knife.

"I have magic hands," she declares. "They're ever so fast!" I remember the magic trick she showed Finch once—a coin appearing out of thin air. "Mmm, clients enjoy them, but they're meant for so much more. They're meant for stealing things. For slipping things into little Birdies' drinks and food. Don't you think it's funny?" She cocks her head. "They said the Mockingbird couldn't keep a secret. Turns out she had the biggest secret of all."

I remember Luc's words the first day he brought me to the museum.

Hush little bird, don't say a word. And she never did. Her fingers do all the talking, but they're far too quick for any of the other Birds to hear.

"Why Flamingo? She wasn't on Raven's level. Or Blackbird's."

"Silly, stupid little Pinky. Only one who ever saw my fast hands. Was going to tell Owl, but I fixed her first."

"Just like Finch." Something snaps inside me as I think of the little girl.

"*You* didn't eat!" Mockingbird accuses me. "I was going to take her under my wing after you were gone." She's almost nose to nose with me, peering into my eyes. "I poisoned your food a lot, but you never ate enough."

The bits of poison must have been the reason for my loss of appetite over the past couple of weeks.

"How did you ever get to Raven after what happened with the others? She would've had a guard."

Mockingbird chews on her index finger. "I had a little help."

"I wish you would give me more credit than that."

I flinch at the sound of the voice. Not because it frightens me, not because it alarms me, not even because it startles me. But because its owner has discovered every way to make me beautiful. Her brush has painted designs on my skin; her hands have touched forbidden places.

I feel like a fruit peeled of its skin. A bird plucked of its feathers.

"Dove..." Her name is almost a plea as I watch her come up behind Mockingbird and cup the girl's shoulders.

"I did everything you told me to, Mummy."

Slack-jawed, I gape.

Dove's perceptive eyes gobble up my surprised expression, and I realize she's come to recognize all of them. All this time, she's spent so much time learning who I am.

"The serpent..." I start. "But you said your daughter—"

"The best lies are hidden in the truth," Dove says, running her fingers through Mockingbird's hair. "There was a serpent, and he did want to bite my daughter, but I ripped out his fangs before he could.

"Remember how I told you I was close to becoming the Swan? There were others before Luc who searched for you. The search for the Swan was passed down from generation to generation by Aviary directors. Mockingbird *was* hatched here. And when she was born, I resolved she would become the true Swan, even though the Temple wanted her. They were going to take her from me." She gazes down at Mockingbird, settling a hand on her daughter's head.

"But you killed the Temple man," Mockingbird says with pride in her voice. "You took your two hands and squeezed all the life out of his—"

"Yes, dear, Mummy's talking now," Dove murmurs before continuing. "I set fire to his car, making it appear the baby was destroyed with him. Then, I left Mockingbird right on Luc's doorstep. Well..." She pauses with a smile, tucking a few strands of Mockingbird's hair behind her ear. "I left her on the doorstep of his house, as it was then. His lakeside retreat. He was only a boy, but you should've seen the first time he held her. He treasured her so. He kissed her. And I knew I would always be able to watch over my little Mock. Now, she'll finally have the chance to spread her wings."

I grimace at the two of them. "She's already spread them. Several times."

"Do you know how many clients Mockingbird has had?" Dove steps toward me, her voice laced with sweetness. "She has what we call repeat clients. Her numbers are few, so what are a few poisoned clients who can't testify?"

Mockingbird raises her hands. Flicks them in the air. "Magic hands. Right, Mummy?"

"Yes, love. Magic hands. The clients won't even feel the effects of the poison until they are outside Aviary borders. And client records are so easy to disappear.

"Can you imagine what I felt? When Luc gave Mockingbird her name when she turned sixteen?" Malice spears Dove's eyes, and I now understand the abhorrence she feels toward him. "After all those years I spent trying to persuade him that she was the Swan without telling him the truth about us? I tried *so* hard, Serenity. But he never saw her. Tell me…did he ever show you the needle marks on his skin?"

I stand up then, remembering how he'd said it was the worst thing he'd ever done.

"I was a healer before this," Dove says. "And I wanted him to die slow. I wanted him to feel the pain I felt seeing my daughter every day without being able to hold her or reach out to touch her." Dove frames the sides of Mockingbird's face. "We had to pretend all the time. I had to pretend my daughter was not my own. If Luc ever found out she was mine, there would've been no chance for her to become the Swan.

"I tried to give him an overdose a few times during his visits, but he'd built up such a high tolerance for Bliss that it never took. I think it helped numb his pain after every kill. But when I saw my Mockingbird visit him in the infirmary for the first time, and I saw the way she coveted him, I knew I couldn't let him die. So I stopped injecting him, and he recovered. The drug left his body. He returned with Nightingale later, and was appointed director."

"You underestimate him," I tell her, remembering the sound of Luc's gun burrowing bullets into bone and burning graphicker flesh and blood.

"Luc is sweet," Dove coos. "He's always watched over his Birds. But when he found his Swan, he got a little too distracted. Soon, he'll have one less Bird to watch."

I take an active stance, ready to fight or run. "Why, Mockingbird? By tomorrow, I'll be in the Temple."

Dove cuts her eyes at her daughter, opening her hand. "Give me the knife, Mockingbird. It's time."

I roll back on my heels, prepared to run. "What's the point of this, Dove? Luc knows who Mockingbird is. He'll never make her the Swan, not even if I'm dead."

"Don't you see?" Dove inches toward me. "Your death will be the culmination. Your death will destroy him. He will be an empty shell without you. And who do you think will comfort him?" Her smile is affectionate when she beams back at her daughter.

Mockingbird grins, licking her lips as she watches her mother come toward me.

"Of course, he won't realize it. Bliss is so versatile. So simple to prepare in food or tea. He hasn't ingested any in such a long time. I will dress her up. I will prepare her just as I've prepared you. Why do you think I requested you? It was a safe way to monitor you—to learn more about you. The viper I painted on your back was the signal to Mockingbird that all was going according to plan. And that plan is turning her into the Swan. In his grief, he'll imagine it's you. And it will be just what I need to blackmail him. Luc's ultimate rule will be broken, and when the Family finds out he's using again, his control will be lost."

Rolling my eyes, I cross my arms over my chest. "He won't grieve me, Dove. I'm just another Bird. An investment. You just dressed me prettier than most. In the end, it was still just a game. He played his part, and I played mine. I'm just a piece, and he played me to the Temple."

Tilting her neck back, Dove laughs. I could reach out and touch her laughter. It's a tangible thing.

"Silly, silly, *silly* girl!" Dove focuses on me once again. "The Temple did not win your auction. Luc did."

I feel my chest seize. "What are you talking about?"

Dove advances toward me again. This time, she roams the area around my body, her words chirruping into my skin. "The Temple was no match for what Luc did. Do you know what that foolish man did? He auctioned off the Aviary."

The words could pitch my body to the ground. That means he chose *my* freedom. Not my parents.

"Unbeknownst to his father, Luc has invested his personal

funds into Aviary stock. He owned the majority of shares without his father's knowledge. And he auctioned every single one off—for you. Congratulations, Serenity. Luc owns you. Pity he won't get a chance to tell you himself."

Dove faces me, raising the knife. "And Director Force now owns the Aviary. He may keep Luc as director or replace him. Even if that occurs, Luc's last recommendation will hold weight. There will be a new Swan—my little Mockingbird."

Before she can bring the knife down, Mockingbird interrupts. "Mummy?"

Annoyance flashing across her face, Dove turns toward her daughter. "Mummy's trying to kill the one last thing that stands in your way."

"Did he really give up the Aviary for her?"

"Yes, Mockingbird." She turns back to me, aiming her words. "The auction was a very private affair. All the girls were supposed to be on lockdown. But Mockingbird is not the only one who can spill secrets. I arranged for the auction to have an audience…well, its result to have an audience. Amazing how violent those girls can be when they hear the Temple now controls the Aviary. So much more competitive. But there will be one less Bird to worry about soon."

Thirty-two
SereNity's StOry

"Mummy?"

Mockingbird interrupts one more time, stepping forward to join her mother's side while I scrutinize them for a gap. With the lake on my left, there's only one way I can escape. I'll have to jump over Gull's body to do it.

"I'm never going to be the Swan," Mockingbird says in a pouty whine.

"I'm giving you the Swan right now," Dove retorts in a sharp voice.

"But I won't be *his* Swan. I'll never be his Swan."

Dove appraises her daughter. "Give him time. He'll have no choice. His Swan will be dead. And you will go to him tonight."

I may be small, but there's enough wildness in my body for me to barrel into Mockingbird, smash her to the ground, and leap over her and back onto the path.

"You can't fly from me, Serenity!" Dove's voice echoes behind me, but I scramble over the bridge, past the waterfall.

Sky is nowhere nearby. For a moment, I'm glad. But I won't leave him behind. I head for the museum. Reaching the closest entrance, I find it bolted tight. The security system must be back online. The only person who can secure or override the system in an emergency is Luc.

I have to push thoughts of him aside. He and Sky can't help me now.

Only the present matters, and Dove's soothing, murderous

voice skewers the air behind me as I press my body against the wall, scuttling into the shadows.

The glass sculpture garden is my nearest hope. I flee to it, remembering the glass Sky and I broke together. It's the closest thing to a weapon I have, and the darkness ravages the garden, lights all turned off due to the lockdown. Dove knows these paths better than me, so it doesn't take her long to catch up, but I slide behind a nearby statue framed by bushes to avoid her notice.

"Serenity," she pants, then catches her breath before speaking my name one more time. "You gave me your name first; do you remember?"

She sways around the glass sculptures, checking each one, scanning the darkness for me. I manage to duck behind a few different birdlike sculptures, their glass wings shading me.

"You can't hide from me. Come out, child."

My feet brush some pebbles. Dove spins around at the sound, but I throw my body against a wide tree, hoping she doesn't see me.

"If you come out now, I'll make it quick. I've waited too many years for this. You never belonged to this life. You never belonged to this world. Just like you told Gull—your land is an island no one can ever sail to."

Dove strays around the shape of one more glass sculpture. She's close enough, but still a good few steps away. Hiding like this won't work for much longer. Nor will running. My best hope is to take her by surprise.

I pray she won't turn around right before I barrel into her.

Dove twirls, but too late. My terror makes me fast, and my petite body is quiet and light, but it's enough to knock her to the ground.

She doesn't drop the knife, but she doesn't have to. From the sound of her scream, I know my plan has worked. I just don't realize how well until I spring back into a crouch, waiting for Dove to flick her knife up again, but she doesn't move.

She coughs a wet cough. When I hear the clatter of the knife, I kneel to examine her. Blood drips down one side of her arm like a ribbon. Drops glitter on cut glass and pavement, and she chokes.

"Out of my way!" Mockingbird screeches. She hurls me

aside, so she can stare into her mother's eyes. "Mum? *Mummy!*" She reaches her just in time to see Dove draw her final breath.

Dove dies smiling at the daughter she could always watch but never know.

Mockingbird screams. Shrill and agonizing, like a banshee.

"I didn't mean to kill her, Mockingbird. I'm sorry," I say honestly. I'd only meant to incapacitate her.

Mockingbird doesn't even spare me a glance before she grabs a large shard of glass, tainted by her mother's blood. She turns on her heel, sweeping around with the shard's keen end pointed at me. Better than any blade, its frosted edge is a smile ready to slaughter.

She lunges at me. Evading her for one moment, I jerk to the side, but Mockingbird wasn't lying. Her hands are magic, and they vault across my skin so quickly I can't even hope to blink.

I wince, grabbing for my shoulder where she cut it. Beneath the torn sleeve of my white dress, there is a tiny line of blood soiling it, redder than a wine puddle.

Mockingbird pauses to admire her work, canting her head to the side before she grins and snaps toward me again, the shard aimed lower this time. I double over from the pain, raising my hand to cradle the bloodied stripe on my chest. It's deep.

I can feel blood pooling in my fingers.

Mockingbird swings her body around in a circle, her laughter riotous in the air.

She clutches the shard in two hands as she dances to her own song. "I always wanted to see a Swan bleed, see a Swan bleed, see a—"

On her next twirl, I lunge for her shoulders, forcing her to the ground, trying desperately to pin her arms, but they are moving too fast. The shard cuts me again.

Pain slices through me, and I grab my side until the tips of my fingers drown in my blood.

First, all I can see is the dark sky above me. And then, nothing but Mockingbird's face, the twist of broken feathers that is her smile, her words pecking at me, and the slow hum of the shard sailing just above my chest where my heart beats.

"See a Swan heart," Mockingbird whispers in my ear.

"Mockingbird!"

The voice startles us both, but Mockingbird drops the glass shard and flutters away into the darkness. It's not the voice I want.

Luc leans over. Cups my face. Heartache steeps his expression, but I know better than to be duped by it. He's manipulated me ever since the moment I first laid eyes on him. Just as he slides his arms underneath my body to raise me, I reach for the shard of glass, get my fingers around it. He doesn't see. Only draws me closer.

Without hesitating for a moment, I aim for Luc's chest and slice. Shocked by my action, he leaps back. Adrenaline pumps through me as I slice again, but I'm having trouble focusing. My eyes turn bleary. I blink a couple of times, more surprised to find Luc not fighting back. He doesn't thwart my attempts whatsoever. Just stands there, one hand clutching his chest, with the other held up in a pleading attempt to prevent me from attacking him farther.

Not to be unsettled by this new and most likely desperate ploy, I raise the shard again, gripping it so tightly I feel the edges cutting into my skin. "Let me go!"

"Serenity, please listen to me."

"You lied to me! You gave me your word!" I thrust the shard at him, and he steps back. Something wet oozes down the front of my chest. Losing blood from Mockingbird's claws. I start tripping over my words, blinking again as my vision dims. "Supposed to free my parents. My mother—"

Holding up his hands, he steps forward. "Your freedom is more important!"

I lunge, slashing at his arm, gratified by the fabric ripping his keen suit and the thin line of blood there. "Move! Take me to the gate!"

"Security's branching out from the back of the Aviary."

"Then, we'll go out the front. We'll take the shortcut through the garden path to the main gate."

Luc opens his mouth to speak, but I interrupt him.

"*Now!*"

He obeys, and I follow his steps, keeping my eyes on the ground because anything else will turn my vision into spinning tops. While pressing a hand against my chest to stem the blood there, I can't help the smug smile from teasing the corners of my mouth. I'm walking right out the front door. Part of me wonders if this is what it feels like to be drunk. As we cross the garden bridge, I sway a little, almost pitching forward. Only one thing doesn't change—the glass in my hand. The pain stinging my palm there keeps me going. That and the adrenaline.

After about a half mile past Luc's bathhouse and through a gap in the trees, I can see the main gate. Not even the sight of the laser barriers will deter me now. In spite of my body's protests, craving just one moment of rest, I grab the back of Luc's jacket and pull him closer, then press the glass weapon into the base of his spine.

"Open it."

The moments I wait for him to connect to his interface are excruciating. The blood on my chest has slowed but not stopped, and the white dress blushes from the fluid staining it. After another moment or two, the gate finally splits apart like bird wings spreading, waiting for me to fly from this coop.

I march right past Luc and the gate without a care in the world. No more plans. No more plots. No more waiting. I'm ready to leave the Aviary even if it means I fall to my knees once I'm outside. It's no surprise to feel Luc's familiar body heat just behind me when I do, but I barely notice when I hear the rumble of a vehicle behind us. It doesn't slow, the spotlights flooding us. Glancing back, I shield my face from the beams just as the limo careens to a halt right in front of us.

Out of the car swoops the one man I will always trust in this life or any other.

"Care for a lift?" Sky motions to the limo until he realizes what's going on, then he practically leaps for me. "Serenity, what—"

"Later," Luc interrupts. "Get her into the car."

Immediately, Sky sets to work. Putting pressure on my wounds, easing me onto the luxury leather, and then searching around for something.

All my adrenaline is depleted now. Pain slams into me. Some star is exploding, dying in my skin, leaving branding meteors in its wake. I can feel the gash, the mutilated skin. It feels like I've lost a river of blood.

"What the hell happened?" Nightingale's voice echoes somewhere across from me. "Will she be okay?"

"You stole Force's limo." Luc sounds shocked, but almost approving.

"Hacked it, yes. Daddy is furious. Overheard him planning to take her by force. Figured nabbing his transportation would be a good idea. Get this thing moving, Luc."

Something registers in my mind. A name I can't quite pinpoint. For the life of me, I can't remember his name. He's just the Vampire. He takes blood. And I've lost too much already.

"Guys, I think she's slipping into unconsciousness," Nightingale warns. "You have to keep her awake!"

Sky slaps at my face, a staccato rhythm in his fingers. Then he grabs hold of my neck to keep my head from rolling. "Ser, Ser, look at me!" He demands my attention, but I don't have the energy to give it.

Luc's hand replaces his on my chest. I want to blush, but I doubt I have enough blood to rush to my cheeks.

"Ser, just hold on. Get me a damn first aid kit, somebody! I'm going to fix you," Sky soothes me, hand cradling my face.

I latch onto one word. "You fix everything."

I can practically hear his smile. "That's right, I do. Except for your mother. I understand why now. I know why her dreams always haunted her." Sky fumbles around, searching again for something. I snap to attention when he holds it just above me.

"Listen," Sky says before he opens the lid and retrieves an object. "Your mother wasn't just rescuing girls all those years in the Sanctuary. She was *searching* for one special girl."

He holds up a photograph. It's me, but not me.

Her eye color is all wrong. It's too dark to be mine. Her hair is not as wild. Not as many curls. And I don't see lightning anywhere. No intensity in her face. No feral glint in her eyes. No subtle curl in the corner of her mouth.

"She's alive, Serenity," Sky tells me. "Your twin sister's alive."

Thirty-three
ConvaLescence

I DON'T REMEMBER PASSING OUT. The last thing I remember is the doctor's hands tearing my dress from me, just as a nurse injected me with something. I remember it wasn't a hospital; it was a private clinic.

But I wake inside a bed. Just across from me is a window with shades drawn. Whoever put me here must have known I'd want the natural light. The view of the lake just outside is stunning.

There are long white bandages across my chest. I don't feel pain anymore, but there's an underlying ache, a sense of gnawing. The wound on my side isn't as deep. I peel back the smaller swatch of gauze there to see…nothing. Of course—the Immortal Treatment. My cells have already regenerated, new skin grown. My hair is damp, and I'm wearing one of the white Aviary dresses. No blood on my skin. Almost as if everything is erased but the memory.

"You're awake," Nightingale says. "Good. You've been sleeping for most of the day."

"What's going on? Where are we?"

"Luc's lakeside retreat. It's a few hours upstate, far away from the Aviary." Sinking onto my bed, she pats my hand. "They want to talk with you."

"Did you dress me?"

"And cleaned you off, yes."

Relief engulfs me, and I nod because there is one thing I definitely remember from the limo. A need for answers bubbles inside me.

I don't get out of bed. Instead, Nightingale leaves to give us some privacy as Luc and Sky walk in.

Both men come to me, but I direct them to sit on the same side so I don't have to look back and forth between them. Neither seems happy about that. An awkward intensity hovers between their bodies.

Once they both establish I'm feeling better, I ask about what Sky told me in the limo. "You said the baby died."

"I thought it was the truth," he says. "Anytime your mother mentioned anything about it, she only said they took your twin from her because she wasn't breathing, and that's the last she ever saw of her. I've left her chest on the table for you. Other than that photograph, I know nothing. The rest is yours to dig through."

I purse my lips. "What about Force?"

Luc straightens to answer. "He and I were the last of the bidders. So, I bid my Aviary shares. Every last one."

Sky crosses his ankle over the opposite knee. "Couldn't very well turn down the whole Aviary, now could he?"

Luc leans over the bed, and I notice Sky tense at the action. "It was worth it."

"What does that make me, Luc? Your property? Your slave?" I challenge.

Luc shakes his head. "It makes you Serenity. Though you will always be my Swan."

"Give her some breathing room, or I'll do it for you." Sky threads his brows low.

Luc turns to Sky. "Don't forget whose roof you are under, Skylar."

"Oh, I think we both know I won't forget anytime soon."

"What's going on between you two? What aren't you telling me?" I survey both of them.

They stare at each other.

"Should we tell her?" Luc asks.

"Obviously, we have to now." Sky rolls his eyes. "You don't ask something like that in front of her without telling her. *Ignoramus*." Sky slides back in his chair, spreading his legs out. He mutters something under his breath. It sounds like, 'known her for sixteen damn years.'

"You are not helping the situation," Luc informs him.

Sky inspects his hand before clenching it. "Situation's already screwed beyond repair. You won't make it any worse by telling her that we're brothers."

"*Half*-brothers." Luc interjects.

As they bicker, I suck in the air around me. It can't be true. It just can't.

"What the hell?" is all I manage to get out.

"I told you we should have told her before," Luc says.

"Clearly, you're the dumb pretty boy in the family."

"Shut up, Sky," I say. "Luc, you're better at talking. So, talk."

"I discovered the information shortly after hiring Sky. It was one of the reasons I promoted him to head of my security, other than the fact he conquered all my other candidates."

"What can I say?" Sky tightens his arm, showing off his brawn.

"I bided my time," Luc continues, unhindered. "Observed him until I could form enough of an impression. I never had much interaction with him as I was older than both him and Larke, who were born from the same mother. At the time of his disappearance, my father was more interested in raising me, the byproduct of the only woman he ever genuinely loved. She passed away giving birth to my younger sister Lea."

I remember her from the Guild visit night.

"Larke was supposed to be watching Sky the night he disappeared—though his name was Lars then."

Sky grunts at the name, but I point a finger at him and invite him to shut it.

"I had my suspicions, but it wasn't until the night you saw the volus in my room that I discovered his connection to you. When I confronted him, I learned we both held one common interest—your safety above all else. And once I learned of Sky's association with the Sanctuary, that he was responsible for securing Blackbird and her child, I chose to inform him of my decision to auction off the Aviary.

"However, we both knew Force would never stop hunting you. It was a grand diversion, but a diversion nonetheless. I provided it while Skylar disarmed the system and took care of you. Dove's involvement was unexpected."

Once he finishes, I remain where I am for the moment, sorting through all the other questions in my head.

"Serenity, I don't regret a damn thing," Sky says, interrupting my thoughts. He sits up in his chair, reaching over to hold my hand. "When I was little, I got lost and took the wrong elevator. The next thing I knew, there was your mother and this pretty little baby."

My concern latches onto one thing. "Where are my parents, Sky?"

"Still in Guild custody. Luc's father is hoping to use them as a bargaining chip, since his three-for-one Temple partnership deal didn't work out so hot thanks to Aldaine here."

That's when I launch myself at Luc. Kindled like lightning at dawn, I spin around and slap at Luc's face over and over again. "You promised me! You said anything I wanted! *Any* favor!"

Sky is the one who grips me by the waist, who pins me back onto the bed while Luc rights himself.

"Stop," he commands. "Your new skin is still growing. As soon as it's finished, you can smack him around to your heart's content. Hell, I'll join you. You did a good number on him already. Not as deep as your wounds, but he still needed stitches."

"Good!"

"If you want someone to blame, blame us both, Ser. We made the choice together."

"I couldn't let you fall into the hands of the Temple," Luc adds, approaching from the other side of the bed.

I grimace when he approaches, but Sky pushes down on me again and scolds, "Be good. And pay attention."

"Force was prepared to make my father a Temple partner," Luc says. "He put up Temple stock shares, ownership titles, everything, but even Force could not bid an entire museum."

"Clever party trick, Aldaine."

Keeping his hands placated at his sides, Luc holds his head high as he addresses Sky. "You're an Aldaine, too."

Sky shakes his head. "Hell will grow icebergs before I become an Aldaine."

I glance back at Luc, study him, compare them for a moment.

The Aviary

"You look nothing like each other."

"Pity for him, isn't it?" Sky snickers. A joke, of course, because we both know how easy Luc is on the eyes, even if I've always found Sky undefeated in the handsome category.

"Does Force have my sister, Sky?" I ask.

He nods once. "Identical twins are exceedingly rare in this day and age. And apparently, Director Force has spent over sixteen years searching for the match to the other twin. Just like your parents have spent their lives looking for their older daughter. When they finally found her, they got captured in the process. Force hid her pretty well. Shame they never thought he'd hide her in plain sight. In the Penthouse."

"What does he want from me?" I bite down on my lip.

"He'll turn you into the Face of the Temple. That much I do know. But I can't begin to speculate about anything else."

Sky backs off when I stop tensing. "Penny for your thoughts?"

I ask for my twin's photograph again, as well as my mother's when she was the Unicorn. The photograph of Mom has old, curled corners. The one of my twin is fresh, but Sky's fingerprints taint the edges.

The Temple is full of blood. And she's some white jewel crusted into its center, my father's hand in danger of shattering her every day.

After I trace the edges of both photographs, I close my eyes. I have to help my family.

Sky and Luc rescued me. Now, it is my turn to do some rescuing.

I glance at the photographs once more.

I'm coming, I tell them silently.

Discussion/Essay Questions for *The Aviary*

*T*HE MAIN THEME OF THE Aviary is identity. In the world of prostitution, dissociative identity disorder is common, though it manifests in different ways to each individual. Consider the struggle of identity with multiple characters from Luc's identity with his Family and responsibilities to Serafina's identity with the Unicorn to Serenity's Swan identity. Consider researching the psychological process of DID and writing on it.

Luc tells Serenity she was not groomed for life in the Aviary and he would need to remake her. Research different grooming methods. Discuss how they play a role in how one can end up in the sex industry. Here are some helpful hints to get you started: poverty, sexual abuse, physical abuse, mental health issues, parental absence, homelessness, modesty culture, respect for authority figures, patriarchy, toxic masculinity, pop culture, and pornography.

1. Consider Serenity's reflections on Sky and how he looks at the girls around him. How he focuses on their eyes. Why is this important in the scope of sexual objectification? Discuss the images of pop culture, media, and advertising and how they may perpetuate drawing the eye to a woman's body or sexualizing her body instead of emphasizing her humanity?

2. When Blackbird explains her background and her mother's debt, it's understandable why she applied for the Aviary. Unlike Serenity, she chose to enter the Aviary, but discuss whether girls should be forced to make such choices. Discuss whether choosing the sex industry vs

poverty is truly a choice. Discuss how society can offer other solutions for families or individuals in poverty so they don't have to make such a choice.
3. During the inspector's testing, Serenity overhears how signs of abuse have been found on the girls despite the beautiful and technologically advanced environment of the Aviary. Research studies and articles on countries where Red-Light Districts are legal and if abuse is prominent in such environments. Discuss possible effects of legalizing prostitution. Would regulations and panic buttons be enough to stem abuses in the sex industry or does it open doors for more abuse to occur? Contrast the Nordic Model of decriminalizing the selling of sex but not the buying.
4. Consider the terminology Serenity uses throughout the book: Breakable, broken, doll. Consider Blackbird's reaction to Serenity's view of her. And then consider Serenity's change of heart when she confronts Luc and reflects on how strong girls in this environment can be and how beautiful they are. Discuss how stereotypes and words—even ones socially acceptable and normalizing ones such as "slut" or "whore"—can harm and impact girls' self-esteem and how they influence their belief about their worth.
5. After Nightingale shares her story, Serenity likens the viewpoint of her time in the sex industry as "paid rape". Contrast Nightingale's background with Blackbird and her character and choices. While Blackbird only came from poverty, Nightingale came from poverty and sexual abuse. Research the backgrounds and psychology of those who enter prostitution or who are vulnerable for trafficking into prostitution or sexual exploitation (i.e. strip clubs, pornography, massage parlors etc.). A good place to start: The National Center on Sexual Exploitation.
6. In light of Nightingale sharing her coping mechanism of singing, research survival strategies of those in prostitution. This can overlap with dissociative identity disorder. What other survival strategies are used in The Aviary, not just in the museum but in other environments as well?

Acknowledgements

First, I have to thank the guys in my husband's unit for talking to the local men in an underground pub in Germany where I overheard the words: Red-Light District. Without them, I would never have been shocked into wanting to know more.

A most sincere thankfulness goes to Benjamin "Benji" Nolot of Exodus Cry for the documentary Nefarious: Merchant of Souls, for talking to me on the phone, for all you and the whole Exodus Cry team do. Thank you, Helen, for your intervention training, for your strength, your grace, and your kindness. Thank you for reacting to my name at Justice Awakening; it was both sweet, encouraging, and humorous!

Special thanks to all my local freedom fighters. For Terri Hands and her networking superpower! If you weren't so busy running around inspiring us, you could write a book! For Adri who read this book in its infancy and thought it was good (even though it was awful!) and all she's done for the cause! For Keith and all your hard work with Trafficking Justice. For Amanda for helping me with my presentation, for telling me the truth, for challenging me, for educating me. For Kjersti and your inspiring kindness and compassion. Your testimony softened my heart, and you've always taken the time to answer my questions graciously. Thank you for your patience as I continue to learn! For Danielle and Justice Awakening which triggered my WORD. For all those working with Trafficking Justice, Breaking Free, Source, Beautiful and Loved, The Link, Action169, and more. A big thank you as well to Anna Friendt for the enchanting Swan artwork. Really hope for more art for the sequels!

For Rebecca "Becky" McDonald. There's not enough room to describe how much you've empowered me and changed me for the better. I know many who agree! For the entire WAR team. For lovely Shelby and all your fangirling over The Aviary. For Tricia and Elizabeth and Hannah and more. We are all WARriors!

To all the agents who rejected Serenity, thank you. Thanks to the beta readers I met along this book's journey. Special thanks to Kate Angelella, who chose me as her grand prize winner for professional editorial services. To Allison Singer, formerly of ZSH Literary Agency, and all her editing/agent skills however short a time. To Carlie Webber and how long she stuck it out with The Aviary. Even though it didn't work out, it wasn't wasted, and I learned so much!

Finally, to the incredible team of Clean Teen Publishing for taking a chance on me and for giving this series a place to shine! Thank you for partnering with me on such a significant issue. You are helping me to #dosomething.

Last but not least, my family—my mom for teaching me to read and write, and to my daddy for always asking me questions about my writing. It matters! For my husband for always raising me up when I fall, for holding me and rocking me, for appreciating my passion, for walking with me on this twelve-year journey!

Ultimately, to my Designer, Inspirer, and Abba who gave me my Princess Vision and my word: M.A.P: Mother/Author/Preventionist.

Resources

NATIONAL CENTER ON SEXUAL EXPLOITATION
https://endsexualexploitation.org/

TRUTH ABOUT PORN
http://truthaboutporn.org/

POLARIS
https://polarisproject.org/

WOMEN AT RISK, INTERNATIONAL
http://warinternational.org/

EXODUS CRY
https://exoduscry.com/

OPERATION UNDERGROUND RAILROAD
https://ourrescue.org/

SHARED HOPE INTERNATIONAL
https://sharedhope.org/

FIGHT THE NEW DRUG
https://fightthenewdrug.org/about/

About the Author

EMILY SHORE IS A MN author with a B.A. in Creative Writing from Metro State University and was a grand prize winner of #PitchtoPublication, which led her to working with professionals in the publishing industry. Her anti-trafficking books Ruby in the Rough and Ruby in the Ruins are her first indie-published books with proceeds benefiting trafficking rescue organizations. She is signed with Clean Teen Publishing for her anti-trafficking dystopian The Aviary. For every book sold, a personal donation will return to Women At Risk, International.

Throughout the years, she has connected with rescue organizations and survivors of sex-trafficking and injects the truths she's learned into her books for youth. She loves motivational speaking on the issue of sex-trafficking and always hopes for more speaking events in schools, churches, and libraries. Please contact her on her website if you are interested in hearing her speak. In her spare time, she loves attending any abolition events, baking, acrylic painting, interior decorating, and spending time with all the little girls in her life.

Emily lives in Saint Paul with her husband and two daughters. Their goal is to adopt a little girl from India.

CPSIA information can be obtained
at www.ICGtesting.com
Printed in the USA
LVHW041017100219
606969LV00006B/6